MAKE YOUR MOVE

A FORMULA NEXT ROMANCE

MELISSA BRAYDEN

Edited by Lynda Sandoval and Avery Brooks

Cover design by Ink and Laurel

First Edition: 2026

ISBN (ebook): 979-8-9928823-3-9

Published by Brayden StoryWorks

For the ones who risk it all — in life and in love

PROLOGUE

"People always think racing is about speed," Reese Maddox said, her tone easy, practiced. She leaned back in the chair, crossing one leg over the other, her race suit zipped halfway, exposing the neckline of a black tee beneath. "It's not. It's about control."

She shifted, the studio lights hot against her face. Someone behind the camera murmured an adjustment, and she gave a quick, camera-ready smile. She knew exactly how to deliver the polished persona they were after, having had lots of practice in front of a lens.

INTERVIEWER: "Control. That's an interesting word. Why that one?"

REESE: "Because it's the one thing that keeps slipping away."

A beat passed. She laughed, soft and self-deprecating. "Not that I'd admit that to my engineer."

INTERVIEWER: "You've got a reputation for charisma—fans love you, social media loves you. How do you feel about that?"

REESE: "Sometimes it seems like that's *all* they love: the smile, the brand deals, the posts. But when I'm on the track … that's the part that still feels real. That's where I remember why I started. But sure, it's not awful."

INTERVIEWER: "Let's talk about that. You've been called the most marketable driver in Formula 2. Do you think that reputation helps or hurts you?"

REESE: "Depends on who you ask. The sponsors love it. The other drivers think I don't belong. The truth's somewhere else entirely."

She shifted forward, elbows on her knees, expression sharpening. "But they'll believe I belong when I start winning. That's the plan, anyway."

She glanced toward the crew, realizing her guard was down. Dangerous territory. "Anyway, control. That's the thing, right? You lose that, and you lose everything."

INTERVIEWER: "You're coming to the end of your second season in Formula 2. You'll likely finish near the top of the drivers' standings. What's next?"

REESE: "Good question." She sat back. She had no shot at winning the season, given her point deficit. But she'd done okay. "The dream's still Formula 1, same as it's been since I was five years old. But dreams get expensive. You run out of sponsors, or patience, or both."

But Reese had no plans to give up. In the last ten years, exactly three women had raced in Formula 1, and none of them had won the world championship. Reese aimed to change that statistic in the next few years or kill herself trying.

"I'm going to be world champion one day," Reese said, staring straight into the camera. "I'm telling you that now."

A pause hit as her words settled.

"Okay. I think we got it," Samara, the interviewer, told the cameraman. She was also the producer of the film and the one who had recruited Reese to the documentary, which followed a handful of drivers on their quest to reach F1. Reese had been part of the project throughout the season, and the goal was to continue following her progress over the next year. It meant squeezing in interviews both before and after races, not to mention little spurts in between to capture scenes from her day-to-day life. It was a bit more of a commitment than she'd origi-nally realized, but it's not like she could have said no. She needed the cash to keep racing. She didn't come from money like so many of the other drivers.

Samara grinned. "Hey, thanks for the sit-down. I know your morning was stacked."

Reese unclipped the lavalier microphone and handed it over. "Wouldn't be my life if it wasn't." She adjusted her race suit, wondering what time it was.

"Think you're gonna fare well today?" They were at Silver-stone that weekend. The iconic track in Northamptonshire, England, was known for its wet weather, and the forecast called for rain that day. A slippery circuit would give Reese the opening she needed to move from her qualifying spot of P3 to, hopefully, P1 and win this thing for her team, Ravensport. God knew their second driver, Kevin Henry, wouldn't finish in the points. His lap times seemed to get slower with each race, leaving Reese feeling the team's success rested squarely on her shoulders. Frus-trating.

"I plan to win today. And not just a podium finish, but P1." Reese said without a moment of hesitation. And she believed she could. "Maybe I'll see you after?" she asked Samara with her best lazy smile. She was an admitted flirt, dedicated to the cause and women in general. Couldn't help it. She and Samara had known each other long enough to have fun with the energy. They hadn't hooked up yet, but the season wasn't over.

A pause. "You just might, Reese Maddox. Tell you what." She looked over her shoulder as she collected her notepad. "You can buy me a drink. One."

Damn, she had pretty eyes. "Anytime, Samara Idris." Reese offered a playful head tilt before walking back to the paddock to prepare her mind and body for all they were about to experi-ence. When she passed a small group of fans waving her over to the barricade, it wasn't like she could ignore them. She chatted with a few, signed their programs next to her photo, and took selfies before finally pulling herself away, probably a little behind schedule now.

"We love you, Reese," a woman with a Ravensport T-shirt yelled.

"Will you marry me?" a teenage boy yelled. She pretended to catch the kiss he blew. She didn't date boys, but the world knew that.

"You're gonna kick ass!" another girl shouted. "Mickels is on pole position today. Overtake him on the straightaway. He sucks on the straights."

She looked back over her shoulder and grinned, purposefully showing off her dimple, aware that multiple cameras were grabbing the shot and wanting to make it good. "You know I will," she yelled to the last girl. But as she walked back to the paddock, she knew she'd lingered too long, and concern blanketed her like the storm clouds already overhead. She'd wanted to be kind to the fans and give them the attention they asked for, but maybe the sacrifice had not been in her best interest or the team's. The prep list was long, and Reese was behind. She had the track map to go over, her physical warm-up, reaction drills, contingency plans, target lap times, plus she needed to eat something and time it appropriately. There would be an official driver weigh-in before the race.

"Hey. Where have you been?" Julie Rennick asked when she arrived at the paddock. Her race engineer wore her blue Ravensport polo and had her dark blond hair up in her customary ponytail. With her cane in one hand and a tablet in the other, Julie was dialed into race day with very little else allowed in her brain. Soon, she'd be wearing a headset and talking Reese through the hour-long race, the only voice in her ear.

"So sorry. The interview ran long, and then I got caught up with a group of fans, entirely on me. Let's get started."

Julie sighed and seemed to press on, when they both knew she wanted to deliver one of her voice-of-reason lectures. At 36 and about 10 years older than Reese, Julie brought big-sister vibes and had earned Reese's respect over the years. Instead of the lecture, Julie pointed at the laminated map on the table, which had red circles at two spots along the track. "Take a look at turns three and seven. Late brake here only if the fronts are in." She paused. "And stop flirting with the media. Flirt with your apexes."

"Yes, boss," she said with an apologetic grin. She also flashed the big innocent eyes for good measure. They tended to make people forgive her.

"I'm glad one of us is smiling," Julie said with her serious brow wrinkle. How did she manage the perfect cartoon furrow? Impressive. But as stressed as Julie seemed now, Reese knew she'd be the picture of calm once the race was underway. It was Julie's gift.

Reese laughed. "It's just that I'm so happy to see you and feel that it's all going to come together for us today, Jules. Something in the air says so."

"Splendid," Julie said as sincerely as possible. "Can we get your head back in the car now? We're short on time." Reese moved to the map, prepared to do whatever Julie asked. While Reese believed fully that Julie would have made a fantastic driver, Julie had been born with a disability that left her with one leg shorter than the other and a pronounced limp. Unfortunately, the condition had prevented Julie from following her driving dreams beyond youth sport. Instead, she'd moved from karting to crew to engineering for Raven, using her encyclopedic knowledge of motorsport to Reese's advantage. They were casual friends, but only off the track. When at work, Julie took her job and wrangling Reese very seriously.

"We can definitely get to work," Reese said, sobering because Julie was right. She should have been more on top of her race prep and would do a better job in the future. At the same time, Reese knew unequivocally that everything would be fine. She'd get out there and win, grab top points for Ravensport, spray some champagne on the podium, and attract the attention of the scouts that would open the door to Formula 1—end of story. Sign her up for world champion. Write the happily ever after now.

"Map then reaction drills," Julie said.

"I'm ready. Let's do the work." They dove into the physical, mental, and teamwide warm-up to get everyone in shape for the hugely important race.

Two hours later, it was go time. Reese was primed. She rolled her shoulders and pressed one elbow to the sky and then the other, reveling in the pull of each muscle. The sun was sneaking behind the clouds, confirming the forecast for expected showers. Didn't matter. There was nothing like a Sunday afternoon to bring home a visit to the podium. Formula 2 races were high-stakes, wheel-to-wheel battles with frequent overtakes. Scrappy, in the best sense, and it just so happened that Reese was made for it. She'd been scrapping since she was in kindergarten, when her dad dropped her in a go-kart for the first time.

"Did you go over your map?" Luke asked, matching her step as she walked to her car. Her older brother was her best friend and constant guardian angel when it came to racing. Ravensport had agreed to bring him on as the crew chief for their cars, which meant he made sure she was not only fast in the pit, but in the safest car possible.

"I did," Reese said, helmet hanging at her side. "Late brakes on turns three and seven, and then I should be able to hold the inside through the straights." She studied the sky once they arrived alongside her car. The cloud cover looked even more ominous than before. Reese grinned and blew out a breath. "No big deal, right? What's Silverstone without a little rain?"

She looked up at the stands, which were only half full. The big crowds weren't here yet, opting to arrive in time for the Grand Prix race later in the day. Formula 1 was, after all, the big show and the main draw. It was when the likes of Sebastian Keller and Luca Hayes would battle it out for the checkered flag finish. The fans who had arrived that morning with their coffee and croissants for the F2 race were the diehards who wanted to soak up every second of race day, and many of them just so happened to be Reese Maddox fans. Her Instagram following proved as much. She'd settle for being one of the most popular drivers on the circuit, if not world champion. That is, for now.

She checked the clock and gave Luke a final nod, their tradition. As crew chief, he would oversee the pit crew and garage, ensuring both cars were in optimal condition. Reese believed fully in Luke and trusted him with her life, quite literally.

She slid on her balaclava, making sure none of her long dark hair escaped. Her earpiece went in snug. She knelt next to the car just as Julie's voice arrived in her ear.

"Radio check."

"Radio's good," Reese said back.

Julie would be Reese's eyes and voice of reason for the duration of the race, having all the data that Reese didn't. She trusted Julie, who'd learned over the years how to inspire Reese, how to calm her down, and how to call her on her bullshit whenever she needed to be. "You're good to go, Reese," she said.

"All right. Let's bring home a win."

"No one wants that more than I do."

Reese grinned, slid into the car, and let the team harness her tight. "Except me." She would make turn three her bitch if it killed her. Luke handed her the steering wheel, which she clicked into place.

The moment the signal went green, Reese eased out of the garage, the car rumbling low and alive beneath her. Out past the pit exit, the track opened up before her. Reese exhaled slowly, taking a moment to absorb the sheer history in front of her while her heart thudded with anticipation. The moments before a race never got old because this was holy ground.

She gave the engine more throttle, feeling the car respond, abrupt and hungry. She was off and picking up speed. This was the reconnaissance lap, to warm up the car and ensure all systems were operational, but it never felt casual. She pushed the car harder on the straightaway, orienting herself to its feel and ensuring it was in prime condition.

"How are my tire temps?"

"Fronts are great," Julie said. "The backs could use a little heat. Watch your grip. It'll be a slippery one in about fifteen minutes when the rain hits."

"Got it," Reese said, from inside her helmet.

"Everything looks good," Julie said in her ear. "Systems are all working and tip-top. Car is slowly warming up."

"Copy," Reese said, making her way to the grid box and the third position starting point. Her crew swarmed the car for final prep, checking the front wings, tires, sensors, and giving her hydration system a final once-over.

"It's a big one," Luke told her, leaning down to the car. "Stay steady and listen to Julie."

"Don't I always?" she asked.

"No," he said with wide green eyes. The shade that closely matched her own had been handed down from their father, whom she missed much more acutely on race days. He'd have been like a kid in a candy store watching her climb into this caliber of car. Her mom would be watching from home in Missouri, too nervous to sit still in the stands when it was her baby flying by at 200 mph. Reese didn't blame her, after all their family had been through. Despite the anxiety race day brought on, her mother supported and loved Reese and Luke through every second of the season, checking in with them multiple times a day and screaming from her couch.

"Well, I will today."

"You'd better. And Roo?"

She closed her eyes and smiled, half-hating, half-loving the clichéd nickname he'd insisted on since she was three, and he was eight and bossy as hell. "Yep?"

He leaned in closer, so his words were just between them. "This is not the time to be flashy. Smart choices." His brows pulled down, and his eyes held concern. It was an important race, and he wanted to make sure she didn't blow it. For all of them.

"Why is everyone so worried?" she asked.

He leveled a stare, and it was all the answer she needed. This was a business, and the higher-ups at Ravensport would not take kindly to her coming up short this close to the end of the season.

"Knock it off," she said. "I got this. *We* do."

When the track cleared at the three-minute warning, Reese felt everything in her relax. She was born for high-stakes moments like these and relished every second of the adrenaline. When the lights in front of them went out, the race was on. Reese leapt off the line in a controlled burst, tires gripping just enough to keep her from spinning. Her focus narrowed, all noise swallowed by the roar of engines and the thrum of her own pulse. She didn't lunge—she calculated. Brake late into Turn 1, defend her inside line, and keep the car ahead in sight like a target, not a threat. This wasn't about heroics in the opening seconds. It was about staying clean, keeping position, and waiting for the pack to settle before she'd pounce. Her goal for lap one: survive the chaos.

"Nice start," Julie said over the radio. "You have Griffin behind you. The gap is 0.6 seconds. Hold your inside line."

"On it," Reese said, poised to defend.

Time behaved differently behind the wheel, slow and fast at once. Reality drifted away as the minutes ticked by, leaving Reese in a dreamlike state where her instinct and reflexes took over as lights, sounds, and colors flew by. It was everything she loved in this world.

By Lap 12, Julie was calling her in for a pit stop. She'd need new tires. "Box this lap, Reese."

She frowned. "I'm in good track position and think I can make a move on Simeon." The car ahead of her was offering too many openings not to snatch one up. "Give me another lap."

"You've got more than a dozen laps ahead. Your tires don't have much left in them, and you're going to lose grip."

"One more."

"Box, Reese. Box," Julie's voice crackled in her ear, sharp and determined. It wasn't a request.

But instead of driving into the pit lane, Reese stayed out. She pressed the throttle and blew past the entry, committing to one more lap. "Reese. What are you doing?" Julie asked. She probably had a few other choice words, but the team radio was public, and the world could hear every exchange.

"Just trust me on this. About to improve our position immensely." Reese had to redeem herself after the last few races, and that meant taking risks. Defiant? Yes. But Julie was being too cautious with so much at stake. She eased to the outside until she was wheel-to-wheel with Simeon, who was such an asshole she'd take pleasure in the attack. He was edging closer, forcing her onto the marbles. The tiny clumps of shredded rubber waited like ball bearings on concrete. Reese kept her foot in, the steering wheel trembling in her hands as her worn tires searched for grip. *Fuck. Fuck. Fuck.* She had to correct, but the tires weren't listening. The car speared toward the barrier, and she knew what was coming and braced. A split second later, the sickening *bang* of carbon fiber meeting concrete echoed in her helmet. She'd put the car straight into the wall.

Then silence. Nothing. That is, until Julie's voice crackled in her ear. "Reese, are you okay? Talk to me."

"Goddammit!" she shouted, slamming her fists against the wheel. Smoke curled from the right rear as marshals waved yellow flags. The car was in bad shape, with the front wings nearly torn off. She honestly couldn't believe what had just happened. This was an absolute nightmare.

Julie's voice came back, cool and clipped. "Copy that, Reese. Race over."

CHAPTER 1
THE OFFER

Sloane Foster picked up her iced coffee—cream, no sweetener—from the counter of her favorite coffee shop in Venice Beach, just a few blocks from her apartment. The Cat's Pajamas was not only funky and homey, but it also served what she considered the best damn coffee in LA. And she considered herself one who would know.

"Excuse me, ma'am. You're going with iced? It's not even 10 a.m."

No way. Sloane turned at the sound of the familiar voice and found herself face-to-face with none other than Veronica Vance, shiny mauve lip gloss and all. Her brain scrambled for context. "This is certainly an unexpected cameo." She quirked her head, a grin tugging at her mouth despite her shock. This was certainly a welcome one. "What in the hell, Ronnie?"

Veronica rose from her seat near the counter, wearing dark, expensive jeans, a hunter green blazer, and heels. She looked undeniably pleased with herself for the perfectly executed surprise. "What can I say? I had to see you. Been too many months." Her dark hair fell in the same glamorous waves, now a couple of sophisticated inches shorter, brushing just below her shoulders. She was still as gorgeous as ever and far more confident than 90 percent of the population.

"Do you ever take those things off?" Sloane asked, gesturing to the pumps. "Maybe in the shower?" It was what they did, tease each other, affection in disguise. She held out her free arm for a tight hug—because damn, she'd missed Ronnie more than she'd realized until right now. They had such a history, coming up together from karting through Formula 2. Eventually, when Sloane had been called up to F1 and Ronnie hadn't been offered a seat, their paths had diverged. Their friendship hadn't, however. Veronica was family to Sloane and always would be. She was one of those humans whom you could go a year without seeing and pick up exactly where you'd left off.

"No," Veronica told her, giving her a warm squeeze. "Heels live on my feet in perpetuity. Are you a touch blonder than the last time I saw you?"

Sloane touched her hair absently. She had it in a purposefully messy ponytail today, a look she was leaning into. "Nah. Just some extra highlights."

"You're looking good, Foster. But since when do you not?"

"Oh, Veronica, I love you. I also have a feeling you didn't come all the way out here to boost my ego, so what's going on?"

"What? I can't visit my good friend and one of the best drivers ever to hit the circuit?"

"Wow. Now a driving compliment?" Sloane narrowed her gaze and held up a finger. "Veronica Vance, as good a driver as she is, is just as savvy a businesswoman and doesn't appear in my city unannounced without an ask."

"I'm wounded, honestly. That's what you think of me?" She bumped Sloane's shoulder to knock a little sympathy her way.

"Hmm no, you're not."

"Fine," she said with a laugh. Veronica could own her shit. She also brought an impressive résumé. Her friend had become a prominent figure in racing over the years, having worked for

Laurens, Ravensport, and even the FIA for a stint before moving into consulting. Veronica excelled at building airtight team systems and commanded attention wherever she went. Her high-gloss look and God-given beauty definitely didn't hurt, and she harnessed both to open doors. Sloane had always been the quieter, less flashy of the two, which was ironic because—as one of the few female drivers in F1 history—she'd received more attention.

"I do have one little thing to discuss, but I did miss you."

Sloane bumped Veronica's shoulder this time. "At least there's that."

"Want to sit?"

Sloane eyed the table by the window where Veronica had been working: a laptop, her attaché case, and a half-empty mug of coffee. She'd been camped out there for a while. What was all of this about?

"We can do that. I don't have any client consults until this afternoon, so I have time. Why not?" She slid into the chair across from Veronica's and waited. This should be interesting if nothing else.

Veronica stared, shifted, then balked. "No small talk at all? You just want me to jump in cold?"

"How's your mom?" Sloane said to appease her, but also because Cassandra Vance was like a Real Housewife, always into something scandalous or expensive. The best stories came from when it was both.

"Still caught up in herself, buying out half of Barney's, but sends you her love." Veronica dabbed the corners of her mouth with a napkin. "She was excited I'd be seeing you this morning and wants me to steal you away for a holiday ski weekend with the family." Aha. So today wasn't a whim at all. Veronica had planned this Venice Beach ambush. She scooped up that clue and continued on.

"Tell her if she'll make her famous hot toddies, I'm there, but no skimping on the good whiskey."

"It's like you don't even know her." Veronica sat back and smiled. "You still working with that European auto company?"

"I consult for a lot of different companies, but they're one of them, sure."

"Because you know cars. Maybe more than anyone I know."

Sloane traced the top of her cup with one finger. "Uh-oh. My ego's going to weigh me down just walking to my car. Veronica Vance, who are you about to contract me to murder?"

Veronica snapped forward, now in full *I'm-about-to-impress-you* executive mode. "Fine. Let's get right to it. I want you to come to work with me this season." She glanced at her watch. "And it starts soon."

Sloane knew the season was starting soon. She couldn't ignore it if she tried. And she had. "At the little experiment you have going?" She'd heard about Veronica's latest project through the rumor mill of their mutual friends—something about developing up-and-coming female drivers who wouldn't normally be given the spotlight they deserved. A noble cause. They both knew how steep the climb was for women in the sport.

"It's not an experiment," Veronica said flatly. "It's a full-blown racing academy, and it's going to elevate the game for a lot of female drivers. We're weeks from launching."

Sloane lifted a brow. "And you're able to fund all of this? How?"

Veronica smiled. "Because the F1 teams are already in."

That got Sloane's attention.

"Not only that, but they're sending people," Veronica continued. "Talent scouts. Performance directors. Engineers. Some of them are fielding junior programs through it, and other teams are backing full academy entries—two-car teams under their own banners. We're talking Ravensport, Laurens, Halo Racing, the big guys. A few have already agreed to reserve-rights deals."

Sloane leaned back. "So this isn't just visibility."

"No. It's also about access. These drivers won't just be racing each other. They'll be racing under observation. Every weekend. We're putting these women on the map."

"And the people who make the decisions? The F1 team principals?"

"Will be watching from day one," Veronica said. "They've been asking for a pipeline like this for years. Now they've got one."

Sloane absorbed that. An academy wasn't new. *This*—this was different. This focused specifically on female drivers.

"So if someone shines," Sloane said slowly, "they don't have to wait to be discovered."

Veronica's smile sharpened. "Exactly. They'll already be on someone's list." Sloane blinked, absorbing the gravity. She would have killed for something like this when she and Veronica were coming up.

Veronica rechecked her watch, all business. She probably had four more meetings that morning. "Which is why I want *you* there. Because when the right driver comes along—and she will —I need someone who understands what that moment actually costs." She placed a hand on the table, and her features softened. "You have a lot of wisdom to impart, Sloane, and a history that will make your words count."

Sloane exhaled, still turning the concept over in her brain. She couldn't deny the excitement that gathered, a quiet current just beneath the surface. "This sport has way too much testosterone, and everyone damn well knows it."

"Exactly. And the more eyeballs we can get on these amazing women, the more we're going to change that. After a few years, we'll have renovated the whole system. I will personally see to that." Veronica was more than capable, and, honestly, there was no one else positioned as perfectly in the sport. "Formula Next," she said, sitting back in declaration. "That's what we're calling the academy. Designed to increase the number of female drivers in Formula 1."

Silence hit as Veronica waited for her response.

"I have to say, you should be proud of yourself. This is amazing, and I see no holes in the plan." Sloane hesitated, not wanting to offend, but also not ready to leap out of her comfort zone and back into a world she made a point to avoid. "But I don't really see how I can help. I don't race anymore, so I don't think my enrolling would benefit either of us." A joke was always good for business.

"I wasn't offering you a seat, weirdo, but you know that, too."

"Then spill. What do you imagine I would do at Formula Next?" Sloane crossed her arms and waited. Everything in her wanted to scream no to whatever the offer was and end the meeting. At the same time, something unnamed tugged and pushed her to listen. The war within was certainly a lively one.

"I want you to come in, get to know the drivers' styles, their personal weaknesses, and provide your expertise. Maybe offer an informal class or two along the way, you know? Talk to them about life in F1. Pitfalls to avoid on the way up. You're not only one of the best drivers I've ever seen, but you know race dynamics in a way no one else does."

Sloane shifted. "You want a mentor for your drivers?"

Veronica didn't hesitate. "Someone who's been there. Yes."

Sloane frowned. She'd backed away from racing for a reason, and the idea of going back to it in any capacity was a nonstarter. It sent white-hot fear through her nervous system just thinking about it. She now devoted her time and skill set to working closely with the cars' designers and manufacturers, far away from an actual race. She enjoyed working for herself, deciding which consulting projects to take and with whom she wanted to work. The one thing all of those contracts had in common? They were miles away from the actual circuit. She shifted in her chair, now acutely aware of the often-present ache along her spine. The metal rod they'd used to put her back together made itself known right on cue, a pointed reminder of a very dark day in her history. She scrubbed the memories from her brain as they swarmed and pulled, threatening to drag her under. To this day, she struggled with panic attacks and worked hard to fight them off. She was in no mood for one today.

"I'm sorry, Ronnie." Sloane shook her head. "I don't think I'm the best fit. Trust me when I tell you to call Jeff White or Melinda Nash. Either would do a fantastic job getting your drivers ready for F1. I'm a distant has-been away from the circuit for far too long to be of help."

"I'm not accepting an answer today. Today is just a conversation." Veronica said it as simply as she would her sandwich order.

Sloane laughed, reminded of Veronica's tenacity. "I didn't realize. Excuse my mistake. I'll tell you no tomorrow instead since it sits better with your schedule."

Veronica held up a manicured finger. "I want you to take a look at my offer first. It'll be in your inbox before you get home."

"Are you planning to throw money at me? I'm a Foster for God's sake." It was challenging to woo the rich. Sloane was the granddaughter of Benjamin Foster, who'd founded Foster Foods in the 1960s. Her brother, Royce, now ran the very successful company, responsible for a variety of hugely popular brands on grocery store shelves. They were a well-known, well-to-do family. Racing was an expensive sport, and without her family's money, Sloane wouldn't have had half the opportunities that had come her way.

"The money is mediocre. I can admit that," Veronica said, as if not pleased with that part. "We're new and not exactly rolling in cash. Yet. I'm hoping when we wow the masses, that will change."

Sloane laced her fingers under her chin and rested her elbows on the table, lured by the glint in Veronica's eyes. "What's your plan for the wow factor?"

"I'm pulling in a few new drivers who might ... garner us some attention. The kind that sparkle."

Sloane narrowed her gaze. "You're padding your leaderboard with eye candy?"

"No, but … yes." Veronica leaned in. "How are women supposed to gain traction in this sport? We have to create our own opportunities, and recruiting a high-profile driver or two into the academy is good for them and good for us. And if they bring their Instagram following with them, even better. Advertisers will love it." She sipped her latte like a cat enjoying its cream.

Sloane was reminded that racing wasn't just a sport, it was a business. "Who do you have in mind?"

"I'll send you the file tonight. I'd love to have you on board."

"I don't want to look at your file." Sloane knew the moment she opened the door to that world, it would be hard to close it. Veronica knew it, too, which was why the ambush was planned. Sloane would have summarily declined the meeting, the way she was declining this file.

"Can we get you two anything else?" Autumn, the owner of the coffee shop, asked. Her red curls were gorgeous today, and her bright smile filled the room with the kind of positivity one couldn't bottle. Sloane really liked Autumn. They'd even gone on one date once upon a time, well over a decade ago, and quickly realized they were way better suited as friends, which they'd been ever since. The Cat's Pajamas was Sloane's favorite haunt when she was home for any stretch of time, her morning security blanket.

Veronica looked up, smiling at Autumn. "I don't understand how this coffee is so good."

Autumn placed a hand on her hip and leaned in. "Because I'm a woman obsessed with my craft."

"It's true." Sloane grinned and sat back. "I've traveled the world and never found anywhere as good."

"I wouldn't mind a second one of these to go," Veronica said with a hopeful look. "It's a lavender latte."

"My specialty. Coming right up." Autumn headed to the

front of the shop and, once she was safely past their table, gestured to Veronica, added a saucy look, then raised her palms in silent question. *Oh.* She wanted to know if Sloane and Veronica were a thing. A romance. A couple. A forbidden tryst. Sloane shook her head emphatically, prompting Veronica to frown and flip around in curiosity. The idea of romancing Veronica Vance, the strongest-willed woman in the world, was laughable. She'd eat Sloane alive. Not that Sloane didn't love her type A, highly driven friend.

"Was that charades?" Veronica asked. "Am I the subject of a silent TED talk?"

"Yes," Sloane said without hesitation as Autumn, wide-eyed, scurried away, caught and convicted in the romance-themed pantomime act. "But as an act of penance, I'll put that second coffee on my tab." She stood. "Thanks for making the trip. I'm sorry to disappoint you about the academy. But here's the thing. I know it's going to be revolutionary in your hands, and I will be cheering you on every step of the way." She meant it, too.

Veronica didn't flinch. "Look at the file, Sloane. For me."

She sighed, crumbling like a sandcastle in high tide. "I'll give it a glance, but only because you once bought my dinner when I left my wallet in that cab that smelled like seaweed."

"Well, thank God for seaweed cabs. And just take a little glance through. That's all I'm asking."

"Will do."

Sloane left Veronica at the Cat's Pajamas, still shocked by her visit and the ripple it left in its wake. Her morning had just been tossed into the air with pieces of herself and memories raining down all around her. She attempted to pick them up, each one a reminder of the past she'd been forced to move on from. Her racing days had meant everything to her, but she had no intention of returning to them. It was a powder keg that was best not to disrupt.

Later that night, after a Zoom call with Honda to go over their new engine upgrades, Sloane poured herself a glass of the

Bordeaux she'd picked up last week in France. She could unwind with that new medical drama everyone was talking about or maybe start a new book. She'd been on a biography kick lately, with the most recent from Michelle Obama having energized her for more. Then she remembered her promise to Veronica and the email she'd seen sneak into her inbox a few hours earlier. She could take a few moments to check that box and officially let Veronica know she wasn't interested in working with the academy's slate of drivers.

Settling in on her ridiculously comfortable cream-colored sofa and careful not to spill her wine, Sloane flipped open her laptop and started to read. Not only had Veronica included the offer, but she had also taken it a step further and attached the schedules, goals, rankings, and dossiers for each driver. Before Sloane realized it, over an hour had passed as she pored through the material, lost down the rabbit hole into a world that used to be her one true love. The pull was still there and just as potent as ever. *Fuck. Fuck. Fuckity. Fuck.* She ran a hand through her blond hair, half aware of the dangerous game she was playing but too hyped up to rein herself in. She scrolled back to the schedule and, just for fun, compared it to her own. Only a couple of actual conflicts because she refused to book herself too far out. She liked keeping her options open, going where the water was warm. She'd had no idea she'd be in France earlier this month until days before. Just how she liked it.

But, wait. Was she actually considering Veronica's offer?

She took a fortifying breath, did something she'd never done, and let herself go there. Sloane closed her eyes and let herself drift back to her F1 days. The roar of engines pressed against her chest like a living thing, vibrating through her bones. The smell of burning rubber and hot oil clung to the air, mingling with the faint tang of sweat. Her hands flexed as she remembered the feel of the steering wheel, slick and warm from countless laps, fingers tightening instinctively around the worn grip. The tires screamed over asphalt, a high-pitched wail that was both terrifying and intoxicating. Wind whipped against her helmet, carrying with it the taste of dust and adrenaline, and she could almost feel the centrifugal pull of corners, her body leaning into the curves as if the car and she were one. For a moment, every worry melted away, leaving only the pure, unfiltered thrill of speed and control. For a brief moment, she lost herself in the sensory over-load. Dizzying. Wonderful. That is, until she remembered how it all ended and shut the laptop as if it were on fire.

"What are you doing right now?" she asked herself and took a quick lap around her kitchen, needing to burn off this extra energy. "This is a bad idea, and you know it." Sometimes hearing her voice out loud served as a wake-up call. But not tonight because it was already too late. Somehow, the mixture of Veronica's words and the lure of the world she used to know had worked their way beneath her skin.

Two days later, she called Veronica.

"I wondered when I might hear from you," Ronnie said instead of hello.

"Yeah, yeah." Sloane paused but only briefly. "So, when do you want me there?"

Reese scanned the beige and blue living room of the junior suite she'd been housed in for Formula Next's opening weekend in Miami. She'd arrived well in advance of race weekend to meet the other drivers in the academy and attend the various events Veronica Vance had arranged. There was a reception on the schedule, a few presentations, some press junkets, and some meet and greets with fans to get everyone excited for the upcoming season.

She pulled her dark hair into a ponytail as she moved through the small space. While the academy felt like a step down from F2, she was also grateful she'd landed anywhere at all after the disastrous end to her season.

While Ravensport wasn't offering her seat back to her for the upcoming F2 season, they were still investing in her. They had agreed to put her on the team for the academy, likely at the urging of Veronica Vance, who'd walked into the paddock that rainy day in England after she'd put the car into the wall.

There'd been a knock on the open door to the driver's room. Reese had been aiming for a little privacy to lick her wounds. "Have a minute?"

Annoyed, Reese had turned at the sound of the voice. Still in her race suit and livid from having to retire from the race, she wasn't in the mood to speak to anyone. But she went still when she saw *Veronica Vance* standing in the doorway. She'd seen her many times at qualifying or on race days, usually with an assistant by her side or a TV camera trained on her face. Everyone knew who she was, a formidable driver from years back, but now a personality that everyone respected. She was a businessperson and a spokeswoman for the sport.

Reese straightened. "Hi." At any other moment, she would have turned up the wattage on her smile and led with her God-given charm. Today wasn't that day. Hi was all she had in her.

"Tough break out there."

"You could say that." Reese paused, unsure what Veronica could possibly want from her in this moment.

"In fact, you've had a string of those. Has Ravensport offered you a seat for next season?"

They hadn't, and today would make the prospect even less likely. She had a feeling Veronica already knew all of that. She shook her head.

"Well, I have one."

Reese arched a brow. "Are you starting your own F2 team?"

Veronica walked further into the room. "You're familiar with Formula Next?"

She'd heard the rumors. Everyone had. "The driver academy?"

"Exactly. Ten teams. Two drivers each. I have it on good authority that I could convince Ravensport to keep you on. Just at the academy, which would provide you with a more direct pipeline anyway."

She blinked, trying to process the offer and the logic. "Formula 1 is my next step."

Veronica passed her a sympathetic smile. "I don't see that happening anytime soon. Without a redemption arc, that is. Your F2 team is about to drop you, not promote you. I doubt that anyone else will pick you up. If you want to be behind the wheel, I'm offering you an opportunity that, with all due respect, I'm not sure you deserve."

"Ouch."

Veronica held up her hands. "I shoot straight. You'll learn this about me."

"I can handle it."

"Good. The academy races exclusively on Formula 1 weekends. Qualifying on Friday. A sprint race on Saturday. And a feature race on Sunday morning. The first race is in the spring."

While Reese hated that it felt like she was moving backward rather than forward, she also knew that the academy might be her last shot. If she wanted to race, she didn't have the luxury of choice. At least, not anymore. She sighed. "And when I take the championship. What then?"

A small smile tugged at Veronica's lips. "You're very sweet, but have you seen my lineup? You'll have an uphill battle in front of you."

"And if I blow past all of them?"

"Then there might be people at the end of the season who want to have a conversation. I make no promises." She still wasn't at all convinced, and that was fine. Reese loved a challenge, and Veronica would see what she was capable of sooner or later.

"And you think Ravensport is in?"

"They will be," Veronica said, like she owned the world. "I have a way of convincing others."

Reese blinked. "I think I just saw it in action."

"Thank you for allowing me to bend your ear, Reese. I envision a beneficial relationship ahead." Veronica extended her hand, and Reese shook it. "My office will be in touch with your agent."

She watched Veronica Vance glide out of the room, having changed the trajectory of Reese's immediate future in the span of just three minutes.

That was four months ago, and here she sat ready to kick off the Formula Next season. All women drivers would make up the grid, unlike what she was used to. In reality, she enjoyed the idea of surrounding herself with top female drivers chasing their dreams. Women, in general, were her absolute favorites. It was just a shame she was going to have to beat all of them on her way to the podium.

"I don't mind taking the couch," Julie said, gesturing to the pullout. As a last-minute addition to her contract, Julie didn't yet have her own accommodations. Reese had agreed to let her crash until Ravensport and the academy officially added her to the team. Reese had worked hard to ensure Julie remained part of her deal, even if it meant sacrificing other small perks. She honestly couldn't imagine anyone else in her ear when she was out on the track, heart hammering, tires hot, engine screaming, knowing Julie's voice would keep her alive—and maybe sane.

"Good, because I prefer sleeping like a starfish." Reese flopped onto the armchair opposite and offered a wink. The Miami skyline glimmered through the sliding glass doors, a reminder of the upcoming weekend and its looming importance. Julie settled onto the pullout, cane leaning against the edge, and already had her tablet open, scrolling through telemetry from practice, the predicted weather, and a tentative strategy. Reese let herself watch for a beat, grateful that this was the one person who would push her, scold her, and—when necessary—save her from herself.

"What time are we due at the reception?"

"Not until six," Julie said.

Reese pushed herself out of the chair and crossed to the window. "You want to grab a fun drink before the official drinks?" she asked. She felt slightly out of sorts. Tonight meant meeting a flood of new people—drivers, academy sponsors, team principals—and the thought of it all buzzing around her at once made her restless. It didn't help that her brother wouldn't be there. Ravensport had elected to keep Luke with the F2 team, which meant that for the first time, Reese was truly on her own.

"I'd love it, but I have our strategy to work through."

"And we have so much time for that. Honestly, Jules. We're in Miami. Shouldn't we take advantage?"

Julie sighed and turned around. "I'm worried you're assuming these women are going to be easily dominated. That you're going to breeze in here and win."

Reese nodded. "You're right." She lifted her shoulders as if to say, *and?* Because she had every intention of blowing these women away once the starting lights went out. She didn't come here to play checkers.

Julie nudged her glasses up her nose. "This cannot be a replay of your stint in F2. You've got to get your head in the game. Less smiling. More work."

The thought sobered her because a replay was certainly not what she intended either. She strolled to Julie and slung an arm around her shoulder. "I will get my shit together. That means doing my homework and preparing every time I pull onto the track, whether it's practice, qualifying, or a race. New leaf time. New Reese."

"I'm going to hold you to it because I honestly think this is our last chance."

"You mean *my* last chance," Reese said. Julie's eyes softened with regret. They both knew it was true. Julie's star was on the rise in the racing world, and she'd be just fine if Reese was never offered another seat. The idea slashed at her, imagining Julie partnering with another driver, one who delivered. Which is why she couldn't let that happen. Reese sighed. "I know I'm capable of more than I've shown people." She scrunched one eye closed. "Just one fun drink? I'll buy."

"You're unbelievable."

"But also, incredibly lovable. Wouldn't you say?" Reese asked.

"Ask me again after you win something."

CHAPTER 2
FALSE START

Sloane preferred sitting at the bar over anywhere else in the restaurant. From there, she had the best view in the house — the chefs moving in practiced choreography, the bartender's easy charm with customers, the front door swinging open to let in the night air and new faces. Drinks arrived faster, the food felt more casual, and she never had to crane her neck to flag someone down. Plus, people-watching was a sport on race weekend, and the bar was the front row.

She checked her watch. The academy's kickoff reception was set to start in half an hour, but she didn't feel the need to be there at six on the dot. Her role that evening was small, which she took comfort in, seizing the chance to ease herself into the world she'd been on the outskirts of for so long. Veronica would introduce her during her welcome speech, and Sloane would then be free to enjoy the reception and get to know the drivers and their teams with whom she'd be working. After that, she planned to slip away at the earliest possible point, having fulfilled her responsibility. Hopefully, this brief pregame would help ease her nerves.

"Hi," a woman from three stools over said, once the space between them was vacated by two men who'd been arguing over the quality of wine in America. She wasn't sorry to see them go. "I don't want to bother you at all. In fact, tell me if I am, but I have an ask." Except it wasn't just a woman, it was Reese Maddox. She'd seen her arrive with her engineer about twenty minutes ago. She was gorgeous and walked through the room as if she belonged there. Long dark hair, sea green eyes that could easily read blue in the right light. She understood why Veronica had recruited her to the academy despite her less-than-stellar record in F2.

"You're okay. What can I do for you?" She tacked on a smile, knowing they'd be working together soon. Perhaps Reese wanted to introduce herself.

"I'm not from around here and was hoping to get a restaurant recommendation."

"Oh." Reese apparently hadn't recognized Sloane, which was entirely okay. "I don't know the area all that well, unfortunately." She turned back to her martini. There would be time for small talk at the reception. After all, this was supposed to be Sloane's quiet recharge time, and she planned to claim it. Polite and short usually did the trick. Reese picked up her drink and slid down two chairs until she was seated next to Sloane. She smelled unexpectedly of vanilla and sandalwood. Sloane would have appreciated the combination if she'd wanted any company at all.

"Are you staying at this hotel?"

"That's kind of a personal question, don't you think?" Sloane said. Where was that engineer to wrangle her?

"Fair enough." Reese tapped her rocks glass with the tips of her fingers, her manicured nails clear with polish. "We don't know each other. Why would you want to share that information? Easy fix. I'm Reese."

"Nice to meet you."

"Nice to meet you, too."

"I'm in town for the week for the Grand Prix." She gestured

with her head out the large picture window that overlooked the Miami International Autodrome. "Race weekend."

"Ah."

"I'm a driver." Reese met her eyes and waited, surely expecting a more pronounced reaction. Sloane had a feeling that the line probably opened up a lot of doors when it came to picking up women. She just hadn't expected to be one of them coming into tonight.

She decided to play along and widened her eyes. "Are you kidding? As in professionally?"

"Yes," Reese said, looking very serious now. "It's what I do for a living. I am a professional race car driver."

"Wow. That's really impressive."

"You should come out and catch a race. The weather's supposed to be beautiful this weekend."

Sloane sipped her drink. "You know, I just might."

"I'd be happy to teach you a few things about racing to, you know, give the experience context."

"Oh yeah? What would you teach me?" This was getting good.

Reese turned sideways on her stool so she faced Sloane. "Well, first of all, the cars all line up on the grid."

"The grid. Got it."

"Then five red lights come on one at a time. Then, when they all go out? That means go. Not before, not after."

"I can imagine that's a big moment."

"Huge. It's all about your reaction time. You jump the start, you get penalized. You're too slow, you're immediately overtaken."

"Well," Sloane said, sitting taller. "I'm glad I have you to guide me. I thought it was all just about going really, really fast."

"There's actually a lot to the sport. Tire management. Strategically timing pit stops. Overtake maneuvers."

"I'm gathering."

Reese opened her mouth, likely to continue her lesson, only

to be interrupted by the woman Reese had arrived with. Sloane recognized her as an engineer from the dossiers Veronica had sent over. She was always one to do her homework, and in this case, it had served her well.

"Oh, wow. Hello," the woman said, coming behind their stools with her cane, her eyes glued to Sloane, her face turning red. "I'm a little caught off guard right now. Forgive me. This is an immense honor." She looked to Reese as if to say, *Can you believe this?* before swiveling back to Sloane. "Ms. Foster, my name is Julie Rennick. I'm Reese's engineer and someone who's meticulously followed every aspect of your impressive career. You've paved the way for all of us."

Reese froze, eyes flicking between Julie and Sloane as if the lights at the club had just been turned on at closing. Her swagger from moments ago faltered, and a bright flush crept across her cheeks. "Wait. You're Sloane Foster?" she said, and the recognition hit her all at once, and it seemed to mortify her in the process. Sloane had to admit that this was wholly satisfying. She couldn't help sending Reese a small, private smile in response. The same driver who had been flirting like a pro and giving her basic racing pointers just minutes ago was now reduced to a flustered, self-conscious mess. Even someone as magnetic as Reese could stumble, and Sloane had a front-row seat. She decided to be gracious because, other than acting like a show-off, Reese had committed no real crime.

"I am. It's a pleasure to meet you officially, Reese. That was a helpful lesson." She faced forward and gestured to the bartender for her check, but Julie was quick to step in.

"Oh, I'll take that," she told the bartender, her brow furrowed in earnest as if this was a mission she simply could not fail. Julie seemed kind and grounded in a way her driver was not. "I'd love to buy your drink. Honestly, it's on my bucket list, if you don't mind."

"I don't mind, if you're sure."

"More than. You're kind of a big, huge deal to me. I hope that's okay to say. I ramble when I'm nervous."

"It is, and thank you," Sloane said, appreciative but ready to get out of there. "Find me at the reception, and we can talk," she told Julie. "I'd love to hear about your career so far." That part was true. Sloane loved talking to engineers, mechanics, and pretty much anyone who interacted with the car. Drivers were a unique breed, but those who comprised the team were always generous and selfless, and their love for the sport was contagious.

"I will definitely do that."

Well, it was time to take a deep breath and head into the fire. The experience at the restaurant had been an unexpected one, and if nothing else, she'd learned that Reese Maddox's arrogance was something to take note of as she worked with the drivers. Tenacity went a long way in racing, but an overarching ego hindered clear decision-making. She stood and, with her cross-body on her shoulder, turned to Reese. "I'll see you at the reception. This was fun ... and enlightening." Reese seemed to be struggling for words, another new development, but with Sloane on the way out, she wouldn't need any. "Take care."

Sloane walked out of the bar and into the hotel lobby, realizing that they were going to have their hands full with that one. Reese was confident, charismatic, and undeniably beautiful in person—sharp features, bright green eyes, and a presence that made it obvious why sponsors swarmed. Sloane had seen the stares and second glances Reese had pulled from practically everyone in the bar. No wonder Veronica had brought her here. She wasn't just a driver. She was a spotlight that would illuminate the academy when it needed it most. But could she back up all that swagger on race day? Only time would tell. Sloane was intrigued and knew one thing for sure. Reese Maddox was a definite wild card, but could she pull off a win when it mattered?

"Just kill me now," Reese said, staring at the door Sloane Fucking Foster had just walked through. Reese placed her palms flat on the bar, attempting to ground herself and will this awful moment away. "I don't deserve to move forward in life. I'm merely a shell of a human who should never race again. I could maybe work in a bakery. I used to be good at helping my mom bake cookies and frost cakes. Why not revisit those tasks?" She took a long swallow of her drink because she now needed it.

"You're going to have to catch me up," Julie said as she signed the sales slip. She turned around and waited for Reese's delayed response because Reese was so far into the land of mortification that she was going to have to build a house there. Maybe a gingerbread one, since she was a baker now.

"I tried to impress her," she said and closed her eyes for a moment. "Flirt a little."

"You flirted with who?" Julie looked around the bar.

"Sloane Foster. And not only did I hit on her, but I did it in this overly confident, very basic, cringe-for-days manner."

Julie blinked about eight times, as if the information had short-circuited her system. "No."

She stared into Julie's overly widened eyes. "Yes. Jules, I offered to teach her the rules of racing and then proceeded to do just that."

Jules winced like a horrified child in the midst of a nightmare. "No."

"Yes, again. I'm going to have to keep saying yes." She shook her head slowly. "I explained to her what lights out meant."

"Please tell me you did not do that." Julie squeezed Reese's wrist, imploring. "Not to Sloane Foster of all people on the entire planet. She's an icon."

"Except I did."

They stared at each other as the realization—no—*humiliation* swirled and settled on Reese's shoulders, a boulder she'd now be forced to carry around for life. Then she did what she always did when something didn't go her way: she deflected. "Maybe she thought it was sweet."

"Sure. One of the most badass drivers this sport has ever seen, a woman who was on her way to winning the world championship if it hadn't been for a crash that never should have happened, thought you not having a clue who she was, and schooling her was *sweet*. I don't know what the statistical likelihood of that scenario works out to be, but let me tell you, it's not in your favor."

Reese sobered. "Point taken." She shrugged. "I'll find a way to win her over. She's probably only here for tonight anyway, a show of support."

"Maybe."

"If I can just make it through this event without bursting into flames, there's a chance I can look myself in the mirror again."

"Just have to survive an hour then. Two tops." Julie nodded, seeming to take comfort in that lifeline. "Let's get through tonight without any more missteps, okay? You have got to be on your best behavior."

"Yes. You're right, and I will be."

"Excuse me, are you Reese Maddox?" a twenty-something in a decidedly low-cut top asked as she slid a strand of blond hair over her ear.

Reese eased into a polite smile and turned to the girl with full attention. She wanted her fans to feel seen, a choice she'd made after drivers she'd idolized had brushed her off when she was a kid. She vowed never to do that to anyone once she'd established a career. "I am. Hi. What's your name?"

"Sophie."

"It's really nice to meet you."

"Would you mind signing a hat for me?" Sophie came prepared and pushed forward a Ravensport team hat and pen, which Reese happily took and used to sign the bill.

"Come on," Julie said, tugging her wrist. "We have a reception to get to. Sorry, Sophie."

"That's okay. So awesome meeting you!" Sophie called.

As she was being dragged away, Reese waved at the soft-eyed woman and held her gaze for a few seconds, watching as she melted and blushed. Sophie had been friendly and sweet, and the fan interaction had been just what Reese needed, helping her forget about the most embarrassing moment of her life. At least, for all of two minutes.

CHAPTER 3
THIS IS FINE

The elevator doors slid open to the 22nd floor with a soft chime, and Reese stepped into a world that smelled faintly of polished marble and expensive perfume. The reception was perched near the very top of the Delacorte Hotel with the city of Miami sprawling beneath floor-to-ceiling windows like a glittering circuit of its own. Neon streaks from South Beach pulsed in the distance, while the ocean caught the fading light of sunset, a watercolor wash of pink and indigo. The view alone was enough to steal her breath. Veronica Vance had timed the event perfectly. Reese was drawn immediately to the windows, eager to soak in the gorgeous view and catch her breath a moment, but the hum of voices quickly pulled her attention back inside. She smiled at the people she passed, nodded politely, and remembered to put on her professional face. *No hitting on anyone. Absolutely do not flirt.* Julie's words were a chant in the back of her brain.

The room had been dressed to impress. Sleek cocktail tables draped in white linen were scattered across the glossy parquet floor, each crowned with flickering votives and delicate arrangements of tropical orchids. *Nice touch.* Waiters in crisp black uniforms floated through the crowd with trays of champagne flutes and artfully plated hors d'oeuvres.

"Those look too pretty to eat," Julie whispered as a server glided by with canapés.

"Yeah, Veronica Vance doesn't mess around," Reese whispered back, feeling intimidated for the first time in quite a while. She couldn't pronounce half these foods.

"I see Rodney," Julie whispered, gesturing toward Ravensport's team principal. Rodney Krauss oversaw both the drivers and the myriad of people supporting them. He was at the top of the pyramid and also their boss, meaning they'd have daily interactions. Academy or not, Ravensport took winning seriously and wanted as many points on the board as possible. "I'm going to go check with him about the tire degradation data we received."

"Okay. Let him know I'm flexible on strategy," Reese said, wanting to start the series as a team player. The one-woman show had never served her well, so her goal was to collaborate more. Not always insist she knew best. She could do that. Right?

Alone now, she studied the room. The buzz of conversation was thick, easy, practiced. Everyone was already slipping into the rhythm of a season that hadn't even begun. Reese spotted a few familiar faces—two drivers she'd tangled with in karting days, one who'd beaten her soundly in a rain-soaked final. Others she recognized only from her late-night Googling before hopping on the plane: names she'd studied, stats she'd memorized, faces that still felt like cutouts from someone else's highlight reel. She blew out a breath and adjusted her posture, trying to project confidence, but the memory of her earlier blunder with Sloane Foster tugged at her like a loose thread.

"Reese, hey."

She turned at the sound of her name to see Delaney Rhodes, one of her truly good friends from when she was just a kid racing go-karts. It had been what, a couple of years since they'd seen each other? Delaney looked awesome as always, fashion-forward with a nod to European trends. Tonight, she wore black pants, sockless loafers, and a sleeveless white blouse that showed off her fabulous arms. Her thick, chestnut hair was loose past her shoulders and shiny, offering the slightest, God-given wave. A lopsided grin tugged at her mouth, the same one Reese remembered from podium photos years ago. Delaney always managed to look effortlessly cool with a sweetness one didn't suspect lurking behind the very chill persona. Reese grinned, a little tension slipping from her shoulders at the sight of a familiar face.

"I was starting to think you'd ghosted me," Reese said, breaking into a grin as she pulled Delaney into an immediate hug. They were headed into the academy as teammates—the two drivers signed by Ravensport—and Reese couldn't imagine a better pairing. Delaney was fast, fearless, and exactly the kind of competition Reese wanted beside her instead of across the garage. The fact that they'd both be wearing Ravensport royal blue only sweetened this new chapter of her career. Their connection had always worked like this: no warm-up required. Time fell away the second they were together, and they slid easily back into the rhythm of talking trash, trading life updates, comparing love-life disasters, and joking about which one of them would cross the finish line first.

"Did you ever imagine us here when we were teenagers? This close to it all?" Delaney glanced around, eyes wide, as if having stumbled into Disney World as a child. "We're on an actual scout list for Formula 1."

"No. I definitely didn't," Reese said. "We're karters." She leaned closer, not wanting to let anyone else in on the imposter syndrome. "Where are the hot dog stands and dollar-fifty beers, because this reception is not that."

"Right? I'm feeling very much out of my league. Looking around this room, I see why they call F1 a rich man's sport."

Reese stepped closer. "Let's make it so they can't use the word *man* in that descriptor ever again."

"I volunteer as tribute," Delaney said to a laugh from Reese, who hadn't felt this relaxed in weeks. Thank God for the friends who knew the real *her*.

"I think I could actually get used to this. F2 was cutthroat, but they didn't throw us too many fancy parties. Make that zero."

"I wouldn't know. I've been stuck in the Indy world and trying to find a way back to civilization."

"All it takes is the right sponsor." Reese wouldn't be anywhere near the cost-prohibitive sport without people willing to back her financially. She didn't come from money the way so many of her competitors had and wouldn't have had a shot without convincing rich people to take a chance on her.

"Easy for you to say." Delaney popped her in the arm. "People love you wherever you go. They want a conversation, a photo, or to join your latest live stream." Delaney tossed her hair back as if to imitate Reese and underline the allure.

Reese laughed. "Well, I happen to like you, so you can come on my live stream anytime you want. And sponsors? You just have to get out there and hustle. Turns out, I can hustle my goddamn ass off."

Delaney gave Reese's chin a shake. "It helps when you look like this cover girl right here. Looks good on an energy drink poster. Correct me if I'm wrong, but isn't that you on the cardboard cutout in the lobby?" It had been. One of her sponsors had it flown in.

"No comment." Reese grinned because Delaney didn't mean any harm, but her spirits took a dip, nonetheless. Reese didn't aspire to be a spokesperson for any product. She didn't want to be known for the cardboard cutout. It was a necessary part of her job to keep the funds flowing. At the very least, she hoped the racing world saw more in her driving than an opportunity to sell a drink. Sometimes she wasn't so sure.

"Hey. You know I'm just messing with you, right?" Delaney asked quietly with her signature arched brow. She must have sensed Reese's energy shift, having always been good at that kind of thing. On the outside, Delaney Rhodes came off like a badass, but underneath, she was a thoughtful, sensitive soul.

"Yes, and you can fuck right off," Reese said back with a shoulder bump, attempting to let her off the hook.

"There's the Reese I know." The two of them shared a smile hung on years of shared experience.

They'd always vibed in the midst of friendly competition that simmered underneath. That was just part of racing. Everyone wanted to win, and that meant taking down the driver in front of you, even if you liked them. Yep, it would be fun to race Delaney again. She was quick and feisty behind the wheel, and the two of them had been known to mix it up. One of their more notorious scuffles ended with Delaney tossing her helmet across the driver's lounge and calling Reese a reckless and selfish dick. They'd made up two hours later over a beer and girl-watching on the Las Vegas strip.

Delaney lifted her chin, which meant they were shifting into shop talk. "Ready for this weekend?"

"Hell, yeah. It's been a minute since I drove under a checkered flag. Feeling a bit of withdrawal from high-adrenaline curves and fighting with assholes like you on the straights."

"As long as you get out of my way."

Reese tilted her head. "Or you could get out of mine. Just an idea."

"Careful, Reese. If you're seeing my front wing, it means you're already in trouble."

"Good. I like starting the weekend in trouble."

Delaney laughed, the sound bright and unrestrained, drawing a glance from a man in a thousand-dollar suit. Reese felt herself relax, reminded that even though the league was new, the heart of it all was still racing. This was her element—and she was among her friends. They were built the same, and there was something comforting in that.

"It's more than good to see you, Delaney."

"Right? Can we hang out later? I can introduce you to some of the others."

"I'd love that."

At that point, the room seemed to quiet, which prompted them both to turn. "If I could have everyone's attention, I'd like to say a few words." Veronica Vance, in a gorgeous, dignified blue cocktail dress, stood before a podium and a microphone.

"First of all, thank you for being here on such a special occasion. Tonight, we celebrate more than just the start of Formula Next's first-ever season—we celebrate the village it takes to be here. Each of you, drivers and team members alike, represents the future of this sport. You've pushed through late nights in the garage, early mornings on the track, and countless moments where most people would've quit. But you didn't."

Reese swallowed, nodding along with Veronica's words because they rang true.

"This league is about more than racing. It's about proving what happens when talent, discipline, and opportunity collide. It's about showing the world that speed, skill, and determination aren't limited by where you come from, what you look like, or who you are." She was a powerful speaker, making eye contact with each person in the audience one at a time rather than addressing the group. "And yes, it's about proving that women belong here—not as exceptions, not as novelties, but as drivers, engineers, and leaders who raise the standard for everyone. When you put on that helmet, when you step out on that track, you are carrying not just your own dreams, but the dreams of every young person who watches you and thinks, *maybe that could be me one day.* That's powerful. Every lap you take sends a message that the next generation of girls doesn't have to ask if there's a place for them in motorsport—they'll know there is."

Reese stood taller, already feeling inspired by the message, and realizing that maybe there was a larger calling here she hadn't fully examined. Veronica's words resonated.

"So, race hard. Race fair. Race with everything you have.

Make this season unforgettable—for yourselves, for your teams, and for the future of motorsport. Now let's raise a glass to a season that will test us, transform us, and remind us why we fell in love with racing in the first place."

The servers were quickly handing out glasses for the toast, and Reese raised hers along with the rest of the room. She and Delaney touched their glasses and locked eyes, the importance of the message having changed the temperature in the room. This wasn't just about them. It wasn't just about the wins, the podiums, or even the thrill of speed. It was about every girl who dreamed of the track and might be watching them now, imagining themselves behind the wheel. The responsibility hit her fully for the first time: their season, their choices, could shape what came next. Racing had always been a passion, but tonight, it felt like purpose. And all the more reason to earn her way to the top, and that meant Formula 1. At any cost.

"She has a way of convincing me of literally anything," Delaney said, turning to Reese. "She could probably get me to sign away my life's savings."

"Good thing I'm here then," Reese said, mid-drink of champagne.

"Here I am imagining smoking every driver in this room, and she brings me right back down to earth, thinking about little girls in the stands and the cause that's more important than all of us."

"It's sweet that you think you could do that," Reese said with a playful wink. "But I'm right there with you about the speech. She knows how to drive home a message. Which I suppose is why she's Veronica Vance. I take it she showed up in your paddock after a race?"

"Ha. No. Paddock visits must be reserved for Instagram superstars," Delaney said with a wink. "She contacted my team principal and my agent like a normal transaction. What's it like to be Reese Maddox anyway?"

"And now that we've celebrated the moment, let's get down

to a little bit of business," Veronica said, precluding Reese from having to answer that question. "Allow me to showcase my team." One by one, Veronica introduced the room to social media directors, hospitality managers, technical heads, race coordinators, and more. "I saved this particular introduction for last," Veronica said, eyeing the crowd. "Some of you have already spotted her. In fact, there was a literal line of people waiting to speak with her just a few moments ago. But let me tell you happily that there will be plenty of time for everyone, because Sloane Foster is not just here tonight as a supporter of the academy, she's joining our team."

Reese went still. *Oh no.*

Delaney swiveled in Reese's direction, her eyes pulled wide in shock. "Get the fuck out of here."

Veronica wasn't finished. "Sloane will serve as Director of Driver Development for the academy. Using her vast knowledge of the sport, she'll offer our drivers insight, group coaching, and individual sessions to enhance their lap times, adjust their mental outlook, use telemetry data to their advantage, anticipate complications on the circuit, and formulate real-world solutions to deal with them accordingly." Sloane pretended to wipe her brow as if realizing she had her work cut out for her, which, of course, pulled a laugh from the crowd. Reese tried to remember to breathe. "You can expect maybe even a behind-the-scenes glimpse of what it was like to be one of the first female F1 drivers in the history of the sport. We're blessed, folks. Join me in welcoming my friend, Sloane Foster."

The applause outweighed anything they'd heard that night. Reese followed the gazes to see Sloane standing a few yards from Veronica, smiling warmly at the room. She didn't have a flute of champagne. Apparently, the one martini at the bar had been enough. Reese felt the mortification from earlier triple as she understood that she could no longer sweep the exchange between them into the closet and close the door. She was an absolute idiot and would continue paying for it. Only one thing to do. Fall on her sword. She would find a way to speak with Sloane later, apologize again. She'd stand in line if she had to. Climb the tallest mountain. Dance the two-step in a monkey costume. Luckily, the first was all it took to stand face-to-face with Sloane.

"Hi," Reese said when it was, at last, her turn. "First of all, I'm excited to hear you'll be joining us."

"Me too. This should be an exciting series."

"Secondly, I'm incredibly embarrassed about our conversation at the bar, and I'd like to apologize."

Sloane nodded and crossed her arms. Finally, she squinted and leaned in. "What conversation would that be?"

Reese exhaled her way to a smile. It was a response filled with grace and kindness that left Reese grateful. Sloane was letting her off the hook. "Thank you for that."

Sloane lifted a shoulder. "I like fresh starts."

"I will prove to you that I'm worthy of your forgiveness. And I promise not to behave like an overconfident bobblehead in the future."

"Prove yourself behind the wheel this weekend, okay?" she said gently. "I want to see what you're capable of. And I don't plan to go easy on anyone. Even bobbleheads."

Reese smiled. "I wouldn't want you to." In the midst of her groveling, Reese couldn't seem to unsee one thing. Sloane's blue eyes were gorgeous, like sunlight breaking through a canopy of trees. There was also a confident, untamed quality behind them, perhaps the same quality that once had her on the way to becoming the first female world champion at 230 miles an hour. Reese lived for untamed. It's what fueled her on her very best race days. Well, until she spun out or put the car into a wall. She'd have to learn to balance untamed with … something else she hadn't yet figured out. "What are your thoughts on tire degradation? Change 'em early or stay out when the other cars pull into the pits?"

Sloane opened her mouth to answer, and Reese held up a hand. "Kidding. I know you have a line of well-wishers."

Sloane didn't laugh. Instead, she watched Reese with interest, and it sent a slight shiver up her spine. This woman had presence for days, but she was hard to read. "I watched your films and have thoughts. Let's chat soon."

They stared at each other for a moment as if trying to figure each other out. "Yes. I look forward to it."

Sloane blinked as if remembering herself. "If you'll excuse me. I should probably ..." She looked behind Reese to the line of other drivers and team members waiting to say hello and introduce themselves.

"Oh. Yes. Sorry. Of course." Reese stepped aside and only then realized that her pulse was racing, her heart like a drum. It was a foreign feeling. She wasn't the type who got nervous. Apparently, Sloane Foster had that effect. When she'd laid eyes on her an hour ago in the bar, she'd been drawn to her immediately. She wondered now if she'd sensed a kindred spirit in Sloane. Don't all drivers have a similar quality? Or maybe it was just how goddamn beautiful she was in person. She stole another look just because. Blond with light green eyes.

"So, she's sticking around," Julie said with a clap to Reese's back. "This is probably the best thing that could possibly happen to drivers at the academy." She must have caught Reese's face that said she wasn't so sure about that. "Except for the whole crash and burn and humiliate yourself at the bar."

"Thanks for the colorful reminder." Reese exhaled, trying to stay positive. How she chose to view Sloane's presence this season would determine how things went. It was essential to readjust and start over. "But actually, it's good. We talked. She's being totally cool about the fact that I hit on her and acted like she knew nothing about a sport she dominated."

Julie grinned. She was a kid realizing a dream. "Because she's Sloane Foster and entirely awesome. I think I've watched and read every interview she's ever given, and she's not just a generational talent, but a gift to the sport. And she's not just brilliant—she elevates everyone around her, Reese. You're going to see. I swear, if she says something about your line, your setup, or your mindset, you *listen*, okay? Because she'll be right."

"I get it. She's amazing. But you sound like you have a fan club in your head just for her."

"Maybe I do. And don't get me started on what she's done for women in this sport." Julie moved forward, leading with her cane. "Honestly, having her in Formula Next? That's a gift. For all of us." Reese wasn't sure she'd ever seen Julie so animated over a human being. Usually, it was data and spreadsheets and tire plans that got her going.

"I will remember that."

"You have to. There's a lot to learn from. Did you know that Sloane always labels her helmet visor inserts with little reminders about cornering lines or braking points?"

Reese turned, impressed. "I sometimes forget that you're an absolute motorsport encyclopedia."

"You're welcome," Julie said with a smile. "Now, shall we mingle? Get to know a few of these other teams?"

"Mingle, you say?" Reese nodded and summoned her crowd-working skills. Because that part she could do with her eyes closed.

CHAPTER 4
LIGHTS OUT

The heat hit Sloane's face before the realization arrived in her brain. Why was she hot? Why couldn't she see clearly? She coughed as the air burned its way to her lungs. Then her orientation flooded back. She had to get out of the car. She blinked, hands still on the wheel, flames inching closer. The car had rotated. She'd crashed. And now it was on fire. *Stay awake. Stay awake.* She heard voices, but they were muffled. The words were impossible to make out, but she needed those instructions. She also had to get the hell out of the car, but she couldn't move. Pain seared from her ankle to her shoulder. The voices retreated. No one was trying to help her. She would die here. "I crashed!" she yelled, desperation coating her tone. "I'm still in the car!" Except she wasn't. Sloane was in her bed, squeezing the sheet beneath her body with both hands, a grounding tactic that reminded her that the crash was all a dream, an echo of a memory from long ago that never quite faded.

"You're okay," she murmured. Another orienting device she'd developed with her therapist years ago. Talking herself through it helped.

Ever since her accident eight years and two months ago, Sloane had noticed a change in her sleeping patterns. Once a deep sleeper who enjoyed sinking into the mattress, pulling the sheets over her bare shoulders, and snoozing as late as her schedule would allow, she was now someone who woke frequently during the night and was up for good before the sun rose. The sensory-rich nightmares were enough to pull her out of bed if the ache from her injuries didn't do it first. Waking up full of fear and adrenaline made it hard to find a way back to sleep. Her new reality was one she'd come to accept.

This morning was different, however. She hadn't woken as quickly from the nightmare, leaving her in the car for longer, lost in the moments that were exaggerated and garish versions of the actual day. Colors were brighter, faces distorted, and sound twisted cruelly whenever she tried to decipher the rescue team's critical words. She'd woken breathless, sweating, and desperate to get out of bed.

"That one was bad," she told herself. Her own voice helped anchor her in the present.

She knew why the nightmare had been so intense. In just a few hours, she'd be smack in the midst of race day, and that knowledge loomed over her like a ghost she wasn't ready to face. "Nope. Get it together, Foster," she told herself in the bathroom mirror with a long, hard look. "This doesn't have to be a big deal. You used to do this every weekend. Suck it up."

After a quick protein bar, Sloane rolled out her mat on the hotel room floor and began a series of long, deliberate stretches, feeling the tightness in her back ease gradually. Her shoulders ached as she reached overhead, her spine lengthening with each breath, a painful necessity. Squats and push-ups followed. Her muscles protested at first before settling into the familiar rhythm. Sweat gathered at her temples, but she ignored it. Her heartbeat synced with the steady count in her head. She always woke her body first—flexing, straining, pushing—trusting that once her limbs were humming with energy, her brain would sharpen, too, thoughts snapping into place as surely as her muscles fired. Nothing fixed her head like a good workout.

Today marked the first of two Formula Next races that weekend. The sprint race was today, with the featured race to follow tomorrow on Sunday morning. It would also be Sloane's first chance to see the drivers in action, to watch how they handled their cars and interacted with their teams under pressure. If time allowed, she hoped to meet some of them personally after the race. For that, she wanted to be focused—clear in her communication, confident in her presence, and ready to make a strong first impression on the drivers she was there to mentor.

On the ride over, she worked to get ahead of her nerves. She still wasn't convinced she'd done the right thing in accepting the position at the academy. Was there time to tell her driver to head straight to the airport instead?

VERONICA

Excited for today?

Veronica's text gave her something to focus on.

Yes, actually. Do they serve Bloody Marys at the track these days?

VERONICA

You're in luck. I'll have one hand-delivered to you.

In that case, I might just stick around.

Doubt pooled and settled uncomfortably in her midsection. She stared out the tinted window as the colorful sights of Miami flew past. At the very least, she could make this a temporary commitment. One season. If things didn't go well at the academy, she'd move on to the next project and wouldn't look back, the same way she'd handled things for the past few years. It was a risk putting herself so close to the action again. But Sloane didn't do things halfway. Her passion, her unrelenting drive, wouldn't allow it. So, she was going to do this thing, which meant meeting her fears head-on and punching them in the face.

She arrived at the Miami International Autodrome well in advance of the sprint race. The atmosphere buzzed from all angles, a hum of excitement zipping through the tarmac itself. Crews darted between garages in coordinated bursts of motion, their headsets crackling with clipped instructions. The scent of fuel and hot rubber already hung in the air, even though engines hadn't yet roared to life.

Sloane took a moment to let it wash over her. She loved this part, and the sensory details took her straight back to her favorite memories of race days. Drivers in their race suits drifted in and out of view, some locked in concentration, others laughing too loudly to mask their nerves. Above it all, the grandstands were beginning to fill, a restless sea of color and flags, as if the world itself leaned forward to watch what would unfold. This was a big day for the academy. Revolutionary in many ways.

"You ready?" Veronica asked, sliding a strand of dark hair behind her ear as she appeared next to Sloane. The sun bathed them fully, signaling good weather for the race. In the midst, Veronica's eyes held concern, which meant she realized what the day might mean for Sloane. She was standing there as Ronnie, Sloane's friend, not Veronica Vance, the academy's director.

"Yeah," Sloane said, meaning it. "I was worried, but now that I'm here, the atmosphere is, I don't know, comforting in a way. Almost like coming home."

"The good old days," Veronica said, easing into a soft smile. They'd had some amazing times back then. "Remember when we'd sneak away from the paddock and toss tennis balls against the back wall and talk for hours, trying to figure out when we'd get the call to F1?"

"Of course I do." Sloane smiled, instantly transported. "Those were some of the best days of my life."

"Mine, too," Veronica said quietly. "And of course your call came first. As it should have."

Sloane had been offered a seat at DeRossi Racing, and on a

rainy Sunday evening, she signed the contract. They'd celebrated with warm peanut butter toast and cheap cabernet and laughed and gaped at each other in disbelief. It wasn't gonna be just a boys' club any longer. Ronnie joined the grid as a midseason replacement, and suddenly they were racing each other every weekend and thrilled about it.

"What matters is that we were there together." Sloane met her friend's gaze, still reveling in all they'd accomplished and all they'd been so close to achieving. "We're part of history."

"Damn right we are. Now, let's help a few of these up-and-coming drivers do the same."

"No. Let's go one step further and make one of them the world champion," Sloane said, focused on a mission greater than all of them. They let the words hang in the air, glistening in possibility, both realizing their importance. Then she offered a smile. "And we can maybe throw a few more tennis balls in the process."

"You're on, Foster. Holding you to it."

Sloane decided to watch the beginning of the race from the Ravensport pit wall, where she could focus on their two drivers, Reese Maddox and Delaney Rhodes. She took her spot in front of a series of timing screens that provided access to sector times and live TV feeds. With her headphones on, notebook open, Sloane waited quietly for the start of race one of two that weekend, her heart thrumming with anticipation as she remembered the adrenaline spike that hit when she slid behind the wheel. The measured control it took to keep her wits about her and her reflexes focused and sharp. Those drivers were experiencing it now.

The cars, following a formation lap, assembled one by one on the grid. Marissa Giovani, driving for Vantera, was on pole position after qualifying in P1. Reese Maddox was in the P2 slot, and thirteen other drivers fanned out behind them. Sloane watched intently, her heart hammering with every bit of excitement those opening moments always brought. Two seconds later, the lights came on one at a time until they were all solid. Three seconds later, it was lights out, and the cars roared to life, leaping forward, surging for space on the track. The crowd erupted as the drivers maneuvered for the best placement possible, the perfect time to overtake another car. Reese attempted to move around Marissa for the very early overtake but was shut out. Sloane nodded. Good for Marissa, defending adeptly.

She flipped to the radio communication for Ravensport to hear Julie Rennick, the engineer, say, "Nice try, Reese. We'll get her soon."

"Copy," Reese said, likely very focused.

"Sprint race, remember," Julie said as a reminder. It was her job to keep Reese focused. "That means twenty-five minutes. No tire changes. Just a push to the checkered flag."

"Got it."

"You're at a good pace. Quicker than every other car. Let's keep an eye on tire temps."

"Who's behind me?"

"Joanna Abrahamian. A half a second slower."

Sloane was interested to see how Reese would fare in the race against this particular group of drivers. Marissa, in front, was hungry. She'd been racing most of her life but had only recently begun to mature as a driver and really come into her own. Her father was an olive oil mogul with a racing fixation. From what Sloane saw in the media and the research Ronnie had sent over, she didn't have an easy time of it with him. If Reese could hold off Joanna and hang in there, P2 would score her team quite a lot of points. Hanging in there didn't seem to be a strong suit of Reese Maddox. She was known to start strong and lose her grip on her lead as the race went on. She checked her watch. Time would tell.

Wanting to cover more ground, Sloane moved on to the next garage, hoping to spend a little time observing each team. It would tell Sloane a lot about how each driver operated in the midst of a cutthroat, high-stakes race. It was while listening to

Emma Vanover report on the radio that she was losing rear grip on Turn 3 that the crowd cheered loudly, then gasped into silence. What had Sloane just missed? She scanned the monitors for the one showing the TV broadcast, which replayed the moment. Reese Maddox had attempted another overtake in which she didn't have enough room, tapped Marissa's front wing, and sent them both careening off track. What an unnecessary waste. Both cars sustained damage and had to be retired from the race, costing both drivers a shot at points.

"What in hell?" she murmured, questioning everything about the decision and the desperation that seemed to motivate it. She watched the replay a second time, and the new angle showed even less room. It had been an unwise call. Reese had been either reckless or unfocused. Maybe both.

"That one's on Maddox," a nearby mechanic said to his buddy. The race stewards must have agreed, because Reese was not only out of this race but also penalized five spots on the starting grid for the feature race the next day. Her truly poor decision-making had now cost Ravensport points in *both races*. Unbelievable. Sloane knew exactly which driver she'd like to start with for her one-on-ones later that day.

Sloane gave Reese time for the post-session weigh-in, the mandatory check to be sure her weight and the car's met the regulations. After that, Reese would need a few minutes with the team's higher-ups, and a little space to decompress in the drivers' room, before Sloane arranged for them to meet in the conference room Veronica had set aside in the paddock.

When Reese finally walked in, she was still in her blue race suit. She'd pulled her dark hair loose from the ponytail—probably in a moment of frustration. It fell around her shoulders, messy but effortless, catching the light in a way that made Sloane pause, without quite knowing why.

"Hi," Sloane said, standing. "How are you feeling?"

"I've been better," Reese said, eyes brushing the ground. She was quite the contrast to the surefire version of herself from the bar. Defeat wasn't easy for any of them, and it would likely hover just over Reese's shoulder until she could get in the car again.

"Well, I'm sorry about the race. The way it ended."

"Yeah, me too." She hooked a thumb behind her. "Um, Ava, the PR rep for Ravensport, said you wanted to have a chat?"

"I did. I hope I didn't pull you away from any postrace responsibilities."

Reese shrugged. "I'm good. Already went before the firing squad." It was a reference to the press and the likely brutal questions Reese would have been doused with. Sloane remembered how the reporters and bloggers would seize on any mistake on the circuit and have a field day making you explain yourself to the world. She and Ronnie used to call them beatdowns.

Sloane offered a smile, hoping to reset the mood. "This is my first chance to see everyone in action, and I thought we could debrief."

"Right. The mentorship." She sighed and ran a hand through her dark hair, tousling it so it fell in a haphazard cascade like a hair product commercial. It was truly something to behold.

"Why don't you sit?"

Reese did, waiting. Sloane didn't want this to feel like a kid called into the principal's office and did what she could to speak as casually, yet as impactfully as possible. A tricky combo. "I could tell you what I saw out there, and maybe we can come up with a strategy for next time. I think that's the crux of my new job here."

"You are incredibly kind. I'll obviously listen to any and all advice, but I think today was just a fluke." It was a form of a brush-off, likely because Reese wasn't ready to take full responsibility for the crash. Interesting and a comment on her confidence level. Or perhaps, she should say, her *overconfidence* level.

Sloane paused, realizing she just had to go there. "Was it, though? Because you also crashed out of your last F2 race, and a handful more throughout last season." She paused and checked her notes. "A higher crash rate than most drivers, and that was in addition to the string of penalties you drew."

Reese exhaled slowly before attempting a smile. "Okay. You know how to kick a girl when she's down." She added a laugh, but the tension remained.

"Not my intention," Sloane said with a hand out to steady their interaction. "But I have to call it as I see it. You have a record of leaving points on the table. Let's get you those points, because trust me, they will add up."

Since she'd arrived, Reese's hands had been in motion—fidgeting with the zipper of her suit, brushing a strand of hair from her face, or tapping lightly against her leg—and Sloane found herself noticing the rhythm of it, almost like a quiet signal of energy she couldn't name.

Reese's gaze flicked up, briefly meeting Sloane's before darting away, and there was a faint scent of melon shampoo mixed with motor oil from the car. It was all so ordinary, and yet Sloane's attention lingered longer than it should have, catching the small details that made Reese feel unexpectedly present in the room.

"So, you think I shouldn't have made the move on Marissa. Wouldn't you have done the same thing? Honestly?"

"Honestly." Sloane sat back, hoping they could relax into the conversation now. "Not with those margins. You had inches. What was the rush?"

"It's a timed race, and I felt like I had to capitalize on every opportunity."

"And some drivers could have pulled that move off, but they're rare."

Reese met her gaze, her green eyes darkening almost imperceptibly. "And you don't think I'm one of them." She gave her head the slightest shake. "I think you're underestimating me."

"It's possible."

Reese didn't say anything, but the corners of her mouth fell almost like a child at the zoo who'd let go of their balloon.

"What I saw today was a driver with true talent and impressive car handling skills who's not afraid to take risks."

She closed one eye, waiting. "But?"

"Someone who lacks maturity when it matters."

Reese's eyes went wide, and her hand went to her heart. "I'm mortally wounded now. I feel like you just punched me in the face."

"I'm not finished," Sloane said, a smile tugging. Her tone wasn't commanding, but it was to the point. She glanced at her notes. "Would you say you're in the best driving shape of your life?"

Reese sighed, not enjoying the question. "I would say that I have a lot on my plate."

"So, that's a no?"

Reese paused before answering, as if gathering the details like pieces of a deconstructed puzzle. "Here's the thing. There are sponsorships, social media collabs, media obligations, networking, and the documentary, which is likely the reason I was even afforded this opportunity. So, no. I'm not able to hop into the simulator as much as I'd like. I could certainly increase my stamina with more gym sessions. I also don't always get enough time before a race to practice my reaction drills. My body is strong, but it could be stronger."

"I hear you. It's a lot. What about your social life?"

"Doesn't suck," Reese said with a sly smile.

Okay, now that was the Reese she had encountered at the bar, all cocky and surefire. But there were other threads to her personality that Sloane was now glimpsing. Veronica had written her off as solely a media darling, but Sloane hadn't. At least, not yet. "I'm sure it doesn't. Maybe you can borrow some time there?"

Reese nodded. "Maybe."

"So what's the plan?" Sloane asked quietly. "To avoid a repeat of today?"

"Execute better," Reese said, as if it would magically happen without the blood, sweat, tears, and prep.

She took a breath, trying not to get frustrated, because there were so many factors Reese was glossing over. She decided to backtrack. "Let's look at today. You had a good position and could have held it all the way. P2 is a fantastic finish. Why not bank the smart points?"

"Because I wanted the win." Reese frowned. "Is that what you would have done when you were driving? Bank points?" It seemed so unchampion-like.

"Yes. It's exactly what I would have done, and would still do, over taking zero."

Reese's eyes went wide but only for the briefest moment. She likely hadn't expected that answer because in her mind, greatness wasn't associated with the conservative approach. That's what a lot of people missed. You had to make big moves to get big results, but only when the time was right. Only when the risk was likely to pay off.

"Here's what I can tell you. You don't become a world champion in one race. It's about consistency. You deliver each and every weekend. You can't afford to blow it when you're sitting in high points."

"But I want to be first. Always." She smiled, owning it.

Sloane caught the fire behind Reese's eyes. She was hungry, but maybe putting the cart before the horse. She needed to back her skills before she put so much on the line.

"You strive for the strongest position possible, always."

Reese leaned forward, satisfied. "It sounds like we're agreeing."

Sloane shook her head, unable to resist a smile. Reese was so infuriating that she almost looped back around to endearing. She was starting to understand why so many doors opened for her. She was someone you wanted to see happy.

"Only to an extent. You want to win, all or nothing. But I'm trying to show you the smarter route. Your risks have to be weighed."

"Fair," Reese said. They held eye contact for a moment, and neither of them spoke. Reese's green eyes studied Sloane's. Maybe she was actually taking Sloane's words to heart. "What else?" she said quietly. For a moment, Sloane forgot to answer.

"Oh, um. Right." What the hell was that about? She flipped her laptop around. "Look at your times on Sectors 2 and 3. That's raw speed. It's impressive in a car like this one." Unlike the F1 cars, the academy cars were all identical. Yet, Reese was able to achieve lap times that no one else was able to duplicate. It honestly made Sloane wonder what Reese would be capable of behind a higher caliber car, backed by the kind of money only F1 paid out.

Reese sat taller. "Yeah? Good. I like this part of the conversation better."

"I thought you might." She scrolled down. "But compare it to the rest of your race—do you know what I see? A lack of dependability. Your times are all over the map. Listen to your engineer."

Reese didn't hesitate. "I do. I trust Julie with my life and my career."

"Really? Because I heard you ignore several of her directives over the radio."

"Well." She paused in exasperation, searching for an explanation. "Because she's not in the car."

"That's the point. And it gives her perspective you don't have. You might want to honor it."

"Yeah. Okay. You make a valid point." But she didn't seem entirely convinced.

It was a roller coaster of an exchange, and at the end, Sloane wasn't sure if she'd made a huge impact or none at all. That's how puzzling Reese Maddox was. She existed in a lot of different columns. Charismatic, beautiful, and obstinate as hell. Sloane decided to call it and hope for a more definitive conversation in the future. It would take some work to get a good read on Reese, and she had a list of drivers to work through that afternoon.

She stood. "I'll let you get back to your team."

"I actually have a—"

"Let me guess. A commitment to a sports drink company?"

Reese's jaw dropped. She was being playful again, which was, at the very least, good to see after a loss. It meant she could roll with the punches. A professional. "I'll have you know, it's racing apparel today."

"Got it." Sloane nodded as she feigned contrition. However, Reese had just proven Sloane's point. Not that a driver like her would ever realize it. She was caught up in the commercial machine. Perhaps Veronica was right about her prospects after all. "But maybe find some time to train after?"

Reese nodded, her smile dimming. "I'll see what I can do."

Sloane spent the rest of the afternoon meeting with the drivers, going over their individual successes and missteps from the race, intrigued by their unique backgrounds and personalities. None of them left quite the impression on her that Reese had, however. She kept coming back to their interactions, the way Reese flicked a gaze or turned a tense moment into a lighthearted one. Sloane was certainly confused by her. But, she knew one thing for certain: Reese Maddox was the most interesting person in whatever room she walked into and that had to count for something.

CHAPTER 5
THE STARTING GRID

Reese returned to the academy hotel after her postrace responsibilities were at long last behind her. She'd participated in the debriefs, the weigh-ins, the rounds of press, sponsorship duties, fan interaction, and even a session with Sloane Foster, who had a lot of opinions to impart, apparently.

Her absolutely everything ached. The day had been a whirlwind of smiling, laughing, and playing the part of the woman they all wanted her to be. But the moment that had resonated with her beyond all others was the question Sloane had raised about her lack of dependability. She sighed, the implications still jabbing at her. It wasn't fucking true. She showed up and did her absolute best during every moment on the circuit.

"There you are." Marissa Giovani poked her head around the corner just as Reese located her key card. She was apparently in the room next to Reese's.

"Yeah. Hey," Reese said and tried not to wince. After all, Marissa would have won the race that day if Reese hadn't attempted that messy overtake. "Awesome driving today. I'm sorry I took us both out."

"Luckily, I excel at forgiving and forgetting. Unless you plan to make a habit out of ending my races early." She'd said it with a playful smile and a hand on her hip. Marissa had these impressive long, dark curls that she'd tossed to the side like a pro.

"I don't. And thanks for being cool about it. I think the wall I smashed into was less forgiving."

"And probably your team's mechanics."

She thought of the car that they were likely still working on. "Fuck. They probably hate me."

"I truly doubt it. Everyone seems to love you, which is why I'm here."

She leaned her shoulder against the door and grinned. "Say more."

"Idea. Want to come over so we can like you, too?" Marissa seemed laid-back and fun. She'd heard a lot about her, but they'd never had more than a quick exchange in the past. "Oh, fair warning. A couple of the other drivers swung by for a bit."

Reese paused because the offer was tempting. The day had taken its toll on her. Losing the race, being beaten up by the press, the dreaded meeting with Sloane Foster, and then smiling the rest of the day for her sponsor obligations that had included two photo shoots and an autograph line that went on and on. She was honestly sick of herself, and her smile muscles ached. At the same time, she wanted the chance to get to know the others, and her FOMO wouldn't allow her to drop into bed. "Maybe just for a little bit. I may crash soon."

"We all will. The feature race is tomorrow, and I don't take corners the same without sleep."

"Then maybe we should stay up after all," Reese said with a laugh. But the reminder of the race, a clean slate, had perked Reese up. A longer race, more points on the line, and a chance to redeem herself in front of Sloane Foster. Correction, *the racing world in its entirety*. She didn't need to single anyone out. Sloane was not in her head.

"Looking forward to it. I could use a redemption arc." She followed Marissa into the room next door while already mentally prepping for the next day. She'd get to the paddock early and go through her reaction drills, study her map, and grab a power smoothie. Everything a successful driver should do to show up in the best shape. Then she'd win the whole thing and take the podium in victory. Glorious. The applause would be thunderous. She'd kiss babies. Crowd surf. She might even give Sloane a nod in thanks for the pressure she'd applied. Record scratch. So, okay, maybe she was in Reese's head.

"Well, well," Delaney said, standing as Reese arrived in Marissa's living room. "We were wondering where you got dragged off to." She had her chestnut hair back in a ponytail, showing off the very subtle blond streaking, and wore yoga pants and a blue, extra-soft-looking sweatshirt with the phrase *What?* in the center. Textbook Delaney.

Reese grinned back, and it hurt. "Ow. Dammit. I have to stop smiling. Do not let me smile." She touched her mouth. "My muscles are killing me. It was an event for Apex." She turned to Marissa. "They do the racing apparel with the triangle logo on them."

"Right, right. They have a huge following."

"Only you would be in pain from oversmiling," Delaney said with a laugh. "Does your ass hurt too from all the kissing?"

"What can I say? Part of my contract."

Delaney shook her head. "I'm lucky if I can sell my own merch on my website one T-shirt at a time, and you're repping other people's as well."

Reese shrugged. "Yeah, well, the harsh reality is it's about the only way I can afford to be here. And there are worse ways to make money."

She turned to see one other driver on the sofa, smiling along. She didn't mean to ignore her. Cassidy Simms. She was new to the scene, a relative unknown in single-seat racing. She'd heard through the rumor mill that Veronica scouted from rally car racing. "Hey. We haven't officially met. I'm Reese Maddox."

"Yes, I definitely know who you are." The blush hit Cassidy's cheeks. "Sorry. Embarrassing, but I was a fan before I ever heard of the academy. I hope that's not weird. I tend to get enthusiastic about things and then, apparently, announce that enthusiasm when I meet the person. So here we are." A small pause. "Sorry if I'm smiling too much. My muscles don't hurt."

"Not at all," Reese said. "It's cool of you to say so."

"I'm Cassidy, which, God, is information I should have led with. I'll work on thought organization for our future interactions." She offered her hand, and Reese stood and took it. Cassidy had her blond hair in a ponytail and friendly blue eyes. Good vibes already. She seemed happy, eager even, and it was contagious. Reese found herself relaxing in her midst, fatigue shoved to the side.

"How was your first race?" Cassidy had finished fourteenth of twenty, if Reese remembered correctly. Not awful for a first time driving a car that must have been very new to her.

"I was a fish out of water, figuring it out as I went, but loving every second of it." A very positive take.

"Embrace that." Delaney turned to Cassidy. "You're exactly where you're supposed to be."

"About three inches from the road." Cassidy laughed. "I'm still getting used to how low you all sit. It might take me a couple more races to adjust to that alone."

"Your ass will definitely get a workout," Marissa said without blinking. Her dry delivery was entirely unexpected. Reese swiveled to Delaney with wide, appreciative eyes. This one might be more fun than had been advertised. "Drink anyone?"

"I'll take a beer. Yeah," Reese said, spotting the array of options on the small bar that resembled the bow of a ship.

"Coming your way."

As Reese caught the can Marissa tossed to her, she noticed that both Delaney and Marissa were drinking diet soda. Cassidy had a bottle of water at her feet. "Fuck. I'm drinking alone? I'm that girl?"

"Don't sweat it. I try to limit my intake before a race," Delaney said. "It sucks, but I want to be as clear as possible."

"My trainer made me promise," Marissa said. "After tomorrow's race, though? All the walls come tumbling down. Oh, and my birthday. There will be a glass of wine, race or not."

Reese turned to Cassidy.

"Oh, I'm new here," she said with a shrug. "I do what they do."

"No, I get it." She glanced at the Tecate she'd already opened. "And I probably shouldn't be partaking either."

"Everyone's different," Delaney said. "Do what works for you."

Reese allowed herself a few sips as the others chatted about the strong crowd turnout for their sprint race and the specific technique Marissa employed to achieve her high velocity champagne spray on the podium after winning. Reese laughed along, slightly on edge because it had been a while since she'd found herself on top of one of those things, and the clock was ticking. Why did it feel like she had so much to lose? Because she did. She ran a finger around the iced rim of her beer. If she didn't start winning, not only would Ravensport likely move on to another driver, but her sponsorships would shrivel up, and her endorsement deals would gradually fade into the distance. When she came back into the fold of the conversation, she realized the others were talking about Sloane.

"How is she so incredibly good at this, though?" Marissa asked. "She saw patterns in my driving after one race and a few films that I'd never even considered, nor had my team. And she was right."

Delaney leaned forward from her blue leather club chair with the pelican throw pillow. "I left that meeting more inspired to work hard than probably any other conversation in my career. Veronica was a genius to bring her on."

"Confession time. I had a poster of Sloane Foster in her race suit on my wall when I was sixteen," Cassidy said. "I skipped high school parties to watch her race. She was just so composed. Even when things went wrong, she had this calm, almost surgical focus. I used to think, 'If I can be even a fraction of that one day, I'll have made it.'"

Marissa raised a sculpted eyebrow. "And now you've met her. Was it everything you dreamed?"

Cassidy laughed and covered her face. "No. It was terrifying. She's amazing, but her eyes? First of all, gorgeous. It hurts to look at her. Second, it's like she's seeing right through you. I kept waiting for her to tell me to go home. I would have."

"She doesn't mince words," Delaney agreed. "But she's the real deal. I think that's why she resonates with us. She's not pretending to be anyone else."

Reese took another sip of her beer and felt the carbonation burn all the way down. The others were right—Sloane *was* the real deal. And she'd read Reese like a book, even though she'd refused to see it in that moment. Dependability. Consistency. All the places she came up short. Her jaw tightened at the thought.

Marissa reached for the bowl of popcorn in the center of the coffee table. Actually, a repurposed nautical wheel painted gold beneath glass, because of course it was. The hotel's decor leaned hard into its theming, from the under-the-sea mural to the lamp made out of a starfish. A little over the top, but somehow charming. The academy wasn't springing for the high-dollar F1 accommodations, which made sense, so they'd take the personality instead. Reese caught sight of herself in the reflection of the coffee table and almost laughed. Four women in matching sweatpants and hoodies, drinking soda and water in a heightened space meant for influencers. Perfect metaphor for their lives.

"All right, enough about Sloane," Delaney said, grabbing the popcorn bowl from Marissa. "We need to talk about the real story. Which one of you actually cooks and can make something happen in these kitchenettes? Because we have weeks of travel ahead, and I'm not built to survive on takeout."

"I'm a solid breakfast woman," Cassidy volunteered. "Like, eggs and toast level. Not fancy. But I can work on sprinkling some cheese and crisping up the bacon."

"I can order from an app like nobody's business," Marissa said. "That's my skill set."

"I'm a cereal girl," Reese admitted. "It's fast and doesn't burn."

Delaney pointed at Reese. "You're the one with all the sponsors. Use your charm and get us a chef deal."

"Please," Reese said. "Half my sponsors are probably about to ghost me unless I win something soon." The words slipped out darker than she'd intended, and silence followed.

Cassidy tilted her head. "Are you feeling extra pressure?"

Reese hesitated, then nodded. "You could say that." She thought about brushing the topic off, defaulting to humor, but something about the relaxed energy in the room, no cameras, no handlers, made honesty easier. "I also had my one-on-one with Sloane earlier."

That got everyone's attention. Delaney leaned forward. "And?"

"And she thinks I need to get my head on straight." Reese exhaled. "Basically, told me I'm inconsistent because I spread myself too thin. Sponsors, media, appearances, all the extra stuff."

Marissa nodded. "I mean … I'm sure it's hard. That caliber of juggling. It's enough for me to focus on the race itself."

"Here's the thing, though. You're not just a driver. You're a brand, Reese," Delaney said. "You've built something big. That's impressive."

"It's exhausting," Reese admitted. "Sometimes I forget why I even started racing in the first place." The confession surprised her as it left her mouth. The others didn't pounce or pity her, though. They just listened. That alone felt like a relief.

"We all get that," Delaney said quietly. "It's the noise. All of it. You've got to tune it out somehow. The season's just starting."

Cassidy smiled. "I know I just got here, but hear me out."

"Hearing," Marissa said, sliding a strand of dark curls behind her ear.

Cassidy sat forward. "Maybe this," she gestured between them, "is how. No cameras. No press. Just us. It's like therapy."

"Four drivers, one golden popcorn bowl," Marissa said solemnly. "We should form a pact."

"A pact, you say?" Reese asked, amused despite herself. It seemed a little bit sponsored by Hallmark, but she was willing to keep an open mind. "Are we still allowed to say fuck?"

"Fuck yeah," Delaney said. "Encouraged even."

"Every city, every race weekend," Cassidy said, her tone growing in excitement, "we meet up at whoever's room has the least weird decor—"

"Impossible," Marissa cut in. "They're all weird."

"The *least* weird," Cassidy continued. "We drink something cold, eat something questionable, and talk about literally anything except lap times." Her blue eyes shone with pride in her idea.

"Why not?" Marissa raised her water bottle. "I'm in."

"Me too," Delaney said. "Even if the food's questionable."

Reese hesitated, then smiled, the kind that felt real, not practiced. It didn't even hurt her face. "All right. Pact accepted."

"I'm calling us The Starting Grid. You don't have to, but I am," Cassidy said. She was certainly a confident new kid. "First race weekend and all."

Delaney nodded along. "Why not? Everything good needs a name."

"That's why we call you Slow," Reese said, only to be smacked hard in the face with a pelican throw pillow.

"All right. The Starting Grid. Who's in?" Marissa asked.

All four cans and bottles clinked together, the sound small but steady. Reese leaned back against the couch, letting the conversation and low music fill the corners of the room.

Tomorrow would come with pressure, expectations, and headlines. But tonight? Tonight was hers.

CHAPTER 6
HAIR DOWN

Samara adjusted her headset as the camera settled into place, the hum of the paddock threading through the air behind her. "For the viewers watching who might be new to the sport," she said, turning slightly toward Reese, "can you define open-wheel racing—and what brought you to it in the first place?"

Reese didn't hesitate. She leaned back against the car, gloves dangling from one hand, already half in race mode. "In open-wheel, all four tires sit outside the body of the car," she explained. "It's part of what makes it so aerodynamic. These cars live on ground force. That invisible pull that keeps us pinned to the asphalt." She tipped her chin toward the cockpit. "People are always surprised by how low we sit. You're basically reclined, almost lying down, inches off the track."

Samara nodded, following Reese's gaze. "So today—reclining, sitting that low—what's going to be the biggest obstacle for you out there?"

Reese rolled her shoulders once, loosening up. "Consistency," she said. "That's the real test today." She gave a quick, self-aware smile. "I get antsy when I'm not leading. That impatience can turn into bad decisions if I'm not careful. I need to settle into a rhythm, find my pace, and be smart."

Samara's brows lifted slightly. "You brought it up," she said. "So let's go there."

Reese laughed under her breath. "Fair enough."

"You've built a reputation for some pretty daring overtakes," Samara continued. "Some say too daring, that you squander your position. Are we going to see more of that risk-taking behavior today?"

Reese grinned as she tugged her gloves on, tightening the straps with practiced ease. "Hopefully, a little less of it," she said. "At least, that's the plan." She glanced briefly toward the pit wall. "My coach, Sloane, reminds me that patience wins races. It's not about diving into every gap. It's about knowing which ones are worth the risk. Points matter. The team matters." Her voice softened just a touch. "I'll be trying to remember that once the adrenaline kicks in."

"That sounds like a shift for you," Samara said.

"It is." Reese exhaled, thoughtful now. "I like to chase. That's how I've always driven—see a car ahead and go get it. But Formula Next isn't about individual moments of glory." She shrugged lightly. "If I take myself or someone else out with a bad move, everyone pays for it. So today's about control. Smart aggression." She smiled. "Not just … aggression."

Samara smiled back. "Smart aggression. I like that." A pause. "You seem calm for race day."

Reese laughed, the sound quick and bright. "Give it ten minutes. Once the lights come on, calm disappears." She reached for her helmet, fingers resting there for a beat. "Then it's just me, the engine, and about a hundred decisions every lap. But yeah, I'm trying to borrow a page from Sloane's book. Think before I send it."

Engines began to growl to life around them, the sound rippling through the paddock. Mechanics moved in close, final checks happening almost wordlessly now. Samara lowered her mic slightly, though the camera kept rolling.

"Good luck out there, Reese."

Reese slipped the helmet under her arm and flashed a quick grin. "Thanks. Let's see if I can actually level up."

"Who's behind me?" Reese asked Julie over the radio. Her pulse thudded in her ears, matching the engine's roar. Adrenaline pumping, Reese was in the zone, dialed in, and flying. She had less than three laps to hold her position and bank some points for herself and her team, and she'd be damned if she let another driver overtake her at the last minute. This was her first feature race for Formula Next, and she wanted that podium so badly it ached.

"You have Danielle behind at 0.8 seconds. She's quicker. Be careful." Julie was advising her to defend, and she would. "Push, push, push."

"Copy that," Reese said, gripping the wheel tighter. Sweat beaded at her temple beneath the helmet. Her eyes flicked to the rearview. Danielle Todd was a go-getter from England—a bold, aggressive driver. A lot of folks had their eyes on her as an up-and-comer, but she was prickly at best. Her tactics behind the wheel were also questionable, if you asked Reese. Right now, she was inching closer, just enough to make Reese's pulse pound harder.

Up ahead, Marissa was pulling away, smooth and confident, completely unaware of Reese's battle behind her.

Reese's instincts screamed at her to go for the overtake, to stay on her tail and then surge past Marissa for the glory. Her foot twitched on the throttle. Just one move, one perfect corner, and she could do it. But Sloane's voice reminded her of the bigger picture. *Points matter.* A reckless move could result in zero and damage to the car. She took a deep breath and focused on the line, forcing her shoulders to loosen, her vision to narrow to the asphalt ribbon ahead. She brushed away the urge to dart for the inside on the next corner.

Danielle tried a move into Turn 7, but Reese anticipated it, defending her line without overcommitting. The tires squealed, and smoke curled as she braked later than Danielle expected. "Fuck no. Not today," she muttered, a grin tugging at her lips.

The final lap stretched out like a test of endurance. Each straightaway, each chicane, Reese balanced aggression with caution, blocking Danielle while resisting the temptation to chase Marissa. Every nerve in her body screamed for release, for risk, but she held steady, the car an extension of her will. The checkered flag waved in the distance, and Reese crossed the line in third, heart pounding, grin spreading wider.

"That's P3, Reese," Julie said. "Nice race."

She'd held her ground. P3 wasn't the win, but it was smart, strategic, and just as satisfying in a different way. She'd made the podium and was damn proud of herself. She'd earned it.

Because she never celebrated without Luke, Reese brought him up on FaceTime as she walked back to the garage.

"Who in the world was that?" he asked immediately upon answering

"I'm trying a few new tricks," she said, unable to hold back her grin. "Not bad, right?"

"That was methodical, Reese, and exactly the kind of drive that's gonna take you to F1."

"You don't think I should have gone for the overtake at the end?"

"I didn't see a safe opportunity. Did you?"

"Sometimes you've got to create your own."

"That's how you spin out and damage the car for folks like me to piece back together again. Trust me. This was better."

"Fine," she said with the extra sarcasm she reserved for him. "Love you. Miss you. Hey, did Mom watch?"

"Through her fingers as she walked through the room every ten minutes."

Reese nodded. "It's her process. Gotta run. Podium soon."

"You earned it."

When she passed Sloane in the paddock later, she made a point to make eye contact. She'd taken her advice and had a better race for it. She couldn't help but wonder if Sloane had noticed her more conservative driving style the way Luke had.

"Was it hard?" Sloane asked with a smile. That smile. God. It was unfair, really—slow-building, genuine, the kind that made Reese feel like the only one standing there.

Reese went immediately warm. "Fucking Mount Everest. I wanted to attack."

"Of course you did," she said, meeting Reese's gaze. "And one day you will. All about picking your moments."

"You coming to the podium ceremony, or do you prefer to pretend like you don't have a favorite?" She was on a high, and that made it hard not to casually flirt with a woman she found dangerously irresistible.

Sloane's mouth curved, slow and knowing. "Oh, I'll be there. My favorite earned it." She looked behind Reese. "Where is Marissa anyway? I need to congratulate her."

"That's a dagger," Reese said, covering her heart. "You know that, right? You did that on purpose to wound me mortally."

"I've met you, and you'll get over it." She tapped Reese on the shoulder as she passed. "Maybe there's a woman at the bar you can teach all about racing."

"And I'm dead. No point in the podium now."

But Sloane laughed, and it was everything. Remarkably so. Reese would take jab after jab if it meant she got to experience the sound again. Light and easy with a melodic tone. She got the feeling Sloane didn't laugh a ton. Reese instantly wanted to change that. She also wanted to know what made her laugh, which movies made her light up, and which foods were her absolute favorites—all of it. And where had that come from? The realization was more than a bit jarring.

"Did you hear what I said?" Sloane asked, quirking her head. "Hmm. I don't think you did. You drifted off to somewhere that actually looked awesome."

"What's that?" Reese straightened from the dreamy posture. "Say it again. Please?" A few of the Ravensport crew passed by, smacking her on the back and calling their congratulations.

They stood in front of each other, and even in the midst of her excitement and continued congratulations from everyone as they passed, all Reese could think about was the way Sloane looked with her hair down. She seemed free. Sexy. Like a day at the beach. It was a small rebellion against her usual polish: loose, natural, and entirely captivating. She had a strand of hair that cut across her forehead, nearly shading one eye. Lengthwise, it brushed a little past her shoulders and was thicker than Reese had realized. She'd been pretty before, noticeably so to anyone with a pulse, but today she absolutely stunned. Reese's brain short-circuited somewhere between professional admiration and something she definitely shouldn't be feeling for a mentor.

"Um. You still in there? Basking in your glory? Think I lost you again." Sloane said with a slight turn of her head. Her tone was teasing, but her eyes—steady, curious—seemed to see right through Reese's scramble to recover. That jarred Reese back into action.

"Sorry. I was, um," she sighed, smiled, and shook her head. "Nothing."

Sloane stepped in. "It was more than nothing. You showed a lot of talent and control out there, a nice balance. Enjoy it." Her hand found Reese's arm in a quick, confident squeeze, which was gone too fast. But the contact lit something low in Reese's stomach that had nothing to do with racing adrenaline. Sloane disappeared into the crowd, and Reese couldn't help but think that control had never looked so damn good. She let out a slow breath, reveling in the moment, loving the win and stomach flutter, a one-two punch that she didn't mind in the slightest.

Sloane was probably on her way to similarly stroke the egos of the top two finishers, and that was fine. This was enough. Because Reese knew she had many more race weekends to make her mark on the academy. And if fate was kind, maybe a few more moments like this one. Turns out, she had a lot more to learn. And maybe she wouldn't mind if it was from Sloane Foster.

74

CHAPTER 7
QUEER QUORUM

Monterey forced Reese to slow down in ways she hadn't expected. The coastal air, the steady rhythm of the circuit, the way every corner asked for restraint instead of her usual bravado, which maybe after all this time had been bullshit. It all demanded a kind of focus she'd been working toward, but thus far, hadn't mastered. She came into the weekend not trying to dominate the race, but to understand it.

So far, so good.

Reese returned to the hotel after qualifying, feeling good about her showing. She'd be starting P4 for tomorrow's sprint race. No, it wasn't pole position, not even the front row, but she'd earned something that mattered more. She'd found a rhythm.

Her laps had come together with a steady precision that felt new, her times dropping one after the other as her confidence grew. She was able to settle in and focus. For once, she wasn't chasing perfection. She was building it, lap by lap. The car felt like an extension of her, her breathing synced to the turns, her mind clear in a way it hadn't been for months. This is what racing was supposed to be.

Now, walking through the quiet hotel corridor with her

helmet bag slung over one shoulder, she could still feel the hum of the track in her bones. Her muscles ached, but it was the good kind. A ghost of engine vibration still tingled in her fingertips, the phantom sensation of speed still clinging.

By the time she reached her room, a small, proud smile tugged at her mouth. She hadn't conquered the field, but she'd conquered herself. For the first time in a long time, she felt like she had a grip on her own destiny rather than making it up as she went each step of the way.

She sat near the corner of the bed, unzipping her suit halfway, the adrenaline finally fading. She knew, deep down, where that steadiness had come from. Sloane's voice had been in her head, urging her to measure her risks and trust the long game. It had sounded so simple when Sloane imparted it, but no one had ever framed it quite that way before.

"Because she's a driver," Reese mumbled, the words soft but certain.

She trusted Julie implicitly and respected her more than others. But Julie had never been in that seat, never felt the surge of fear and exhilaration as the world blurred at 200 miles an hour. Sloane had. And somehow, Reese could feel that difference every time Sloane spoke.

She lay back on the bed, the mattress squeaking beneath her weight. The room's decor didn't help her find peace. She was surrounded by the world's strangest ode to ocean science. Was this place owned by the same folks from Miami? Perhaps a marine biologist had discovered their passion for interior design. A massive jellyfish mural glowed faintly blue across the wall, and a mobile of plastic clownfish rotated lazily near the air vent. The bedside lamp was shaped like a coral reef, and when she walked through the hotel lobby, she was greeted with the sounds of whale calls. Even the carpet looked like someone had printed satellite images of the Great Barrier Reef and called it a day. Veronica's assistant, Miranda, whom she heard was responsible for booking accommodations, certainly had an affinity for unique spots.

Before she could get even the slightest bit comfortable, there was a knock at the door. "No. Go away," she called, her voice muffled by a pillow. Her body had hit too many adrenaline peaks and valleys today, screaming for stillness. "Immediately."

"You're sending me away? Me?!"

Delaney. Reese softened instantly and laughed, imagining her friend's incredulous face. "Well, not you." She sat up with a groan and swung her legs off the bed. "I'll get up for you. But understand, I don't move around for many people."

She opened the door to find Delaney leaning against the doorframe, smirking. "I guess I'm honored to be on the VIP list."

"Is that code for teammate? Because you're my only one of those."

Delaney grinned as she stepped in. She'd finished qualifying P5 for the race tomorrow, which meant they'd start practically side by side, two neon-blue blurs defending their turf.

"You looked good out there," Reese said, collapsing onto the small couch in the living area. It had a coral reef pattern that seemed to vibrate under the lamplight. "Very *Finding Nemo* chic in here, in case you hadn't noticed."

"Oh, I had," Delaney said, kicking off her shoes. "I was happy with my time, but Sloane got me thinking. I don't want to settle for midfield. I want to win races."

"The great Sloane Foster got to you, too?"

"How could she not?" Delaney raked a hand through her hair. The light streaks in the dark strands popped nicely tonight. Reese was jealous. "She's an effective speaker. For someone who comes off kind of contained. I didn't expect that. But, fuck. I gotta get it together."

Reese groaned and covered her face with her hands. She felt her filter falling away. She was too exhausted not to be honest. Especially with Delaney. "Pretty sure I hit on her."

"I'm sorry. What did you just say?" Delaney blinked. "You're definitely not talking about Sloane Foster."

"I am. I've hit on her twice now." She winced. "I have a problem. And her name is Sloane. She does things to me."

Delaney opened her mouth, then shut it. "I have too many questions to form words."

Before she could recover, there was another knock at the door. Reese dropped her hands and stared, wide-eyed. "What's happening right now?"

"It's Cassidy and Marissa," Delaney said, heading that way. "I invited them before I knew this was a VIP teammate-only party full of unbelievable confessions. I didn't know those were a thing."

"They're not. Let them in. We have that pact, remember? The grid thing that Cassidy said."

"Right, right, right. Excellent, because at this point I need backup—and witnesses."

"Witnesses? I didn't murder anyone," Reese called after her.

Delaney swung open the door. "Yeah, well, this is equally shocking."

Marissa frowned, holding up a grocery bag. "What is? I brought snacks. Good ones."

"Our friendship continues to improve," Delaney said, grabbing a bag of Doritos as Marissa passed.

Cassidy followed with a grin, carrying two sacks of what looked to be sparkling water, cold brew, and Gatorade Zero. "And multiple hydration options."

"You're both hired," Delaney said, stepping aside. "Grab a spot. There's news."

Cassidy flopped down on the couch beside Reese, eyeing her. "Why do you look like you can't decide whether to nap or host a rave?"

"It's been a lot," Reese said.

"What's the news?" Marissa asked, already unloading her spoils onto the kitchenette counter. Pop-Tarts spilled forth in every flavor known to humankind—chocolate fudge, strawberry frosted, cookies and creme, peanut butter and jelly—like a pastry rainbow had just unfolded in Reese's hotel room.

Reese blinked. "Did you rob the convenience store? What in the world is happening over there?"

"It's a whole thing. I get ridiculously hungry after driving," Marissa said, utterly unapologetic. She tossed Reese a box of Brown Sugar Cinnamon, the best one, obviously. Reese tore it open and pulled out a silver-wrapped pair like it was a sacred treasure.

"The news," Delaney said, raising her voice over the crinkle of foil, "is that Reese apparently hit on Sloane Foster."

Silence fell. Even the air vent seemed to pause.

Reese froze midbite. "What? Is that … awful?"

"Only you would wonder that," Delaney said, arm outstretched in mystification. "You have such absurd luck with women that I don't think you even recognize the concept of 'out of your league.' You're completely unmoored from dating reality."

"I dispute that," Reese said, chewing. "I know she's out of my league. But I've had, what, four or five encounters with her now, and each time I'm more and more attracted to her."

Cassidy nodded thoughtfully. "That's understandable. She's beautiful."

Reese squinted at her. "Wait—are you gay? I don't mean to pry, but considering we're eating Pop-Tarts in an underwater theme park of a hotel, it feels like the right moment for radical honesty."

"Valid," Delaney said, biting into her own Pop-Tart.

"I dated a woman back home for a while," Cassidy said.

"That's a pretty gay thing to do," Marissa said. "You're in the club."

Reese held up her pastry like a toast. "Well then, we have a queer quorum. I can officially dish all."

"Thank God," Marissa said, leaning on the counter. "Now,

tell us exactly what you said to her and the specific tone you used."

Cassidy narrowed her eyes. "And was your hair up or down? That affects the entire vibe."

"Good point," Marissa said gravely. "Hair context is important. How are we supposed to know if you had that windswept quality or not?"

"You might be mocking me." Reese sighed and sank deeper into the couch cushions, clutching her Pop-Tart like a stress ball.

"I definitely am," Marissa said. "Cassidy's serious. These are the details that keep her going."

Cassidy nodded like a straight A student. "She's figured me out fairly quickly."

Reese nodded, enjoying their differences. "Okay, but you have to promise not to judge."

Delaney snorted. "Oh, that's absolutely not how this works."

Marissa raised a hand solemnly. "But we will judge quietly."

Cassidy nodded and squeezed Reese's hand. "And supportively."

"Fine." Reese sighed. "The first time was in the bar before the opening reception. I informed her that the race starts when all five lights go out."

The room went silent.

"You did not," Delaney said in shock.

Marissa's head snapped up. "Wait, back up." A smile tugged. "I want to make sure I have this straight."

"I get it," Reese said. "I'd probably enjoy hearing this story, too."

"You tried to teach Sloane Foster—Sloane fucking Foster from the lore of F1—how a race starts?"

"I didn't know it was her!" Reese said. Damn, hearing the whole thing out loud was almost worse than living it. Almost. "In my head, she was this beautiful, unassuming woman in a bar. And I was hoping to impress her with my job. It's worked before."

Delaney wiped the quiet tears. "So, your big opening move was to mansplain racing to a near world champion?"

Reese closed her eyes in shame. "When you say it like that, it sounds even more mortifying."

Cassidy grinned. "Yet, you hit on her again?"

"Maybe," Reese muttered. "Today, after the lecture. I offered to show her my abs."

Marissa nearly fell off the armchair. "This is real life?" She looked to the others. "I think it is. And it's too good to be true."

Reese covered her face, now laughing with Delaney at her own ludicrous move. "In my defense, it was supposed to be a funny quip. Lighthearted."

Delaney wiped another tear. "Okay, there's lighthearted, and then there's thirsty with a gym membership."

"Don't feel bad." Cassidy clinked her Pop-Tart against Reese's. "At least when you crash and burn, you do it spectacularly. There's really no other way."

Reese stared at the wall. "She's never going to take me seriously."

Marissa smirked. "Maybe not yet. But if she ever asks to see those abs ... call us immediately."

Reese shrank. "Yeah, I'm sidelined."

Delaney looked thoughtful. "I guess my question is, are you seriously interested?"

Reese hadn't allowed herself to go there. She was attracted to Sloane without question. Honestly, who wasn't? But anything more formal seemed like buying a winning lottery ticket. The odds of success were slim to none. "In a perfect world, I'd love to get to know her better. Are you kidding? But even I know she's beyond reach."

"Sorry, pal," Delaney said. "We're mere mortals and Sloane Foster is a goddess on earth."

"With a resumé I'd trade my grandmother to have one day," Marissa said. She held up a hand. "But she's a mean grandma who screams at me in Italian, so don't feel too bad about it."

Reese set her jaw. "I guess I'll just keep my little crush in my pocket then. Know my place."

Delaney grinned. "That's right, pal. Keep it in your pants."

That pulled a laugh from the group, who were honestly becoming the kind of people Reese hadn't realized she needed. Instead of tiring her out after a long day, they gave her energy. The laughter lingered in the air, warm and easy, like it had been waiting all day to show up.

As the noise faded and the Pop-Tarts disappeared, Reese sat back and let herself breathe. For so long, her world had been engines, telemetry, pressure, and proving herself. But here—in this absurd ocean-themed room with its jellyfish glow—she felt something new. Belonging. These women, these drivers, got it. The chaos, the competition, the craving to be better. And they still made space to laugh at themselves.

Her chest softened. This was her crew. Her people. Her soft place to fall.

And Sloane ... well, Sloane was the opposite. Terrifying in so many ways, but also a preoccupation she couldn't turn off even when she actively tried. It was like once they'd met, there was no undoing the Sloane effect. She was clean lines, heat, and a voice that made Reese want to rise taller. Which meant, for everyone's sake, she needed to stay professional, focused, and dialed in. Whatever ridiculous sparks Sloane Foster lit in her, they'd have to stay the hell out of the way. At least for now.

She finished the last bite of her Pop-Tart and smiled faintly. Tomorrow, she'd drive. Tonight, she'd let herself rest.

***

Sloane was a dirty martini kind of woman. Always had been. Cold, clean, a little salty—just like she liked her evenings. She didn't indulge as often as she used to, but that night after qualifying, she found herself heading down to the hotel bar anyway. She wasn't ready to turn in just yet.

She took a moment to look around, invest in her surroundings. The place was trying desperately to have a personality. Seashell sconces. Blue lighting. A chandelier shaped like a school of fish, for God's sake. Monterey, apparently, had taken its ocean affinity very seriously. The academy hotels, midrange at best, always came with extra flair. Sometimes she wondered if Miranda was pranking them all with these finds. Luckily, the drinks were better than the decor.

She settled into her seat at the bar and exhaled, letting the day slide off of her, leaving something unnamed. She felt different this week—restless, maybe. Being back in the fray had done something to her. Reawakened something? She wasn't sure. But watching the young drivers tearing around the track, full of heat and hunger and half-formed discipline, had stirred an ache she thought she'd buried. It reminded her of the woman she used to be, the one who thought talent and adrenaline were enough to outrun time.

And maybe that's why she was here, perched on a barstool instead of tucked in her hotel room with a book and a cup of tea like she should be. Maybe she just wanted to feel the hum of life again.

She stirred her drink, absently watching the olive shift in its pale green sea, and was surprised when a second martini appeared beside it. She looked to the bartender, who nodded toward a woman across the room—a brunette raising her own glass in silent toast. Interesting. Yet, she didn't immediately reject the notion of company. Also new.

Sloane hadn't been planning on a second drink, but, honestly, why not? She nodded her thanks. The woman smiled, slow and confident, and began walking over. Sloane felt her stomach tighten in that old, familiar way. It had been a while since she'd been with anyone. Maybe too long.

The woman was attractive—mid-thirties, maybe—with dark hair that fell in soft waves around her shoulders and eyes the color of espresso. Her white linen shirt was casually half-tucked into black slacks, collar open just enough to make you look twice. Sloane did. Everything about her said composed, intentional. The kind of woman who didn't have to try hard to draw attention; she already knew she had it.

"You looked like you could use company," she said, voice warm and low. "I'm Talia."

Sloane gestured to the empty stool beside her. "Talia, you're observant."

"And you're a mystery," Talia countered with a smile that was all invitation. "Mind if I try to solve you?"

Sloane almost laughed at the line. It had also been a long time since she'd allowed someone to flirt with her. But something about the curve of Talia's mouth made her consider it.

She took a sip of her martini, its crisp bite grounding her. "You can try. I haven't had much luck."

Talia's gaze lingered. "So, what brings you to our little aquarium of a bar? Business or pleasure?"

"Work."

"The serious kind or the fun kind?" she asked, her tone suggesting she already knew which answer she preferred.

For a heartbeat, Sloane let the question hang between them. She could say *fun*. She could lean in, test the waters, let her body remember it still belonged to her.

But then, unbidden, came the flicker of a grin. Brown hair, green eyes, a spark of defiance, a challenge thrown like a gauntlet across a lecture hall. Reese Maddox. A driver. Too young. Too reckless. Too close.

She blinked it away and lifted her glass to Talia's. "The serious kind," she said lightly, though her voice betrayed a touch of regret.

Talia tilted her head. "Pity. You strike me as someone who could use a little fun."

Sloane smiled faintly. "You might be right." But when Talia's hand brushed hers, she didn't move to take it. The wanting was there in an undeniable way, but it wasn't for this. Not for Talia. Not tonight.

"Thanks for the drink," she said softly. "Really."

Talia read the tone, gave her a kind nod, and drifted back into the crowd.

Sloane watched the fish chandelier glint overhead, light rippling across the glass, and exhaled. Okay, so she wasn't dead. Not yet. But apparently, she was alive in all the wrong directions.

Three hours later, as Sloane watched Reese unbutton her shirt one button at a time, revealing her blue satin bra, she knew she was exactly where she was supposed to be. She sat back on the bed, watching intently, the ache between her legs demanding attention. She throbbed. She was in need. And the show was almost too much, except it was perfection. This was everything she didn't know she'd needed. When Reese had knocked quietly on the door, Sloane almost hadn't let her in. It was late, and she'd had the martinis, and let's be honest, she had no business getting entangled with the likes of Reese Maddox. Now, she was more than glad she'd opened that damned door. Reese pulled down the cups of her bra, allowing her breasts to spring free, and Sloane's mouth watered. Before she had a chance to so much as touch, lick, or lavish them with attention, Reese was easing Sloane's legs apart. She was wet, so wet, and Reese would see that. The idea only turned her on more. Her underwear was slid down her legs as Reese grinned, gorgeous and so fucking sure of herself. Her fingers moved between Sloane's legs, featherlight and then with more assurance. It was so fucking satisfying that Sloane wanted more like she'd never wanted anything in her life. Her breath hitched as the pressure climbed and climbed, the friction undoing her.

"Hey," Reese said in her ear.

"Yes?" she managed.

"Are you ready to be fucked?" Reese whispered as she stroked her with more authority, owning the moment, owning Sloane, the rhythm hypnotic, the yearning intense.

Sloane met her eyes and nodded.

"Okay, then." Reese slid her fingers deep inside with unencumbered purpose. It was when she began to move inside Sloane that the world came undone. No sensation compared to this one, the need, the wonder, the fucking amazing feeling of Reese inside her, filling her fully, fucking her, taking her higher and higher with each thrust to places she hadn't dared imagine she'd ever get to again.

But then it was dark.

The world disappeared, and Sloane found herself sitting upright in her hotel room, alone and on fire. She checked the clock. It read just after 3 a.m. "My God," she murmured, shocked and affected by the dream in a manner she wasn't sure how to handle. It had seemed so real, down to the throbbing that still lingered between her legs—throbbing for release. For the touch of one person. For Reese.

Sloane fell back against the pillow, eyes wide open now. She'd kept her distance all this time for good reason, but her subconscious clearly hadn't gotten the memo. And as much as she tried to dismiss it, one truth pulsed beneath it all: Reese wasn't just under her skin. She was in her head, and that was far more dangerous.

CHAPTER 8
ALL YOURS

"Are we taking bets on our winners today?" Veronica asked.

"Should we?" Sloane turned from her spot in front of the second-story window over the garage. It offered a gorgeous view of the circuit. The drivers had taken their individual walks around the track as Sloane looked on, wondering what the day of racing would bring. The air outside already smelled like breakfast sausage and fried dough as the vendors set up for a day of racing. Mechanics and pit crews shuffled about like busy bees below, prepping the cars, doing warm-ups and drills to prepare for the fastest pit stops possible. The F1 Grand Prix would take place later that afternoon, and this place would be overrun with enthusiastic race fans. The stands would be *mostly* filled for the Formula Next and F2 races, as the majority would want a full day of racing for the price of their ticket.

"Who do you have?" Sloane asked.

"Marissa's going to take it all." Veronica came to stand next to Sloane at the window. "That is, if her father will give her some room to breathe."

"I don't think that's in his DNA." Marissa Giovani was a

bright light of talent, who Sloane had noticed dimmed considerably when the pressure from her father, who owned part of the team, came down. "But he's definitely doing more harm than good. Marissa's a good driver who needs more racing hours under her belt to grow. His presence makes her shrink instead."

"Maybe she needs some extra cheerleading from the academy."

"I was thinking the same thing."

Veronica turned. "Speaking of growing, Maddox had a solid finish at P3 yesterday. Another podium. Do we have you to thank?"

Sloane laughed. "I don't know. Reese is hard to reach. She's not only a people pleaser, which allows her to be pulled in fifteen different directions, but she's a hardheaded one."

"Hardheaded? Wow." Veronica shook her head. "I don't know anyone like that. Nope. Not a soul."

"Stop that. If you're comparing me to Reese, you could not be more off base." But she was smiling. Probably because the idea was ludicrous. Sloane was steady and methodical. Reese was chaos and fire.

Veronica crossed her arms. "I don't know what it is, but the more I'm around her, the more I see glimpses of you ten years ago, before you got serious and took us all down."

"Then maybe there's hope for her yet." She took a sip from her paper coffee cup. "Let's see where she finishes today."

Veronica turned her body to lean sideways against the railing. "If she makes podium again, we might have something interesting and very unexpected on our hands."

"I'm all for it," Sloane said with a shoulder lift. Her gaze fell to the circuit, where even though the other drivers had recessed back to their respective team garages, Reese was now jogging the track, likely working up a sweat in a little prerace workout. To say she looked good doing it was an understatement. Sloane purposefully looked away. Not a show for her. And probably not at all helpful to her cause.

"Well, it will be up to you to teach her the way. Reese is all yours."

Veronica's words, braided together with the dream that had jolted Sloane awake last night, landed like a live wire. All yours. The phrase alone was gasoline.

In the dream, Reese had been close—so close Sloane could feel the warmth of her breath against her thighs, could smell the melon of her shampoo when she'd leaned in, reckless and hungry. It had felt too real: the slide of hands, the low hum of laughter, the sound Reese had made when she—

She stopped the thought dead in its tracks, pulse quickening anyway.

"Lucky me," she said lightly, hoping Veronica didn't notice the edge in her voice.

If she did, she didn't comment. Instead, she gave Sloane a knowing half-smile before turning back toward the pit lane, leaving Sloane to wrestle with the vivid echo of the dream still playing behind her eyes.

Down on the circuit, Reese had finished her jog and was stretching in the morning sun, shirt damp at the collar, her hair falling from the ponytail in wisps. There was an ease to her, so unaware of the effect she had, unbothered by the eyes that followed her.

Sloane swallowed hard, knowing she should drag her gaze away. Professional. She was supposed to be *professional*. But as Reese bent to tie her shoe, sunlight catching the curve of her smile, Sloane couldn't help the heat that flared low and insistent, whispering that the dream hadn't been nearly enough.

She turned sharply, too fast, the motion meant to sever the thought. "I'll be in data analysis," she muttered, mostly to herself, and started down the stairs toward the paddock. The air was cooler there, the space shadowed, full of the metallic scent of fuel and brake dust. They were familiar and grounding smells that usually steadied her.

She pulled her tablet from her bag and forced her focus onto telemetry numbers, anything but the memory of Reese's mouth on her skin. Line graphs. Corner speeds. Brake pressures. Facts. Data. Control. Lions and tigers and bears. Her brain was full and jumbled with it all. And when she finally looked up, Reese was crossing the paddock toward her, towel slung around her neck, eyes bright and easy.

Sloane's fingers tightened around the tablet.

"Morning," Reese called with that disarming grin.

Sloane's reply came a beat too late. "Morning," she said, crisp. "Ready for today?" She set her tablet on a nearby table to give Reese her full attention. "You should have good weather."

"Yeah, I'm stoked about that. The forecast didn't look promising as of yesterday. But sun's out and conditions are great. I also feel like I'm in a good headspace. And hey, you'll enjoy this part," Reese said, leaning in.

Sloane folded her arms, holding her ground and trying not to notice their close proximity. "Tell me."

"When one of my endorsements, this key lime lip balm that's actually pretty great—"

"You'll have to give me the name."

"You got it. Well, they wanted me for an hour to record a reel."

"Of you applying their product?" Geniuses.

"Exactly that. I told them I couldn't make that work until tomorrow. *After* the race." She straightened, looking incredibly proud of herself. It was actually cute, which is not a word she often applied to Reese. But in this moment, she very much was.

"Well, well," Sloane said. "Impressive. And what's been the payoff?"

"Space to get my body and head right before flying around that circuit like a madwoman on a mission to make history."

Sloane laughed, and something flickered behind Reese's eyes. She liked it.

"It makes a big difference," Sloane said.

"You know, Sloane Foster, I'm actually starting to believe you."

"Thank God."

Reese took a step closer, and Sloane noticed a droplet of sweat on her collarbone from the workout. She forced her eyes to meet Reese's. "But don't tell anyone I said that. I'm known for my ego and want to keep it that way."

"Your secret is safe."

"I'm off to start reaction drills." She turned back as she walked, as if to say, *Can you even believe it?*

"Who are you?" Sloane called.

"I know!" Reese called back.

Sloane went back to her tablet, but it was only a moment before Veronica walked into the garage and paused. "What has you smiling like that?"

Sloane hadn't even realized she was. "Oh. Race days still have a way of …"

"Of?"

She searched thoroughly for the end of that sentence. "Getting me all excited. For the drivers."

Veronica smiled. "Okay, well, lean into that. Because if that's what this is, it looks good on you."

"Yeah?"

"I mean it, Sloane. There's a new energy. It's like the old you is back." She raised a shoulder, marveling. "And it's really nice."

Reese crossed the line with her hands steady on the wheel, heart hammering hard enough to rattle her ribs, but, for once, her head was clear. No panic or reckless instinct screaming at her to prove something. Just pace and consistency, both of which took a lot of restraint.

"And there's the checkered flag," Julie's voice came through the radio.

Reese whooped, the sound wild and unfiltered inside the cockpit. "Yes! Come on!" She smacked the steering wheel once, breathless and grinning. Yesterday's P3 sprint finish had felt good, but this? This felt like it belonged to her on a whole different level.

The radio crackled again. "That's P2, Reese," Julie said, jubilant. "Brilliant drive. No dive-bombs. No chaos. Just pace and patience. You did it."

Reese laughed into the mic. "Didn't even hit anyone this time."

"Even the wall was safe," Julie said. "Don't make me emotional."

Reese rolled into parc fermé, engine popping as it cooled. The moment she climbed out, the sun hit her face, warm and blinding. She tugged off her helmet, shook out her hair, and turned toward Julie, who was easing her way across the pit lane with her cane, smiling despite herself.

Julie didn't hug. Reese knew that. So when Julie stopped beside her, eyes bright with pride, Reese didn't push it—just grinned wide and said, "That felt good, huh?"

Julie nodded once. "That looked *different*. Last weekend, you were fighting the car. This time, you managed it. You kept your head. The race threw everything at you, and you didn't blink."

"Trying something new," Reese said with a wink. "Still trying to find what works best for me."

"This," Julie said way too quickly. "Solved it."

"Well, okay. Your opinion is noted for the record. Guess I'm growing up," Reese said, teasing.

Julie smirked. "Don't get cocky. But yeah … maybe a little."

"Guess I should get ready to do this thing." Her stomach fluttered with nervous energy. Reese looked back toward the podium setup in the distance, watching Danielle's team swarm around her car. "She's fast," Reese said quietly. "And ruthless. Her overtake on Marissa today was questionable."

"Yeah," Julie replied. "And she has zero regrets about that

kind of shady move. But listen to me." Reese turned and met Julie's earnest gaze. "Danielle Todd's been doing this longer. But she's not as naturally quick as you are. You just needed to prove it to yourself."

Reese glanced toward the paddock, where Veronica stood a few feet away, sunglasses on, phone in hand, but her attention clearly fixed on Reese. She wasn't smiling, exactly, but the slight nod she gave was unmistakable. Approval.

Julie noticed, too. "Looks like someone upstairs just started paying real attention."

Reese followed her gaze and gave a crooked grin. "About damn time."

Julie tapped her cane lightly on the ground. "You keep driving like that, and they'll have no choice."

Reese tilted her head, still flushed from adrenaline, proud of herself, but wanting more. "P2 today. P1 next time."

Julie's grin sharpened. "It's feeling possible now."

"Yeah," Reese said with a nod. "A lot of things are."

The officials were already waving them toward the podium area, where the crew had set up the step and repeat and mics for the press. Reese followed, the crowd noise a low roar beyond the barriers. Julie walked beside her, cane tapping on the asphalt.

"Remember," Julie said. "Smile. Be gracious. Don't take the bait. No matter what she says." She was referencing Danielle Todd and her hobby of trolling her competition.

Reese smirked. "You're saying that like I might."

Julie's look said everything.

Reese laughed under her breath and joined the other two drivers behind the podium. Danielle stood in the center, unzipping her suit halfway to reveal her fireproofs, her expression cool and satisfied. She was everything the British press said she was —razor-edged and unrelenting.

"Nice drive," Reese offered, genuinely impressed. "You claimed that one."

Danielle's gaze slid sideways. "Did I? Or did you just decide to play influencer today instead of driver?" She smiled for a photographer.

Reese blinked and forced a smile for the shot. "Excuse me?"

Danielle relaxed and turned to Reese. "Oh, don't pout. You're very good at the whole brand thing, posting selfies like a pro. I suppose that's its own kind of talent, am I right?"

Before Reese could answer, a marshal gestured them up the stairs. Danielle brushed past her, the faint scent of victory champagne already in the air.

On the podium, Reese forced her shoulders back and her grin wide as the announcer's voice boomed through the speakers. Marissa passed Reese an encouraging smile and raised her trophy first, then Reese's turn as the second-place finisher, and finally Danielle lifted hers to a mix of cheers and scattered boos. Apparently, the crowd hadn't loved her takeover either. The fans didn't miss a thing.

Champagne sprayed, cameras flashed, and Reese's mind barely tracked the moment. Julie was watching from the edge of the paddock, her expression unreadable. Veronica stood a few rows back, sunglasses glinting, arms folded.

When the postrace interviews began, the top three drivers were lined up in front of the cameras. Danielle went first.

"Danielle, that was a dominant drive from lights to flag. What made the difference out there?"

She smiled thinly. "Experience, mostly. You can't fake that. Some drivers still think it's all about being *seen*. But I prefer to do my talking on the track."

Reese's jaw tensed, but she kept her expression bright. When it was her turn, she leaned toward the mic.

"I think we *all* did our talking on the track today," she said easily. "Danielle drove a great race. Marissa killed it, and as for Ravensport, Delaney Rhodes came in strong with a P5 finish, which is great for us. I'm proud of how far our team's come this weekend and that's what matters to me."

Julie nodded slightly from the sidelines, approving.

Veronica's lips curved into something like a smile. Interest, confirmed.

And when the cameras swung away, Reese caught Danielle's eye one last time. She didn't say a word, but the message was clear.

Keep underestimating me. See how that works out.

CHAPTER 9
HEAT OF THE NIGHT

Marina Bay in Singapore was already lit like a city that never slept, heat hanging thick in the air. Reese stood beside the Ravensport car on the circuit, helmet resting against her hip as the film crew made final adjustments before her practice session. She was minutes away from sliding behind the wheel, and anticipation surged through every vessel, but she'd agreed to come in a night early for this interview and needed to make good on the deal.

Samara stepped behind the camera and settled in for her first question. She always took a deep breath first. Reese figured it was part of her process. "For spectators who might be new to racing, can you explain what qualifying means and why it matters so much?"

Reese nodded. "Qualifying is how we decide where everyone starts the race," she said. "We go out and run the fastest laps we can, one at a time. The quicker your lap, the closer you start to the front. The fastest lap is awarded pole position." She shrugged. "It's where everyone's dying to be. Me included."

Samara nodded, as if considering what more she might need for her storytelling. "Talk a little about why qualifying at the front of the grid matters at Marina Bay in particular."

She glanced down the pit lane, where the track disappeared between concrete walls. "Starting position matters everywhere, but especially here in Singapore. This is a street circuit. It's narrow, there aren't many places to pass another car, and mistakes are expensive. If you start near the front, you stay out of trouble. If you start farther back, you spend the whole race trying to fight through traffic. It's rare to move too many positions from where you start on a street circuit."

"So, during qualifying, it's not about racing other drivers yet," Samara said.

"No," Reese agreed. "It's about racing the clock. You're pushing for one clean, fast lap without overdoing it." She smiled faintly. "Too careful and you're slow. Too aggressive and you end up in the wall."

"What's the hardest part?"

"Trusting yourself," Reese said. "You're driving inches from barriers at high speed and telling yourself the car will stick, that you'll hit every corner just right. There's no fixing a mistake in qualifying. You only get what you earn."

A call crackled over the radio, summoning drivers to their cars. Engines fired around them, sharp and impatient.

Samara stepped back. "Good luck at qualifying."

Reese picked up her helmet and slid it on, her voice calm, certain. "Thanks. A good starting position will make everything easier."

Later that afternoon, Reese buzzed with extra energy. She was thrilled to be back with her friends again. She'd begun to miss the three of them in the space between race weekends, their presence like fresh air to her lungs. The Starting Grid set up a four-way group chat to stay in touch with each other while they were apart, which helped. But nothing compared to getting the gang back together again with real voices, real hugs, real chaos.

Singapore only amplified the feeling that something exciting was happening. The circuit was tight, twisty, and utterly unforgiving, one of the rare night races held through the glowing streets of downtown.

Reese spotted Cassidy first, standing in a long, sleepy line for a cappuccino at the hotel's little café. "Oh my God. Finally," Cassidy said, immediately abandoning the line and throwing her arms wide. Given that she was Cassidy, and the kindest person Reese knew, they'd likely let her cut anyway. Those big blue Bambi eyes could probably get her out of a federal crime.

"It's beyond good to see you," Reese said as she pulled her into a tight squeeze. Cassidy might've been new to single-seaters, but she was making waves at the academy. She'd held her own against drivers with years more experience and had just snagged her best finish at P9 last week, finally earning her first points of the season.

"She's a spark plug," Reese had overheard Veronica say to one of the lead mechanics the week before. "She might just shock us all. If not this season, then next. Mark my words."

Veronica was likely right. Drivers got only two seasons in Formula Next before they were kicked out of the nest to make room for newcomers. Cassidy would be more than ready by then. Hell, they all might be scrambling to get out of her way. The funniest part? She had the temperament of a barista prepping everyone's oat-milk latte, presenting as peaceful, adorable, and decidedly non-cutthroat.

"Are we all doing dinner tonight?" Cassidy asked, bouncing a little on her toes. "There's a great place on the corner. I've asked about eighteen people for recommendations, and they all agreed."

"I'm in," Reese said. "Are the others here yet?"

"Marissa's flight is delayed, and Delaney should be here any—"

"You're nothing if not accurate," Delaney said, appearing as if conjured, wearing a whole lot of black and a duffel slung casually over her shoulder. She honestly rocked any look she attempted. "Damn, it's good to see you people."

Reese practically leapt into her arms and held on. "The team is back together again."

"Why, thank you for that headlock," Delaney said, patting her back. She turned to Cassidy. "Ready to get back at it?"

"God, yes. I'd spring into a cartwheel, but I'm in the coffee line," Cassidy shot little beams of excitement off in every which direction. "But I'm learning the car more and more, and I even missed it a little this time. I think that means we're bonding."

"Just wait till you get your shot at F1. Every car is different there." A difference Reese couldn't wait to experience herself one day.

"Would you sign this for me, please?" a woman asked, stepping forward to Reese with bright eyes, a pen, and the commemorative program.

"Of course," Reese said, taking it. The others waited patiently while she signed and snapped a selfie, beaming like she'd won a prize.

"It really doesn't matter what country we're in, does it?" Delaney said, shaking her head, as they started walking again. "You'll always be our resident superstar." She ruffled Reese's hair affectionately, and Reese ducked out of the way, laughing.

Later that night, after Marissa arrived at the hotel, the four of them caught up over steaming bowls of laksa and plates of chili crab that required a team strategy. The restaurant was tucked under a string of lanterns along the waterfront, the humid air carrying the smell of lime, ginger, and grilled seafood. Reese laughed so hard at one of Delaney's stories that she nearly dropped her chopsticks. Something about a karting rival, an eel, and a very startled official.

"Why does stuff like that only happen to you?"

Delaney shrugged, cracking a crab leg with surgical precision. "I have an approachable face for chaos."

"Someone has to be the cautionary tale," Marissa added.

Reese was wiping tears from her eyes when the air in the room seemed to shift. Not dramatically. Not in a way anyone else at the table noticed. More like a subtle change in temperature, a prickle down Reese's spine. An awareness. Her gaze lifted instinctively toward the entrance, and then she understood.

Sloane had just stepped inside. Her hair was slightly damp from the humidity, pushed behind one ear in a way that looked unfairly good. Why was her glisten so much better than everyone else's glisten? She wore a simple black dress, nothing elaborate, just clean lines and confidence. Veronica walked beside her, elegant and composed in a slate-blue dress that hung off her tan shoulders. Two race officials followed in close conversation, one checking something on his phone, the other pointing out a table across the room. They were dining as a foursome, but Reese saw none of the others at first. Only Sloane.

She felt her heart give one clean, traitorous thud.

Cassidy kept talking beside her, but Reese heard only the soft, distant hum of the restaurant—cutlery, chatter, the clink of glasses—as if someone had turned the world down a notch.

Then Sloane's gaze landed on their table.

The reaction was small, but Reese caught it: a pause too long to be casual and a flicker of something unguarded in her eyes before she shifted her attention back to Veronica. Professional mask in place. Shoulders straight. Nothing out of line. She was hard to read.

Yet she kept glancing back. Just enough to betray that something was pulling at her.

Reese sat back in her chair, pretending still to be a part of their table's conversation. She laughed at Marissa, nearly missing her flight because she couldn't live without her favorite travel pillow, and was ready to sacrifice all to go back for it. "No. I get it," Reese said. "Some things are sacred." But all the while, she couldn't shake the feeling that maybe whatever preoccupation she had with Sloane Foster wasn't entirely one-sided. They were sitting across the room from each other, but the sizzle of whatever bounced between them was palpable. She no longer believed she was imagining it. Reese took a very slow inhale.

"Okay, why are you staring at a wall?" Delaney asked, leaning into her line of sight.

"What?" Reese blinked. "I'm not."

"You absolutely are." Delaney took a strategic sip of her lime soda. "I'd ask if you saw a ghost, but ghosts don't usually wear strappy dresses."

"Delaney," Reese said, a word of warning.

Before Delaney could push further, Cassidy's eyes widened. "Um. Veronica's here and walking this way."

They turned and smiled like dutiful soldiers as Veronica owned the room on her way over. Her designer dress and the way she wore it turned quite a few heads. "Popular place," she said as she arrived at their table.

"Cassidy finds us all the best spots," Delaney offered.

"Well, welcome to Singapore. How are the accommodations?"

"I don't have any complaints," Marissa said, "but I do have four twin beds in my room."

"I have five," Delaney offered.

Veronica nodded. "Miranda does have a knack for choosing the most interesting locations."

You can say that again, Reese thought. She also had an army of twin beds and a feeling that Veronica had upgraded her own lodging and was likely at a five-star hotel, sipping top-shelf cocktails. It also made her wonder where Sloane was staying, which of course made her imagine Sloane's hotel room, and then Sloane's bed, which was a train of thought she needed to get in front of before it spiraled out of control in the presence of a room full of people she was supposed to be socializing with.

"Well," Veronica said, touching the table, "don't leave without trying the pandan chiffon cake. It's a national treasure. In fact, I'll send over a couple. My treat."

"Thank you," Reese said.

"That's incredibly thoughtful," Marissa chimed in.

"My pleasure," Veronica said. "All I ask is for one amazing race weekend to show the world who we are. Think we can manage it?"

"That won't be a problem," Reese said and exchanged a fist bump with Delaney, who would be right there with her, aiming for more points for Ravensport.

"I think they're ganging up on us," Marissa told Cassidy.

Veronica grinned. "A little competition is healthy. I'd better get back to my dinner companions. Don't stay out too late." But she said it in a singsongy tone that said she thought they might anyway. Not Reese. She wanted to be rested and clear-eyed when it came time to fight for starting positions tomorrow.

While her friends waited for the desserts, Reese slipped away from the table, weaving through clusters of diners until she reached the dimly lit hallway near the restrooms. The hum of conversation faded behind her, replaced by the soft splash of a fountain and the distant clatter of dishes.

She pushed open the door and stepped inside, letting it click softly behind her.

For a moment, she just stood in front of the mirror, tugging at a stray lock of hair and taking a slow breath. The humidity had tousled her hair, her cheeks still warm from laughing too hard, and she allowed herself a small grin. Alone, at last.

The stall next to her opened. Reese froze.

Sloane stepped out, calm, poised, everything Reese knew her to be. But there was a spark in her eyes. She moved to the sink beside Reese, glancing at her reflection before flicking a smile to Reese.

"Practicing your prerace look, or just checking if Singapore's humidity has defeated you?" Sloane teased.

Reese blinked, caught off guard. "Uh ... both?" she said, forcing a laugh. "Humidity always wins."

Sloane raised an eyebrow, clearly unconvinced. "Always? I'm

pretty sure you could survive a monsoon with that hair and still look like you own the place."

Reese smirked, leaning slightly closer to the mirror. "That's a very specific compliment. I'm flattered ... and slightly intimidated."

Sloane shrugged, eyes twinkling. "Good. Intimidation is part of my charm."

Reese's grin widened. "Ah, so *that's* what I've been missing all this time."

Sloane laughed softly, the sound low and easy, and leaned against the counter. "Don't tell me you're finally admitting I was right about something."

"Nope. I'd have to hand over my hardhead card, and that's not likely to happen." A pause, as they smiled at each other. Reese turned to the mirror and attempted to fix her hair. "This humidity is a lot."

Sloane leaned slightly, peering at Reese's hair. "You know, I kind of like the tousled look. Makes you look dangerous."

"Dangerous?" Reese echoed. "I don't think anyone's using that word about me yet."

Sloane grinned, a slow, deliberate twist of her lips. "A day to put on the calendar."

"For a lot of reasons." Oh, she was just speaking freely now. Sloane had yet to turn and go, and that said something. "I guess we should get back to our respective tables, but it would be nice if we had dinner together sometime. I'd love to hear about your racing days. War stories."

Sloane's smile dimmed a touch, and Reese wondered what had caused it. "Tell you what. You win a race, and you're on."

"Wait. Really?"

"Yep."

Reese turned to Sloane fully. "Let me make sure I understand this clearly. I take P1 in a race, and you'll agree to have dinner with me. Just the two of us?"

"Yes. The answer is yes." She didn't hesitate.

"I can't decide if you're agreeing because you think I'll win or because you're confident I won't."

Sloane touched her shoulder on the way to the door. "Sometimes a little mystery is good."

Reese laughed outright this time, the tension from earlier replaced by warmth—and a thrill. "Well … I'll take my chances. And Sloane?"

Sloane's eyes lingered a beat longer than necessary. "Yes?"

"I'm definitely going to win."

Her expression was dialed to I'll believe it when I see it, but Reese had never been so fired up about a race in her entire career. "Enjoy your dinner, Reese."

"You, too, Sloane."

Reese wasn't sure if she'd imagined it, but just before Sloane disappeared back into the restaurant, her gaze drifted from Reese's shoulders to her toes. "She just checked me out," Reese murmured to the empty restroom before following Sloane back into the restaurant with a smile on her face. Things were starting to get so very interesting.

The visor of Reese's helmet caught the reflection of a thousand city lights as she settled her car into the third grid slot. She'd take P3. She could work with that starting position.

Singapore at night always looked like a celebration, unless you were strapped into a race car with your pulse hammering harder than the engine beneath you. Reese took a deep breath to settle her nerves while still hanging onto the adrenaline she'd need to advance her position.

Julie's voice filled her helmet. "Clean start. Be patient with Marissa ahead of you."

Reese nodded out of habit, even though Julie couldn't see her. Patience wasn't exactly her defining trait, especially not tonight. Not with the deal she'd made with Sloane humming under her skin like electricity. A win meant an extended conversation. One-on-one time in a dimly lit restaurant. A chance to get to know each other. Hold eye contact. The thought alone sharpened every sense.

Five red lights came on one at a time. Reese gripped the wheel. Then they went out.

She launched hard, tucking in behind Marissa as the cars threaded through the impossibly tight first corners. The walls blurred past, inches from her tires. Fuck, this was tight. Singapore never forgave overconfidence, and Marissa drove like she planned to block every inch of track for the entire race. Why did she have to be so fucking good? If Reese didn't like her so much, she'd really hate her right now.

But a quarter of the way into the race, Reese noticed it, the faint twitch of Marissa's rear tires on the corner exit, the kind that meant her grip was fading.

Julie must have caught it, too. "She's sliding. Set her up for Turn 7."

"You got it."

Reese waited one more lap, letting the tension coil through her shoulders. The humidity pressed in. The heat was almost unbearable in the car. She'd been climate training for two weeks to prepare for this. Time for some self-talk: just another day on the exercise bike in a ninety-five-degree room. She just needed to turn off her brain and its reaction. Though it was probably the most uncomfortable she'd ever been inside a car. Singapore didn't play.

When the moment came, she took it without hesitation.

Marissa drifted wide by a fraction, and Reese dove for the inside. The overtake was quick and almost surgical, done before Marissa had time to defend. She'd buy her dinner to apologize. Hell, she'd buy them all dinner if this went her way.

"P2."

"Let's go," she called back to Julie.

"Nice one, Reese. One more. Let's go get Danielle."

She focused on the turquoise-and-white car ahead of her. Only Danielle Todd remained in her forward view. As always, she was fierce, stubborn, blisteringly fast. The kind of driver who'd rather scrape the paint off her car or run them both into a wall than give up a position. *Well, fuck her.*

Reese allowed herself a small smile in the absolutely sweltering heat. *Game on.*

A few laps later, chaos erupted behind them. Two midfield cars tangled, one spinning into the barrier in a shower of sparks. Yellow flags waved instantly, and the safety car rolled out.

Julie didn't miss a beat. "Safety car. Box now. Fresh tires. Box. Box."

Reese obeyed, pulling into the pit lane. Her stop was slick and fast, and she rejoined the track glued to Danielle's rear wing. Danielle hadn't pitted — a gamble that might pay off or might crumble. How much faith did she have in those tires?

Julie's voice steadied her. "She's losing traction. Trust me. She'll slip up. Wait for it." Patience seemed to be a running theme these days, and though it was hard for Reese, she was working on it. She silenced the urge to make an immediate move and waited. Another five seconds passed. Another three. This was killing her.

And then Danielle made the mistake.

Coming out of a slow corner, she went for the throttle too early. Her car snapped sideways for the briefest moment. Not a crash, but just enough of a stumble to crack the door open.

Reese made her move.

They tore down the narrow straight wheel-to-wheel, the walls crowding in as if daring them to shift an inch. Reese held her line with icy focus. Danielle had to back out or risk the wall. Sweat ran down her face as she gripped the wheel.

Finally, Reese pulled ahead.

The last laps blurred into a mix of adrenaline and bright city lights. Was this actually happening? Was she this close to winning her first race in Formula Next? Reese managed her tires, her breathing, her nerves, all enhanced by the thought of the people who would be proud of her. Her mother. God, she couldn't wait to talk to her. Julie. Her team. *Sloane.*

When the checkered flag waved, she let out a raw, involuntary shout.

Julie laughed in her ear, warm and relieved. "That's a win, Reese. A damn good one."

Reese slowed on the cooldown lap, her breath catching in her throat. Her voice lowered, almost a confession to herself. "I did it. I actually did it."

The very next thought? Guess she was getting that dinner.

CHAPTER 10
LAST OF THE BEST

Well, well. Race weekend in Singapore was certainly shaping up to be an interesting one. Sloane had spent a good portion of it with the drivers from Dominion Racing, which meant time dedicated to Danielle Todd, who was talented as hell but unnecessarily aggressive in her approach. If Sloane could convince her to value the rules of racing and drive fairly, there was a bright career ahead of her. If not, no team was going to trust her with their multimillion-dollar cars in F1. She had a choice to make moving forward. Unfortunately, Sloane wasn't convinced Danielle believed her.

As she walked back to the paddock after watching Reese accept her first-place trophy atop the podium, she was stopped by a determined reporter.

"Hey, Sloane, you got a second?"

"Sure. What can I do for you?"

"Quick question. As a veteran driver, who are you rooting for this season?" The microphone was thrust in front of her face.

"I work for the academy. I don't play favorites."

"Yeah, but you're human. Who do you pull for?"

Whether she wanted to admit it to herself or not, she *was* starting to root for one woman in particular, and nothing she did seemed to stop it. Reese's triumphant smile when she waved to the crowd had done surprising, electric things to Sloane's body, whether she wanted to admit it or not. For now, she was a professional at work and would stay that way.

She offered her most practiced smile. "If I told you, I'd have to kill you."

It had been a while since she'd talked to the media, but she was surprised at how easily it came back—the switch flipping, the charm sliding into place.

"Fair enough. Who has the best shot at the drivers' championship?"

"Too soon to say. Ask me in another two weeks."

"You know we will. Thanks, Sloane."

"No problem."

She continued toward the paddock. Teams were already breaking down their setups. Mechanics rolling tool carts, crates slamming shut, crew members peeling tape from the concrete. The loud, frantic rush of race day softened into a tired hum as the night deepened.

All except Ravensport.

Their side of the paddock still buzzed with bright lights and leftover celebration. A speaker had been turned up, crew members were laughing, and someone was spraying down a champagne-sticky floor. A first-place finish did that.

Sloane smiled and scanned the scene just in time to spot Reese near the front of the garage, talking with Delaney. Delaney, calm and cool as always, stood with her arms loosely crossed, listening more than speaking. She'd finished P5—solid points for the team—and carried her success with her usual understated confidence.

Reese, by contrast, was still effervescent. Flushed from the podium, trophy tucked against her hip, she gestured animatedly as she recounted something from the race. Her hair was slightly mussed from the podium ball cap she'd worn, a loose curl stuck to her temple in the humid Singapore air. Sloane had the faint, ridiculous urge to brush it back. She could stand there and watch Reese forever.

Delaney noticed Sloane first. Her eyes flicked over, then she gave Reese a small nod, subtle but encouraging.

Reese turned, and when she saw Sloane, her whole face lit up. The smile hit Sloane square in the chest like a fastball.

Delaney murmured something. Probably *Go.* Reese dipped her head in acknowledgment and stepped away from her teammate.

"Hey," Reese said when she reached her, a little breathless. "Did you see the race? Please tell me you saw the race."

"Totally missed it." Sloane winced immediately as Reese's smile dropped hard and fast, like someone pulling the lights in a room. Guilt punched her straight in the gut. "Stop that. I'm kidding. Of course I watched. You were brilliant. Measured when you needed to be, aggressive when it was called for. A balanced, solid drive. You should be proud of yourself."

Relief returned slowly to Reese's features, softening her shoulders. "It was honestly a very satisfying race." Her green eyes moved back and forth as she searched for the right description. "It was almost like I could, I don't know, hold it in my hand." She raised her gaze to Sloane's. "I have no idea if that makes any sense."

"It completely does," Sloane said. "You were thinking just as much as you were feeling your way through. It takes both to win races."

Reese's mouth curled. "Turns out I actually don't know everything." Sloane hadn't meant to laugh out loud, but she did. Reese brightened at that. "Well, until now, of course." She flashed a sly smile. "Where are we eating?"

Sloane went still, and doubt filtered in. "I think they still have food in your hospitality room, but I've already had lunch."

"Our *dinner*," Reese said pointedly, holding eye contact like she had no intention of letting Sloane wiggle out of it. Reese excelled at eye contact, always so steady and confident, a little too intimate for Sloane's peace of mind. A shiver traced down her spine.

"Oh. Right. About that." Sloane rocked forward and back on her heels, suddenly very aware of her body. "Weren't we just playing around?"

"We definitely were not," Reese said instantly. Her brows pulled in like rain just invaded her picnic. "But we can keep it 100 percent professional." A beat. "If you want."

It was the first time either of them had acknowledged there was a spark bouncing between them. Saying it out loud made Sloane want to run screaming, because *none* of this was ideal, and she definitely couldn't lean into it. She was here to coach, guide, set boundaries. And the last thing she needed, given her history, was to get involved with a driver.

But another part of her stirred too. The part that had been quietly, stubbornly imagining what would happen if she let herself linger on this crush she'd developed on this hardheaded, drop-dead gorgeous—

She cut the thought off so abruptly she nearly felt the whiplash.

Sloane cleared her throat, gaze darting briefly toward the garage as if a distraction might magically appear. "Look, Reese … it's probably not the best idea now that I think about it. The season's long."

"And eyes are on you. On both of us. I get that." But she didn't pull her gaze away. "Let's keep it simple. Dinner next week. There's a little place just outside of Suzuka. Wooden tables. Handwritten menus. No one we know would possibly show up. I'd love to hear about your racing days. That's it. That's all."

Sloane nodded, and a smile crept in. It honestly sounded kind of nice. Time with Reese didn't have to be scary or carry greater implications. It also didn't have to mean anything beyond two people with a shared interest having dinner. Sloane was a grown woman, and there were no laws against getting to know one of the drivers. Even the attractive ones. She'd passed Veronica having coffee with Danielle Todd at a café that morning. Networking was a real and vital part of the women's experience in this male-dominated sport. They needed each other as allies.

She turned to Reese. "Next week in Suzuka it is. Let's do it."

Reese offered that same smile that sold a million sports drinks. It was worthy of every damn one. "Now I have something to look forward to."

"How about focusing on the race tomorrow first?"

"It's like you are programmed to keep me focused."

Sloane laughed. "Someone has to be."

She walked on, aware that she'd just agreed to something that could change her entire season if she wasn't careful. The Singapore night pressed in around her, loud and electric, and Sloane realized that the heat wasn't fading anytime soon.

Reese had waited a long time for a win that felt this right, and she took the time to truly savor the victory. Winning was everything. It felt like alignment, talent, patience, and belief finally pulling in the same direction.

But her brother hadn't been there. That was Reese's only regret about the win in Singapore. For years, her brother had been a part of every high and low she'd experienced in her career—her hype man, her analyst, her reality check. And while the victory had been electric, part of her longed for the familiar grounding of family.

By the time she finally returned to the driver's room and powered her phone back on, the screen lit up like a fireworks show. Missed calls. Voicemails. A string of texts from both Luke and her mom.

MOM

You never stop impressing me. I watched the
last few laps because Luke told me I'd kick
myself if I missed a win, and he was right.
Hugs. Kisses. Love to you.

Reese pressed the phone to her chest, eyes falling shut for a beat as warmth pooled through her. The next message was pure Luke.

LUKE

Fuckin' killed it. I was worried on turn 5 but you
flipped the whole thing around after the safety
car. Raising a glass to my little sis tonight. Call
soon.

It wasn't an in-person hug. It wasn't Luke yelling at her in the garage or Mom squeezing her so hard her ribs protested. But it helped. It was something. And given the time difference, they were probably brushing their teeth and falling into bed after staying up half the night to watch her. She'd call them in the morning, when she could string coherent sentences together.

The circuit around her was shifting into exhale. Crews packed up gear. Media stragglers hustled toward exits. Only Ravensport seemed immune to the slowdown—still celebrating, still loud, still claiming their corner of the paddock like they'd never leave it. She wandered anyway, letting the noise fade the farther she moved from the team's hub, until she could just be a spectator again.

She slipped into the stands for F1 qualifying and found herself cheering alongside thousands of diehards who'd flocked to the circuit for the main attraction. The roar of engines vibrated through her, the lights strobed across the track, and she watched the drivers carve through the corners with a precision that felt almost mythical.

What must it be like to sit behind the wheel of one of those cars for the big show? To feel that speed, that pressure, that world watching? The longing clawed at her, powerful enough to steal her breath.

And, knowing that if anyone in Formula Next was getting the whisper of a call-up, it would be someone like Danielle Todd, lit a new fire in her gut. Not jealousy. Not quite. More like a challenge. A dare.

She wasn't done yet. Not even close.

When she walked back to the paddock to grab her bag, most everyone had already cleared out. The lights were dimmer now, the air less electric—victory celebrations having tapered off one garage at a time. As she passed Vantera's on the way back from Ravensport's, a sharp exchange of voices cut through the quiet, making her pause.

One was Marissa's.

The other—louder, angrier—was her father's.

Dammit. That fucking guy always showed up on race days. He flew in just before lights out, made a bunch of demands, and disrupted Marissa's flow like it was his personal hobby. Reese couldn't imagine what it must be like to have an overbearing parent like Leo Giovani, while also having him be one of the team's biggest investors. He was a VIP and acted like it.

"It's still a podium," she heard Marissa say, calm but tired.

"Don't, for a moment, let yourself feel good about P3. You hear me?" Leo's voice snapped like a whip. "P3 is last of the best. You want to be last? Not on this team. Not on my team."

"I don't know what more you want. I did everything I could," Marissa said, her voice thinning with exhaustion.

"Then what went wrong? This isn't F1. You're all in the same car. Figure it out." Something clattered—metal on concrete—as if he'd purposely knocked something over on his way out. His footsteps stormed down the corridor.

Reese's jaw tightened. She wanted nothing more than to explode into that garage and tell that man exactly how phenomenal his daughter was—not just behind the wheel, but as a human being. Instead, she made herself breathe and waited a few beats before appearing in the doorway.

"Hey," she said softly.

Marissa turned. Her attempt at a smile wavered. She'd changed into her street clothes already, her long dark hair pulled into a ponytail. She looked wrung out, like she'd spent the better part of the last hour justifying a result seventeen other drivers would have killed for. "Want to ride back together?"

Reese nodded. "Hundred percent. Let's get out of here."

Some of the tension slipped from Marissa's shoulders, and together they walked out into the humid night. The full moon hung low, glowing brighter by the minute. Heat clung to Reese's skin, heavy and sticky, and despite the long day, she wasn't even close to ready for sleep. They raced again tomorrow ... but one drink couldn't hurt. She'd sworn off any more than that during the season.

"Want to grab a cocktail?" she asked. "I know you don't drink on race weekends, but maybe we could make it a mocktail?"

"Reese. I want a drink right now more than I've ever wanted anything." And this time, Marissa's smile looked real. "We're having one."

They found one of the academy cars and rode back to the hotel, a quick drive punctuated by silence that didn't feel awkward, just needed. Inside, they posted up at a small, out-of-the-way table in the lobby bar, away from the remaining buzz of the night.

"You had a great race today," Reese said once their drinks were delivered—a glass of wine for Marissa, a beer for her. "Your dad not appreciating it doesn't change the facts."

"Ah. So you heard him?" Marissa's cheeks flushed with embarrassment. "Nothing I'm not used to. He has impossible standards. It's been that way my whole life. He's rich, entitled, and expects everyone to bend the second he snaps his fingers."

She swirled her wine, watching the liquid catch the light. "What are your parents like?"

"My dad died when I was eight," Reese said quietly. "And my mom is poor and awesome, which sounds like the exact opposite of your dad."

Marissa blinked. "I didn't know you'd lost yours."

Reese shrugged. "I don't talk about it much. He was my hero. A good guy who maybe put racing in front of the things that mattered more. He loved it so much that he died doing it."

"In a race?" Marissa asked, eyes wide. Every driver's worst nightmare sat between them now.

"Nothing official. It was a street race." Reese shook her head. "He should've known better. It was reckless, and he could've hurt someone. Wound up hurting himself. And us. In the end, my mom had to figure everything out on her own with basically nothing."

"I'm sorry," Marissa murmured.

"Oh, that's okay." Reese forced a small smile. "I guess we both had dads who made some choices that weren't great for their families."

Marissa nodded slowly. "I think about that a lot. How one decision, made in an instant, can completely redirect a life. Sometimes I wonder what would happen if I just told my dad to fuck off."

"Would you?"

"I might." Her gaze drifted past Reese to some point far away. "I don't quite know what my plan is."

"For him?"

"For me." Marissa exhaled, a soft huff. "I love racing. It's all I've ever known. But sometimes I think … maybe there's more out there, you know?"

Reese was confused. The words didn't compute. "Like what?"

"Hard to say. Maybe I could be Veronica Vance. Or one of the race officials." Marissa sat back, lighter with a faraway look in her eye. "Hell, sometimes I think I'd make a great sports journalist." Then it seemed like reality came crashing back in. Her eyes dropped to the table as if she regretted saying any of it aloud. "Anyway."

Reese stared at her, stunned. Marissa Giovani, of all people, not fully committed to racing? Marissa, who drove like she was born for it? But the thing was … Reese believed her. And she believed she could do any one of those things brilliantly.

"You'd be a kick-ass reporter," Reese said, leaning back in her chair, "now that I've seen you hold your own with literally anyone. You ask good questions. You never get rattled under pressure. And you actually listen when someone talks, which is more than I can say for most people."

Marissa looked up, surprise flickering across her face like she hadn't expected kindness, at least not today. Maybe not ever, coming off a race.

"You really think so?" she asked, voice softer than before.

"No. I know so," Reese said simply. "You'd be great at whatever you picked."

Marissa didn't speak right away. Instead, she took a long sip of her wine, staring straight ahead as though absorbing the idea piece by piece. The lobby was quiet except for the faint hum of an air conditioner and the muted chatter from the bar. It made the moment feel oddly suspended. Untouched.

Finally, she exhaled. "No one's ever said that to me. Not like that."

Reese blinked. "Said what?"

"That I could be great at something outside of what I'm expected to be." Marissa gave a small, lopsided smile, more honest than any she'd worn today. "It's nice."

Reese's chest tightened, something warm and protective blooming there. "Well, it's true. And you deserve to hear the truth every now and then."

Marissa laughed softly, but there was no embarrassment in it this time. It sounded more like relief. "You're turning out to be a really good friend, you know that? Not gonna lie. It's not what I expected of Reese Maddox."

Well, this was interesting. "What did you expect?"

"No. It sounds awful."

"Even more reason to just say it." Reese sat back, smiling, and waited. It wasn't the first time she'd been misjudged.

"I expected you to be surface-level. Very caught up in yourself and glued to a mirror."

"God."

"I know!" Marissa shook her head, mystified. "I was guessing you took all the media gigs and Instagram collabs because you were so into yourself and your image. I didn't ever imagine it was because—"

"I was trying to pay my way?"

"Exactly. Yes." She winced. "I'm an embarrassed, entitled asshole."

"I don't fault you. I'm finding out that it's a pretty common assumption."

"From people who were brought up with too much of everything," Marissa said. "Racing is a sport designed for rich people. Let's be honest."

"Maybe you'll change that one day. Bring awareness in your capacity as a sports journalist."

Marissa grinned. "Maybe I will. In the meantime, I don't mind saying that I was dead wrong about you, Reese." She swirled her wine and took a sip. "I'm glad I was wrong. I'm even more glad you're my friend."

The word *friend* hit Reese in a place she hadn't realized was empty until now. She nodded. "Right back at you."

For a while, they sat quietly, not needing to fill the space with chatter. Just two drivers in the late-night calm, letting the day settle. The moonlight spilled through the lobby windows, and the weight of earlier conversations lifted between them, replaced with something steadier. Trust, maybe? Or the beginning of it.

Marissa set her glass down gently. "Thanks for staying with me tonight."

"Anytime," Reese said. And she meant it.

The friendships she was forming with these women after just a few weeks were staggering. There was something special about the academy. Maybe it was the mission, maybe the shared grit of women carving out space in a world not built for them. Maybe it was the simple fact that they were all here, together, wanting the same impossible thing.

Whatever the reason, Reese knew with startling clarity that these friendships weren't temporary. They were the kind that rewired you, that marked the before and after in your life. These friendships were the beginning of something lasting. Something she'd carry with her long after the season ended.

CHAPTER 11
JUST DINNER

Sloane couldn't believe she was doing this. Was she really going to do this? She picked up her hairbrush and then set it down again. Alarm bells sounded as she fluffed her hair in front of the mirror and watched the blond layers fall and mingle in a tousled result. Not bad. She surveyed herself in a red V-neck top, dark jeans, and two-inch black wedges. When she'd agreed to make good on her deal with Reese and go with her to some out-of-the-way restaurant, it was a day on the calendar in the future. But fast forward a week and a plane ride to Suzuka, and she was one cab away from a cozy dinner for just the two of them. Did that send a ripple through her midsection? Hell, yes. Did that make it a better idea? She sighed. The answer was a resounding no, but something in Sloane wouldn't let her cancel. She'd picked up her phone to do just that several times. But she'd always put it back down again. Quite frankly, she was curious and more than a little intrigued. Regardless, it felt like she was pulling on a loose thread that might unravel the whole neatly woven sweater she'd come to rely on. "Maybe keep your hands off the thread," she murmured as she grabbed her bag, the designer one her mother had sent her for Christmas the year before. She dared not look up how much it was worth.

When she arrived at the quaint little restaurant that was everything Reese promised, a small part of her relaxed. It was just a dinner. Why had she agonized about the meetup? Sloane fully believed she'd overreacted. Well, right up until she saw her.

Reese sat alone at a table by the window, the fading light pouring over her like it had been creatively designed for this exact moment. She wasn't even doing anything remarkable. Just … watching the sunset. But somehow that made it worse, because Sloane suddenly understood what it meant for someone to be stunning without the slightest intention. She swallowed at the insistent tug.

Reese's dark hair was down, loose around her shoulders in a way that caught the orange-pink glow outside. A soft, sheer gloss warmed her lips, making them look even more impossibly smooth. They were slightly parted, like she'd been caught midthought. Breathtaking. The sleeveless black top showed off the contour of her arms, and she wore jeans that made her look both casual and impossibly put together. Black leather heeled sandals with narrow straps showed off just enough skin to feel effortlessly stylish in the Suzuka heat. Her posture was relaxed as she waited, almost unguarded. Totally Reese.

But it wasn't the outfit. It wasn't even the way the light gilded her cheekbones. It was her expression that was so soft, faraway, and contemplative. Like she was somewhere else entirely, somewhere tender and private that Sloane had never been invited to before. Somewhere Sloane suddenly wanted to know far too much about.

And the sight of it hit Sloane like a hand to the sternum.

God, Reese was beautiful. Not because she tried, but because she simply existed in a way that made everything else feel less interesting by comparison.

She gestured toward the table to let the host know she had spotted her dinner date.

As she approached, Reese turned and broke into a smile that could end wars, which left Sloane grinning right back. Her chest did something traitorous and warm. It really was good to see her. "Hi. Welcome to Japan." Reese placed her napkin on the table and stood without hesitation.

"Thank you." She looked around the small dining room with so many personal touches. It seemed family-owned, with thought put into each piece of art or decor. "This place is great."

"Right? I thought it would give us space without fifteen people we know seated all around us." She remained standing until Sloane took a seat. "And I just can't believe you agreed to go on a *date* with me."

Sloane's eyes went wide, which pulled a laugh from Reese, who held out a hand. "I'm kidding. I promise. You can relax."

"You do that a lot," Sloane said, gaze narrowing. "Kid."

"I can cop. I'm definitely the cutup in this duo." Her grin showed off that damned dimple on her right cheek. She had a small one on her left, but it was the right one that did Sloane in.

"And now we're a duo?" She arched a brow.

"Oh, yeah. The moment we were at odds in your talk to the drivers, we became a duo."

"God, if that's all it takes, I'm in a lot of duos."

Reese leaned in. "But are any of them this good? You, a former driver who made history. Me, a current driver about to."

She passed Reese a smile. "Don't get ahead of yourself, Maddox."

Reese's cheeks dusted pink at the use of her last name. Well, look at that. Sloane had unnerved her. A first. After letting the moment slide over her, she studied the menu and easily chose the salt-grilled salmon with a side of gyoza. Reese was more adventurous and picked the yakisoba stir-fry, which she promised to let Sloane steal a bite of. They were relaxing around each other, which, honestly, was like much-needed air.

When the server delivered Reese's nonalcoholic beer and Sloane's warm sake, she couldn't help but pick up on the parallel. She and Reese were as different as those two drinks, but here they sat anyway.

"Now," Reese said, her glass in hand, "tell me about F1. Everything. No detail must be spared. I worked hard for this intel."

"Oh, that," Sloane said. It was a wash of good memories and more difficult ones. "It's not for the weak, especially when you're female. I'll tell you that."

"You are an absolute badass behind the wheel, so it makes sense that you were one of the few of us to make it to the top of the game. So what's the hard part?"

"Let's see. Most of the men don't think you belong, are sexist, and have their own boys' club." She eased a strand of hair behind her ear. "The media has a separate set of expectations for female drivers, and the public is absolutely unforgiving of the tiniest misstep."

Reese shook her head. "That's awful."

"And I don't think much has changed."

"That stuff shouldn't still exist at the highest level of motorsport."

"I can tell you it's worse. But you know what?" She met Reese's green eyes as a wash of nostalgia came over her. "It was still the coolest thing I've ever done. There's nothing like F1."

"Now the best part."

She relaxed into a grin because the answer was undeniable. "That speed. Nothing compares to those cars. Nothing. The vibration of the road beneath your steering wheel with that kind of power, constantly reminding you that you're one of the best in the whole damn world. It's a drug in the best way."

"Damn," Reese said, sitting back with a face full of wonder. "What I wouldn't give."

"I remember winning my first Grand Prix in Monza, crossing the finish line beneath that flag, hearing my team losing their minds on the radio as the fireworks burst in the sky."

"Fucking mind-blowing," Reese said, shaking her head as if just imagining being in Sloane's shoes was too much.

"It was. It was fucking mind-blowing," she said, leaning in

with a laugh. It felt surprisingly good to let herself go back there. Not many people in the world could appreciate the magnitude of such a moment, but Reese could. Sloane recognized the same hunger in Reese that she'd experienced on her way up, and in that moment, she wanted nothing more than to help Reese achieve her dream. "Could be you one day if you land a few more P1 finishes. I will admit that your high profile doesn't hurt. Teams want a driver who will pull in investors. But none of that matters if you can't score points."

"I'd give anything." She tapped the table, something tugging at her. "The academy, however, has put things in perspective."

"Oh, yeah? In what sense?"

"There are a lot of us, and we're all talented. If an F1 team pulls up someone from the academy, it could easily be someone else." She took a drink of her beer.

"Which is why you don't leave it to chance. You give them every reason to select you." Sloane took a breath and decided to level with Reese. "You're a well-known driver, and that works in your favor. You pair that with winning the championship for this season, and it's a hard combo to turn down, provided they need a driver." That was the thing about F1: it was a constant game of musical chairs. Two drivers per team, and if all the seats were filled, there'd be no reason to promote from a lower level. Unless she wowed them to the point they couldn't resist, and Reese Maddox had that wow factor. Sloane had experienced it firsthand.

As they enjoyed their meal, Sloane felt herself loosen considerably. Partly a result of the easy give-and-take she and Reese had when away from the academy, partly the sake and its potent effect.

"So, what's it like coming from such a well-known family?" Reese asked. "If this feels too much like an interview, just say so, and we can stare into each other's eyes instead," she offered a wink to let Sloane know she was kidding, but they both knew only partly.

"Less pressure than you might think. The members of my family are very determined people, but very much focused on their own goals and endeavors. My uncle introduced me to racing because it was his hobby. My parents threw money at it because it kept me busy and out of the way."

"Not incredibly hands-on then?"

"Let's just say they weren't in the stands more than they had to be."

"Oh," Reese said. Sloane didn't blame her. What did one say when you announced that your parents were uninvolved in your childhood and left you to coaches, nannies, and tutors?

"It's okay. We still exchange Christmas presents. Very expensive ones."

"We had completely opposite childhoods."

"Your parents were awesome?"

A pause. "Well, until my dad died. My mom did everything she could to fill his shoes, which makes her an amazing human being. No money though. No childcare, so my brother had to help. The two of them are the only reason I'm here."

"Wow. That sounds like a lot to take on." A pause. "I'm sorry about your dad. Was he sick?"

"He died in a street race after a semipro career never took him where he wanted it to, but he introduced me to racing. Put me in my first kart."

"Oh, Reese. I'm sorry."

"It's okay," Reese said with a reassuring smile. "If I were eight, you were probably what, nine?"

"Smooth. Very smooth." She'd done the math. She was eleven years older than Reese, which meant she'd have been a teenager.

She did, however, remember something in the write-up Veronica had given her about Reese coming from a racing family. How had she missed such a key detail, the kind that could shape a person and their entire career, their outlook from behind the wheel, their risk assumption or lack thereof? Those things contributed.

"I'm sure that still has an impact on you. His legacy and what happened to him."

"Every day of my life. I don't start a single race without thinking about him. Hoping that I'm making him proud, wherever he is."

"He's with *you*," Sloane said simply. There was no doubt in her mind. "In that car."

The smile started small but then blossomed into an image Sloane knew she'd never forget. It softened Reese in a way she rarely let the world see, without the bravado she put on like a second fire suit.

"Thanks," Reese said quietly, eyes lowering to her hands. "Most people don't know what to say about it. Or they focus on the tragedy part and not everything else."

"What else?" Sloane asked.

Reese lifted her gaze again, and there was a surprising steadiness there. "He loved racing more than anything. He died doing what he lived for. Do I wish he would have thought of us? Sure. Yes. But I also understand that drive."

Sloane nodded, understanding the sentiment maybe too well. "There's honor in that. And courage."

Reese huffed a soft laugh. "Maybe. Or maybe we're all just a little unhinged for choosing this life."

"Both can be true," Sloane offered, a small smile tugging at her mouth.

Reese's expression turned playful for a heartbeat, a flicker of her usual spark returning. "You would know."

"Yeah," Sloane conceded. "I would."

The words lodged for a moment, catching on something sharp in her chest. She wasn't sure if Reese was alluding to her accident, but it was right where Sloane's brain went. She pushed past it. Coming back to the academy had been risky, closer to the action than she'd been in years, and sometimes the sounds alone could tilt her back into memories she'd spent a long time learning to survive. But this wasn't the moment for that. She forced her focus back to Reese, steadying herself and focusing on the beautiful woman in front of her, a puzzle she couldn't help but want to solve, dangerous or not.

For a moment, the noise of the restaurant faded. The low hum of voices, the clink of cups, the hiss of the espresso machine. All she really registered was Reese across from her, the light outlining the curve of her cheekbone, the weight of something unspoken settling between them. Something real.

Reese tapped a knuckle lightly against the table. "I don't talk about him much. But I did a week ago with Marissa."

"Because you trust her. She's your friend from what I've seen."

"More than I ever would have guessed when I arrived. But I went there with you, too."

Sloane met her eyes. "Because you needed to. And I listened."

Reese considered that, then nodded once. "Yeah. You did." They stared at each other for longer than two regular people were supposed to, drawing a giant arrow sign over the unique tension that seemed to underscore their interactions. "You do realize I've developed a huge crush on you."

Sloane usually would have dodged such a comment, keeping her head on straight. Tonight, the out-of-the-way location that made her feel far removed from the real world loosened her grip on the practical. "Is that true?"

"And this conversation, this meal, the way you're looking at me right now …" Reese let out a breath that sounded dangerously close to a sigh. "It's not helping."

Sloane felt her pulse thrum once. She should shut this down, redirect, and remind them both of the boundaries she was here to uphold. That was the smart thing. The necessary thing.

But Reese was still watching her, eyes bright and open in a way that stripped Sloane's defenses down to their foundations.

"I'm looking at you," Sloane said carefully, "because you're being honest. And because you matter. That's all."

Reese's lips quirked, not quite a smile. "Doesn't feel like 'that's all.'"

God, she wasn't wrong. The space between them felt charged, humming with something Sloane had no business entertaining.

"I work for the academy," Sloane reminded softly, a quiet tether to reality. "We have rules. Lines."

"Lines can exist," Reese said, voice low but steady, "and there can still be … whatever this is."

The candor was disarming. So was the courage behind it. Sloane pressed her palms to the underside of the table, grounding herself.

"Reese," she said, gentle but firm, "you're incredible. And I'm not pretending I don't feel an attraction. But I can't step over that line. Not here. Not now."

Reese took that in without flinching. "I didn't ask you to step over it. I just needed you to know."

Sloane exhaled, something inside her easing. "Okay," she said quietly. "Now I know."

Reese nodded once, the tension between them softening, settling into something less unnerving. "Good," she murmured. "Feels better already."

It did. And it didn't. In equal measure.

Sloane reached for her napkin, more to give her hands something to do than anything else. "We should get going," she said, her voice softer than she meant it to be. "Long day tomorrow."

Reese nodded, pushing her chair back. "Yeah. Makes sense."

They stood, and for one suspended second, simply looked at each other again, an acknowledgment of everything said and everything that couldn't be.

Sloane gestured toward the door. "Come on. I'll walk you out."

Reese smiled, small but real. "I'd like that."

It turned out Sloane had been booked into the same hotel as the drivers, which was a first. As far as Reese knew, Sloane usually preferred to snag a place away from the chaos that came with race weekend. The upside of the change? They could ride back together.

As the sights and sounds of Suzuka streamed past the car windows, Reese felt lighter than she had in years. The driver had his window cracked, and the warm night air rushed in, lifting strands of her hair every few moments. She closed her eyes and grinned, letting the sensations wash over her. She enjoyed the wind, the motion, the lingering adrenaline from the day, and the quiet awareness of Sloane beside her. When she opened her eyes again, Sloane's gaze rested on her profile. In the darkened car, Reese pretended not to notice. She enjoyed it too much.

"What floor?" Sloane asked fifteen minutes later as the elevator doors slid open in the lobby.

"Eighteen," Reese said.

"Impressive." Sloane tapped both their buttons. "I'm on five, which is … less so."

"You have to make friends with Miranda."

Sloane raised a brow. "You think I haven't tried? And of course *you* have. I'm sure you've successfully charmed your way into her good graces. I forget who I'm dealing with."

Reese smiled and rocked onto her toes as the elevator doors closed, sealing them in together. She savored the quiet, the last few seconds of their evening. She hated to see it end. She wondered if the honest, refreshing rhythm they'd slipped into tonight was a one-off born of travel, exhaustion, and their simple proximity, or the first step toward something that could unfold into more.

Did she want to undress Sloane slowly and make her crave things with white-hot intensity? Hell, yes. But she'd settle for platonic if it meant more moments like this. She'd take whatever she could get.

Someone somewhere must have been listening to her thoughts, because the elevator abruptly shuddered, sputtered, and stopped with an ominous metallic bang.

"Oh no," Sloane murmured, stepping forward. "I'd hit a button, but I'm afraid I'll send us plunging to our death."

Reese's eyes widened. "Let's maybe not put that out into the universe." She glanced up at the ceiling panel, then down at the seam in the doors as if clues might reveal themselves. "Maybe I could pry the doors open? Check if we're near a floor?" She shifted forward, bracing her hands—

Sloane's palm closed gently around her bicep. "Not sure this is the time for heroics."

"I feel like it's always time for those. No?"

"No," Sloane said flatly. "But maybe we should ring the bell."

"We can try that first," Reese conceded. She crossed her arms to keep from wrestling their way out of this. The emergency call connected to a maintenance worker who spoke only Japanese, which neither of them understood, but his tone was calm and reassuring.

"Well, now what?" Sloane asked—just as the overhead lights flickered and switched to dim, humming emergency fluorescents. They exchanged a look.

Reese lowered herself to the floor. "It might be a while. The last time this happened, it was over an hour."

"The last time?" Sloane echoed, sitting beside her. "You've been trapped in an elevator before?"

"Four times."

Sloane stared at her, incredulous. "Remind me never to get on one of these with you again. The elevator overlords have cursed you."

Reese grinned. "No. They just like me."

"That cannot be your answer to everything," Sloane said, but a smile tugged at her mouth.

Reese slid a little closer. Not enough to crowd, just enough to be unmistakable. "I think you find it endearing. I'm hoping you find all of me that way."

"I don't think it matters if I did. Your confidence knows no limits."

"Then you don't know me as well as you think you do," Reese said softly. "Because I care very much what the great Sloane Foster thinks. And," she added, "I also care what *you* think."

Sloane went quiet. The uneven lighting cast shadows across her face, softening some features, sharpening others, revealing nothing.

"It's interesting," she said finally, voice low, "that you differentiate the two. I'm not sure most people do."

"I'm sure there's overlap," Reese said, her knee brushing Sloane's lightly. "But yeah, there's a difference."

Sloane's gaze flicked down at the quick, unmistakable contact. She didn't move away. In fact, she shifted almost imperceptibly closer, as if pulled by something she wasn't ready to name.

The quiet in the elevator changed. It tightened. Thickened. Reese felt it settle on her shoulders, warm and heavy and full of possibility.

"You're confusing," Sloane said finally. Her voice was soft enough that Reese had to lean in to hear it. "And I don't get confused easily."

"That feels like a compliment," Reese murmured.

"It wasn't meant as one," Sloane replied, but her eyes said otherwise. The dim emergency lighting caught a flicker of something. Interest, maybe? Curiosity? Whatever it was, it was new. And it was aimed directly at Reese.

Reese let the moment stretch. "You know, you don't have to keep pretending you don't like me. Or are we leaving all of that back at the restaurant?"

Sloane's brows lifted, but she didn't deny it. She didn't

deflect. She didn't joke.

Instead, she exhaled, slow and steady, as if Reese had knocked the air from her. Her hand, resting on the floor between them, curled just slightly. Nervous? Or fighting the impulse to reach? Reese couldn't tell. She only knew her own pulse was thundering in her ears. Had she ever found any woman on earth this wildly attractive?

"Reese," Sloane warned, but the warning wavered. "This, whatever this is, we're not supposed to go there."

"Because of some undocumented rule?" Reese asked quietly. "Or because you're afraid of where it might lead?"

Sloane met her gaze head-on then, and the world beneath Reese's rib cage tilted. "Maybe a little of both," Sloane said. A confession she probably hadn't intended to give.

Reese swallowed. "You know what's funny?" she said, leaning in, her shoulder brushing Sloane's now. "I've been trying all night to decide if I should sidestep whatever this is. If I should ignore the way you look at me sometimes."

"I don't—"

"You do," Reese whispered. "You're doing it right now."

Sloane froze. Completely still. Completely caught.

And Reese—God, she wanted to touch her. She wanted to trace her jaw with her fingers. Unbutton that blouse and watch it fall from her fingertips. She settled for sliding her hand an inch closer on the floor until their pinkies nearly, almost touched.

The elevator hummed around them, a soft mechanical heartbeat. Time felt suspended.

Sloane's voice came out barely audible. "This is a terrible idea."

"Probably," Reese said. "But it doesn't feel terrible."

For a moment, for one breathless second, Sloane seemed to grant herself permission to look. Really look. At Reese's mouth. At the bare inches between them. At the closed space that suddenly felt too intimate in all the right ways.

And Reese knew: if the elevator stayed stalled even one

minute longer, one of them was going to make a choice they couldn't take back.

Sloane's gaze dropped once more to Reese's mouth. Just a flicker—but enough to feel like gravity had shifted direction and decided Reese was the new down.

Reese's breath caught. "Sloane ..."

"Don't," Sloane whispered, though her body swayed closer as if her instincts had not received the memo. "Don't say my name like that."

"Like what?" Reese asked, her voice barely more than air.

"Like you want—" Sloane cut herself off, jaw tightening, as if the rest of the sentence was too dangerous to speak aloud.

But Reese heard it anyway. Want *me*.

Reese didn't move at first. She waited. She let Sloane feel the weight of her wanting, the safety of it, the invitation without pressure. She let the moment fill every inch of the dimly lit space.

And then, slowly, carefully, like testing the edge of a cliff, Reese slid her hand along Sloane's cheek, into her hair.

Sloane inhaled sharply.

That tiny spark of contact traveled straight up Reese's arm and settled low in her belly. Sloane didn't pull away. She didn't speak. She only watched Reese, eyes dark and wide, as if she was actively losing a battle with herself.

"Tell me to stop," Reese whispered.

Sloane closed her eyes. "I can't."

That was all Reese needed.

She reached up, a slow, deliberate lift of her hand, giving Sloane every chance to retreat. But Sloane didn't move. If anything, she leaned in first.

Their lips met in a soft, startled collision. Not urgent. Not practiced. Not anything Reese had expected.

Just real. Carnal. Amazing. This should have been the moment the elevator burst to life, stealing this very important moment, but it didn't. They were left to explore it, deepen it, breathe in the shock of how right it felt. Sloane's hand came to Reese's jaw, tentative at first, then certain, guiding her closer. Reese melted into the touch, into the kiss, into the way Sloane kissed like she'd been holding herself back for far too long. The world narrowed to warmth and breath and the soft press of mouths learning each other in the dim, humming quiet of the elevator. For a suspended, perfect moment, nothing existed outside the two of them. No rules, no roles, no impossible lines drawn between who they were supposed to be.

Just this.

Just them.

They came apart breathless and a little shocked. Silence settled as they watched each other, still hungry, still wanting. "There are probably cameras," Sloane said finally.

"I suppose there are." Reese's eyes never left Sloane's. But she was right. The last thing either of them needed was some assistant shift manager at the hotel selling the footage to one of the racing outlets. "I'll stay over here," Reese said.

"You haven't moved," Sloane pointed out, the beginnings of a smile tugging her lips.

"Oh, right," Reese said, her cheeks warming because her brain had clearly not returned to its full function. She slid to the other side of the elevator, which, honestly, was only a few more feet. "So." A pause. "How's your day been?"

That pulled a laugh, and Reese understood that she would spend an entire lifetime trying to earn that sound again. Something warm and certain settled in her chest. She loved Sloane's laugh, the way it softened her, brightened her, cracked her open in ways Reese had only ever imagined. And suddenly, more than anything, she wanted to be the reason Sloane laughed, over and over again.

She wasn't sure what to do with that realization, so she held it quietly for herself.

Before either of them could speak again, the elevator jolted with a violent shudder. Reese's hand instinctively shot out to steady Sloane, who grabbed her arm in return. Then the machinery groaned, hummed, and miraculously began to move.

They both stood quickly, straightening clothing, smoothing hair, clearing throats like teenagers caught doing something they absolutely shouldn't.

"Great timing," Sloane muttered.

"Elevators respect drama," Reese whispered back.

That earned her another tiny, involuntary tug of a smile.

The doors slid open to the *lobby*, not a midfloor landing, proving the universe had a sense of humor and liked to weaponize it. A few guests milled about, including Delaney, who froze mid-text the moment she spotted them stepping out of a stalled elevator together, hair mussed, faces flushed, looking profoundly *not* normal.

Delaney's eyes narrowed slightly, just enough for Reese, who knew her well, to notice.

Sloane cleared her throat. "I'm, uh, going to take the stairs." She pointed vaguely toward the stairwell as if announcing a fire exit. "Five floors. Good cardio."

"Right," Delaney said. "Cardio is always a good idea."

Sloane gave Reese one last look—quick, soft, and absolutely devastating—before ducking away with the brisk efficiency of someone escaping a crime scene.

Reese stepped out, trying very hard to appear like a woman who had *not* just kissed someone she shouldn't in a stalled elevator. She failed.

Delaney watched Sloane disappear, then turned back to Reese with an expression far too knowing.

"So," Delaney said slowly, sliding her phone into her pocket. "Anything you want to tell me?"

Reese swallowed. "About what?"

Delaney's eyebrows lifted. "Uh-huh. That's what I thought."

CHAPTER 12
BOUNDARIES, PENDING

Reese Maddox shocked them all that weekend with back-to-back wins in Suzuka.

It wasn't just that she won—it was how she won. With precision she'd never shown before, discipline that made the pit crew stand taller, and a kind of electric assuredness that rolled off her in waves. Every lap seemed to focus her, pull new possibilities out of her. By the final checkered flag, even the skeptics were leaning in, whispering about her potential, wondering if this was the start of something bigger.

Reese handled the attention with that maddening ease of hers, grinning for cameras, slinging an arm around her crew, basking in the high without letting it swallow her. And every time Sloane caught a glimpse of her with her helmet tucked under one arm, hair damp, eyes bright with triumph, something warm and dangerous twisted in her chest.

Which was precisely the problem.

After their first night in town and the eventful stay in an elevator, Sloane had kept her distance. She had to. She needed room to get her bearings and figure out how she was supposed to proceed where Reese was concerned. And she damn well couldn't do that with Reese—radiant, magnetic, infuriating Reese—anywhere in her proximity.

She'd learned that much from a single kiss. Reese Maddox scrambled her logic, blurred her lines, and made every carefully drawn boundary feel flimsy and optional. Sloane needed space, silence, a room without the gravity of Reese's presence tugging at her. Because when Reese was near, Sloane forgot the rules. She forgot reason. She forgot why wanting her was such a spectacularly bad idea.

Worse, Reese didn't seem upset or confused or tentative after what had happened. She just looked … lit up. Like kissing Sloane had flipped a switch inside her.

Sloane wasn't sure whether that terrified her or thrilled her. Possibly both.

They crossed paths in the paddock late Sunday morning, the usual storm of personnel, media, and logistics swirling around them. Reese slowed as she approached, her expression brightening like seeing Sloane was the best thing that had happened to her all day. That didn't help.

"Why don't we debrief before you leave town tomorrow?" Sloane asked, tone clipped, professional. At least she hoped so. Reese still had meetings with her team principal, with Julie, and the press. A technical breakdown could wait until the world stopped buzzing around them.

"How about tonight? After the Grand Prix?" Reese countered easily. The F1 race would hold everyone's attention, and Sloane was surprised Reese wouldn't want to watch with her team, eat, celebrate, then fall into bed for twelve hours.

"Are you sure you'd be up for it then?"

Reese's smile edged into challenge. "That sounds like a no."

"Then let's do it," Sloane said, hearing her voice dip into something warmer, something familiar. "I'm free if you are."

"I'll see you in the hospitality suite."

"Perfect." Sloane kept walking, but something made her glance over her shoulder.

Reese was still standing there. Still watching her walk away. Still wearing that look.

"Stop that," Sloane said, forcing herself not to smile as she continued on.

"You can't make me," Reese called back.

A busy afternoon followed, longer than usual. Sloane spent most of it with Cassidy Simms, helping her understand the nuances of driving on different compounds and how tire evolution changed over a race distance. The rookie listened like every word mattered, eyes sharp with hunger.

Sloane had to give it to her. The girl was determined to learn her sport and learn it quickly.

"Cassidy Simms," Sloane said as she stepped into Veronica's onsite office.

Veronica looked up from her laptop. "What about her?"

"She impresses me. She finished in the points today."

"I caught that," Veronica said, removing her glasses and raking a hand through her always-gorgeous hair. "When she arrived for race one, I wondered if we'd get a gee-golly kid, in over her head. She's not even close."

"She's a tiger in sheep's clothing. That's the beauty of it. They don't see her coming, Ronnie. She inches up the drivers' standings every weekend. Give her a couple of years, and she might be starting at the front of the F1 grid."

"Let's not get crazy."

"I'm not even close. Don't underestimate hard work."

Veronica sat forward, elbows on her desk. "Speaking of, I don't know what you said to Reese, but she's been putting in the time since the last race, and now look. Two wins?"

Sloane leaned a hip against the desk. "Say more."

"Helmut, the assistant team principal over at Ravensport, says she's been the first one in and the last one out. Living in the simulator, hitting the gym, doing climate conditioning. Putting in real hours. Not show. Not optics. Not smiling for selfies with the fans. Work."

A tug of pride surprised Sloane, hitting her low and warm.

Reese was trying. Really trying.

And tonight, she'd have to look her in the eye and somehow discuss racing, professionalism, boundaries, while pretending her pulse didn't trip every time Reese so much as looked at her.

Sloane exhaled slowly.

"Where did you go just now?"

"I was just thinking about Reese and the progress you mentioned. We saw it on the track today."

"No. Uh-uh." Veronica sat back in her chair. "That faraway look was anything but work-related. Did you almost bite your lip? I think you almost bit your fucking lip."

"You're imagining things," Sloane said. She tossed in a laugh, but it sounded manufactured and only hurt her cause.

"You're seeing someone."

"No. I'm absolutely not." Sloane headed for the door before she spilled one detail too many.

"Then you're lusting after someone, and it's good. It's soap opera good. I can tell. Do you know how long it's been since I've had sex?"

Sloane's hand went still on the doorknob. "I don't. Are you gonna tell me?"

"Too damn long, Sloane, and if you're getting some, then I need to hear the sexy stories that will surely give me hope that good old-fashioned lust in a handbasket is waiting to carry me away to Smutville. So, can we do the girl talk thing now?"

Sloane wanted to say yes because this was her friend, but the subject of her R-rated thoughts these days was the very reason she couldn't. What would Veronica say if she knew it was one of their drivers? And not only that, it was the overly hot one. I mean, how cliché could Sloane be? Not that there wasn't more to Reese. She'd seen it.

Sloane hesitated, searching for a diplomatic exit. "You know what? I can't. Not today."

The brightness in Veronica's eyes dimmed a fraction, quick,

almost invisible, but Sloane caught it. A flicker of something like disappointment slid through the space between them before Veronica straightened, smoothing it over with practiced ease.

"Right," she said lightly. "Of course. You're busy. We're all busy."

It was meant to sound breezy. It didn't.

"I just have a lot on my plate," Sloane tried, but it came out stiff. Defensive, even. *Dammit.*

Veronica lifted one shoulder, a half-shrug that didn't match the sharpness suddenly settling into her posture. "No explanation needed, Sloane. I get it. Boundaries and all that." She reached for her glasses, turning them in her hands instead of putting them on. "Go. Do your … work thing."

The pause before "work" was small but unmistakable.

Sloane's chest tightened. She wanted to fix it, bridge the gap she'd just created, but doing that meant opening a door she absolutely could not open. She just wasn't equipped yet.

"I'll see you after the race," she said instead. "Or maybe even in the morning. I might turn in early after I finish my last meeting." The meeting.

Veronica nodded without looking at her. "Sure. I hope it's a good one. See you then."

Sloane slipped out, pulling the door closed behind her. The click sounded too final, too loaded for what should have been an ordinary conversation.

But the air in the hallway felt heavier, confirming what she already suspected: Veronica didn't buy the brush-off.

And she wasn't thrilled about being shut out. Ronnie wasn't one to hold long-term grudges, but it was clear her feelings had been hurt, and Sloane hated that she made her feel unimportant.

Sloane scrubbed a hand down her face and exhaled. Great. Perfect. Add that to the list: a friend she'd just hurt, a driver she couldn't stay away from, and a night ahead she wasn't remotely ready for.

And in a few hours, she'd have to walk into that hospitality suite and pretend none of it was unraveling her from the inside out. Piece of cake.

Reese watched the Grand Prix from along the Ravensport garage, toes practically against the yellow pit-lane line. The air vibrated with engine noise, each car shooting past in a blur that tugged at her and got her blood pumping. This was the kind of thing Reese lived for, and she was itching to be a part of it all. But out here, close enough to taste the fuel in the air, she could almost fool herself into thinking she was part of the race. She relished every twitch of the cars under braking, every surge of acceleration, every breathless gamble through the corners.

Fuck, this was good stuff.

When the midfield battle hit the trickiest turn on the circuit, known as Degner 1, she leaned forward instinctively, reading the body language of the cars like text. Too close. Too bold. This wasn't good at all. Her stomach dropped half a second before one car snapped loose and spiraled across the track.

The other had nowhere to go. She braced, knowing what was coming.

The impact cracked through the air, a metallic roar swallowed instantly by screeching tires and a plume of carbon fiber shrapnel. "No, no, no," Reese murmured, shoving a hand through her hair as she watched in fear.

Both cars spun out, one burying itself nose-first into the gravel trap, the other slamming hard against the barriers. Marshals were already sprinting. Hospitals would be prepping. And Reese couldn't breathe. This was every driver's nightmare. Her own family knew all too well.

Her fingers gripped the railing so hard her knuckles blanched. The smell of scorched rubber reached her a beat later, acrid and unmistakable. A few mechanics behind her swore. Someone else began whispering a prayer.

"Come on … come on …" she whispered, eyes locked on the ruined machines for any positive sign.

Then, movement. A driver shifting in the cockpit. Pushing the steering wheel off. Climbing out with help from the marshals. Seconds later, the second cockpit opened, and another driver pulled himself free, shaken but standing.

A whoosh of release rippled down the pit wall, a tense exhale shared by everyone.

Reese let her grip loosen, breath finally slipping out of her. Racing was a monster and moments like this carved a truth into her bones: if you weren't careful, this sport could take everything.

Almost three hours later, when Reese stepped back into the academy's hospitality suite, her pulse was still buzzing from the race. The suite had been cleared out for the night, which meant the staff would be back the next day to pack up. It also meant she and Sloane could relax and be themselves without worrying about crew and office staff milling about. It was likely the group had headed out to dinner, an invitation that Reese had politely declined, much preferring to take this meeting with Sloane, both for personal and professional reasons. First of all, she hadn't spent any one-on-one time with her over race weekend, barely an exchange since the kiss she'd relived about a hundred times. She needed to look Sloane in the eyes and make sure they were okay. Beyond that, every good thing that was happening in her professional world right now could be traced back to Sloane Foster holding her feet to the fire, and Reese was prepared to absorb her advice like a dutiful sponge. Dinner could wait.

But she didn't make it very far into the dimly lit room before she realized someone was in distress. She could tell immediately from the breathing pattern. "Hey, are you okay?" Reese asked before the figure leaning over in a chair shifted. It was Sloane. "Hey," Reese said, moving to her and kneeling at her feet. "What's wrong? Oh, no. Talk to me."

"Sorry," Sloane managed, but her jaw was tight, almost like

she couldn't unclench it. "I wasn't expecting to …" She trailed off, leaving Reese to guess what had set off what looked to be a full-on panic attack.

But Reese didn't guess. She didn't press. She just stayed close, knees on the carpet, posture relaxed so she wouldn't add to the claustrophobia tightening Sloane's chest.

"It's okay," Reese murmured softly. "You don't have to explain anything. Just breathe with me."

Sloane shook her head a fraction. "Can't." The word came out strangled. Her hands clutched the armrests like she was trying to keep herself anchored to the chair. Or to the world.

Reese slid one hand, slowly and deliberately, over Sloane's forearm. Not gripping, just offering a point of contact. A light-house instead of a rope.

"Hey. You're right here. I've got you."

A shudder ran through Sloane. Her breaths were rapid and shallow, her pupils wide, unfocused. Panic lived in her posture, shoulders curled inward, throat working like she couldn't get air down far enough.

Reese kept her voice low, level. "Match me, okay? Just match what I do." She inhaled slowly, exaggerating the rise of her chest so Sloane could follow if she wanted. Then she exhaled, long and steady.

At first, nothing changed.

Then, a faint, shaky inhale from Sloane tried to follow hers.

"Perfect," Reese said. "You're doing great."

Sloane braced her elbows on her knees, pressing the heels of her hands to her eyes like she was trying to squeeze back the memory, the trigger, whatever image had clawed its way into her head. "I knew … coming back … being this close would be … stupid." Her breath hitched. "I thought I was, you know … past it."

Reese shook her head. "You don't have to be past anything. And it's not stupid. You got hit with something big. Anyone would react."

Sloane huffed out a broken laugh. "Not like this."

"Especially like this," Reese countered gently. "Your body remembers danger even when your brain doesn't want it to. Today was a nasty reminder."

Sloane's hands lowered slowly. Her eyes were glassy, embarrassed, and angry at herself. "You saw it, too? The crash?"

"I was near the pit lane when it happened." Reese swallowed. "It shook me. So, I get how it could hit you even harder."

Sloane blinked, breath finally lengthening. Not steady yet, but no longer spiraling. "I haven't had one of these in a while," she whispered, the words small like a confession. "No one's ever actually … seen it."

Reese's chest tightened with something warm and fierce. "I'm glad I'm here, then."

That made Sloane go very still, like she didn't know what to do with someone not running for the door. Like she expected them to.

Reese shifted just enough to get on the edge of the chair beside her, careful not to crowd her. "Is it okay if I stay?"

Sloane nodded once, barely perceptible. But it was enough.

Reese remained right where she was. Silent when silence helped. Breathing slowly until Sloane's breath unconsciously aligned with hers. The room was dim and quiet around them, like the whole world had agreed to give them space.

After a long stretch, Sloane let out a breath that didn't shake. They were making progress.

"I'm okay," she murmured, not convincingly.

Reese answered anyway. "I'm here, either way. Nowhere I need to be. We could sit here all night if you want."

And for the first time since Reese walked in, Sloane looked at her fully, her eyes tired with vulnerability.

"Thank you," she said, voice almost a rasp. "Really."

Reese gave a small, soft smile. "Are you kidding? This is what we do. Sit in dim elevators and hospitality suites together. It's our thing."

Sloane's mouth tugged a little, a hint of a smile threatening.

It was honestly everything to Reese.

The moment hung between them, quiet and fragile. The kind of moment that Reese hadn't expected but was glad she was here for. Finally, she reached out her hand, and Sloane took it, their fingers threading automatically. Reese was amazed at how perfectly they fit. She wasn't sure how long they stayed that way, holding each other's hand in the silence, but quite a while.

"How do you do it?" Sloane asked finally.

Reese turned toward her. "Do what?"

"Climb into that car day after day after losing your father the way you did."

"Oh." Reese's breath left her in a slow exhale. "I definitely think about his crash. I think Luke does even more. He was there. I wasn't."

She rubbed her palms on her knees, gathering her words from somewhere deep. "But I think the love of racing didn't die that day. Not for me. My dad … he always said fear doesn't mean stop. It means pay attention. And I do. Every lap. Every time I strap in. I know the risk. I don't pretend it's not there."

Sloane watched her, expression soft but intent.

Reese went on, her voice quiet but steady. "But the thing is, when I'm in that car, the love outweighs the fear. Every time. It's not that I'm not scared. I am. Sometimes more than I let anyone see. But the second my wheels are rolling, it feels like choosing the part of my life that's still bright. Still mine. And I can't let the worst moment of my family's life take that from me."

Sloane's throat worked, emotion tightening her features. "I wish I could see it that way."

Reese shook her head softly. "You don't have to. Your crash wasn't some abstract risk on a screen. It happened *to you*. Your body remembers that. You're allowed to carry the fear differently."

Sloane looked away, blinking hard.

"But," Reese added, "you're here. You came back. Even when it scares you." Her voice softened. "That's brave as hell, Sloane."

Sloane let out a slow breath, shaky but real. Reese didn't break eye contact.

"And hey," Reese said gently, "you don't have to power through alone. You have people in your life. Colleagues all around you. Friends like Veronica. And you have me."

That landed. Reese saw it in the way Sloane's posture loosened, the smallest crack in her emotional armor. Not collapse, just maybe, permission.

Sloane swallowed, her voice rough. "Thank you."

Reese squeezed her fingers lightly. "Anytime."

The silence that followed wasn't heavy anymore. It felt like something else entirely. Unfinished, charged, or the kind of quiet that hinted they were dangerously close to crossing another line.

Sloane was the one to break it, her voice barely above a whisper. "We should ... probably talk boundaries at some point."

Reese's smile was small and wry because this was Sloane's default. "Yeah. Probably."

But neither of them let go of the other's hand.

And that said everything.

CHAPTER 13
NOT NAKED MODE

Monza carried its own kind of electricity. God, it was good to be back. Sloane was unexpectedly invigorated to return to Italy and to a circuit where she'd scored the most significant race win of her career. So many memories came flooding back as she stared out at the now-empty track. She could see and hear it all play out in front of her. The sound of the crowd when she emerged from her car. Her team hanging over the fence as she passed beneath the checkered flag. The sheer exhilaration of winning the whole damn thing. She wasn't sure she'd ever experience a moment that compared.

All around her now, the air thrummed with the sound of engines even when they weren't running, as though the circuit itself remembered every lap ever laid down on it. Sloane liked that about Italy, the history, the reverence, the way the locals spoke about racing like it was religion.

But this weekend, she had something else to look forward to.

She hadn't realized exactly how much the absence would settle under her skin until she stepped into the Formula Next paddock and spotted Reese-fucking-Maddox leaning against the wall outside the conference room—early, of all things. She was scrolling through something on her phone, one ankle crossed over the other, posture relaxed in a way that said she had nowhere more important to be. And Sloane felt it, that quiet pull in her chest she'd spent a week pretending wasn't growing. But it was. God, Reese was a sight for sore eyes.

She looked up just as Sloane approached, a slow, warm grin curving her perfect lips. "Hey, you."

It hit harder than it should have. "Morning," Sloane said, grateful her voice came out steady. "Didn't expect you yet."

"Impressed?" Reese grinned, proud of herself, but there was something careful beneath it. "Figured I'd be on time for once." A beat. "Did you miss me?"

Yes. "What constitutes miss?" Sloane asked with her best quizzical look.

"Imagining me naked."

And there went all the air from her lungs. "Seriously?" Sloane said, pausing with the doorknob in her hand. But her skin prickled, and heat slid down her spine. She was instantly turned on and all too aware of her inner thighs. The idea of being naked with Reese was enough to short-circuit her morning.

"I'm kidding."

"No, you're not," Sloane said, dropping her tone.

"No. I'm not," Reese echoed, the grin fading from her face.

Something flickered across Reese's expression—pleasure, maybe, or relief—but before Sloane could define it, footsteps and conversation rose from behind them. Two other drivers rounded the corner, filtering toward the conference room, greeting Reese as if she'd simply been waiting there quietly the whole time rather than tossing Sloane's morning on its head … or rather onto its back. There were more voices down the hall, reminding Sloane that it was four minutes until nine o'clock and she had notes to look over before her talk with the drivers.

Sloane swallowed her smile and nodded toward the entrance. "Let's get inside."

A few minutes later, Sloane stood at the head of the compact conference room inside the Formula Next suite of mobile offices, kicking off what would be a more informal chat, heavily based on Q and A. The space was sleek and efficient, comprised of a long table, mounted screens, and the faint hum of air-conditioning battling the late-summer Italian heat. The rest of the drivers filed in, taking their seats with the low chatter of people who'd spent enough time together to know each other's rhythms. These women were becoming friends, enemies, and everything in between. Typical of any driver lineup.

Reese settled halfway down the table, posture relaxed but eyes unmistakably focused. And every so often, Sloane felt those eyes drift to her like a quiet pulse of heat.

She inhaled, smoothing her palms down the front of her blazer. She could do work mode, even with Reese Maddox looking at her like that. Work mode, *not naked mode.*

"All right," Sloane began, projecting her voice just enough to fill the room. "Let's talk more about what being a driver looks like beyond the circuit. Most of you signed up to go fast. That's the simple part. Everything else?" She offered a wry smile. "That's where the real learning begins."

A few nods around the room. They'd had a taste of it at the lower levels, but F1 was its own animal.

Cassidy leaned forward, elbows on the surface, eager as ever. "You're referencing the media?"

"Yes," Sloane said. "Media, sponsorship obligations, fan engagement, charity appearances. In Formula 1, you're a public figure whether you intended to be or not. Your team and their marketing department will help shape your calendar, but you need to understand the identity you're putting out into the world."

She glanced down the table. Reese was listening—the real kind of listening, the kind that said she was fully dialed in. Her focus landed squarely on Sloane, and the attention felt different this time. Purposeful. Present.

Sloane forced herself to continue. "You'll build a brand whether you plan to or not. The key is making sure it reflects *you.* People can smell inauthenticity from a mile away, and it's hard to keep up a persona that's not who you actually are."

"That true, Maddox?" Danielle asked. "Is it hard?"

Reese rolled her eyes. Delaney turned around, gaze narrowed. "Not at all necessary," she told Danielle. "Let's pretend to be a grown-up for the rest of the day."

"My mistake," Danielle said with a proud grin. She turned back to Sloane. "Right. Didn't mean to detract, but I do have a question. Do we get a say in our branding? Or is that on the team?"

"Both," Sloane said. "The team will guide you. But what you choose to highlight—your values, your personality, how you show up—has to come from you. Or it won't stick. I remember arriving for a session with a reporter, prepared to talk all about my last race, only to find myself at a loss for words when the questions were about me. The interview came out, and it was horrific. I came off like a hostile witness. My team marketing manager took me under her wing from that point forward." She folded her arms. "Moral of the story. Learn from my mistakes. Pay attention in media training."

Another question came. Then another. And Sloane fielded each one, crisp and steady. But every few heartbeats, her attention tugged toward Reese again, head bowed as she jotted a note, fingers drumming lightly on the table, eyes lifting every time Sloane shifted.

It was infuriatingly distracting. And exhilarating. Reese made Sloane feel alive again, and, honestly, she'd forgotten what that was like. "Remember," Sloane concluded, "every interaction reflects on your team and on your future. Treat the work outside the cockpit with the same focus and intention you bring to your qualifying laps."

Marissa grinned. "So basically: don't be an asshole?"

"That's the short version," Sloane said, a smile tugging at her mouth. "And now, take time to get yourself ready for quali. If that means eating something healthy, do it. If you need extra reaction drills to get your reflexes firing, make sure it happens." She lifted her shoulders. "I can't wait to see who comes out on top."

That brought on a few overly confident murmurs, which tracked. You needed an ego to reach this level.

The conference room emptied slowly, chairs scraping back, drivers chatting among themselves as they filed out. Sloane answered a last question from one of the rookies, then gathered her notes with mechanical precision.

Professional. Calm. Steady.

Except none of that matched what was happening inside her chest. Reese hadn't left with the others. Of course she hadn't. Her notebook was tucked under her arm. Her long dark hair was pulled back today, exposing that sharp jawline Sloane absolutely wasn't staring at.

Sloane swallowed. Her hands felt warm. Too warm.

"Good session," Reese said quietly.

Just that. Simple. Normal.

Except it wasn't simple or normal because Sloane felt the echo of last week's panic attack still connecting them like an invisible thread. She remembered acutely the way Reese had sat with her in the dark, holding her hand, breathing her back into the world. No one had ever seen her that undone. No one had stayed.

Sloane cleared her throat. "You're a good group."

Reese nodded. "But better when you talk to us. Look at my lap times."

"Is that why you were early?" Sloane asked.

Reese stepped closer, not close enough to crowd, but close enough that the air shifted. "No," she said softly. "I was excited to see you."

Sloane's breath caught at the honesty. No games or performance. Just the truth, spoken like it was the easiest thing in the world.

She looked up. Met Reese's gaze.

And a door she'd welded shut years ago, clicked open half an inch.

Not enough for anything dangerous. Just enough for light. There was nothing here she had to run from. Nothing here was going to hurt her. With that reminder, she relaxed, and it felt good.

"Sloane," Reese murmured, "you don't have to say anything."

But Sloane already was. Just not with words.

She reached out, intending to brush a nonexistent speck of lint off Reese's sleeve, something harmless, but her hand lingered an instant too long. Her fingertips grazed warm fabric, then the warm forearm beneath it.

Reese inhaled softly. Sloane met her eyes.

God, what am I doing? What am I starting?

She stepped back half a foot, breaking the moment, fighting for sense. "This is a terrible idea," she whispered. "You know that, right?"

Reese nodded, eyes steady. "I know."

"And dangerous."

"I know that too. Still don't care."

"And I'm not looking for serious." The words were quiet, raw, more honest than she meant them to be. "Not emotionally."

Reese took the smallest step toward her, not pushing, not asking, just there. "Who is? I think we're two people who are drawn together. Just let whatever this is be what it is. Real."

Real. That word resonated. And tempted. Sloane shook her head, enjoying their proximity immensely. She could smell Reese's shampoo, melon again. It was becoming her drug. "You're very bad for my self-preservation, Reese."

Reese's grin was soft. "Maybe. But you're very good for mine. Also, I like it when you say my name."

Sloane felt the pull, the gravity, the terrifying comfort of it.

She didn't kiss her.

But she stepped close enough that her breast brushed Reese's arm when she reached to pick up her notes from the table. Close enough to feel Reese's breath. Close enough that the space between them wasn't space at all. And Reese didn't move away.

For this moment, that was enough.

Sloane wasn't ready to fall.

But she was starting to lean.

***

"What is *happening* out there lately?" Delaney asked, clapping Reese on the shoulder hard enough to rock her forward. They stood in the Ravensport garage, still buzzing from the aftermath of qualifying, mechanics and engineers weaving around them with the kind of barely contained excitement that only victory could generate. "This is epic. You're starting on pole? *Again.* And at Monza no less. You're on a streak that doesn't quit."

"I know," Reese said, eyes wide, cheeks flushed from the adrenaline that hadn't yet worn off. She still felt the vibrations from the last lap, every apex clean, every braking point sharp, every risk she'd taken paying off. Her body remembered it all, even as her brain still tried to catch up. "It's fucking rad, and I don't want to do anything to jinx it."

"What changed? I need the recipe so I can join you on the front row of the grid." Delaney had qualified in P6, which would still give her a good shot at finishing in the points for the team.

"I'm not even sure. There have been a variety of factors, but I'll tell you one thing: I've been working my ass off." She shook her head. "I was too complacent before. Headstrong and thought I knew exactly what I was doing."

"You?" Delaney oversold a scoff. "No. That can't be."

"I get it." She shrugged. The lighthearted back-and-forth was easier than admitting how close she'd come to stalling out her own career. "Turns out there might be, like, two things I don't know in life. It's fine." She flashed a smile, still riding high from quali.

"But let's be real." Delaney arched an eyebrow in a way that suggested she had further suspicions. "It's her, isn't it?"

"Who?" Reese asked, attempting casual innocence but overshooting it by a mile.

Delaney simply crossed her arms. Waiting. Knowing. *Dammit.*

Reese sighed. Why was she fighting the inevitable? "Fine. Yes. Maybe."

"Say more. All the words, please."

Reese kicked at the concrete and exhaled. "She made a lot of valid points about how I was spending my time. We ... disagreed about it at first. There was all this tension."

"Of course there was," Delaney said with a smile. "Here we go."

"She recommended a stronger work ethic," Reese continued. "Fewer selfies. Cutting back on brand deals when I could. More sim time. More gym time. Basically: grow the fuck up. Get serious."

"And that's all it is?" Delaney asked. "Just her helping you become a better driver?"

"Delaney ..." Reese warned, though a smile tugged at the corner of her mouth. "What exactly are you asking?"

Delaney stepped closer, lowering her voice like they were discussing state secrets. "We know you hit on her. Has it progressed from there?"

Reese stared at her, contemplating whether to go there or not. This felt like standing at the edge of a cliff.

"Are you sleeping with her? Confirm or deny."

"No," Reese said immediately.

"But you want to."

"Well, who wouldn't?"

"Valid." Delaney nodded. "She's beautiful and amazing and so out of your league I feel like I should prepare a PowerPoint about it."

Reese threw up her hands. "Everyone keeps saying that.

Constantly. Relentlessly." She hesitated, then shrugged. Her chest tightened, the thrill tangling with something more vulnerable. "But ... yeah. I think there's a spark. A sizzle. Something. We kissed once."

Delaney froze. Squinted. The world just exploded. "Are you kidding me? When? You—no. No. I refuse. You buried the lead entirely. You have no future in journalism, and I am filing a formal friendship complaint."

Reese turned and started walking toward the quieter stretch of pit lane, knowing Delaney would follow. F2 drivers swarmed around their cars, preparing for their own qualifying, the air buzzing with energy but blessedly free of anyone listening too closely. The space gave Reese room to breathe, to let the moment settle instead of ricocheting away from it.

"You're telling Marissa and Cassidy," Delaney said, hot on her heels. "Immediately. I'm not carrying this burden alone."

"Who said I haven't told them?"

Delaney's eyes went wide. "You told them and not me? I'm your friend. Your only teammate. We go back to childhood. I don't even know—"

"Relax. I was fucking with you. You're the first."

Delaney went still. "I'm going to have to murder you a second time."

"That's not even a thing," Reese said, leading the way back to Ravensport's suite. "You can't die twice."

"*You* will. It will set a record."

"At least I'll finally hold one." She smiled as she said it, but the truth lingered underneath: pole position, records, wins. They were starting to matter differently now. Not just as proof she was fast, but as proof she was becoming someone worth believing in. And for the first time, that felt like an ending she wanted to stand inside, not outrun.

CHAPTER 14
NO MORE PRETENDING

The sun had barely dipped behind the trees when Reese and Delaney followed the winding path through Parco di Monza toward Villa Mirabello. The Pirelli reception was already underway, with soft music drifting on the warm evening air, the faint clink of glasses, and a low hum of multilingual conversation. Reese slowed without meaning to, taking it in the way she always did, like she needed a second to recalibrate. It all felt impossibly elegant for something happening a stone's throw from the deafening chaos of the racetrack.

Pirelli supplied all the tires for Formula Next and was well respected in the racing world. With their corporate headquarters in Italy, they rolled out the red carpet for an industry party most wouldn't forget. Reese had learned by now that "industry party" was code for breathtaking excess. The budget could probably bankroll Reese's living expenses for a year or two. Maybe more, if she were smart about it.

She'd grown up counting things. Hours, dollars, favors. She still did, out of habit if nothing else. There was always a moment at events like this when she felt it acutely—the quiet awareness that she hadn't come from money or connections or a last name anyone recognized. She'd come from grit and borrowed gear and sleeping on couches, from believing hard enough that talent might eventually tip the scales.

She glanced sideways at Delaney, who was taking in the villa with the same careful fascination, like she was mentally cataloging exits and snack tables all at once. That helped. Delaney never pretended this world was normal, either. They were both visitors here, standing at the edge of luxury, belonging and not belonging in equal measure.

And yet. The invitation had her name on it. She'd earned the right to walk this path, to step into this space, even if part of her still expected someone to stop her and ask for proof.

Cassidy and Marissa waited near the entrance, both looking unfairly polished for people who'd spent the afternoon sweating through practice sessions. Cassidy, in a navy jumpsuit that looked tailored to her form, lifted her glass in greeting.

"There she is," Cassidy announced. "The woman of the hour. The prodigy. The future tire poster child of Italy."

"Oh, God. Please don't call me that." Reese adjusted her black spaghetti strap top. She'd paired it with black pants and a pair of heels, but she was suddenly aware of how underdressed she felt amid all the glossy fabrics and subtle perfumes. "I'm probably going to be informed this whole thing is a mistake, and I should pack my bags for home."

"Sure," Marissa said, stepping forward to link arms with her. She wore a gorgeous red cocktail dress and black heels. Sexy as hell. Her versatility was really something. More than a couple of people turned their heads as she passed. "Keep pretending the entire paddock isn't whispering about your pole streak. Very cute."

Reese rolled her eyes, but couldn't stop the grin that tugged. The air was warm, scented with garden roses and the faint waft of truffle arancini from a passing server. Lanterns hung across the courtyard, casting a honey-colored glow over everything, including old stone walls, crisp white linens, and polished shoes moving across centuries-old tile.

"Anyone else surprised they let us in here?" Reese asked, taking in every last impressive detail. The room was already full, drivers from all levels mingling and sipping expensive wine. Veronica held court in the corner. Reese scanned the room for Sloane but was disappointed not to spot her. Maybe she wasn't coming.

"Wow. Look at Sloane," Cassidy said and grabbed a glass of prosecco from a passing tray. "That dress, though."

Reese swiveled and went still.

Sloane stood near the far side of the terrace, half-turned toward a small cluster of executives, a champagne flute loose in one hand. She wore an ice-blue cocktail dress that looked like it had been poured over her rather than sewn. The color sharpened everything about her, throwing her blond hair into brighter relief and making her blue eyes startlingly vivid. Her hair was swept back at the nape, a few soft strands loose around her temples, leaving her face open and impossible to ignore. The neckline on the dress offered a glimpse of the tops of her breasts, round and full, which almost did Reese in. Quite simply, Sloane devastated. "Yeah, that dress," Reese murmured, captivated as she watched from across the room.

Sloane was on, but she wasn't performing. She listened, head tilted slightly, a thoughtful line between her brows that smoothed when she smiled. People leaned toward her without realizing they were doing it.

She laughed at something someone said, low and brief, and Reese felt it land in her chest. She wondered what they were talking about. This wasn't paddock-Sloane in team gear, or mentor-Sloane with her arms crossed and her patience worn thin. This was Sloane, polished and effortless, fully aware of her gravity.

Then Sloane glanced up, her gaze moving across the terrace and finding Reese.

For a suspended heartbeat, the world narrowed to that exchange. The conversation, the music, the clink of glass all faded for Reese. Sloane's expression shifted, something warmer and sharper flickering through her eyes, and the corner of her mouth curved, just slightly.

Reese forgot to breathe.

"Anything you want to share with the class?" Delaney asked well within earshot of the others. Reese reluctantly pulled her gaze from Sloane and the impact of her beauty to see Delaney smiling expectantly at her.

"What?"

"Can we tell Cassidy and Marissa?"

The other two exchanged a glance that said they had no idea what was going on.

Reese blinked. "Okay. Well, um, in the name of friendship and transparency," Reese forced her brain to rejoin the group, "I should probably tell you that there was a kiss. A good one."

"I get the feeling this isn't new for you," Cassidy said. "That you kiss a lot of people. But I'm happy for you that this one seemed to resonate."

"Ask her who she kissed," Delaney said and tapped her lips. She was definitely ready to dish on this with other people.

"Someone we know? One of the drivers?" Marissa frowned and turned, scanning the crowd. When her gaze fell in Sloane's direction, she went still. "Surely not with …"

Delaney rocked back on her heels.

Understanding descended like an excited lightning bolt. Marissa whirled back. "Oh my God, it *was*. You stop that right now."

"Reese, you and Sloane!" Cassidy said.

"Maybe not so loud," Delaney cautioned.

"Have such a great working relationship," Cassidy said, trying to course-correct at triple the volume for anyone who might be listening in. "What a mentor she is! The grandness of her advice. The knowledge and experience she brings to the table is a gift to us all." She added an exaggerated sweeping of her arm.

"You're out of control," Marissa said calmly.

Cassidy turned to Reese and broke into a huge grin. "But that's amazing," she said, quieter this time. "And it makes total sense. The chemistry between the two of you fills the whole room like the sexiest elephant at the zoo."

Reese frowned. "You might need to tweak your similes."

Cassidy waved her off. "Translate me. You always do."

And Reese did, because they were genuinely all good friends now, even though they wanted to wipe the floor clean with each other on race days. "Every day," Reese said, placing a hand on top of Cassidy's head.

Cassidy was definitely enjoying this, a new energy having come over her. "There's this romance novel tension that surely bubbled over until neither of you could stand it." She wasn't wrong. A thought seemed to occur. "I have to tell my Aunt Stevie. She lives for this stuff."

Reese held up a hand. "Aunt Stevie is probably fine. But we keep this to ourselves for now. There's no academy rule against fraternization. I looked it up. But I think we'd both like to remain discreet."

"What now?" Marissa asked with a sly smile. "Are you two moving toward a full-fledged relationship? Do you have a girlfriend, Reese Maddox?"

"No," Reese said automatically. Even she hadn't thought that far. "I think we're just enjoying ourselves. Life is short, right?"

Delaney stared at Reese like she wasn't even close to buying it. "I know what you're like when you're only enjoying yourself, and this isn't it. You're in this."

Reese tossed an arm around her teammate's shoulder. "Then you're just gonna have to trust me."

"Mayday. She's looking this way," Marissa said. "Oh, and now she's walking by. Should we wave her over?" Marissa stood taller and adjusted her posture.

"Why are you pushing your boobs out?" Reese asked. "Stop that."

"These aren't for Sloane," Marissa said. "I share them with the room." She followed up the quip with a playful wink.

"Already protective," Delaney said with a satisfied raise of her brow.

Reese laughed. "Not at all."

Cassidy leaned in. "Do you want me to come up with some questions about the car to ask Sloane? It's a good excuse to get her over here."

"No. How about I just go say hi like a regular human?" Reese said.

"She has the best moves," Cassidy murmured, as if taking notes.

Reese ignored her. Or tried to. She finished her prosecco and handed the empty flute to a passing server, like that settled something.

"Be right back," she said, already stepping away.

She made it three strides before Sloane turned, excusing herself from the small cluster of executives with an apologetic smile. She didn't rush. She never did. She crossed the terrace with that same unhurried confidence Reese had learned meant she knew exactly where she was going.

Including toward Reese.

"Hey," Reese said when Sloane stopped in front of her, her voice softer than she meant it to be.

Sloane smiled immediately, warm and familiar. She was happy to see Reese, and it showed. "Hey, yourself."

They stood there for half a second longer than necessary, the sounds of the party rushing in around them.

"You look so good," Reese said, then laughed quietly. "I had a better line planned, but it disappeared."

Sloane's eyes softened. "I like the honest one."

She glanced Reese over, the attention sending a flutter through Reese's midsection. "You clean up nicely, too. I almost didn't recognize you without a helmet."

"Devastating," Reese said. "I'll try harder next time."

"No need. You're gorgeous."

They stared at each other as Reese did everything in her power not to let her eyes dip to that neckline she so wanted to drink in.

"Come walk with me?" Sloane asked, already turning.

Reese followed easily. "I was hoping you'd ask."

"Well, tonight is your lucky night," Sloane said, glancing back with a smile. Reese raised a brow at her choice of words, which won her a "stop that."

"Whatever you say."

They drifted toward the far side of the terrace. Lantern light caught in Sloane's hair and glowed against the side of her face.

"You were good today," Sloane said. "Not just fast. Smart. I really enjoyed watching you drive."

Reese leaned her forearms against the cool stone. "High praise."

"It's sincere," Sloane said, nudging her lightly with her shoulder. "You're fun to watch. In a lot of ways."

"Do tell." That warmth settled low in Reese's chest.

Before Sloane could respond, someone called her name. A sponsor. Sloane sighed quietly and touched Reese's wrist. That touch was everything. So simple in nature, but intimate enough that she never wanted it to end.

Reese smiled. "Do you have to go? It's nice out here. Just us." The moments when it was just the two of them were turning into Reese's absolute favorite of each week. She craved more *them* time and was becoming increasingly aware of it.

Blue eyes met hers. "I wish I didn't. Maybe I'll run into you later."

"I really hope so." Sloane turned to go, and Reese's eyes fell to the smooth skin of her shoulder. "Sloane."

"Yes?" she asked, turning back. The breeze lifted the loose strands of hair around her face.

"Just … enjoy your evening."

The night fractured after that.

Reese talked. She networked. She answered questions. Laughed with her friends about why Delaney was so uniquely superstitious when it came to race days, right down to the brand of socks she wore. Time slid sideways, measured in moments instead of minutes. Sloane, from across the courtyard, lifting her glass at Reese; Sloane sending her a glance before turning back to her conversation with Veronica; Sloane leaning in close to murmur something dry that made Reese laugh before being pulled away again.

It was a jumble of very concise moments that added up to a night that had Reese pressed to her limit with pent-up desire. The ice-blue dress was doing things to her that she couldn't name in public. She wanted her lips on Sloane's shoulders and her hand beneath that hem. She wanted it so badly she ached. Instead, she took a deep breath.

When the reception began to wind down, and Sloane brushed past Reese on her way out, her fingers ghosted Reese's hand, barely there, but unmistakable.

Reese closed her eyes for half a second, savoring the tiny shred of contact.

Sleep was not happening tonight.

***

The elevator doors slid shut behind Sloane back at the hotel. She exhaled, rolling her shoulders as she stepped into the quiet hallway, grateful for the silence after a night of laughing politely at everyone's jokes and pretending she hadn't spent every second acutely aware of Reese's eyes on her.

She reached her door, digging through her bag for the key card. When she looked up, she stopped cold.

Reese leaned against the wall a few doors down, barefoot, her heels dangling from the loose curl of her fingers.

Well. That was certainly a sight she'd never forget. She blinked again to be sure she wasn't a mirage.

"Not your floor," Sloane said, heart thudding. She knew exactly what was happening, and just as clearly, that there was nothing she could do to stop it. They were an avalanche already breaking loose, too much momentum to undo now.

"No," Reese said, pushing off the wall.

"And you lost your shoes."

"Confession. I wear them because they look good, but I've never actually been a heels kind of girl."

Sloane's gaze dropped despite herself—long legs, painted toes, the faint sway that came from hours of smiling and a little too much champagne. "Trust me. No one would ever know."

Reese's smile softened. "Except you." She took a step closer. Then another. Each one thickened the air between them. "And I have a feeling my secret's safe."

"What brings you by?" Sloane asked. The voice that came out barely sounded like hers.

"I figured we got pretty good at the circling-each-other thing tonight." Reese stopped just inside Sloane's space. "Thought maybe we could try something else."

She didn't give Sloane time to answer.

Before the last word fully left her mouth, Reese leaned in and kissed her, sure and warm, with the kind of confidence that made it clear she'd been thinking about this all night. All season. Her free hand settled at Sloane's waist, steadying them both as their mouths met, the impact immediate and disorienting. The heels bumped softly against Sloane's thigh, grounding her just enough to notice how the hallway tilted, how everything narrowed to the press of Reese's lips and the heat gathering low in her belly.

Too good. The kiss was too good for Sloane to process all at once. It bypassed thought entirely, lighting her up before she had the chance to resist. She'd been fighting this—*them*—for far too long, and her body seemed relieved to finally stop pretending otherwise.

"Inside?" Reese murmured against her mouth.

Sloane nodded, fumbling the key card from her bag. Reese took it from her, opened the door in one smooth motion, and then they were inside. Reese's arms were already around her, walking her backward, kissing her without breaking rhythm.

Holy hell. Her brain couldn't catch up with her body. They were a hurricane, colliding in a rush of urgency and want.

"What are you doing to me?" Reese breathed, just before her mouth found Sloane's neck.

Sloane's head tipped back on instinct. Her fingers slid into Reese's thick hair—hair she'd imagined gripping for weeks—and the sensation sent a desperate, needy pulse through her. Her center throbbed, almost painfully so.

She slid her hands to Reese's hips and stopped them both, not to pull away, but to anchor the moment. Reese stilled immediately, breath warm against Sloane's skin, waiting. That alone did something intense to her.

Sloane leaned in and kissed her, slower this time, deeper, letting herself feel it fully. Reese made a quiet sound of approval and melted into her, but Sloane kept the pace, kept control. It felt good. She threaded one hand into Reese's hair and tugged just enough to make the point, just enough to make Reese's breath hitch.

There. That reaction. That was hers.

She walked Reese back a step, then another, until Reese's shoulders brushed the door. Sloane pressed closer, letting Reese feel exactly how affected she was, how little distance remained between intention and action.

"Tonight was torturous," Sloane murmured against her mouth. "You and those bare shoulders."

Reese smiled, slow and wicked. "I was hoping you'd do something about it."

Oh, Sloane wanted to.

She kissed her again, open-mouthed and sure, hands roaming now with purpose, along Reese's arms, her waist, memorizing heat and shape and the way Reese leaned into every touch like she'd been waiting for permission she no longer needed. Reese's heels slipped from her fingers and hit the carpet with a soft thud, forgotten.

The sound made them both laugh, quiet and breathless, until Sloane was kissing her again, harder this time, her tongue in Reese's mouth, momentum surging back into place. Desire gathered low and intense in her body, tossing away her every inhibition.

Yes. This was still a hurricane. But now Sloane was standing in the center of it, choosing not to step aside.

Reese's hands were at Sloane's waist when they stilled, the room settling into a taut, expectant quiet.

Her fingers slid along the seam of Sloane's dress, slow enough that Sloane felt every inch of it. The zipper moved with a soft, unmistakable sound.

Sloane sucked in a breath.

Reese didn't look down. She watched Sloane's face instead, tracking the reaction, the flicker of something unguarded crossed Reese's features before control snapped back into place.

"Still okay?" Reese asked, low and steady.

Sloane nodded once. Then she reached back and finished unzipping the dress herself, the motion decisive. The fabric loosened, cool air brushing skin that had been held too tight all evening.

Reese's jaw tightened, no longer playful. Focused. Hungry. Her gaze locked on Sloane's breasts as they were revealed, bare under the low hotel light.

"Fuck," Reese breathed, the word rough and low. "Look at you."

Sloane stepped closer, closing the last breath of space between them, letting Reese feel the heat radiating off her skin. She tilted her head, voice soft but coated with challenge. "What do you want to do?"

Reese's hands rose, slower this time, palms hovering just shy of contact like she was savoring the anticipation. Then they settled—firm, warm, thumbs tracing the soft outline in a slow, deliberate sweep. "I've been thinking about getting my mouth on them," she murmured, eyes dark and unwavering on Sloane's face. "About how they'd feel under my tongue. How you'd sound when I suck hard enough to make you arch."

Her thumbs brushed higher, circling the tightening peaks without quite touching, drawing a sharp inhale from Sloane.

"They're perfect," Reese added, voice dropping to a rasp. "Full. Sensitive."

Her thumbs brushed the undersides first, slow and deliberate, as if learning the exact weight and curve by touch alone. She exhaled shakily, eyes fixed on the soft swell, the faint flush already spreading across Sloane's chest. "Christ," she whispered, voice rough with something close to reverence, before she dipped her head and pressed an open-mouthed kiss just above one nipple, lingering there, letting her breath fan hot across the tightening peak. Sloane's back arched on instinct. Reese took the invitation, cupping one breast fully in her palm while her lips closed over the other, tongue circling slow and wet, then flattening to draw the nipple deep. She sucked gently at first, testing, then harder when Sloane's fingers tightened in her hair. Reese seemed to savor every small tremor, every hitch in Sloane's breathing, like she was memorizing the exact rhythm that made her unravel.

Sloane pulled Reese's lips to hers and kissed her, deep, unhurried, claiming ground inch by inch. Reese answered immediately, matching her pressure, her breath, the intensity climbing in controlled increments. This wasn't fumbling. These were two people who knew exactly what they were doing and exactly what it meant.

When Reese's mouth left hers, it was only to drag along Sloane's jaw, her throat, lingering at Sloane's pulse. Her fingers curled reflexively into Reese's hair, holding her there.

"Yes," Reese breathed, almost reverent.

Sloane closed her eyes. To let herself feel how far this had already gone, how impossible it would be to turn back now. To let the arousal wash over and imagine Reese satisfying the already growing throb between her legs, and then to give pleasure right back.

This wasn't a game.

It was a choice—made, owned, and accelerating.

She wanted to be fucked.

She pressed her breast into Reese's palm, her nipples pebbling, her center aching. As Reese gently squeezed, she felt the wetness between her legs grow. When Reese pulled her mouth away, focusing her gaze on Sloane, now only wearing her bikinis, she felt the heat of the stare everywhere. But they weren't anywhere near even with Reese still in her clothes. Time to change that.

Sloane eased the thin straps of Reese's top down her arms, exposing tan shoulders that had looked untouchable all night. The fabric followed slowly, and Reese's breath hitched in surrender.

The imbalance shifted.

She slid her hands over Reese's shoulders, thumbs brushing warm skin, then guided the top over her head until it fell to the floor. Reese stopped helping after that. She let Sloane unclasp her bra, let herself be undone, her lips parted as she watched. It turned her on. Sloane could tell.

Sloane stepped closer, close enough to feel the heat coming off her. She traced a slow line down Reese's side, mapping territory she'd imagined too many times to count, feeling the answering tension beneath her touch. With one finger, she circled Reese's nipple. Her breasts were round and full. Beautiful. She lifted one and pulled the nipple into her mouth, swirling it with her tongue.

Reese's hands came to Sloane's waist, firm now, grounding, but she didn't take over. She held on, as if bracing.

That did something dangerous to Sloane.

She unbuttoned Reese's pants and lowered the zipper slowly.

Then, with slow deliberation, she slid her hand down the front of Reese's pants, inside her underwear, into warmth and wet. She closed her eyes to remember this moment, to fully absorb it. The quiet whimper Reese let out shattered what little restraint Sloane had left, the sound sinking deep and settling there. "God, you feel good," Sloane said in her ear. "Do you like being touched like this?"

Reese nodded wordlessly, her hips beginning to rock, to press into Sloane's hand. She was asking, and Sloane had every intention of delivering. She began to stroke Reese, setting her own even rhythm, encouraged by the little gasps of air Reese offered to punctuate each pass. But this wasn't the way she wanted to take her. "Lie on my bed," Sloane said.

Reese didn't hesitate, but she also didn't rush. She eased back onto the bed with deliberate slowness, settling against the pillows, topless, legs slightly parted, eyes never leaving Sloane's. The lamp's warm light traced the curve of her collarbone, the gentle rise of her breasts still flushed from Sloane's mouth, the faint tremor in her thighs that spoke more of anticipation than impatience. She looked vulnerable in the best way, open, trusting, already giving Sloane everything.

Sloane slid off her bikinis and followed, crawling onto the mattress with the same measured care, straddling Reese's thighs without pressing down yet. She braced her hands on either side of Reese's head, leaning in until their foreheads touched, breaths mingling in the quiet space between them.

"You've been so patient," Sloane whispered, voice thick with something softer than lust. "All this time, waiting for me to stop running."

Reese's eyes fluttered closed for a second, then opened again, dark and shining. "I would've waited longer."

Sloane's heart squeezed. She kissed her then—slow, deep, tender—pouring everything unspoken into it: the months of tension, the fear, the certainty that this was right. Reese answered with the same quiet intensity, one hand sliding up

Sloane's back, fingers tracing her spine like she was mapping something sacred.

When they parted, Sloane sat back on her heels, gaze traveling over Reese's body. "Beautiful," Sloane murmured, almost to herself. She leaned down and pressed a slow, open-mouthed kiss to the center of Reese's chest, right over her heart, feeling it thunder beneath her lips. Then she moved to one breast, tongue circling the peak in lazy, worshipful strokes before drawing it gently into her mouth.

She kissed her way lower, pausing to nip softly at the sensitive skin below Reese's ribs, then hooked her fingers into the waistband of Reese's pants. Reese lifted her hips without being asked, letting Sloane draw them down—along with the soft underwear beneath—in one careful glide. The fabric whispered over skin, and when it was gone, Sloane paused, simply looking.

Reese lay bare beneath her now, flushed and trembling faintly, legs parted just enough to reveal how ready she was, glistening, swollen, aching. Sloane's throat tightened with something fierce and tender all at once.

She settled between Reese's thighs, hands sliding up the insides of her legs, thumbs brushing the soft crease where thigh met hip. "Tell me if it's too much," Sloane said quietly, voice rough with emotion.

Reese reached down, cupping Sloane's face. "It's you. It'll never be too much."

Sloane lowered her head and kissed the inside of one thigh, then the other—slow, deliberate, working closer until her breath ghosted over the most sensitive skin. Reese's hips lifted on instinct. Sloane pressed a steadying hand to her stomach, then dragged the flat of her tongue in one long, reverent stroke from entrance to clit. That earned her a quiet moan.

Reese's entire body arched, a soft, broken sound escaping her. Sloane hummed against her, the vibration pulling another whimper, then sealed her mouth over her swollen clit, sucking gently, tongue circling in slow, patient patterns. She slipped two fingers inside, curling them upward on each slow thrust, finding the spot that made Reese's thighs quiver and her breath hitch in sharp, needy gasps.

Every movement was careful, attentive—Sloane listening to every sound, every shift, memorizing what made Reese tremble, what made her fingers tighten in the sheets, what drew those quiet, almost reverent moans. When the rhythm built and Reese's walls began to flutter around her fingers, Sloane didn't rush. She stayed anchored, tongue relentless but tender, drawing it out until Reese shattered with a long, shuddering cry, back bowing, name falling from her lips.

Sloane kissed her through the aftershocks, soft licks and gentle presses of lips until Reese's trembling eased. Then she crawled back up, gathering Reese close, foreheads touching again as their breathing slowly synced.

Reese's arms wrapped around her, holding tight. "I've wanted this for so long," she whispered, voice raw. "Not just your body. You."

Sloane pressed a kiss to the corner of her mouth, then her temple. "Me too," she said simply.

They stayed like that for a long moment. Skin to skin, hearts pounding in tandem before Reese's hand slid down Sloane's side, fingers tracing the curve of her hip with the same careful wonder.

"My turn," Reese murmured, eyes soft and dark with promise. "Let me show you how much I've wanted you."

Sloane smiled, small and sure.

Reese shifted above her, settling between Sloane's thighs with a slow, deliberate grace that made Sloane's pulse stutter. No rush, no fumbling, just the even weight of Reese's body pinning her gently to the mattress, one hand braced beside Sloane's head, the other sliding down her side in a single, possessive stroke.

Sloane had pictured this too many times: Reese's green eyes locked on hers, that quiet command in her voice, the way she'd take without asking because she already knew Sloane wanted to be taken. The fantasy had always ended with Sloane surrendering completely, and now it was happening, authentic, warm, and overwhelming.

Reese's mouth found hers again, deep and unhurried, but there was new purpose in the kiss. When she pulled back, her thumb brushed Sloane's lower lip, parting it slightly. "Tell me what you need," Reese said, voice low, almost a command. This was the version of Reese who dominated races, who handled a car like no one else. She was handling Sloane now.

Sloane's breath caught. She'd spent months dodging this exact vulnerability, but the words came anyway, soft and honest. "I need you to fuck me. Like you've been waiting to. Like I've been yours all along."

Reese's eyes darkened, a flicker of something fierce and tender crossing her face. She didn't speak, just leaned down and kissed Sloane's throat, then lower, teeth grazing the sensitive skin above her collarbone in a gentle bite that made Sloane arch. Reese's hand continued its path, cupping one breast, thumb circling the nipple until it ached, then sliding down her stomach, over her hip, between her legs. God, she was good at this.

Sloane was already soaked, embarrassingly so, and when Reese's fingers finally began to explore, she let out a broken sound she couldn't hold back.

Reese paused, forehead resting against Sloane's, breathing her in. "You've been thinking about this," she murmured. It wasn't a question. Her fingers circled Sloane's clit once, twice, light enough to tease, firm enough to promise. "About me touching you here. About me inside you."

"Yes," Sloane whispered, hips lifting into the touch, searching for more. But Reese wasn't ready to give it. "God, yes."

Reese kissed her again—harder this time—as two fingers slid inside, curling on the first slow thrust to find that perfect spot. Sloane's hands flew to Reese's shoulders, nails digging in as pleasure spiked sharp and bright. Reese didn't speed up. She set a stable, deep rhythm, thumb pressing rhythmic circles over

Sloane's clit, each stroke building the heat without mercy. Sloane loved every second of this. She loved Reese fucking her.

It was exactly what Sloane had fantasized. Reese in control, focused, unrelenting, but never cruel. Every movement felt deliberate, like Reese was memorizing her—how she clenched, how she gasped, how her thighs trembled when the angle shifted just right because it was so dizzyingly good.

"Look at me," Reese said quietly.

Sloane's eyes fluttered open. Reese was watching her with raw intensity, like nothing else existed. The sight of it, Reese above her, inside her, claiming her so completely, tipped Sloane over the edge faster than she expected.

The orgasm hit like a slow wave at first, then crashed. Her body tightened around Reese's fingers, her back bowing, a soft, helpless cry tearing from her throat. Reese didn't stop. She kept the rhythm through every pulse, drawing it out until Sloane was shaking, oversensitive, clinging to her like she'd fall apart without the anchor.

When the aftershocks finally eased, Reese eased her fingers free, pressing soft kisses along Sloane's jaw, her temple, the corner of her mouth. She gathered Sloane close, rolling them so they lay side by side, limbs tangled, hearts pounding in sync.

Sloane buried her face in Reese's neck, breathing her in—sweat, skin, the faint trace of champagne still on her.

"I've wanted that for so long," Reese whispered, voice raw. "You. Like that."

"Me too," Sloane said. "And I'm not done wanting you." Reese's arms tightened around her.

They stayed wrapped together, quiet now, the room settling into a warm, sated hush. Sloane felt something shift inside her. It wasn't just release, but relief. Like a door she'd kept locked for months had finally swung open, and on the other side was Reese, waiting. And it made her so incredibly happy.

Reese traced lazy circles on Sloane's lower back, the touch so light and soothing. Sloane nestled closer, her cheek pressed to

Reese's shoulder, listening to the consistent thump of her heart-beat slow from frantic to calm.

"I used to lie awake thinking about this," Reese murmured into Sloane's hair, voice hushed like she was afraid to break the quiet. "Not just the sex. Just … you falling asleep next to me. Hoping I'd wake up and you'd still be here."

Sloane smiled against her skin, true and unguarded. "I thought about it too, even if I didn't want to admit it. I'd tell myself it was safer to keep the distance, but every time you looked at me across a room, I'd imagine this exact thing—your arms around me, no more pretending we weren't heading here."

Reese's fingers paused, then resumed their slow path. "No more pretending," she echoed softly. "I like the sound of that."

A comfortable silence settled between them, broken only by the faint hum of the hotel air-conditioning and their matched breathing. Sloane felt the last of the tension drain from her body, replaced by a deep, bone-level warmth she hadn't known she was missing.

"Stay," she whispered, the word slipping out before she could second-guess it. "All night. Don't go."

Reese pressed a kiss to the top of her head. "I'm not going anywhere."

Sloane let her eyes drift closed, the rhythm of Reese's heart-beat lulling her like a slow tide. Reese's hand kept moving in those gentle circles, steady and sure, until Sloane's thoughts soft-ened at the edges, blurring into the simple safety of being held.

The last thing she registered was Reese's quiet exhale, almost a sigh of relief, and the way her arms tightened just a fraction, as if she, too, was finally allowing herself to believe this was real.

Then sleep took them both, wrapped together in the dark, exactly where they were meant to be.

CHAPTER 15
THE COST TO LOSE

The red light on the camera blinked on.

Reese shifted in her chair, rolling her shoulders once, twice, settling the way she'd been taught—relaxed, but not careless. The backdrop was neutral, deliberately so. Nothing to distract from her face, her hands, the way she occupied space.

Samara sat just off to the side of the lens, tablet balanced on her knee, voice calm and conversational in the way that suggested this was not her first time asking a question that could change someone's life.

"So," Samara said, a small smile curving her mouth, "you've probably heard the rumors by now."

Reese's lips twitched. "Depends which ones."

Samara laughed softly, the sound meant to disarm. "Fair. But there's been a lot of chatter lately about Formula 1 paying close attention to the academy. Specifically, to the drivers' standings as they make decisions for next season." She glanced briefly at her tablet. "And right now, you and Danielle Todd are essentially neck and neck at the top."

Reese didn't react right away. She tipped her head, eyes flicking toward the camera lens—not into it, but close enough to acknowledge its presence. The machine. The audience.

"Danielle's a hell of a driver," Reese said, immediate and unforced. "She's consistently fast. Smart. And a risk taker. You don't get to the top by accident."

"You two don't like each other. That's pretty well-documented. Can you speak on that relationship?"

Reese laughed to ease any tension and searched for a way to remain diplomatic without dodging the question entirely. "We have different styles both on the circuit and in how we deal with people. That part is true." She was trying to be careful while still giving them enough to make their narrative accurate and interesting. "Do I have notes for Danielle?" She blew out a breath that said she didn't even know where to begin. "Sure, but she has them for me as well. Bottom line, she's quick out there, and I'm sure that makes me quicker."

Samara nodded, encouraging. "Does that kind of rivalry sharpen things? Knowing that if Formula 1 *is* watching, every tenth of a second counts?"

Reese leaned back slightly, confidence easing into her posture. "It does," she said. "But not in the way people like to frame it. It's not about beating Danielle. It's about not giving anything away. To anyone." She shrugged, easy again. "If people are watching, it means what we're doing here matters. But rumors are just noise unless you're backing them up on the track. And standings?" A quick smile. "They don't lie. Not for long, anyway."

"Good points." Samara consulted her notes. "Can you share a little bit about what silly season is and what it means to drivers?"

Reese nodded and raised a brow. "Silly season is definitely upon us right now. It's the point in the season through summer when contracts are expiring, negotiations are happening behind the scenes, drivers are jockeying for any open seats, and the press speculates wildly. It's basically a game of musical chairs for drivers."

Samara studied her for a beat. "So, as we sit here in silly season, you're not thinking about what a call-up might mean?"

Reese's smile returned, bright, practiced. "I'm thinking about the next race."

Samara had been right. Everyone from the higher-ups at the academy, all the way down to the entry-level mechanics, had heard the rumor. The one that said the team principals had been having closed-door meetings about the future of their teams, and that the names of academy drivers had been in the mix. No one knew if it was true. But everyone at the academy level was extra excited and working to prove themselves every time they slid behind the wheel.

From the top of the standings, Reese felt like she had a lot to lose. But she also knew one thing for sure: if the F1 teams were watching, she was going to put on a show. The first race in Monza had been a close one, but Reese had edged out Marissa for the win by 0.4 seconds, with Danielle falling down the order after a penalty for forcing another driver off track, her overly aggressive defense drawing the stewards' attention. Word around the paddock was that she'd lost it on her team, thrown her helmet, and blamed everyone she laid eyes on for the loss. Except herself. Danielle would be out for blood during the feature race, which meant Reese needed to be more alert behind the wheel than ever. She'd just increased her lead in the drivers' standings, and Danielle wasn't going to like that one bit.

Then there was Sloane.

Reese had spent years convincing herself that wanting someone, really wanting them, might be a liability. That it would cost her focus, dull her edge. But as she crossed the paddock, she realized the opposite had happened. What she felt for Sloane hadn't taken anything from her. It had clarified things. Made the noise quieter and the stakes cleaner. She was driving with nothing to prove and everything to protect. Her heart squeezed, and she let herself enjoy it.

"Enjoy it," she heard from a distinct English accent behind her when she walked from the podium back to the Ravensport garage. She turned around and met Danielle's fiery hazel eyes, arms crossed as she stared at Reese. "It's only temporary."

"Isn't everything?" Reese asked, shrugging and smiling. She wasn't the type to engage and knew very well how many eyes were on them right now.

"Flash-in-the-pan bitch," Danielle said as she walked toward her team's garage, probably too loudly on purpose.

Reese whirled around, shocked but not.

"Keep walking," Delaney said, approaching from the Ravensport garage, two down. "It's not worth it."

"It's not," Reese said. She much preferred to beat Danielle Todd on the circuit in front of thousands of people, where it would hurt the most.

"Your washed-up girlfriend teach you that in one of her cute classes?"

Reese froze. "What did you say?" Her blood ran cold, both from shock and offense. She turned back and waited.

"Sloane Foster. You're fucking her, right? I saw you leave her room. Got a good laugh. How ridiculous."

"You don't get to say her name."

Danielle placed a hand on her hip. "Guess it makes sense. Sloane couldn't hack it when it mattered, so now she fucks the girls who can and pretends that's mentoring. Is she as boring in bed as she was behind the wheel?"

The words landed like a slap. Reese moved before she thought. One sharp step forward, fist clenched, pulse spiking so fast it made her dizzy. The noise of the paddock fell away, replaced by the rush of blood in her ears.

"Don't," Delaney snapped, grabbing her arm and holding back the swing. Several crew members from inside the garage ran out to help. Danielle just stood there smirking, making Reese look like the violent animal ready to attack her, and damn if she wasn't still ready to do just that. Her body thrummed with heat, anger, the ugly need to protect. She stared at Danielle, her expression gone flat and cold, every ounce of humor stripped away.

"You're both an embarrassment," Danielle said and shook her head. "Look at you."

"Watch yourself," Reese said, voice low and dangerous.

For a beat, it was clear how close Danielle had come to getting precisely what she wanted: Reese out of the academy and out of her way to the driver's championship. And fuck her for that. She exhaled and straightened her race suit, gathering her control.

There were a lot of people swarming now, doing what they could to defuse the tension. Rodney Krauss, her team principal, was one of them. *Dammit. Of course he'd been there for this.*

"My office," Rodney said, fixing her with a level stare. "Now."

Reese closed her eyes and shook herself free of the hands holding her back. "I'm fine. Let me go. Okay? I'm good." She wasn't. Her face burned, adrenaline roaring through her veins, every instinct screaming to lunge for Danielle and let her fists finish what her mouth hadn't.

"Listen to me," Delaney murmured close to her ear. "Don't even sweat it. She's the worst kind of person and not at all worth what you'd pay for that punch."

"She's a lowlife," Reese snapped. "She doesn't deserve restraint." She met Delaney's gaze and found not judgment, but understanding. Fire recognizing fire. Delaney had her back. Always had.

"Fuck her," Delaney said quietly. "But think about your career right now."

Reese exhaled hard. "Okay. Okay. Yep. I'll try."

She stormed into Rodney's office and dropped into the chair

opposite his desk, heart still pounding, muscles tight with left-over fury.

Rodney stared at her, jaw clenched, eyes hard. "What in the hell was that?" His voice was louder than Reese had ever heard it. Rodney was usually reserved, a man who carried pressure without broadcasting it, and Reese respected him for that. She liked him as a boss. Trusted his instincts. Trusted the calls he made on strategy. This was different.

"I don't know what that was about," he continued, "and I don't need to. But that kind of behavior does not represent this team."

"I hear you," Reese said, blinking as she forced her breathing to slow. "But she was so far out of line."

"That was schoolyard bullshit, Reese. And it doesn't fly." He leaned forward, palms pressing into the desk. "She wanted to get in your head—and you let her."

Reese bristled. He wasn't wrong, and that stung worse than the reprimand. It didn't mean she'd change a thing if she had the moment back.

"Look what you just handed her," Rodney went on. "We don't need you rattled over some juvenile driver squabble."

Reese's jaw tightened. "Understood. Won't happen again."

"You've been warned," Rodney said flatly. "This team has a lot on the line. I need your focus on winning races, not personal vendettas."

"Got it."

Rodney exhaled and leaned back in his chair, some of the rigidity easing from his shoulders. When he spoke again, his voice had shifted. Quieter, more measured.

"Off the record," he said, "you've shown real talent out there. A lot of improvement since the season started." He studied her carefully. "Your instincts are rare. And now that you've paired them with discipline, you're dangerous to them."

He gestured toward the door. "The extra time on the sim? It's paid off. I see it."

Reese looked up, genuinely surprised. "Thank you. It's helped."

"I don't say that lightly," Rodney continued. "You're faster than you were six months ago in F2. I've pulled the data. Smarter, too. You're making better decisions under pressure, and that doesn't happen by accident."

She swallowed and nodded once.

"But you will lose your ride if something like this repeats," he said, the steel back in his voice. "Don't let that happen. Not after the progress you've made. Not when you're finally putting all of it together."

He held her gaze, the warning settling into something steadier. "And for the record, I don't give a flying fuck who you spend time with in your personal life. That's none of my business." His expression sharpened. "Just keep it off the track. Out of the garage. Don't give anyone an excuse to question what you've earned."

"Yes, sir," Reese said quietly, a thousand thoughts colliding without finding purchase.

Rodney stood, signaling the end of it. "Good. Now go cool off. You've got another race to win tomorrow."

Sloane had already made it back to the Formula Next offices by the time the altercation between Reese and Danielle had unfolded in front of what seemed like half the academy. By the time she arrived, the entire suite was buzzing. Conversations dropped a notch whenever she passed, everyone carefully skirting around the comment Danielle had apparently made about her.

Veronica, however, wasted no time. She ushered Sloane into her office, closed the door behind them, and gave Sloane the full version of what had transpired out there. Unfortunately, it was even worse than what she'd been hearing.

"She actually said that?" Sloane asked, incredulous.

Veronica nodded, tenting her hands on the desk. She looked caught between two roles—head of the academy and longtime friend—and for the moment, she leaned into the former. "It was unprofessional, completely out of line. I'm sorry she dragged your name into it. She'll be spoken to, by the academy and by her team. I promise you that."

Sloane studied her for a beat. "Okay. Now tell me what you really think. I want Ronnie, not Veronica."

Veronica's shoulders dropped, tension easing as she exhaled. "I want to shake that girl and ask her where the fuck she gets off. How clueless do you have to be to go after a legend like you? I'm offended on your behalf. I think she needs a reality check, and I'm not sure I want her back at the academy next year. Fuck her. She's an ungrateful brat who has no idea the doors that have been opened for her by women like us."

"Oh, I like it when you're you."

"Good, because I'm unapologetic about it." She sighed, rubbing a hand over her face. "She's not likely to return to the academy anyway if she keeps pulling points. Winnaker's F1 leadership is desperate to reinvent itself and get out of the basement. Word is, they're circling Todd."

"They want to offer her an F1 seat?" Sloane blinked, processing. "It is what it is," she said evenly. "Though I think there are better options."

Veronica watched her for a moment, eyes narrowing slightly. "She's the reason you've seemed lighter lately. The better option. Reese."

Sloane could have deflected. Could have pretended it wasn't true. But Ronnie wasn't just her boss—she was her best friend. Hiding felt pointless.

She nodded. "Yes. I promise you it was unexpected."

"Okay. I believe you."

"It's not that I was trying to keep it from you, but I needed to figure it out for myself first."

A pause. "How serious is it?" Veronica asked, coming around the desk, a tennis ball already in her hand.

Sloane accepted it and tossed it against the wall, catching it on the rebound. "It's not like that. She's not my girlfriend. We're just … um, having a good time." The description didn't seem to do them justice, but it was all she had.

Veronica arched a brow. "In bed."

Sloane winced. "Yep. There was one of those," she admitted. She lobbed the ball back to the wall, and this time Ronnie caught it. It went on like that for a little while, tossing the ball back and forth between each other and the wall, neither one of them speaking until …

"She was ready to throw a punch for you out there," Veronica said, looking over at Sloane.

"Yeah? I'm not sure violence is the green flag you think it is." She added a smile to show she was being playful, refusing to look too closely at the way all this made her feel. Reese having her back. Caring enough to risk it all because someone had insulted Sloane. Not to mention the fire, the passion, the grit that made Reese uniquely herself. Hadn't that been a part of the attraction?

Veronica squinted. "I think you understand my point."

"Yeah, I do," Sloane said, sobering, something important blossoming in her chest. "There are a lot of reasons *not to* fully go there with her." A beat. "She's younger than I am."

"There's that. Eleven years is something to consider." Another throw of the ball. Veronica caught it. "You also have a professional relationship to think about."

Another throw. Sloane's catch. "And I don't want to be a cliché, chasing after the hot, beautiful, young driver."

"Well, you're also the hot one, in case you haven't heard the chatter." Veronica caught the ball, held it to her chest, and turned. "But don't overlook the reasons to leap at the same time."

"Wow. Coming from someone who wasn't a Reese fan when she got here? This is a shocking turn of events."

"I was always a fan, just not so much a believer. She might be changing my mind one race at a time."

Sloane stared at the ground, as if it were a lifeline, needing it to articulate this next part. "She's in the perfect spot to get called up, Ronnie. I … I can't go back to that world. That's the main thing that's holding me back." The reality was that F1 was its own animal. The cars were faster, the demands greater, the pressure higher than ever, and that resulted in more close calls, more crashes, more injuries. Sloane swallowed the uncomfortable lump in her throat, clocking the pickup in her heart rate and trying to dodge the panic.

"So you're holding her at arm's length because you can't watch her get hurt the way you did?"

"Or worse," Sloane whispered because her voice was overcome. Her breath hitched as she tried to find the oxygen. "On one hand, I don't think I should get too attached, and that's hard because … it's there for me. I feel it in every sense. I really like her, but …"

"Hey," Veronica said, realizing the severity of Sloane's fear. "You're safe. This is not eight years ago, and the FIA has made a lot of safety improvements since … since we were racing," Veronica finished softly. She stepped closer, voice lowering. "I know your brain doesn't care about statistics when it remembers how it felt. But this isn't the same world. It just isn't."

Sloane shook her head, eyes still fixed on the floor. "It feels the same," she said. "Every time she straps in, it's like my chest tightens before the lights even go out. I watch her take risks, and all I can see is the worst-case scenario."

Veronica leaned back against the desk, giving her space but not distance. "That's not nothing," she said gently. "That's someone who's already lost something important and doesn't want to lose again."

Sloane let out a shaky breath. "I don't want to be the reason she hesitates. Or worse, the reason she thinks she has to prove something. She's so close, Ronnie. One call. One seat. I can't be a complication."

"You're assuming she's fragile," Veronica said. "And she's not."

Sloane looked up at that.

"She's strong," Veronica continued. "Headstrong, yes. Occasionally impulsive. But she's learning. She listens. And today? She showed restraint. That matters."

"She almost hit someone," Sloane said, half a protest.

"But she didn't," Veronica countered. "Because she knew what it would cost her. That's growth."

Silence settled between them, heavier now, but steadier.

"You don't have to decide anything today," Veronica said finally. "You don't have to leap. You don't have to run. But don't shut the door just because you're scared of what's on the other side."

Sloane swallowed. "I don't know how to want this without being terrified."

Veronica's mouth curved into a knowing smile. "Welcome to caring again."

Sloane huffed a weak laugh, pressing a hand to her chest as her breathing finally evened out. Outside the office, the academy buzzed on. Engines revving, radios crackling, the world moving forward whether she was ready or not.

"I should check on her," Sloane said quietly.

Veronica nodded. "You should."

"And Ronnie?"

"Yeah?"

"Thank you. For not pretending this is easy."

Veronica met her gaze. "If it were easy, it wouldn't be worth it."

Sloane opened the door and stepped back into the noise,

carrying equal parts fear and something else now. Something she hadn't felt in a long time.

Hope.

CHAPTER 16
ON THE OTHER SIDE OF THE DOOR

Sloane found Reese in her driver's room, sitting on the bench along the wall, hunched forward with her elbows on her knees, staring at the floor like it had personally betrayed her.

"Knock knock," Sloane said, peeking in through the half-open door. "Can I come in?"

Reese looked up, surprise flickering across her face before she nodded. "Yeah. Of course."

Sloane slipped inside the small room reserved for Reese and closed the door behind her, the click of it sealing them off from the rest of the Ravensport team. Her presence would probably raise a few eyebrows, especially after Danielle had run her mouth, but Sloane didn't care. In this moment, there was only Reese, how she was feeling, and what she was carrying.

"You okay?"

Reese stood and tossed a few things into her bag with a little more force than necessary. "Define okay."

Sloane sighed. "She shouldn't have come after you that way. She was pissed about her own lousy finish and took it out on you. She's jealous."

"She can say whatever she wants about me." Reese whirled

around. "But when she said your name? No. Not gonna happen." She shook her head, her body still coiled with fury.

"So," Sloane said lightly after a weighted moment, "other than that, Mrs. Lincoln, how was the play?"

That pulled a ghost of a smile. Reese scrubbed a hand over her face. "I almost forgot I won a race today." She tugged her hair loose from its ponytail, letting it cascade past her shoulders. "I'm guessing you heard the details of what was said out there?"

"The whole world heard," Sloane said. "It's the talk of race town."

"Is that what they call it?"

Sloane grinned. "Yes. I named it." She tossed in a wink.

"You know," Reese said, eyeing her, "you're a lot more playful than I would have guessed."

"Oh, see, I like keeping people on their toes. Aren't surprises more fun?"

"In this moment, I can't argue with that." Reese's mouth tipped down again. "I'm sorry you got dragged into it out there. That's the part I hate most. You caught a stray bullet, and it wasn't fair. If I could erase anything, it would be that."

Sloane crossed the room and sat beside her, their knees brushing. "Here's the thing, though, Reese." She paused, teasing. "Can I call you Reese?"

Reese shot her a look. "Oh, you have jokes now, too?"

"Occasionally. I use them to deflect."

Sloane placed her hand on Reese's leg, warm and secure. "So, here's the thing. I'm a big girl. I know this sport and the world around it. Racing eats headlines for breakfast and spits them out by dinner. If we're interesting today, tomorrow someone else will be."

Reese squinted one eye shut. "Why do you always have better perspective than I do? It's deeply annoying."

"It's my gift," Sloane said solemnly. "Perspective. Followed by irritation." A pause. "Boobs aren't bad either. At least that's what I'm told."

That finally did it. Reese smiled—a real one, the kind that softened her eyes and loosened something tight in Sloane's chest. Seeing it felt like winning something herself. "That part's true. I can attest."

"That's right. You can." They shared a smile.

"Did you see my podium?" Reese asked quietly.

Sloane lifted a brow. "You mean when you assaulted that champagne bottle like it owed you money?" She shrugged. "Yeah. I saw it."

Reese laughed, breathier now. "Race wasn't awful, right?"

"Not terrible," Sloane agreed. "Though I might've pushed a little harder through Turn 4."

Reese leaned closer, voice dropping. "Julie was in my ear, telling me to play it safe. And what do you always say about listening to my engineer?"

"No idea," Sloane deadpanned.

Reese shifted, angling her head, hovering just shy of Sloane's mouth. "That I should pay attention to those trying to keep me safe. I like to pretend it's because you like how I look in my race suit."

Sloane's gaze dipped, then lifted again. "I don't think you have to pretend." She pulled back just enough to breathe. "But I can't kiss you in the driver's room," she whispered, standing and putting a sliver of space between them. "As much as I may want to. I don't like going hours without kissing you."

"Yes, you can," Reese said, standing too. "And you definitely should. We're so good at it."

"There are people everywhere," Sloane said, her cheeks warming. "Right on the other side of this door, in fact."

"This door?" Reese stepped in and pressed Sloane's back gently against it, the heat between them immediate and unmistakable. She didn't stop there. She rolled her hips forward in a slow, deliberate grind, slotting one thigh between Sloane's legs so their bodies aligned perfectly. The friction was instant, electric. Reese's breasts crushed softly against Sloane's, her hips pressed firmly, teasing in a way that made Sloane's breath hitch.

Sloane's conviction cracked wide open as her center ached.

"They'll survive," Reese murmured against her jaw, voice low and rough, still moving in that maddeningly controlled grind.

"They might not," Sloane managed, gaze dropping to Reese's perfect mouth—the same one that had given her multiple orgasms. She was especially a fan of that bottom lip. She wanted to suck on it, and that would just be the opening act.

Reese tilted her head toward the door, still pressed flush, still rocking subtly. "I could ask. Actually, I will. Hold on."

"Don't you dare," Sloane said, grabbing Reese by the front of her race suit and holding her there.

Reese's smile turned slow and dangerous, her hips giving one more lazy press.

"What are you doing to me right now?" Sloane asked, closing her eyes, trying to ignore the throbbing between her legs. "How do you get me so turned on so fast?"

"I could take care of that for you." Reese watched Sloane carefully as she slipped her hand between Sloane's legs, palming her through the fabric. Even through the material, the heat radiated. Sloane's hips jerked forward on instinct, chasing it.

Reese didn't waste time. She popped the button of Sloane's pants with a flick of her thumb, tugged the zipper down just enough, and slipped her hand inside—past the waistband of Sloane's underwear, finding slick, swollen heat waiting for her. Sloane bit her lip hard to stifle the sound that tried to escape.

"Fuck," Sloane breathed, head tipping back softly against the door, careful not to let it make a sound.

Reese pressed two fingers inside her in one smooth glide, curling them just right, thumb settling over her clit with practiced precision. Sloane's knees buckled slightly. Reese used her body to pin her upright, thigh still wedged between Sloane's legs for extra leverage.

"Ride my hand," Reese whispered against her ear. "I've got you."

Sloane didn't need convincing. Not in the state she was in. She rocked forward onto Reese's fingers, then back, setting a desperate, shallow rhythm that rubbed her clit against the heel of Reese's palm with every grind. They were in luck. The fucking door didn't rattle. It was her favorite door ever. Sloane's hands clenched Reese's race suit, anchoring herself as pleasure coiled tighter and tighter.

Reese kept her pace even, unrelenting, curling deeper with every forward roll of Sloane's hips, thumb circling in tight, perfect strokes. She watched Sloane's face the whole time, likely following her cues.

"Look at you. You're almost there, aren't you?" Reese murmured, lips brushing Sloane's earlobe.

Sloane could only nod, a broken little sound slipping out.

"Shhh," Reese soothed, even as she pressed harder, fingers stroking that spot that made Sloane's thighs tremble. "They're right outside. We can't have everyone knowing what I'm doing to you."

The words, the risk, the pressure, the way Reese's fingers filled her, all pushed Sloane over the edge. Her rhythm stuttered, hips jerking forward as she came with a choked, muffled gasp, clenching hard around Reese's fingers. Reese held her through it, palm grinding slow circles against her oversensitive clit until she whimpered and sagged against the door.

Reese eased her fingers out gently and pressed a soft, lingering kiss to the corner of Sloane's mouth.

"How did I do?" she asked, quietly.

Sloane opened her eyes, still dazed, cheeks flaming. The grin on Reese's face said it all. "Look how proud you are of yourself."

"I mean, I feel like I've earned that kiss," Reese said. "Thoughts?"

Sloane didn't argue. She surged forward and kissed her, immediate and decisive, no hesitation, no second-guessing.

Reese made a low sound of surprise before melting into it, hands coming up automatically, one sliding to Sloane's waist to pull her closer.

Sloane smiled against her mouth. "There she is."

Reese laughed softly, breathless, and kissed her again.

The knock hit the door hard behind them.

"Reese? You in there?"

They froze, eyes wide, foreheads pressed together, breaths uneven.

"You have *got* to be kidding me," Reese muttered.

"Driver debrief," Delaney's voice continued. "Rodney wants to start in five."

"Got it." She exhaled in defeat. "I'll be there."

"Are you doing okay?" Delaney asked. "Do you want to talk about what happened out there?"

"I'm fine. Just taking a minute to feel," her gaze fell to Sloane and her eyes softened, "like myself again."

"You got it. I'll meet you in there."

Sloane rested her forehead briefly against Reese's shoulder, smiling despite herself. "That's my cue. You've got to get to work, and so do I."

Reese stole one more quick kiss. "I'll see you later?"

"Mm-hmm," Sloane said, touching her good-and-kissed lips. "I have a dinner thing with some old friends. We get together whenever I'm in town."

"I'm gonna hang with mine, too. *After*?" Reese bounced her eyebrows.

"You're incorrigible." But Sloane knew that she owed Reese and would delight in making things even between them later.

"Can't say that's new. Can't say it will ever change, either," Reese smiled. "But I'm charming, right? People *always* say I'm charming."

"You're a little charming."

"See?" Reese's playful smile dimmed to sincere. "Seriously, though. Thank you for coming in here. I do feel better, and it's because of your presence. Your words." She looked skyward. "I guess we just wait out the possible scandal."

"Can't say I'm often a part of one of those."

She laughed quietly. "Welcome to Reese. I'd better go."

Sloane took a seat. "For discretionary purposes, I'll hang back a few minutes."

"You look good in my room," Reese said, eyeing her on the bench.

"Get out of here," Sloane said with a smile.

She did. Once alone, Sloane let it all settle. She hadn't given herself space to think about the fallout of the very public argument yet. Not really. She'd been too focused on Reese, on making sure she was okay, and then of course, they'd gotten carried away.

But people would be looking at them differently, trying to decide if the rumors were true. They'd assess, speculate, and decide what version of the story they preferred. Sloane had no intention of showing favoritism among the drivers, yet others would watch and wonder. It wasn't a great spot to be in, but could she walk away from what she'd started with Reese? No. She wasn't sure how to hit the off switch on something that had made her feel alive for the first time in years, and she didn't want to.

Sloane exhaled slowly and reminded herself of a few important things.

First: nothing about what was happening felt wrong. Not the quiet conversations. Not the laughter. Not even the passion that had bubbled over and lingered with her even now.

Second: she was allowed to want this. Whatever *this* was becoming.

And finally, and most importantly, she didn't need to solve it all today.

She stood, smoothed her jacket, and caught her reflection in the small mirror by the door. Her eyes were bright. Her smile came easily. That said something.

"It's all okay," she murmured to herself, not unkindly. "You've got this."

And for the first time since Veronica had arrived in LA and offered her this job, she believed it.

By the time Reese realized the cactus mural on the hotel room wall had *crowns*, she was already on her second sparkling water. She was a party animal tonight, it seemed.

But they were everywhere—painted across the turquoise wall behind Delaney's bed, tall and squat and lopsided, each one topped with a crooked little gold crown like they'd all been quietly knighted. The longer Reese stared, the more convinced she became that one of them was smirking at her.

"This one," she said, pointing, "knows my secrets."

Delaney, stretched out across the bed with her booties kicked off, and her socks aggressively mismatched, didn't even look up from her phone. "That's King Prickles. He judges everyone."

Cassidy snorted from the floor, where she was leaning back against the couch, nursing a soda and stealing popcorn straight out of the bowl Marissa held in her lap. "You're projecting."

"I am *not*," Reese said. "Look at his face."

Marissa, curled into the armchair that looked more decorative than functional, tilted her head. "He does look smug."

"Thank you," Reese said.

Delaney finally glanced up. "He's a solid cactus. Probably has healthcare and a 401(k)."

"Does Italy even have cacti?" Reese asked, squinting. "I've never seen one. This is weird."

"Of course it does, especially in the southern regions," Marissa said automatically. They all swiveled in awe of her very specific knowledge. "What? I'm a proud Italian. You know this."

"I don't think you've told us enough. Again, please?" Marissa threw a throw pillow that smacked Delaney square on the cheek. She didn't even flinch. Reese wanted to be just like her.

Somewhere behind them, the ceiling fan clicked rhythmically, one uneven sound per rotation.

Cassidy nudged Reese's ankle with her foot. "For the record, my room has *none* of this personality."

"That's tragic," Marissa said. "This room has lived."

"This room has opinions," Reese corrected.

The day had been a long one, and though Reese craved time with Sloane, she was grateful for the chance to unwind with The Starting Grid.

They'd been in town long enough now that the edges had softened. No more jet lag, no more frantic unpacking. Just the quiet hum of being midseason—press done for the day, no simulator sessions, nothing urgent pulling at Reese's attention for the first time in hours. And after the horrible incident with Danielle, Reese just wanted to hide out and unwind.

She leaned back on the couch beside Cassidy, letting her shoulder rest there without thinking about it. Someone had put music on, something lazy with a beat that didn't demand anything.

This was the part Reese always loved. The in-between, where no one expected her to perform. Her ever-present smile could take a break, and she could just … be.

Delaney's phone buzzed on the nightstand.

She ignored it.

It buzzed again.

Reese felt the shift before Delaney reached for it. Yep. There was a subtle tightening in the room. Marissa stilled. Cassidy's eyes flicked over.

Delaney frowned and picked it up. Her expression didn't collapse or spike. It just sharpened into concentration.

"What?" Reese said. "What's with the look?"

Delaney scrolled once. Then again.

"Oh," she said.

Cassidy straightened. "That's never good. The singular oh."

Marissa sat up fully. "What happened?"

"Tyler Lock." Delaney looked up, eyes moving between them.

Reese's stomach dipped. He was an F1 driver. "What about him?"

"It says he flipped his car during a practice session. A concussion and a broken right foot. Surgery is expected," Delaney said.

Reese swore under her breath. Tyler Lock didn't make mistakes. Tyler Lock didn't get hurt. He was the kind of midfield driver who felt invincible. Laurens Racing had depended on him for years.

Cassidy's phone chimed. She stared at it for a beat longer than necessary. "And there it is. He's out."

Marissa sucked in a breath. "*Out* out?"

"For the season," Cassidy said, scrolling. "Laurens just made the official announcement."

The ceiling fan clicked.

Reese felt heat rush through her chest, sharp and sudden. "That means—"

"They're putting the reserve driver in," Cassidy said, eyes lifting to Reese now. "Yep. Right here. Marco Faz is taking over the seat effective immediately."

Delaney's phone buzzed again, like it couldn't stand the silence. "Which means," she said carefully, "there's now a reserve driver spot open."

No one spoke.

"Reese. You're bound to be a conversation people are having," Marissa said. She exchanged a look with Delaney, who nodded in agreement.

"You're at least *on the short list*," Delaney said. "Especially, if they've had their eye on the standings and your steady climb."

"You could be the first woman in F1 in … years," Marissa said.

Reese pressed her hands together, grounding herself. "I don't want it like this."

"I know," Delaney said gently.

"But," Marissa offered, because she always was the one to say it, "it's still a door."

Cassidy studied Reese, a slow smile tugging at her mouth. "And you're very hard to ignore when doors open."

Reese slid onto her back and stared up at the ceiling. "I don't know. I'm afraid even to consider the possibility." But she had to. It was her job to move herself forward in her career, and Marissa was right. You don't shy away from opportunity, no matter how unfortunate. Reserve drivers didn't see the action and were mainly relegated to public appearances, team marketing, and fan photo ops. All things she could handle. But it would get her behind the wheel of an F1 car for practice sessions, an absolutely invaluable shot she didn't have anywhere else. Those cars were monsters and miracles all at once, all carbon fiber and fury. They were faster than anything she'd ever driven, more sensitive, more demanding. Blink wrong, and they'd bite you. Get it right, though, and they took off singing.

Reese rolled onto her side, letting herself go there for a moment and imagining herself behind that wheel. "I don't want to be excited," she said quietly.

Cassidy bumped her knee with Reese's. "Too late."

Delaney sat on the side of the bed now, elbows on her knees, grounded and secure in a way that always made Reese feel less like she might float off into panic. "No one's saying this is happening tomorrow," she said. "But if your name comes up, you're mentally ready."

Marissa nodded. "You didn't claw your way up the standings for nothing."

She shifted on the couch, and without comment, Cassidy's arm came up, loose and easy, settling behind Reese's shoulders like it had always belonged there.

"You wouldn't be alone," Delaney said. It wasn't a pep talk. It was a fact.

Marissa nodded. "Not for a second."

Cassidy tipped her soda can toward Reese. "We'd be insufferable about it, actually."

Reese laughed, surprised by how close it was to a choke. The room felt warmer now, not from the temperature, but from the way they were all oriented toward her, like she was the center of something solid.

She'd spent so much of her career pushing forward on her own, bracing for impact, assuming support came with strings attached. This didn't feel like that. This felt like hands at her back, ready whether she leapt or hesitated.

"I don't know what's going to happen," Reese said.

"That's okay," Delaney replied. "You don't have to know tonight."

Cassidy squeezed her shoulder. "Tonight, you just get to exist."

Reese leaned into it because it was clear she wouldn't be facing it solo. Somewhere between the sparkling water and the mediocre hotel lighting, these women had become more than teammates or travel companions.

They were her people.

And because of that, Reese felt less afraid of the door opening and more grateful for who would be standing beside her if it did.

CHAPTER 17
HOTSHOT

Sloane should have known this was coming. The quiet she'd come to rely on had been slashed apart when the news that Tyler had been truly hurt hit her phone. He was a veteran of the sport, and they'd shared the track for two seasons. He was one of the most respected drivers in the lineup, careful, measured, and talented. Injuries were part of the sport, but they landed differently now. Heavier.

Each new report pulled her back into her own accident: the impact, the long recovery, the months of rehab, and the final, irreversible loss of her ability to race. In the end, it hadn't been the physical damage that sidelined her. She could have come back from that. It had been the emotional wreckage. No matter how many times she slid behind the wheel, she couldn't complete a full lap without the panic setting in, which made her a danger to herself and to others. To drive at that level, you needed a clear head and nerves of steel. She no longer had either. The biggest tragedy of her life.

By the time she made it back to the hotel, Sloane had barely had a few minutes alone before Reese knocked on her door. Her mouth curved into a smile. It had only been a few hours, but she already missed the green of Reese's eyes, the sideways glance she deployed so expertly when she was being funny, and the way her eyebrows dipped when she was deep in thought.

She took a breath, let it calm her, then crossed the room. When she opened the door, Reese was still mid-knock, her hand hovering awkwardly in the air. She dropped it, grinning, unrepentant.

"Hey," Sloane said, like they hadn't already spent half the day together. She felt so much better just for laying eyes on Reese, her shiny dark hair loose and gorgeous tonight. It cut across her forehead just shy of her left eye.

"I love the way you open doors."

Sloane paused. "I can't say that's a compliment I've ever received."

"Well, you should hear it more often. You have door flourish." Reese demonstrated with an exaggerated sweep of her arm. "Confident. Decisive. Strong hinge work."

Sloane stepped aside to let her in, suddenly aware of how small the room felt once Reese crossed the threshold, how easily she filled the space just by existing in it.

Reese glanced around, taking in the aggressively neutral furniture and forgettable art. "I didn't examine your room the last time I was here."

"Well. We were … occupied. Have at it." She folded her arms and waited as Reese walked the perimeter.

"Thrilling accommodations," she deadpanned. "Very corporate retreat chic. I notice the absence of a single cactus painting."

"Ah, yes. I'm told the club-level rooms were remodeled," Sloane said, adding a deliberately superior wince. Teasing Reese was quickly becoming one of her favorite pastimes. "The rest of the hotel is aspirational."

Reese spun around, eyes wide and blazing. "You're club level? Do you have a lounge?"

"I'm afraid the first rule of club level is you don't talk about club level."

Reese's eyes went wide. "You brought it up."

"I have no idea what you're referring to," Sloane said, flashing her slyest smile.

Reese's mouth fell open. She then grabbed Sloane's hand and gave it a small, decisive tug, pulling her closer. "What is happening right now?"

"I think it's you getting all hot and bothered because my room is nicer."

"That's not why," Reese said, and then she kissed her.

It was quick, sure, and unmistakably Reese. Sloane leaned into it without hesitation.

"You taste like strawberries," Sloane said when they parted, genuinely delighted by the discovery.

"It's how I get my women."

Sloane lifted a brow. "Your women?"

"So many," Reese said solemnly. "ChapStick groupies. They can't resist the strawberry."

Sloane laughed. "I genuinely can't tell if you're serious."

"I'm rarely serious," Reese said. "But the truth is, I've never had much time to date. Being on the road for ten months a year isn't ideal for nurturing a mature, emotionally complex relationship. I have standards, Foster."

"It's known to work well for hookups," Sloane said, then immediately wished she hadn't. Or maybe she wished Reese wouldn't agree. The thought of Reese with other women tightened something low and uncomfortable in her chest. "I mean, you're young. Sought after."

"Are we going there?" Reese asked with a tentative look in her eyes.

Sloane met her gaze and made a decision. "Why not?"

"Okay. So, here's the truth. Once in a while, I spend a night with someone." Reese shrugged. "I'm a bigger flirt than I am anything else. I don't think I was built for casual as much as I wanted to be."

"I suppose I'm still figuring that part of you out," Sloane murmured, brushing her thumb over Reese's bottom lip.

"That's fair." Reese's expression softened, sincerity dialed all the way up. She hooked a thumb behind her. "But here's the truth. That version of me you met in the bar in Miami? She's brave and flashy and has a few smooth moves—but she's all show. I go home alone most every night. By choice."

Sloane nodded slowly. "And is that what you still want?"

She hadn't earned the right to ask that, but she asked it anyway.

"No. I don't want to be alone," Reese said simply. "But being with the wrong person is worse. So I guess I want to find the right one—and never let her go."

She threaded their fingers together and held on.

So maybe this wasn't just sex to Reese. And if Sloane was honest, it wasn't feeling that way for her either.

"Suggestion."

"I'm listening."

"Why don't we take this one day at a time," Sloane said quietly, "and see where we end up?"

"You might have a hard time shaking me," Reese replied in earnest. "I'm really drawn to impressive door openers. Bonus points if they can also drive fast like you. It's a whole thing."

Sloane huffed out a laugh. "You're impossible."

A beat.

"But not wrong," Reese said.

"Well, I can promise consistency on *one* of those counts."

"Time will tell. The audition continues." Reese moved to Sloane's bed and plopped down on her stomach, chin in her hands. Oh, Sloane liked her there very much. Not only was the visual sexy as hell, but it felt startlingly natural, like she belonged in Sloane's space. "How was dinner?"

Sloane came to the bed and sat on the edge near Reese, like a magnet unaware it had no choice. "Longer than I'd planned, but it was nice to catch up with some old friends. Denny was my engineer back in the day, and his wife is currently expecting their second child. A little girl that they're going to call Theodora. Theo for short. We've been through a lot together."

"He's your Julie."

Sloane nodded. "And just as good at his job." A pause. "We got the news about Tyler while at the restaurant."

"Right. I wondered." She watched the smile fade from Reese's lips. "And how did that affect you? I imagine it was jarring. I'm glad Denny was there."

Sloane went still.

She'd expected Reese to leap immediately into a discussion about the available seat and her chances of snagging the reserve spot. And why wouldn't she? It was the obvious pivot, the big talking point, the undisputed headline everyone in the paddock would be dissecting by morning. Instead, Reese had thought first of *her*—of Sloane and her headspace. The realization landed hard enough that Sloane swallowed, the words she'd been ready to say stalling on the tip of her tongue, stunned into silence.

"What's up?" Reese asked, her brows drawing together as she studied Sloane's face. She shifted, pushing herself into a seated position so they were eye to eye, close enough that Sloane could see the concern etched there.

"Just really thoughtful of you to ask," Sloane said finally. "You've got a lot going on."

"So do you," Reese said automatically. "And I know how you respond to incidents on the track." Sloane flashed to another time. Reese in a quiet suite, holding her hand, talking her through the panic that had wrapped itself tight around her. "How did you feel?"

Her therapists—there had been several over the years— would have encouraged her to take this moment, this sincere opening, and say the thing out loud. To name it. Sloane dropped her gaze to the bedspread, focusing on the navy stitching that formed neat four-inch squares. "Uh … at first, everything went a little tight," she said. "My chest, especially. That's usually my cue to remind myself to breathe. To tell myself I'm safe."

Reese lifted Sloane's hand and turned it over, examining her palm as if it required careful study. The simple gesture siphoned off some of the pressure, making the words easier to access.

"I looked around the restaurant to orient myself and forced a deep breath. That's usually the moment when the panic either takes hold—or it doesn't."

Reese traced the lines of her palm, slow and purposeful, grounding in a way that felt almost deliberate.

"I was worried it would be bad," Sloane admitted. "But being there with Denny helped. It added a level of safety. I was lucky."

"I'm sorry that happened," Reese said softly, lifting her gaze to meet Sloane's. Her eyes held kindness, and something deeper —understanding. Reese knew exactly what they put on the line every time they climbed into a car. She understood the stakes in a way most people on earth never could. And still, she took them on. Because she loved the sport.

And so did Sloane. To this very day.

"When I took Veronica's offer to work at the academy, I was worried about stepping back into the world."

"I can imagine."

"But meeting you? It's helped." Reese's lips parted ever so slightly. "Because whatever is happening between us has been a bright spot. A tether that made me feel … well, stronger. Like I'm not in this alone."

"You're not. And I'm not either." She squeezed Sloane's hand.

"So, my thesis statement is that I'm grateful for you on this journey, Reese, and—"

Reese's phone lit up and vibrated, pulling attention from both of them.

She looked down at it and then back to Sloane, eyes wide. "It's Jeremy."

"He's your agent, right?"

Reese nodded solemnly. "He's probably just calling to tell me about Tyler. But I should take it just in—"

"Go, go, go," Sloane said. "Take it in the hall. Give yourself space."

Reese nodded dutifully and excused herself to the hall for whatever news was about to come their way. Time seemed to stretch on for years, when in fact it was only five minutes. Sloane sat on the edge of the bed, unsure what to do with herself. She straightened the hangers in the closet, fixed her hair in the bathroom mirror, and made sure the TV's remote was next to the bed. Anything to keep herself busy because the anticipation was almost too much. When Reese returned to the room, her face gave nothing away. In fact, it was carefully blank.

"Is it what I think it is?" Sloane asked, her heart hammering. "Was it *the* call?"

She wanted this for Reese because it was what Reese wanted, but that didn't stop the fear from twisting low in her chest. Did she have it in her to watch Reese, this woman she was growing to care for so deeply, step into a world where the margins were razor-thin and the risks so unforgiving?

Reese didn't answer right away.

She closed the door behind her with more care than necessary, like even the sound of it might shatter something fragile in the room. Her phone was still in her hand, screen dark now, the call ended.

She leaned back against the door and let out a long, shaky breath, like she'd been holding it for miles. "Yes," she said. "I can't believe it, but yes."

The words landed heavily.

Sloane crossed the space between them without thinking, stopping just short of touching her. "Yes," she echoed, softer. "As in—"

"As in Laurens Racing wants me as their reserve driver," Reese said. Her mouth curved, but the smile didn't quite land yet. "Jeremy says they're moving fast. They want me available immediately. Luckily, I'm already here. No plane to catch. We're meeting in the morning."

Sloane forgot how to breathe.

Pride surged first, intense and almost painful, followed immediately by fear, then awe. This was it. The thing Reese had been chasing. The door everyone pretended didn't exist for women in recent years, cracking open once again right in front of them.

"That's ... Reese," Sloane said, her voice giving her away. "That's huge. Congratulations!"

Reese nodded, eyes bright but unfocused, like she was still halfway inside the call. "I know. I keep waiting for the part where he calls back and says, 'Just kidding.'"

Sloane let out a breath that was half-laugh, half-sob. She reached out then, fingers curling into the sleeve of Reese's jacket, grounding herself as much as Reese. "They don't joke about things like this."

"No," Reese said quietly. "They really don't."

They stared at each other for a moment, suspended. Then something softened in Reese's face—a small smile, tentative at first, then blooming into something real. It filled the room. It filled Sloane. The fear receded, just for now. There would be time for that later.

Right now, Reese needed to be celebrated.

"Come here," Sloane said, opening her arms. "This is amazing news."

Reese moved immediately, and just before they came together, Sloane caught the tears gathering in her eyes. It stole her breath. She'd seen Reese under pressure, in pain, in moments that demanded steel, but never this. Never tears.

"After wanting this for so long, I just can't believe it's finally happened," Reese said against her shoulder. "I'm an F1 driver. Reserve or not. I'm in F1."

"You earned it. You should be incredibly proud of yourself," Sloane said, holding her tight. "You've worked so hard." She pulled back just enough to look at her. "And don't get me started on the raw talent. That part is wildly unfair to the rest of us."

Reese huffed a quiet laugh. "Stop. You're one of the most talented drivers alive."

Her fingers slipped to the first button of Sloane's blouse, undoing it with deliberate slowness.

"What are you up to?" Sloane asked, amused, watching Reese move to the second button. "What are you doing?"

"Celebrating," Reese murmured. "Yes?"

Sloane laughed softly. "Mm-hmm. But I have an idea. How about you just relax and enjoy? My turn."

Reese's brows lifted, surprise flickering into delighted interest. "Your turn?"

"You just got the call of a lifetime." Sloane leaned in, lips brushing the shell of Reese's ear. "That deserves a proper reward. And I think I know exactly how I want to give it to you."

She felt Reese's quick intake of breath, the way her body instinctively arched toward the words. Sloane's fingers found the hem of Reese's shirt, tugging it upward inch by inch, exposing warm skin and the quick rise and fall of her ribs.

"Lift your arms," Sloane whispered.

Reese obeyed instantly, letting Sloane peel the shirt over her head and toss it aside. The motion left Reese's dark hair mussed and wild, framing eyes that were already dark with anticipation.

Sloane took a moment just to look—really look—at the woman in front of her: flushed cheeks, parted lips, the faint tremor of excitement running through her. Then she closed the distance again, kissing Reese slowly and deeply while her hands mapped the newly bared skin, thumbs tracing the underside of Reese's bra, teasing without rushing.

Reese made a small, needy sound against Sloane's mouth.

Sloane smiled into the kiss. "Patience, hotshot. We've got all night."

"Oh, a new nickname," she breathed.

Sloane laughed quietly. "Well, it is now."

She guided Reese's hands to her own shoulders for balance, then dropped slowly to her knees, lips following the centerline of Reese's stomach. Reese's fingers threaded into Sloane's hair, gripping lightly—not pushing, just holding on.

And then Sloane began.

Outside, the world kept moving. Inside, they celebrated exactly the way Reese needed. When the orgasm ripped through her with Sloane still buried deep, it felt like Sloane was right where she was supposed to be.

"How do you do that so … well?" Reese asked some time later, as Sloane, lying naked on top of her, kissed her neck. "I don't think I've ever come that fast."

"You inspire me to do great things," Sloane said, smiling against her skin.

"You're dangerous when you decide to celebrate someone properly," Reese murmured, voice wrecked in the best way.

Sloane pressed a lazy kiss to her temple. "Only when it's you."

CHAPTER 18
HELLO, F1

Morning arrived gently.

Reese surfaced a little at a time, aware first of warmth, then of weight—Sloane's arm draped over her waist, her breath a steady, familiar rhythm against the back of Reese's shoulder. Sunlight filtered through the thin hotel curtains, painting everything gold and unhurried.

For once, Reese didn't feel the need to move right away.

She lay there, cataloging the quiet details: the faint crease in the pillow where Sloane's head rested, the way her fingers curled unconsciously, as if even in sleep she was making sure Reese was still there. The night before hadn't been dramatic or rushed or heavy with consequence. It had been easy. Laughter and conversation and a closeness that had settled in naturally, like it had always meant to.

Reese smiled to herself.

"Good morning," Sloane murmured behind her, voice still rough with sleep.

Reese's smile widened. "You're awake."

"Have been for a minute," Sloane admitted. Her thumb brushed a lazy arc along Reese's hip before sliding up to her right breast and cradling it. "Didn't want to break the spell."

Reese rolled onto her side so they were face-to-face. Up close, Sloane looked softer, more relaxed, and more beautiful than ever, the edges of her usual composure eased by rest and morning light. Reese reached up, smoothing a stray lock of hair back from Sloane's forehead.

"You okay?" Sloane asked.

Reese nodded without hesitation. "More than okay."

"Me too."

The certainty in her voice did something quiet but profound to Reese. It was everything she wanted to hear.

"One thing you don't know about me yet, is how much I enjoy the morning."

Reese raised a brow. "Yeah?"

"Can I show you?"

Reese nodded as Sloane slid down the bed. When warm lips found her center, Reese closed her eyes and swore. She parted her legs to give Sloane better access, aware that the orgasm was only right around the corner. Sloane's tongue circled her clit, teasing, until Reese began to rock her hips, seeking the payout she now desperately needed. Her body went warm and tight when Sloane started to softly suck, coaxing her closer and closer until the dam broke and pleasure raced through her with a force she hadn't been prepared for. "Fuck," she cried out, her fingers through Sloane's hair. "Oh, fuck. Oh, my God." Sloane continued to play as Reese rode out the remaining shock waves.

"See? I think that's kind of the perfect way to say good morning." Sloane then slid out of bed and walked naked, stunning and unapologetic, toward the bathroom. "Gonna grab a shower. See you soon."

"But I didn't get to repay the very sexy favor. Get back here. Or at least walk across the room naked again. In fact, always do that."

"Later!" Sloane stuck her head out. "You have an important morning, and I wanted to send you off right."

"I think you aced that one." Reese blew a strand of hair off her forehead and lay there an extra moment, her body heavy and happy on the cool sheets.

Sloane's voice floated in. "Also, I love the noises you make just before."

"I don't make sounds."

"God, you so do."

Reese laughed and turned over, grabbing her phone. She'd called Luke and her mom the night before and texted the news to The Starting Grid to ensure her friends would hear it from her before any of the race outlets, which she knew would be reporting that morning.

She took a look at the messages now, smiling at them.

Marissa had been first.

MARISSA

Fuck yeah, you saucy little race minx. You actually did it! Do you know how hard I'm going to hug you tomorrow?

Delaney must have seen the message early that morning, probably on her way to work out.

DELANEY

Literally shaking right now. Are you kidding me? Let's fucking goooooo!

Cassidy had yet to chime in, which meant she was probably not up yet, the resident sleepyhead of Formula Next. She'd once slept through her own practice session.

Room service arrived, Sloane's doing, and Reese, in her underwear and a black tank top, nursed an orange juice as she watched the sun rise higher and higher in the sky. Fresh from the shower and wearing a fluffy robe, Sloane came to stand behind her, her cheek pressed to the side of Reese's shoulder. "Excited?"

"Nervous."

"Pshh. Since when do you get nervous? This is a good thing," Sloane said finally, low and sure. Not the voice she used on pit walls or in meetings. This one was just for Reese, intimate and familiar. "No matter how it shakes out."

Reese nodded, though her chest felt too tight for words. "I keep thinking I'm going to walk in there and they'll squint a minute and realize I'm not what they ordered, like an erroneous Big Mac."

"They won't," Sloane said immediately, without hesitation. She tipped her forehead to Reese's. "And if it's not a fit, that says nothing about you. Remember, this is a business as much as it is a sport."

Something in the center of Reese's chest loosened, and she relaxed. Sloane had a way of adjusting her perspective right when she needed it. "You always know what to say. You're too wise. You've gotta stop it."

Sloane huffed softly. "Untrue. I just know *you* more and more each day."

For a few seconds, the world narrowed to the space between them. The hum of the hotel faded. The pressure of what came next paused, suspended.

"This has been a good morning."

"I couldn't agree more." Sloane brushed her thumb along Reese's jaw. "Go get ready," she said, gentler now. "Walk in there like you belong. Because you do."

Reese leaned in, pressing a quick kiss to Sloane's mouth— warm, grounding, full of promise and restraint all at once. "I'll see you after? Say yes."

"I feel like that's becoming your signature line." Sloane's smile was soft but sure. "I'll be right here."

Reese lingered one heartbeat longer, then stepped back before she could overthink it. Before the moment asked for more than either of them could give. It was perfect as it was.

Forty-five minutes later, Reese had just finished pulling on her jacket in her own room, nerves buzzing under her skin like static, when the knock came.

She frowned at the door, not expecting anyone.

When she opened it, Cassidy launched herself forward into Reese's arms. "Well, hi," Reese said with a laugh.

"Oh my God," Cassidy said, wrapping Reese in a fierce hug, her cheek pressed hard against Reese's shoulder. "You did it. I mean—you haven't done it yet—but you *did it*. You're gonna do it. I'm so proud of you that I can't stand it."

Reese laughed. "I hope to do it, and thank you."

Cassidy pulled back just long enough to grin at her, eyes bright and unapologetically damp. "I just saw the message, or you would have heard from me sooner." She shook her head, smiling helplessly. "The Starting Grid thread should come with the sound of an alert for important moments."

"Nope," Reese said cheerfully. "This is perfect information control. I'm enjoying the staggered celebration."

Cassidy hugged Reese again, tighter this time, rocking them both slightly like she couldn't help it. "Did I mention that I'm exponentially proud of you? You're going to walk in there and be brilliant and charming, the quickest on the track they've ever seen, and they're going to fall over themselves trying to figure out how they ever almost missed you."

Reese swallowed around the sudden lump in her throat. Cassidy spoke with such conviction that she was almost convinced it was true. "You really think so?"

Cassidy pulled back, hands still on Reese's arms, utterly sincere. "I *know* so. And also—" Her voice dropped conspiratorially. "If they don't, I will personally fight them. I'm slight, but I'm scrappy."

Reese laughed again, this time steadier. "I believe you."

Cassidy beamed, clearly pleased. "Good. Now go. Be amazing. Text the chat the second you're done because I'm going to be pacing laps around the garage waiting to hear. Oh, wait. Who's racing today for Ravensport?"

"One of the academy reserves they're pulling in from F3. Julie will engineer. I'm going to try not to be jealous."

"The web of drivers is a complicated math problem I'm still learning."

"You'll get there. Look how fast you've learned to drive a single-seater. One of the best defenders on the academy circuit."

"You're going to make me blush." Cassidy squeezed her once more, then finally let go, backing toward the hallway. "No matter what happens," she said, softer now, "this is huge. Don't forget that. Enjoy your moment. Eat some chocolate. Do a cartwheel."

Reese watched her go, heart full and humming. Cassidy was pure light, and she continued to prove it over and over again.

When the door closed, Reese stood there for a second longer, breathing in the support, the love, the fragile sense that everything was lining up just right.

Then she squared her shoulders, grabbed her keys, and headed out to meet her future.

The Laurens Racing hospitality suite was all clean lines and curated confidence, intimidating in the way it felt like grownups lived here. Glass, brushed metal, and the quiet hum of money doing what it always did best. *Well, well, Dorothy. You're not in Kansas anymore.* Reese took a breath before stepping inside, rolling her shoulders once, the way she did before climbing into a car.

Ready.

Shanelle Laurens was already there, standing near the windows with a tablet tucked under her arm. She turned as Reese entered, her smile sharp and appraising in a way that felt deliberate rather than unkind. A Black woman in a sport dominated by white men would surely have her work cut out for her, but Shanelle knew the business of racing more than anyone. She was well respected, but it hadn't always been that way.

"Reese," Shanelle said. "Right on time."

Reese returned the smile. "I try to be."

"Good to see you and thanks for heading straight in." Shanelle gestured toward the table. "We'll get started in a minute. I want you to meet someone first."

A man leaned back in one of the chairs, arms crossed, posture relaxed in the way of someone accustomed to taking up space. He stood when Reese approached. Tall, dark-haired, trimmed beard, immaculately put together in Laurens' team gear. She recognized Marco Faz right away. The reserve driver she'd be replacing. He now had Tyler Lock's seat for the rest of the season. This was just as big an opportunity for him as it was for Reese.

"Marco," he said, offering a handshake that was firm but brief. He sat down immediately. His eyes flicked over Reese in a quick, dismissive sweep before settling back on her face. "I drive for Laurens."

Reese blinked, caught off guard by the abrupt greeting. "Reese Maddox. The new reserve, apparently."

Marco's mouth twitched. "We'll see."

There it was. Subtle enough to deny later. Loud enough to hear clearly. Shanelle tossed a look her way, likely assessing if Reese had the thick skin she'd need in this environment. She did.

Reese smiled at Marco anyway, projecting calm. "That's usually how these things work."

Marco tilted his head, studying her now, curiosity edged with something sharper. "You've got quite the following," he said. "The internet likes you, which I suppose, is why Laurens does."

"All right, Marco," Shanelle said. It was a quiet warning. Shanelle didn't miss the implication. Neither did Reese.

"What?" he said, breaking into an oversized grin. "I'm just kidding around with the new kid in school."

"I like to give people something to watch," Reese said evenly.

Marco let out a quiet laugh. "Sure. But this isn't karting. Or the girls playing make-believe at the academy thing. This is Formula 1. Pressure's different."

Reese held his gaze. "So I've heard."

"But I'm sure you'll look good on camera."

For a beat, the air between them tightened. Marco was clearly waiting for Reese's nerves to kick in, for bravado, for Reese to overreach. She gave him none of it.

Shanelle stepped in smoothly. "Marco, Reese's data from the academy speaks for itself. We didn't bring her in for optics, so let's move past it."

Marco shrugged. "You got it, boss."

But his eyes said something else entirely.

Shanelle gestured toward the table. "Let's get started. Reese, I want to walk you through what the reserve role actually looks like. Expectations. Access. Opportunity."

Opportunity. The word landed with weight.

Reese took her seat, spine straight, pulse even. She didn't look at Marco again—not because she couldn't handle him, but because she didn't need to.

If he wanted to underestimate her, she'd let him. She was playing the long game and planned to win.

The meeting wrapped up with polite efficiency, handshakes, and a few smiles that felt authentic rather than forced, and then Shanelle Laurens stood, smoothing a hand over the front of her blazer as if she were mentally shifting gears.

"Race days move fast," she said. "No point pretending otherwise. We'll get you set up to observe from the garage."

Reese nodded, heart ticking up a notch. *Garage.* This was getting real.

A team coordinator appeared almost immediately, badge already in hand, and Reese had just enough time to sling her bag higher on her shoulder before she was being ushered down a hallway that smelled faintly of coffee and something metallic she'd never been able to name but always associated with racing.

Samara and her crew stood off to the side to get some B-roll of Reese's first day in Formula 1. As always, she pretended they weren't there, resisting the urge to wave to Samara and shout that she'd actually done it.

They moved briskly past glass-walled offices, past engineers bent over laptops, past doors marked with names Reese recognized from broadcast graphics and Wikipedia rabbit holes. She caught glimpses of monitors flashing sector times and weather overlays. The sport she loved, stripped of glamour and humming with urgency. She was already addicted.

As they neared the garage, the sound hit first.

Engines snarling to life. Radios crackling. Impact guns barking. It was louder than the academy paddock, sharper somehow, like everything had been tuned one degree tighter.

"This is home base," the coordinator said, handing Reese a headset. "You'll stay behind the line. No stepping forward unless someone waves you in."

Reese slid the headset on, breath catching as the world of Laurens Racing unfolded in front of her.

The cars sat like coiled animals, bodywork gleaming under the lights. *Beautiful.* Engineers swarmed with practiced choreography, hands, tools, and voices overlapping. It was chaos, but the kind that made sense if you knew the language.

"Does anyone know who won the Formula Next feature race?" she asked.

One of the engineers slid his headset behind his ear. "Delaney Rhodes by 0.4 seconds."

Reese sucked in air and hooted loudly, which pulled quite a few head swivels. "Sorry. Big win is all. Her first this season." It was like Delaney knew it fell to her now, and Reese couldn't have been prouder. Did she proceed to do a little silent dance in front of her chair? Hell yeah, she did. She fired off a text message to The Grid so it would be there when her friends retrieved their phones again. She imagined the look on Delaney's face when she'd emerged from the car, all of it likely having happened during her meeting inside, and felt a pang of regret.

Across the garage, she made eye contact with Marco Faz as

he slid into the Laurens's car, which prompted him to wink at her. And not the friendly kind. Ezra Fernandez was the second driver for Laurens. He paused in front of her on his way to his car.

"Nice driving these past few weeks," he said, and shook her hand. "Glad you're joining us. Let me know if you need anything. I got a few hot tips on this car."

Reese stared at the absolutely gorgeous car Laurens had developed, a car that she'd now be meticulously learning around the clock. She was scheduled for sim time later that day and would be afforded a few practice sessions as soon as possible. She adjusted her red Laurens ball cap and smiled, relieved to be on good terms with at least half of the team's driver population. "I'll take whatever you have. Have a good race, Ezra."

The next ninety minutes passed in a blur.

Formula 1 didn't breathe the way the academy did. There were no feel-good exchanges or pauses where adrenaline ebbed. Everything here moved with intent. Even stillness felt deliberate.

Reese stayed behind the line, headset snug over her ears, absorbing the rhythm. Voices layered over one another discussing strategy, tire temps, and when to overtake—all spoken in shorthand so efficient it felt almost private. In F2 or F3, she'd understood every word instantly. Here, she caught most of it, enough to know how much more there was to learn.

And no one slowed down for her. That, more than anything, was the difference.

She wasn't the story or the focus here. Conversations skimmed past her on their way to bigger moments. No one cared if she looked composed or rattled. They cared about the day's results.

By the time the checkered flag waved, the garage nodded along with the midfield results. Ezra had finished late in the points, and Marco had finished P21, scoring none for the team. There was a meeting here, a quiet word there about what could have been executed better, and already the focus had turned forward. Data to review. Decisions to make. Another race always waiting.

Reese pulled off her headset slowly, still in a bit of a daze. This is what these folks did week after week.

Around her, Formula 1 continued on without pause, vast and unbothered by her presence. And somehow, that made her chest ache in the best possible way.

She wasn't visiting this world. She wasn't borrowing it.

Standing there, surrounded by noise and purpose and history, Reese Maddox realized something that hit softly but resonated.

This was her life now. And, damn, if she wasn't ready to get behind the wheel and earn her place.

CHAPTER 19
WINE, CHEESE, AND MONZA

Sloane sat in the small room that had been converted into her office inside the academy's mobile suite, decompressing from the chaotic weekend where more had happened than she'd ever imagined possible. She'd arrived in Italy as one version of herself and would be leaving feeling entirely altered by so many unforeseen events. Monza had a way of accelerating everything: speed on the track, speed in decision-making, speed in life changes, and there was nothing to do but roll with each new development. She was proud of herself for not reaching for control, but instead bracing herself for whatever came next.

"It couldn't have come at a better time," Veronica said, breezing into the room in black yoga pants, designer tennis shoes, and a Formula Next tee. She handed Sloane a bourbon on the rocks to cap off what had been a whirlwind of a Sunday. It had somehow morphed into their once-a-week tradition. From tennis balls to hard liquor in the office. They'd come a long way.

"What couldn't have?" Sloane asked, swirling the stormy liquid, as if she were a workaholic from the 1960s.

"Well, I only talk in headlines."

Sloane laughed. "Obviously. You're Veronica Fucking Vance. I take it we're talking about Laurens pulling Reese?"

"See? You're with me. And it's not just great for Reese's career and the academy's legitimacy, but for you."

"Why? Because now I don't have to go out of my way to make sure there's no bias in how I work with the drivers?"

Veronica touched her glass to Sloane's. "Exactly. You get to have your Reese and eat—"

"I'm going to pause you right there."

Veronica laughed, carefree and melodious. "Live it up, Sloane. Enjoy every minute of this dalliance. You deserve the fun more than anyone else I know."

"Fun." Sloane stared at her glass, examining the word.

Veronica watched her, thoughtful. "Unless it's more than that. I shouldn't presume."

The truth was that Sloane's feelings for Reese were growing much faster than she was prepared for. They were scary, jumbled, wonderful, and somehow had a mind of their own. Sloane felt like she'd boarded the most exhilarating roller coaster and just wished someone would hand her a map of the twists and drops. Even now, she was checking the clock, wondering when she might hear how Reese's day had gone with Laurens, her heart squeezing with hope that it had been a good one. She wasn't at all used to this feeling of her happiness tethered to another person's.

She exhaled slowly, prepared to be forthright. "It might be more than that."

"Yeah," Veronica said quietly. "I'm picking up on that now."

Sloane took that first startling sip, and the liquid burned a trail down her throat and made her lips buzz. But she'd earned it. Their day had been killer, packed with a team principal meeting, a round of press, a quick check-in with each duo of drivers, and, of course, the race and podium celebration, where Delaney Rhodes had risen to the occasion, leading her team to a P1 finish like a damn pro. Sloane liked seeing the wealth shared and a driver like Delaney finally get her moment to shine. It was good for all of them.

"I missed her today at the academy. I kept expecting her to come around the corner, and then when she didn't, my chest tugged a little bit, and I wondered if her day was a good one."

"Oh, I'm enjoying this very much," Veronica said, tapping her bottom lip with her finger. "You should see the faraway look you just got in your eyes when you talk about her, like the sexiest scene in the movie just came on."

"Well, that's because in my brain, it did."

"And the sex?"

"Veronica. Shockingly good." She dropped her tone just in case. "I mean, I've had good before. James from back in the day was fine, and then Kristin right before the accident was amazing."

"Oh, I remember Kristin," Veronica said with an appreciative eyebrow raise. "She loved fruit. Everywhere she went, she looked for a bowl of it."

"We had a lot of chemistry. I didn't think sex got better." She closed her eyes. "It does."

"Well, now I have goose bumps. And I need the best sex ever." She looked around the room as if she might find it. "You're making me intensely jealous."

"Don't be yet. You ready for the flip side?"

Veronica made a circular gesture with her glass. "Why rain on this glorious parade?"

"Focus."

Her shoulders sagged. "Fine."

Sloane paused for a moment and regrouped. "She's young. That gives me pause."

"She's not that young. Her frontal lobe is fully formed."

Sloane shot Veronica a look. "Grasping and you know it."

"I realize she's a twenty-something, and you find yourself pleasantly nestled in your thirties."

"Nestled? God. Is it worse than I thought?"

"I don't think your ages are a deal-breaker. You may have to stay up on all the current lingo, however. It will take effort, Sloane, to be cool."

"I think you just slapped me across the face."

"In the name of advice, I did. The good news is that you *look* amazing. Hotter than I've ever seen you if we're being honest."

"Now we're talking." Sloane smiled around her glass, feeling a tiny bit taller. Then the cloud settled over the room, threatening to ruin it all. Didn't matter. She had to go there. "What if I can't handle her behind the wheel in F1? Putting herself in the same danger I know firsthand doesn't always end well." Veronica opened her mouth to speak, but Sloane raised her hand to stop her. "Because, and just entertain me here, what if her story has an even more final ending than mine did?"

"Final." Veronica paused. "Okay, I get it. You don't want to be sitting in the stands, cheering on the woman you love, only to watch a horrific crash that takes her life."

"It could happen."

"Of course it could. But it won't."

"You don't know that, and I'm not sure I have it in me to find out." She closed her eyes for a moment, absorbing the brunt of the concern, working to control her breathing, and then opened her eyes again. "What if I don't? What then? Maybe I get out now before my heart is fully gone."

"Is that what you want?" Veronica watched her. "To be free of this?"

"No. But I'm saying the quiet part out loud. To you. Because you're a safe zone."

"I think you also have to say it to Reese, who needs to know how you're feeling."

Sloane shook her head. "No. Uh-uh. I don't want to steal this moment from her. Do you remember what it was like when we were called up?"

"Easily the happiest day in my career."

"See? She deserves that same carefree celebration."

"Then let her have it. When the glow wears off, have a realistic conversation. The communication alone will make all this easier."

Sloane tapped the side of her glass with her nail. "Maybe."

There was a knock at the door. "Hey, in there. It's me."

"Reese," Sloane said quietly.

Veronica stood and opened the door. "Perfect timing," she said to Reese as she exited the office.

"Are you two drinking?" Reese asked, breaking into a smile. "I feel like I just busted into your secret clubhouse."

"You did, but you're allowed," Veronica said with a pat to her shoulder. "How are the big leagues treating you?"

"Not for the faint of heart," she said with an exhale. "But I think I'm finding my way."

"Let me know if you need anything. I know Shanelle Laurens and will pick up the phone and call in a favor if need be."

"Thanks," Reese said with a nod. "The academy has been great. I owe you a lot, Veronica."

"I provided an opportunity. You did the rest," Veronica said with a lift of her shoulder.

Reese looked in Sloane's direction. "I might have had a little help by way of ass-kicking, but I'm grateful for your kind assessment."

Veronica tapped the doorframe on her way out. "Haha. Have fun, you two."

Reese stepped into the office, and Sloane moved to close the door behind her. "Hi," she said, placing her back against the door. "How are you? Inquiring minds have been dying to know. And it's me. I'm the inquiring mind."

"Well, you. I'm mentally exhausted. Still a little nervous. In absolute heaven." A smile took over her whole face, and Sloane melted. "And three times happier now that I'm standing here with you."

"Yeah?" Sloane asked. "You're really beautiful when you're happy, Reese."

"Thank you." Reese slid a strand of hair behind Sloane's ear. "Can we get out of here?"

"Where are we going?"

"Anywhere you want. I just feel like open air."

"Then let's take a walk. It's our last night in Monza."

"Yes, please. I love that idea." Luckily, Sloane had already slipped out of her official academy-branded attire and into her favorite navy athleisure set. She grabbed a baseball cap for good measure and pulled her ponytail through.

Reese went completely still. "I had no idea how much I would love you in a ball cap."

Sloane touched the bill and laughed. "It's a limited engagement. Come on."

They left the paddock behind and slipped into the long, tree-lined paths of the park, where the Autodromo threaded through the green. The roar of engines had faded to a memory, replaced by cicadas and the soft crunch of gravel underfoot. Every so often, a stretch of fencing appeared through the trees before the path curved again and swallowed it whole.

"So," Sloane said, hands tucked into the pockets of her jacket. "Day one at Laurens."

Reese rolled her shoulders, like she was finally setting the weight down. "It was a ride." She smiled to herself. "Shanelle runs a tight ship. Clean and efficient, the whole machine. I spent the morning learning about their procedures, data flow, and who talks to whom. I was pretty invisible. But not in a bad way."

"That matters," Sloane said.

"It does." Reese kicked at a pebble. "The engineers were solid. One of them, Damon, walked me through everything like I already belonged there."

Sloane nodded, waiting.

Reese exhaled. "And then there was Marco Faz. Oh, Marco was interesting."

Sloane slowed, the path widening as the trees opened briefly to a glimpse of the track, now empty, sun glinting off the curb. "What about him?"

"He wouldn't look at me," Reese said. "Answered questions like I wasn't the one asking them. Asked if I was brought in for 'visibility.'" Her mouth tightened. "Shanelle corrected him. Calmly. But I think it's safe to say he didn't love my presence."

Sloane's expression went cool. "He sounds like an asshole. I already dislike him."

"He's not loud about it," Reese added. "Just dismissive. Like I'm an inconvenience."

"That's still a problem," Sloane said.

"I know." Reese's tone softened. "But it didn't shake me. I didn't feel out of my depth. Not once."

That won her a proud look. "Good. Because you're not."

Reese's mood lifted visibly. "I was thinking," she said, "we could head into town. I heard there's a place that does local cheeses—nothing fancy. Just very authentic. We can feel Italian for a little while."

Sloane's mouth curved. "Italian cheese and maybe some Italian wine after race day in Monza, Italy sounds less like a suggestion and more like a requirement."

"Oh, say Italian again."

"Italian," Sloane said in her most authentic accent.

"Well, that's incredibly sexy." Reese smiled, leaning closer as the park gave way to streets and storefronts, quaint and beautiful in the waning light. "Let's do it."

Behind them, the circuit rested, quiet and waiting, while Monza opened its doors. In a way, it felt like they were leaving the world they knew behind and setting off, just the two of them. When Reese took her hand, it felt like the most natural thing in the world, while also filling Sloane with a sense of wholeness she couldn't quite put into words. Her eyes filled and she blinked back the tears before Reese could discover them. What a sap she was becoming over something as simple as a field trip to town while holding hands. But it felt important to her.

"What's going on over there?" Reese asked.

"Nothing," Sloane said faster than she meant to. She turned away and blinked rapid fire to clear the evidence. "Nothing at all. Definitely not tears. More like stray moisture."

"Why in the world are you crying?" Reese gasped, fairly horrified.

"I don't know. You are to ignore me immediately and pretend this never happened. Pay no attention to the woman behind the tear curtain."

"What?"

"Are you too young for the *Wizard of Oz*? Oh, God. You are, aren't you?" She face-palmed. "What am I doing?"

Reese laughed. "I'm not at all sure what is happening right now, but I've seen the *Wizard of Oz* twice. Is that not enough? I can add five more watches this week if it will make you stop crying. Fifteen?"

Sloane gave Reese's hand a tug and brought them to a stop on a quiet sidewalk on a side street. A gelato shop sat on the corner. A barber shop was next door. She loved the city's quiet charm at the end of the day. "I was misty because I was happy. I'm thrilled for your new trajectory, for your success, and I'm enjoying the time we're spending together." She looked skyward to find the right words. "My life has been more than a little stagnant these last few years, and now it feels very much awake. Those tears come with gratitude for right where I am."

Reese didn't pause. She didn't ask questions. She didn't smile. She kissed Sloane softly, immediately, and with intention, stunning her silent. "Do you know that none of this would have happened for me without you walking into my life?" Reese said, cradling her face. Another kiss, unrushed. "And it wouldn't be half as wonderful without you here to experience it with me." The intensity of the moment rushed over Sloane, and she memorized what it felt like to be seen and appreciated by someone who was becoming incredibly important to her.

"Okay, that was beautiful, but if you keep talking that way,

I'm going to cry again—and I've officially hit my quota for one Italian sidewalk."

Reese laughed. "Got it. Emotional regulation break." She squeezed Sloane's hand. "We'll walk. We'll eat gelato. I'll try not to make you cry on every block."

They continued on, slower now, drifting toward the center of town where the streets widened, and the smell of bread and wine replaced the sweetness of sugar. Reese brushed her thumb over the back of Sloane's hand, casual but intentional, like she was testing a theory.

"You okay?" Reese asked, softer this time.

Sloane nodded. "Yeah. I'm great. But I wish it wasn't our last night."

"It's not." Reese bumped her shoulder. "So many other cities to explore together. So many."

A pause as they walked. "Is that what you want?"

"Without question."

"Good. Me too." Sloane meant it. She was sure about Reese, about this, about them. It was the future beyond that still scared her, the idea of standing trackside someday, heart in her throat, watching the woman she loved disappear behind the wheel at speeds that had already taken so much from her once before.

They found a small enoteca tucked between two shuttered storefronts, its door open, shelves crowded with bottles and wheels of cheese wrapped in paper and twine. Outside, a couple of tables spilled onto the sidewalk. Someone had strung lights overhead, and the glow was soft and comforting.

They ordered a glass of red each and a plate of local cheeses, the owner explaining each one with reverence and very exuberant gestures before leaving them alone.

"I think he feels strongly about the cheese," Sloane said. "So don't you take any wild cheese stances while we're here. You will *lose*."

"No, I wouldn't. I'm confident he wakes up in the morning, decides it's going to be another cheesefest of a day, and celebrates it in his kitchen. Probably with cheese. And then declares proudly, there'll be more cheese later. It's his work. It's his life. He's a cheeseman."

"Monger."

"That's a weird word."

Sloane raised her glass. "To more cheese." She took a bite of the hard Grana Padano and grinned. "And to your first day."

Reese took a sip, then studied her. "First of all, this wine is amazing. Very grapey. That's a technical wine tasting term. Write it down."

"Oh, immediately. I learn so much from you."

They sat in comfortable silence for a few moments, and Sloane caught Reese studying her.

"You might be overthinking again."

"Am I that obvious?"

"Only to me," Reese said gently. "You don't have to have it all figured out."

"I know." Sloane smiled, small but real. "But I like knowing you're here while I don't."

Reese reached across the table and laced their fingers together. "I'm not going anywhere."

The words landed quietly.

Sloane felt it then, that sense of wholeness again, familiar and warm, like something clicking into place. Monza had accelerated everything, yes, as Monza always did. But sitting there, wine between them, cheese for days, the night unfolding at its own pace, she realized something else too.

Some things didn't need speed.

Some things just needed time and the right person to hold your hand through town.

CHAPTER 20
THE DANCING DOTS

F1 was everything Reese had hoped it would be. It was fast, exacting, dazzling. It was relentless.

It moved like a small city that never slept, governed by its own rules and rhythms. The days blurred together in a flurry of events and schedules, with little give. The energy from the fans was electric, and the culture was like nothing she'd ever been a part of before. F1 was a huge fucking deal, and Reese now lived in that world.

The only problem was that she wasn't exactly *participating*.

As a reserve driver, her role lived on the outskirts. Reese was visible without being essential. She was presented to sponsors, ushered through fan events, left smiling for cameras, while the two actual drivers disappeared into strategy briefings and closed-door sessions. Reese became the face they could spare. The one who shook hands, answered questions, and posed beside the car for photos. In other words, the work no one else had time for.

She took it in stride. Publicly, at least.

Privately, she worked like someone trying to earn oxygen. Every spare minute went into her body and her brain—brutal workouts that left her shaking, hours logged in the simulator until the track burned itself into muscle memory, reaction drills that pushed her reflexes to their limits. She trained for heat and altitude, practiced in the Laurens car during the precious, tightly controlled sessions she was granted, and treated each lap like an audition that never really ended.

If they were watching, she wanted them to see everything.

Between races, her relationship with Sloane slipped into the long-distance category, which Reese quickly discovered she hated. What they had built in close quarters didn't translate cleanly across oceans and time zones. They lived now in the thin space of texts and voice notes, missed calls, and FaceTime conversations snatched when their schedules briefly overlapped.

Sloane had kept her client roster and returned to consulting during the week, filling the gap left by the academy with work that demanded just as much of her. Even at home, she was pulling long hours, bouncing between meetings and deadlines, her days packed tight.

Reese, meanwhile, was based at Laurens's headquarters in Enstone, England, a place she was still getting used to. The time difference did them no favors. When Reese's days finally slowed, Sloane's were often just hitting their stride.

One night, Reese lay on her back in the dark, sheets twisted around her legs, her body sore from way too many lower-body reps. The room was silent except for the low hum of the heater. England slept.

She picked up her phone and stared at it for a moment, thumb hovering, before typing.

> Send me photos of your living room.

The reply came faster than she expected.

SLOANE

> My living room?

Reese smiled to herself.

> Yes. Right now. I need to see it.

There was a pause, long enough for Reese to picture Sloane glancing at her phone, one brow lifting in that sexy way she had when her interest had been piqued. God, Reese wished they were in the same room right now.

SLOANE

> That's a new one. And not at all the kind of photo I thought you were about to ask for.

Reese rolled onto her side, hugging the pillow.

> I miss where you are. I want to see it.

A beat. Then another message.

SLOANE

> You know, I could've taken that in a very different direction.

> I know. 

Reese laughed as she typed.

> I wish you would.

The photos came through a moment later.

The first was a wide shot featuring Sloane's couch and low coffee table with late-afternoon light slanting in through the windows. She had curtains, not blinds. The second shot was closer, messier. A throw blanket draped over the arm of the sofa, the corner folded the way Sloane always folded it, without thinking.

Reese's chest tightened.

She typed before she could stop herself.

You still do that with the blanket.

The reply was immediate.

SLOANE

Yeah. Habit.

Reese pressed the phone lightly to her sternum, the ache settling in.

I miss that. 🩶

There was no joke this time. Just:

SLOANE

Me too.

The dots danced. Reese loved those dots, especially when they were coming from Sloane. She'd wait on them all day if she had to, the flutter in her abdomen her new favorite drug.

SLOANE

Four more days 'til I see you.

I'm staring at the clock. I hate clocks now. They move too slowly.

But something interesting had happened in the time they'd been apart. They got to know each other. Not just the big stuff, but the little things that made a person a person. When you text with someone all day, every day, even staying up into the middle of the night to do so, the pretense comes down in the most wonderful kind of reveal.

Reese learned the patterns of Sloane's days the way you learned a track, by paying attention. She knew when Sloane's morning caffeine hit because the texts got sharper, more decisive. She knew when the day had gone sideways because Sloane stopped using punctuation altogether. She learned that Sloane paced when she was thinking, that she folded laundry while on calls she didn't want to be on, that she hated being idle but loved being still.

Sloane learned Reese, too. Not the public Reese from the polished interviews or the grin that she used to sell for sponsors, but the one who overthought everything at 2:17 a.m. The one who needed reassurance that she pretended she didn't. The one who talked through corners in her head when she couldn't sleep, replaying laps she hadn't even driven yet.

> SLOANE
>
> You're spiraling.

> I am strategically analyzing.

> SLOANE
>
> You're catastrophizing.

> Wow. Rude. Accurate. But rude.

They became each other's first text of the day and last at night without ever naming it as such. In a way, it felt like she was never quite without Sloane, even if she was very much without her.

> I think the rear grip issue isn't the car.

Reese had sent the message just after midnight.

> I think it's me hesitating.

Sloane didn't answer right away. Then:

> SLOANE
>
> You don't hesitate. You check twice. There's a difference.

That one stuck with Reese. She carried it into the next practice session like a talisman. Sloane had been right. Of course she had.

They talked through everything. Reese's frustration at being sidelined. Sloane's exhaustion. They shared photos of hotel rooms, airport lounges, bad catering, a particularly aggressive espresso machine. Once, Reese sent a blurry picture of the sky out her window.

Can't sleep.

SLOANE

Me neither. Tell me what it looks like.

Reese did. She described the color, the quiet, the way the world felt as if it had paused. And Sloane listened. Really listened. The way she always did.

Sloane wasn't just her girlfriend; she was Reese's person.

It wasn't dramatic. It wasn't declared. But it was unmistakable. This was a new phase built on messages sent from different time zones, across oceans, in the quiet certainty that whatever happened next, they were no longer doing it alone.

"Welcome to Madrid," the gate agent said as Sloane stepped off the jet bridge. Heat met her immediately—not the sticky kind, but dry and heavy, carrying the smell of pavement and jet fuel. Sunlight flooded the terminal in a way that felt almost aggressive after California's softer glow, bouncing off glass and steel and making everything look newly polished. This city didn't ease you in. It announced itself.

Normally, Sloane would meet up with Reese at the Grand Prix circuit, in this case, the Madring. But after the past two weeks apart, Reese had messaged that she'd meet Sloane at the airport, choosing not to wait a second longer than she had to for them to be together again.

It felt strange to say, but these two weeks apart had only made her feelings for Reese grow. She had become part of Sloane's everyday life. It was Reese she told if she spilled a jar of marinara sauce in the kitchen or laughed with about whatever ridiculous thing Marco Faz said during his interview with *Grid and Glory*. Sometimes they called just to briefly hear each other's voices. The distance had been brutal, and the constant messaging felt like trying to warm your hands over a screen, comforting, but never enough.

Sloane made her way to baggage claim, her heart hammering with excitement as she scanned the throngs of people waiting for luggage, squinting at screens, or trying to find their loved ones.

Then she saw her.

Reese was impossible to miss, not because she was taller or louder than anyone else, but because she looked *different*. Sharper. Stronger, somehow. Maybe it was the easy confidence in her stance, but whatever it was, it hit Sloane low and immediately. She was dressed in training gear, which today meant a fitted T-shirt, track pants slung low on her hips, and a ball cap pulled down over her eyes. But there was nothing casual about the way she filled the space. Reese looked *beautiful* in a way that stole air, the kind of beauty that wasn't about effort but about being exactly Reese.

Sloane briefly forgot that they were in an airport. The noise, the chaos, the rules all fell away. All she could see was Reese, strong and tan and devastatingly familiar, her mouth curved into that half-smile Sloane knew was a tell. The one Reese wore when she was trying not to show how much she felt.

The moment their eyes locked, Reese stopped moving, like the world had been put on pause just long enough for Reese to take her in. A full smile blossomed on those ridiculously kissable lips.

For two weeks, they'd lived in pixels and time stamps, in jokes typed at odd hours and long silences filled with imagining what the other one was doing or wearing. None of it had prepared Sloane for this.

Reese crossed the distance first.

She didn't hesitate or slow. She dropped her phone somewhere near her pocket and caught Sloane by the waist, momentum carrying them together. Sloane barely had time to breathe before Reese's arms wrapped around her in a devastatingly familiar fashion. She never wanted to leave that embrace.

"There you are," Sloane breathed, forehead pressed to Reese's collarbone, aware of her warmth, the press of muscle, and the smooth skin she'd missed so desperately.

"I can't believe you're finally here," Reese said. "Hi."

"Hi," Sloane whispered, holding her tight, memorizing every detail. The familiar smell of her clean cotton laundry detergent, the melon of her shampoo, the warmth of her skin. She'd missed all of it.

They stayed like that longer than was reasonable or probably polite as travelers maneuvered around them. Reese's hands slid up Sloane's back, thumbs pressing in as if checking that she was real. Sloane's fingers curled into the fabric at Reese's waist.

"You look—" Reese started, then stopped and shook her head. "I had sentences earlier. Real ones. They made sense. They were good. Now, nothing." She pantomimed her thoughts floating away.

Sloane laughed softly, still a little stunned to be standing in front of Reese in real time. "You flew all the way here and forgot how to talk?"

"I forgot everything except you," Reese said, then leaned in again, forehead touching Sloane's. "I missed this. I think we can't be apart anymore. I'm declaring it."

"Oh? Are you moving to Venice Beach between races?"

"Or you could come to Enstone and pick up an accent. British Sloane is wildly intriguing to me."

Sloane laughed. "I do make a mean blueberry scone."

"Do you know what that does to me? Domesticity, when you

live the kind of travel schedule that we do, is maybe my sexiest fantasy."

"Let's see what we can establish in Madrid."

Reese was officially lodged by Laurens Racing at a neighboring hotel to the one booked by the academy, but Sloane couldn't imagine a world where she and Reese didn't stay together for the length of their time in Madrid. She knew one thing for certain: it wouldn't be long enough.

The ride into the city felt suspended in time, the two of them tucked into the back seat while Madrid streamed past the windows in flashes of color and motion. She caught scooters weaving through traffic and café tables spilling onto sidewalks. Reese sat close enough that their knees brushed every time the car slowed, close enough that Sloane could feel her warmth without touching. They talked easily, laughing about nothing and everything, the sound of Reese's voice filling the space like it belonged there. Every so often, Sloane caught herself stealing a glance at Reese's profile or her hands folded loosely in her lap, at the sideways tug of her smile, and each time, the sight landed fresh and disarming, like she'd forgotten all over again how much she liked being near her. She was feeling lucky, incredibly lucky. Outside, the city hummed and honked and lived, but inside the car, it was just them, happy and unguarded, already counting the minutes until they could be alone.

"What's on your schedule?" Sloane asked, which was code for *how much time do we have?*

"I have the fan zone at four. Samara's coming to film the whole thing. We'll probably do a quick one-on-one on camera after. A meeting in the paddock after that. A quick round of press where they'll ask me the same questions about being female in a—"

"Male-dominated sport," Sloane finished. "I wish I could tell you that it eventually goes away. It doesn't."

"I think that just means we need to pull up the others, invade

F1 as a group." Reese smiled against the headrest. "That's where you come in."

"I will do everything in my power to make sure that happens. Speaking of, we already know Marissa's at the top of her game, but Delaney, since you moved up, has really been turning up the heat. Danielle is going to have her hands full as she finishes out the season."

"I still hate that she's going to win the whole thing."

"If Marissa can consistently make podium and Danielle falls completely out of the points for a couple of races, it's mathematically possible she won't emerge as drivers' champion."

"Stop talking dirty to me," Reese said with a shake of her head. A pause hit. "I can't wait to see them."

"The Starting Grid? You girls." She kind of loved their group chat name and the way Reese had found a core support system within the drivers' ranks. "You all have gotten really tight. Reminds me of coming up with Veronica. That bond is unique and strong." She squeezed Reese's hand. "I'm happy you have them."

"It feels very full circle, especially since Veronica brought us all together. I owe her a lot." She kissed the back of Sloane's hand, making it clear it wasn't just The Starting Grid she was grateful for. "Now, how far away is this hotel anyway?"

"Why ever are you so impatient?"

"You'll find out," Reese said with a look that left absolutely no doubt she had plans and very little intention of waiting long for them. Sloane had absolutely zero complaints.

CHAPTER 21
VISIBLE, NOT ESSENTIAL

Reese laid out her clothes for the fan zone event later that afternoon while Sloane sat on the edge of the bed, blinking at her open laptop. She needed ten minutes to catch up on all she'd missed in the air, and then she and Reese had a little time to themselves. Reese couldn't wait until Sloane was all hers. She looked amazing with her hair in a messy pony, her crystal-blue eyes bright, and that *gonna handle it* attitude that drove Reese wild. "It sounds like Veronica's team meeting has morphed into a champagne reception. Apparently, she's landed a big fish."

"By fish, do you mean sponsor?" Reese asked, straddling Sloane from behind, and sweeping her hair to the side, exposing her neck. She was obsessed with Sloane when she had her work face on, all focused and dialed in. It made her want to undo every ounce of that concentration. She placed a slow kiss on her collarbone. Just that slight contact prompted Reese's entire body to come alive. Sloane smiled as she studied her inbox.

"I do mean sponsor. She's very excited and wants to celebrate. If I had to guess, sending an academy driver to F1 has certainly garnered them some clout."

Reese kissed higher, taking her time. "Mm-hmm. Wonder who that could be."

"No idea. Some brunette with amazingly talented lips. It's warm in here," Sloane said, looking around. "I think I'm gonna take this off." She began to unbutton her forest green top, leaving her in the black, low-cut tank top beneath. The generous line of cleavage slammed Reese in the throat. She swallowed and slid closer behind Sloane, her hands settling at Sloane's hips like they belonged there. "You do that on purpose," she said softly, voice rough around the edges. "You know I'm addicted to your breasts. And it's totally working."

Sloane glanced back at her, utterly unbothered. "What did I do?"

"Wear a tight top that shows off amazing amounts of cleavage that make me want to lick and kiss all over your body until you scream my name." Reese leaned in again, her mouth brushing the skin just below Sloane's ear.

"Oh." Sloane swallowed.

"Mm-hmm." Another kiss just under Sloane's jaw. She smelled vanilla and citrus. "You're wildly sexy right now, and I'm wondering how fast I can make you come. But slow might be more fun."

Sloane sucked in air. "Well. I have no idea how you can do what you just did to me with words, but here we are." She closed the laptop slowly before setting it aside. "Good," she said. "Because after that email, I'm officially off the clock."

Reese's hands tightened, just slightly. "Finally."

Sloane turned and slid her arms around Reese's neck, close enough now that their lips nearly touched. "You've been patient while I worked," she murmured. "I appreciate that."

Reese smiled, all promise. "I've been *counting the minutes* until I fuck you properly."

Sloane closed her eyes, wrapping her arms around Reese as she kissed Sloane's neck with precision.

"Do you know that I've been undressing you in my mind

since the moment I saw you? I have. So maybe it's me who will be doing the fucking."

Reese's eyes went wide, and she allowed herself to be lowered onto the bed with Sloane in that fucking black tank top on top. That tank top was going to taunt her for months. It was going to replay itself in sharp, merciless flashes: the way the fabric dipped low enough to make her mouth go dry, the faint sheen of skin she'd memorize without meaning to, the soft pull of gravity every time Sloane leaned over her. Months from now, Reese would see that same cut in a mirror or on a stranger, and her body would respond instantly, remembering black cotton stretched warm over round breasts, Sloane's weight above her, and the exact moment her control had slipped clean through her fingers.

"Take off your pants for me," Sloane said, sliding to the side. "I want to watch."

Oh, Reese liked that very much. Wordlessly, she slid her thumbs beneath the waistband of her track pants, Sloane's eyes on her movement, focused and unmistakably hungry. If she wanted a show, Reese would enjoy giving it to her. She eased the pants down her legs, kicking them off, and waited for further instruction. "Those, too," Sloane said, eyes on the black bikinis that matched her bra. Her wardrobe was full of sets that she'd found Sloane appreciated very much.

Reese slid the fabric down her legs inch by slow inch. She felt Sloane's gaze like a physical touch, tracing every revealed curve. When the bikinis joined the track pants on the floor, Reese stayed kneeling on the bed, naked now except for her bra, waiting. Heart hammering. Already slick with anticipation.

Sloane's voice came low, reverent. "Look at you."

The words landed like a spark straight to Reese's core. She bit her lip, fighting the urge to squirm.

"Reese. You're beautiful," Sloane continued. "Arch for me a little. Let me see you."

Reese obeyed instantly, clasping her wrists at the small of her back, chest lifting, offering herself up. The position made her breasts strain against the lace, nipples hard and visible through the thin fabric. Sloane's eyes darkened.

"Beautiful," she murmured. "Can you turn around for me? Face the headboard."

Reese's breath caught. She shifted slowly onto all fours, deliberately—making it a show because she knew Sloane liked to watch. Palms planted on the mattress, knees spreading just enough, ass up, back dipped in a gentle curve. Vulnerable. Exposed. And so fucking turned on that she could feel the heat between her thighs.

Sloane moved behind her without hurry. The bed dipped as she knelt there, close enough that Reese could feel the warmth radiating off her body. A hand smoothed up the back of Reese's thigh, light at first, then firmer, possessive. Reese shivered.

"Spread your knees a little more," Sloane instructed gently. "Just like that. Perfect."

Reese complied, opening herself wider. The air felt cool against her wetness, heightening every sensation. *God.*

Sloane's fingers traced lazy circles over Reese's ass, then dipped lower, skimming the sensitive skin at the crease of her thigh. Teasing. Never quite where Reese needed her most. It was excruciating in the most wonderful sense.

"Please," Reese whispered, the word slipping out before she could stop it.

Sloane placed a kiss on the small of her back. "I love when you ask so sweetly."

Her hand finally slid between Reese's legs, palm cupping her fully for a moment, letting Reese feel the pressure without movement. Then two fingers parted her, stroking slowly, gathering slickness. Reese's hips rocked back instinctively, chasing more.

"I've got you," Sloane said. Her free hand pressed gently at the small of Reese's back, holding her in place. "Let me take care of you, okay?"

Reese whimpered but obeyed, trembling as Sloane's fingers

circled her clit, slow, deliberate swirls that built the ache without mercy. Then they slid lower, pressing inside her in one smooth glide. Reese gasped, walls clenching around the intrusion. Sloane didn't thrust right away. She curled her fingers instead, stroking that perfect spot inside while her thumb kept lazy pressure on Reese's clit.

The rhythm built gradually, coming in unhurried strokes from behind, each one dragging against every sensitive nerve. Sloane's other hand roamed: gripping Reese's hip, sliding up to palm her breast through the bra, pinching a nipple just hard enough to make Reese moan.

"You feel so good like this," Sloane murmured, leaning forward so her chest brushed Reese's back. "All open for me."

Reese could only nod, words lost in the mounting pleasure. Her arms shook, and her thighs burned from holding the position. But she didn't move. Didn't dare.

Sloane's pace quickened, just enough. Fingers curling harder, thumb circling faster. Reese's moans turned desperate, body tightening, coiling.

"Come for me," Sloane whispered against her ear. "Right here, just like this."

The command tipped her over. Reese shattered with a broken cry, pulsing around Sloane's fingers, hips jerking despite the hand still holding her steady. Waves of pleasure rolled through her until she was spent, forehead dropping to the sheets, breath ragged.

Sloane eased her fingers out slowly, soothing with gentle strokes along Reese's back and thighs. She pressed soft kisses to the curve of Reese's spine, then helped her collapse onto her side, curling around her from behind.

Reese turned her head, seeking Sloane's mouth. The kiss was gentle, almost reverent. Their lips lingered in soft, open presses, no rush, no demand.

"You just wrecked me," Reese managed, shaking her head. "I came so hard. Fuck."

"There *was* fucking," Sloane smiled against her lips. "I hope you liked it."

Reese laughed breathlessly. "God help me, I did."

They stayed tangled like that for a few quiet minutes, Sloane tracing idle patterns on Reese's hip, Reese's fingers laced with hers. That is, until Reese's thoughts turned to Sloane's body, her curves. Her hunger slid back into place, and she slid on top. Sloane landed on her back beneath her, that black tank top still clinging.

"Just what is happening now?" Sloane asked, staring up at Reese.

"I think it's your turn."

"Oh yeah?" Sloane asked, blue eyes darkening.

Reese settled her thighs on either side of Sloane's hips, palms braced beside Sloane's head. She dipped low, brushing her lips against Sloane's ear. "You've been so patient. But I can feel how worked up you are."

Sloane's hips lifted instinctively, seeking friction and finding none. "Reese ..."

Reese slid one hand down Sloane's body, over the taut fabric of the tank top, across the soft swell of her breast, thumb circling a hard nipple through the cotton until Sloane gasped. Then she focused lower. Reese dipped her fingers beneath the waistband of Sloane's pants, finding her soaked through her underwear.

"You're so wet," Reese whispered, voice reverent. She pressed the heel of her palm against Sloane's clit, rubbing slow, firm circles over the damp fabric. Sloane's thighs parted wider on a shaky exhale.

"I'm—fuck, I'm already so close," Sloane admitted.

Reese's eyes darkened with satisfaction. "Then let me finish what I started."

She shoved Sloane's pants and underwear down just far enough, not bothering to remove them completely. Two fingers slid through her slickness, gathering wetness, then pressed inside in one smooth glide. Sloane arched hard, a low moan tearing from her throat. Reese curled her fingers immediately, stroking that same perfect spot she knew so well, thumb finding Sloane's clit and rubbing in tight, relentless circles.

It didn't take long.

Sloane's hands flew to Reese's shoulders, nails digging in. Her hips rocked up to meet every thrust, breaths coming in sharp, desperate pants. "Reese—right there—don't stop—"

Reese leaned down, capturing Sloane's mouth in a kiss as she drove her fingers harder, faster. Sloane broke—body locking tight, a choked cry muffled against Reese's lips as she came hard, walls fluttering and clenching around Reese's fingers.

Reese kept the pressure present through the aftershocks, drawing it out until Sloane went limp beneath her, chest heaving.

When Sloane finally opened her eyes, they were glassy, soft. She reached up, cupping Reese's face with trembling fingers.

"You're … unfairly good at that," she managed, a breathless laugh escaping.

Reese grinned, pressing a final, lazy kiss to Sloane's swollen lips. "Only with you."

They stayed tangled like that, sated with heartbeats slowing, until the demands of the world outside the room started to creep back in. But for now, it could wait.

By midmorning the next day, Reese had learned the exact weight of a Laurens team polo.

It wasn't heavy in the hands, but it carried expectation. Or the idea of it. She tugged it straight as she stepped into the fan zone, smile already in place, as the cheers hit. She waved, she high-fived. This was all a part of it.

"Reese! Over here!"

"Can you take a photo with my daughter? She loves you!"

She signed caps, cards, and even the occasional forearm

thrust eagerly over the barrier. Phones everywhere. Parents nudging kids forward. She crouched to eye level, answered questions about how hot the car got, simulator hours, and what it felt like to stand in the F1 paddock wearing *that* logo. She gave them the version of herself that they wanted, even if it zapped every ounce of her energy.

Because it was her full-time job now.

After that, a PR rep peeled her away for a quick media hit. Two questions. Three minutes.

"How does it feel being part of the Laurens race weekend?"

"Incredible," Reese said without hesitation. She tacked on a big smile. "I'm learning constantly. Watching the data, listening in on strategy meetings. Um, it's everything you want at this level."

"And any chance we see you in the car today?"

The question landed lightly. Carelessly, even.

Reese smiled anyway. "Not today. But I'm ready when my number's called."

The answer was clean and professional, because she'd practiced it.

The pit walk came next. She moved with purpose through a corridor of noise with her headset on. Mechanics nodded. Engineers barely glanced up. She belonged there enough not to be questioned, but not enough to draw focus. And that was okay.

She stopped at the garage threshold, her gaze drawn to the car. She ignored the pit in her stomach, knowing it was still out of her reach. The ache of not knowing the next time she'd race was starting to gnaw at her. This was the order of things, though, and no amount of longing would take away the gratitude. Still … the ache persisted.

Someday. She told herself that as she watched the final checks, the choreography of a team preparing for battle without her. Four months ago, this would have felt impossible, so she could suck it up.

Still, a quieter thought followed.

When do I race again?

The question tightened her chest before she could stop it. She swallowed it down and forced her shoulders back. This wasn't the moment for impatience. This was everything she'd ever wanted, and wanting more might ruin it.

As she turned, she caught the look.

Marco Faz, already suited up, helmet under his arm. His gaze slid over her, dismissive and smug. A flick of the eyes that said *marketing hire.*

Reese held it. Didn't blink. Didn't smile.

Then she stepped past him, deeper into the garage, knowing her time would come soon. And when it did, no one, least of all Marco Faz, would be able to look past her again.

Later that night, while Sloane was buried in long, strategic meetings with Veronica, Reese went looking for the only people who understood. She found her friends holed up in Marissa's hotel room, and they all arranged in what could generously be called a circle. There were two of them on the beds, one cross-legged on the floor, one half-perched on the arm of the chair, all surrounded by the wreckage of room-service casualties.

Reese tried to articulate the struggle within. "It's my dream, and it's here, but …"

"It's still just out of your grasp," Delaney said, nodding like she knew. She did. They were all wired to be behind the wheel of a car, doing what they loved. It was one of the reasons they had such an easy shorthand. The three could complete her thoughts before she had them because they were their thoughts, too.

"It's only temporary," Marissa said, meeting her eyes. "And who knows when you'll get a break from the wheel like this again. Put it to use. Get yourself in absolutely impeccable shape both mentally and physically."

"But you know what?" Cassidy said. "It's okay to miss it, too." She reached up and squeezed Reese's hand from her regular spot on the floor. She definitely preferred it to furniture.

"And it's okay to bitch to us about it, because we're your people and we will bitch right back."

"I'd like to bitch about jet lag math," Marissa said, stretching her neck. "I don't know what time it is, what country I'm in, or why my body thinks it's 3 a.m."

Delaney didn't look up from her phone. "Time zones don't care about your feelings." She pointed at them with her bottle of sparkling water. "I'd like to bitch about this morning's meeting with my PR team. Apparently, my brand is 'approachable but mysterious.' I don't even know what that means."

"But you're so cute when you're brooding and mysterious," Reese said.

"I'm not aiming for cute," Delaney pouted in a move that was damn near a smolder.

"Too late," Reese said, ruffling her hair with nothing but unbridled affection.

Cassidy reached for a fry. "I answered an interview question today and realized halfway through I was still in yesterday. Like, spiritually."

Delaney nodded seriously. "That explains a lot."

"And why," Reese continued, sitting up now, "do all hotels either feel like sleeping on a cloud or a personal attack?"

"Fucking spite mattresses," Marissa said immediately. "That's what they are. Designed by someone who's never had hips. I figured that part out early in my career. It's criminal."

"And the pillows," Cassidy added. "Six decorative ones you're not allowed to touch, and zero that actually support your neck. I've written letters." A beat. "I've never sent them."

"The decorative pillows are there to judge you," Delaney said. "For moving them."

For a moment, no one spoke. The AC hummed.

"I know we complain," Reese said finally, softer now. "But I still can't believe this is our life."

Delaney's expression shifted. "Yeah. Same."

"Not sure I'd trade it, ya know?" Cassidy offered with a smile tugging. "Even for better pillows."

"The Starting Grid forever," Reese said, leaning into the cheese and placing a hand over her heart.

"Daily," Delaney laughed.

"Obsessively," Cassidy added.

Marissa smiled. "In this thing."

Reese let the moment settle because this was it. This improbable, hard-won life.

She could want and complain all she wanted, but she looked around the room and understood. She really was the luckiest.

CHAPTER 22
THE LONGEST MINUTE

Two weeks later, Sloane arrived at the Red Bull Ring in Austria, the mountains rising steep and green beyond the barriers, the crisp air a welcome change from the paddock heat. The track wound tightly through the hills, a contrast to Madrid's wide, flowing turns, demanding precision and patience on every corner. One wrong move and a driver would end their race instantly.

She moved through the garage with ease, absorbing the rhythm of the teams, the hum of engines, the scent of burned rubber always in the air. It felt good to be back. More than that, it felt settled. Somewhere along the way, she'd found her footing at the academy, no longer just surviving it, but belonging.

Plus, she was back in the throes of racing, the sport she loved with an intensity that had never dulled. Even after the accident. She worked alongside her best friend, someone who could finish her thoughts before she realized she was having them. And she was seeing a woman who, quietly and steadily, was becoming the center of her world.

She'd sent Reese off to work two hours earlier with a lingering kiss in the doorway of Sloane's hotel room, the kind that promised there would be more later. They'd allowed themselves a semi-lazy morning first, lounging in bed, tangled sheets, conversation drifting everywhere and nowhere.

"I know you love sliced apples," Reese had said, absently tracing patterns on Sloane's stomach. "You eat them every afternoon. I've seen it. But what other fruits?"

"Grapefruit gets a bad rap," Sloane replied. "People hate it unnecessarily. It just needs a sweetener."

Reese sat up abruptly, clutching the sheet to her chest. "No, no, no. Tell me that's not true. I don't know if I can be with a grapefruit fan. There are lines that shouldn't be crossed."

Sloane propped her head on her arm, smiling. "Look how cute you get when you're outraged. Drop the sheet and do it again. I'll even say it louder. Grapefruit is a stellar fruit!"

"You stop that right now," Reese warned, grin betraying her. She let the sheet fall and crawled toward Sloane, unapologetically topless.

"What are you going to do about it? Grapefruit. Grapefruit. Grapefruit."

"Oh, it's on," Reese said, sliding a thigh between Sloane's legs and grinding into her. The onslaught of sensation, the pinpricks of pleasure, forced Sloane's eyes closed. "And you're wet. You *do* like grapefruit."

"I think maybe it's you naked. I like the way your breasts sway when you crawl."

Reese must have appreciated that. Moments later, warm breath traced the inside of Sloane's thighs, teasing, unhurried. Reese took her time, tracing lazy circles with her tongue around Sloane's center until her lips found Sloane's clit and gently sucked. Sloane rocked her hips, finding a perfect rhythm, reaching until the tension snapped and she came apart, gripping the sheets as pleasure tore through her—clean and bright, like a jet slicing through the night sky.

They'd lost the better part of an hour to each other, making up for time spent apart, finishing with Sloane taking Reese from behind—something that had become a favorite. One of many discoveries. Being with Reese had taught her that she loved trying new things, especially with someone who was, impossibly, the hottest woman she'd ever met. Confident in her body for days. And the funniest. The kindest. The list grew longer every day.

Now, Sloane stood at the pit wall at Redline Racing, eyes locked on Cassidy Simms as she began Lap 45 of the feature race. She'd moved from P11 to P6—all fought for and earned. No chaos. No safety car miracles. Just clean, continuous progress toward the front.

The thing was, Cassidy was patient in a car that rewarded discipline over bravado. She threaded through traffic without forcing moves. When she made mistakes, she learned from them and never repeated them. Raw talent, honed fast. She wasn't driving at the car anymore. She was driving with it.

On Lap 47, Cassidy made her move. Late but controlled. A lunge that only worked if you knew exactly how much the car would give. It held and rotated beautifully. The pass was so clean it felt ordained.

Sloane smiled, more than a little impressed. "Fucking brilliant," she murmured, earning a nod from the team principal.

That was racecraft. That was growth. Cassidy wasn't just surviving the academy anymore. She was becoming a problem for the others. And Sloane, who had seen hundreds of talented young drivers flame out for lack of adaptability, knew this when she saw it.

Cassidy Simms wasn't done climbing. Not today. Not ever, if she kept learning like this.

She passed Veronica on her way out of the paddock. "Simms," Sloane said, nothing more, the look doing the rest.

"I know. I saw." She shook her head. "I took a chance on that one. I had no idea how nicely it would pay off."

"That's why they hand you the big bucks, Vance."

Veronica's eyes sparkled. "Why, thank you, Foster. But they could honestly pay me a little more."

"I have a feeling it's coming." The attention on the academy had exceeded everyone's expectations, and Veronica was the woman of the hour. As she should be.

"How's Reese?" Veronica asked, sliding a strand of dark hair behind her ear.

Sloane paused and recalled their last conversation that morning, when Reese was gutted not to be heading off to race that day like her friends at the academy and her teammates at Laurens. "I think she's restless. She misses the action." She shrugged. "Selfishly, it buys me some breathing room."

Veronica gestured for her to walk, guiding them away from curious ears. "You're not relishing the idea of her driving in an F1 race."

"I'd be thrilled to see her behind the wheel, living her dream," Sloane said quietly. "And absolutely terrified at the same time. I keep telling myself it's a problem for Future-Sloane."

Veronica gave her a look. "Is that going to work long-term? If you want this to last, you probably need to talk to Reese about it."

Sloane exhaled slowly. "Probably not. But every time I think about that conversation, my heart rate spikes and I start checking where all the exits are." Her jaw set, body going rigid. The thought of something happening to Reese was unbearable.

Veronica studied her as someone who understood the cost. "That fear never goes away," she said finally. "You just decide it's worth it. We've all been there."

Sloane nodded, gaze drifting back to the circuit where the echo of engines still hung in the air.

"Still," Veronica added lightly, "if Reese is restless, she's right where she needs to be. Drivers hate waiting. It's a good thing. Means they're hungry."

Sloane smiled despite herself. "She's starving."

"Talk to her."

"And ruin all this?" Sloane murmured. "I care too much about her. Feels selfish."

"Well, you're not."

"Ms. Vance?" The documentary crew that followed Reese hovered nearby. "Could we grab you for a second?"

"Sure." Veronica turned back to Sloane. "We're not done."

"I wouldn't presume."

Alone again, Sloane checked her watch. The F1 Grand Prix would be starting soon. She wanted to catch the race, cheer for her girlfriend's team, and, just for today, take comfort in the knowledge that Reese would not be behind the wheel.

There were only so many pit walks, sponsor obligations, and polite media smiles a person could endure before the edges frayed. Reese was there. She watched her teammates climb into the car, yet again, with a familiar ache, adrenaline humming uselessly in her bloodstream. Waiting, it turned out, was harder than failing.

The academy's sprint race was in progress in Austria that morning. She'd grabbed a prime spot to take in the action, enjoying cheering for her friends between obligations. Marissa was flying, leading the pack with Danielle hot on her heels. With Delaney in P3, the race was shaping up to be an exciting one with the win up for grabs. Halfway through, Samara tapped Reese on the shoulder. They'd been following her that morning, grabbing footage of a day in the life of her new reserve role. "Can we do a quick Q and A with the race happening in the background. We've got a setup over there if you're willing. Five minutes."

"Yeah. Okay," Reese said, reluctant to be pulled away from the action and not wanting to miss a pivotal overtake. "But we have to be quick. It's just getting good over there."

They got her set up in record time, and, honoring her request, Samara jumped right in.

"You do a lot of fan interaction for Laurens. What's the one thing you hear from the fans the most?"

Reese didn't have to think about it. Her smile came easily, spreading before she even realized it was there. "I hear from so many young girls who now believe they can grow up and be an F1 driver, too. And if my presence helps spark that belief, then I can't imagine wanting anything more. It's become a theme, and I don't mind it at all. In fact," she added softly, "it fills me up every single time."

"I love hearing that," Samara said, taking a moment to enjoy the sentiment. "Now let me ask you about the day that—"

Behind her, the world detonated.

The sound came first—an explosive *crack* of metal on metal, followed immediately by a deep, concussive *boom* that punched the air from Reese's lungs. She was confused. Her brain couldn't keep up with her senses. Heat washed over her back as a plume of fire erupted trackside, bright and violent, sending debris skittering across the asphalt. Screams tore through the crowd. Reese spun just in time to see a car cartwheel through smoke, flames licking hungrily at shattered carbon fiber before it slammed to a halt in a cloud of sparks. For a moment, everything froze. No numbers, no colors, no recognition—just the sickening certainty that someone she loved was in that wreck. Her pulse roared in her ears as marshals sprinted past, extinguishers raised, and Reese stood rooted in place, heart hammering, unable to breathe until she knew *who* hadn't climbed out.

"No, no, no," Reese murmured, her eyes scanning the scene for any kind of information.

The fire didn't die down. It *fed* on something, flames curling higher as the car sat twisted against the barrier, one wheel still spinning uselessly. Marshals swarmed it, yellow flags snapping, but no one was moving inside the cockpit. No hand. No helmet. Nothing. Reese took an unconscious step forward, Samara's hand catching her elbow as the crowd noise dissolved into a low, terrified roar. Her brain began its cruel inventory—*Marissa was leading. Delaney was P3. Cassidy had been behind them. Where was Cassidy?* She hated herself for the way the question landed like a verdict.

Seconds stretched past reason. The fire finally faltered, smoke rolling low and black as marshals hesitated, then leaned in, working fast, urgently. Reese's heart hammered so loudly she couldn't hear the commentary anymore, only the sharp, frantic command of her own thoughts: *Move. Please move.* But the cockpit stayed sealed, the car lifeless in a way that felt wrong, and the absence of motion became unbearable.

Then the marshals reached in—and pulled a body free.

Cassidy came out limp, her helmet lolling forward, arms slack as they hauled her from the wreckage and laid her carefully on the track. No sound. No attempt to sit up. Reese's stomach dropped through her shoes as medics rushed in, shielding Cassidy from view, hands moving with brisk, practiced efficiency that only made the silence worse. It was a bad dream. It was all of their worst nightmares. Only it was coming true right in front of them. Reese stood frozen, breath shallow, unable to look away, knowing that for far too long, Cassidy hadn't moved at all.

In that moment, Reese didn't do anything heroic. She didn't run. She couldn't. Her feet felt welded to the concrete as medics worked around Cassidy's still form. The red flags came out, and the circuit fell into a stunned hush. Someone was talking to Reese—Samara, maybe, or a team liaison—but the words slid past her without landing. Reese's hands shook, useless at her sides, and she curled them into fists just to feel something solid.

Her first instinct was to count. Breaths. Seconds. The rise of Cassidy's chest—*was there one?*—and when she couldn't see it, panic clawed up her throat. She forced herself to stay where she was, knowing she wasn't allowed on the track. She'd only be in the way. That knowledge didn't help. It just made her feel smaller.

Then training kicked in. Not driving training, but *survival* training. She reached for the radio clipped at her waist with clumsy fingers, thumb hovering before she pressed it, because saying it out loud would make it real. "Who was that?" she asked, voice tight, stripped of bravado. The pause on the other end stretched too long. Reese swallowed hard and added, quieter now, "Tell me who it was."

When the answer didn't come right away, Reese turned away from the wreck so she wouldn't break apart in front of the cameras. She pressed her forehead briefly to the cool concrete wall and breathed through the terror one shallow inhale at a time, waiting for news, for movement, for anything that might tell her whether the silence she was standing in was temporary or permanent.

CHAPTER 23
IS THIS THING ON?

Sloane's hands shook as she stood along the pit wall where she'd been watching timing screens, so she slid them into her pockets. The circuit speakers crackled to life, the announcer's voice stripped of its usual enthusiasm, flattened by caution. "Attention please. The race has been red-flagged following a serious incident on the track." A pause followed. "For safety reasons, the sprint race will not be restarted. Results will be declared based on the last completed lap." The words echoed across the grandstands, across the paddock, across the stretch of asphalt where the wreck still smoldered. No name was given and no update was offered. Just the quiet, unmistakable finality of it: the race was over, and nothing else mattered anymore.

The announcement carried across the paddock just as Sloane finished scanning a timing screen, her attention snapping to it on instinct. *Red-flagged. Serious incident. Race will not be restarted.* The words landed with brutal efficiency, slotting themselves into the part of her brain trained to respond, not react. She was already moving, issuing clipped instructions, confirming logistics with Cassidy's team, checking with Veronica that medical protocols were in motion—because that was the job, and the job was the only thing keeping her upright. It wasn't until someone said *transport to the hospital* that her chest tightened, a familiar ache blooming behind her sternum, sharp and unwelcome. She kept her face neutral, hands hidden, even as the crash replayed unbidden in her mind: fire, speed, and then silence. She told herself this wasn't about her. That it was about her driver. And still, her pulse refused to slow, her body remembering what she spent years teaching it to forget.

"I'm coming with you," Sloane told Veronica, falling in step alongside her as she moved to the waiting car.

"Of course," Veronica said, taking her hand and holding it tightly. All the while, Sloane scanned the paddock for any sign of Reese. She wanted to touch her, make sure she was okay, and ground herself in Reese's presence. But she was nowhere to be found.

They'd gotten out ahead of the ambulance. Neither she nor Veronica said much on the ride. Her brain seemed to function on individual facts rather than on linear thoughts. Stray bits of information were all she could manage. Cassidy had been wheel-to-wheel with Greta Novak when the contact had sent her car up and over. Marissa would be declared the winner. The sky had been blue, with only a few clouds. The last thing Reese said to her that morning had been, "Let's hope for a good day." But it wasn't. And it had the potential to get much, much worse.

"Is her family in town?" Sloane asked.

Veronica shook her head. "I called immediately. They were watching at home in Florida, which must have been awful. They're getting on the first flight they can find. From what I understand, they're a tight-knit family."

"Good. She'll need support." If she makes it, Sloane thought to herself. It was the quiet that no one dared to say out loud. But it was there in the car with them.

More silence.

"Marissa and Delaney were white as sheets," Veronica said. "The four of them are such great friends. How's Reese doing?"

Sloane shook her head. "I wish I knew. I should send her a

message. I hope she's with the others." But her hands were shaking so much she couldn't type. She just needed a little time to get her own emotions under control. She could do this. She could do this. She *had* to do this.

She and Veronica waited in the far corner of the blue-and-white holding area, a glass-walled box overlooking the ER entrance, fluorescent lights buzzing softly overhead. The air smelled faintly of antiseptic and something metallic, clean but unsettling for someone who'd spent a good deal of time in a hospital. When Cassidy was rushed through the doors, surrounded by EMTs, the squeak of gurney wheels cutting too loud through the space, Sloane's breath caught. Cassidy's head and neck were fully stabilized, eyes closed, her stillness making it impossible to tell whether she was sedated or worse. "That didn't look good," Veronica murmured, squeezing Sloane's hand. They had already spoken with the nurse's station, arranging to stand in for Cassidy's family, and the doctor was notified almost immediately. The update came far sooner than Sloane expected—and she clung to that small mercy with everything she had.

The doctor who approached them looked barely older than Cassidy herself, her expression composed but careful, hands tucked into the pockets of her coat. "She's conscious," she said, and Sloane's shoulders eased by a fraction.

"She's got superficial burns to both hands. The suit did its job there and protected her from the worst of the fire. That said," she paused, choosing the words carefully, "burns can evolve. What we're seeing now may not be the full picture."

She shifted her weight, the tablet creaking faintly under her grip.

"We're more concerned about internal injuries. There was significant force involved. Right now, we're seeing signs of internal trauma, but it's too early to say how extensive it is."

"Does she seem to be in pain?" Veronica asked.

"It's being managed," she replied. "She's responsive, but disoriented. That's not unexpected."

Sloane's gaze flicked down the hall toward the trauma bay, then back again.

"She'll be monitored closely hour by hour. The next twelve are crucial. If her numbers change or if she doesn't respond the way we expect, we'll move quickly to surgery."

A beat.

"The suit saved her," she said again, quieter this time. "Without it—" She stopped herself, clearing her throat. "We'll know more by morning." Then she nodded once, professional and brief, already halfway gone. "I'll come find you when there's an update."

The uncertainty in the news slowed time. It felt like hours passed before the others arrived, but in reality, it was only about twenty minutes. Marissa and Delaney were first through the doors, but when Sloane caught sight of Reese behind them, the weight of the night finally settled in. Sloane was on her feet immediately, closing the distance and pulling Reese into her, one hand behind her neck, the other firm at her waist—as much for herself as for Reese—needing the solid proof that she was here, upright, breathing.

"How is she?" Reese asked, her voice low and tight.

"She's conscious," Sloane said. "That part is huge. How are you?"

"I don't even know. I can't seem to get my brain to stop replaying the moment."

"Yeah. I know what you mean."

"Why don't we sit?" Sloane turned to the others, who looked exhausted and unsure, caught between standing and falling apart. They dutifully assembled in the corner of the room away from the only other small group in the space.

"We heard from the doctor, and we're in a wait and see. But the fact that she was awake is encouraging," Veronica said, leading with the good news. The information had a collective impact as each one of them seemed to breathe a little deeper with the knowledge. Veronica updated them on all they'd learned from the doctor, and the wait and see hours ahead of them.

Sloane nodded, but her fingers twitched at her sides, brushing against her own pockets, then her jeans, then fidgeting with the hem of her jacket. She kept her eyes on the double doors, trying to even out her breathing, but it came in sharp, uneven bursts.

"She's alive," Sloane said, and her voice cracked on the word *alive*, despite her best effort to keep it clipped and professional. She swallowed hard. "That's what matters right now." But inside, she was twisted and hollow because she knew very well what a risky game this whole thing was, and that the next time they could be sitting here for any one of the others. And that included Reese. The thought nearly strangled her. Yes, it was what they'd all signed up for, but for Sloane, for where she was in her life presently, maybe that was too high an ask.

Reese's gaze kept flicking in her direction, an incognito check-in. She knew Sloane's personal struggles, her triggers, and was making sure she wasn't in distress. "I'm okay," she mouthed to Reese, who looked at her like she didn't quite believe it, which tracked because it was a lie. Sloane was held together by adrenaline and a sense of duty, but felt like a house of cards about to come tumbling down. That couldn't happen here, not when these women needed her as much as she needed them.

They spent the next few hours talking and not talking. The vending machine got a workout. Someone ordered sandwiches. Coffee cups came and went. So did the roster of other drivers and crew members. They'd come in, stay awhile, and eventually head back out again when no word came. The five of them hadn't discussed it outright, but no one seemed intent on going anywhere. How could they?

"I didn't see it," Marissa said, running a hand through her

long curls, her hair extra unruly, a metaphor for the chaos. "They had to tell me on the radio."

"I saw," Delaney said. "The two cars had been battling. It was no one's fault. Just scrapping for position. It's what you do."

"I feel like Greta's going to take this hard," Reese said. "I would."

"That's why it's important that her community show up for her, just like we have for Cassidy," Veronica said. The others nodded, valuing her wisdom. "You're ready to tear each other up on the circuit, but off? No one knows your life like another driver."

Reese nodded, her eyes pooling with tears. "Isn't that the truth of it all? I feel like we're all cut from the same cloth. That's pretty special, if you ask me."

"Even Danielle Todd?" Delaney asked with a sly grin.

"Let's not get carried away," Reese said, hand up. The comment had helped to break the tension, and they'd needed it.

Time lost its edges after that. Minutes stretched, then snapped back into place, marked only by the occasional opening of the trauma doors or the chime of the elevator. While the others slept or visited the cafeteria, Sloane paced the length of the glass-walled waiting area until Veronica gently steered her back to a chair, her hand firm at Sloane's elbow.

"Sit," Veronica said quietly. "You're going to wear a trench in the floor."

Sloane tried. She lasted maybe thirty seconds before she was on her feet again, heart thudding, every nerve buzzing as if she were waiting for impact instead of news.

When the doctor returned, it felt abrupt, like a door opening into cold air.

"She's holding," the doctor said, and Sloane hated how much she clung to the word. "Vitals are stable. The scans show internal bruising and some bleeding, but nothing that requires imme-diate surgery at this moment."

At this moment.

Sloane caught that, the way you catch a loose thread and know better than to pull.

"She's still disoriented," the doctor continued. "That's expected. We've got her sedated lightly now to let her rest. The next few hours are still critical, but right now, this is ... cautiously positive."

It was a good report.

Veronica asked the practical questions—ICU access, overnight protocols, when family could see her. Sloane stood there, arms crossed tight across her chest, the answers sliding past her without fully landing. She focused instead on the doctor's face, on the absence of urgency in her posture, on the fact that she wasn't rushing away this time.

That was something.

Cassidy's parents arrived a few hours later, bleary-eyed, still wearing travel clothes, her mother clutching her phone like it was the only solid thing left in the world. Introductions were made softly, as if everyone was afraid of speaking too loudly in case it changed the outcome.

"I feel like I know each of you from all Cass has told us," her mother said. She squeezed Marissa's hand. "She sees you all as family, so we do, too."

"She was disoriented but talking earlier," Sloane said, because someone had to say it first, and because she needed to hear herself say it out loud. "She's alive. She's stable. The fireproofing saved her."

Cassidy's mother nodded, tears spilling freely now, her hand flying to her mouth. Her father closed his eyes for a long moment, shoulders sagging before he straightened again, resolve settling in where shock had been.

"Thank you for staying with her," he said, his voice rough. "It means more than you know."

Sloane didn't trust herself to answer; she nodded instead.

With the family there, the energy in the room shifted. There was nothing left for the team to *do*. No more updates to chase.

No roles to play. Just waiting and, ultimately, leaving Cassidy with her family.

Veronica checked the time. "We should get everyone back to the hotel. Tomorrow's going to be long."

No one argued. They just looked tired. Wrung out. Sloane felt like she was about to fall over. Her limbs ached and her head throbbed.

Outside, the night air felt wrong, too cool, too normal, as if everything was okay when it wasn't. Reese walked beside Sloane without speaking, their shoulders brushing occasionally. Sloane was aware of every step, every sound, her body still braced like something else was coming.

The cars arrived, and there was a quiet, awkward shuffle—who was riding with whom, promises to text, to update, to meet in the morning. Sloane watched Reese hug Marissa and Delaney, murmuring reassurances she wasn't sure she believed herself.

When Reese turned back to her, Sloane felt a sudden, irrational spike of panic, which Reese was quick to spot.

"Hey, I know today was hard for you in a different way than it was for us." She touched Sloane's cheek. "You were great in there."

The answer lodged somewhere behind Sloane's ribs, sharp and unmanageable. She nodded anyway. "Yeah. It was hard to hold it together. I'm also just … tired."

"Then let's get out of here."

As they pulled out of the hospital parking lot, the city lights streaking past, Sloane kept both hands locked on her knees, jaw tight, heart still racing like she hadn't quite escaped the crash herself. The worst part—the part she couldn't shake was the thought that kept circling back, uninvited and relentless: *This could have been Reese.*

And once that thought took hold, it didn't matter how stable Cassidy was, or how good the doctor sounded, or how quiet the road was beneath them.

Something in Sloane had shifted tonight.

And it wasn't going back.

The rest of the weekend in Austria was overcast and gray, the sky a fitting backdrop to the reality they were living. Reese went through the motions. Shaking hands, shooting Instagram promos with a practiced smile, running reaction drills just in case she was needed, answering reporter questions about the mood around the paddock, "given the crash and condition of Cassidy Simms." They said her name as if it belonged to a stat line or a grid graphic, not the lovable, silly, huge-hearted woman Reese knew so well.

Cassidy's parents did a remarkable job of keeping everyone updated, and the news, still cautious, was moving in the right direction. She'd been awake and responsive in short stretches, grumpy about the burns on her hands and already asking questions about the race she'd missed. The last part made Reese smile. The internal injuries were being monitored closely, and the doctors chose their words with precision. But each update carried a little more steadiness than the last. Late Saturday evening, her mother texted to say that if everything stayed on course, visitors would be allowed on Sunday. Reese read the message three times, her chest tightening with something wonderfully close to relief, and held onto the prospect as she moved through the weekend.

Sloane had been quieter than usual, which worried Reese. She reminded herself that Sloane had a soft spot for Cass and that everyone was processing what happened in their own way. While she wanted to give Sloane the space she needed, another part of her wanted to do everything in her power to make the world seem okay for Sloane again. To show Sloane that she was safe and loved.

Loved. Because she was that.

Okay, so Reese had yet to loop Sloane in on her feelings, but there would be plenty of time. It didn't make it any less true. She had fallen hopelessly in love, and it felt so amazing she almost couldn't believe she could be this blessed.

But she had her eye on Sloane this weekend. Even if she was more reserved, she still smiled every time their eyes met. Still reached for Reese's hand whenever they stood close enough. At night, they talked in the darkened hotel room long past their bedtime and held each other as a reminder that neither of them had to carry the weight alone.

The morning of the Grand Prix had them both up early.

Reese was ready first and watched from the bathroom doorway as Sloane applied lip gloss in the mirror. She was stunning in these peaceful, everyday moments. Reese's chest squeezed pleasantly at how very much at home she felt. "Want to walk over together?" she asked quietly.

Sloane smiled, ran her fingers through her hair, and gave herself one last check in the mirror. "I would like nothing more than to walk with you," she said, turning. "Maybe we could grab a smoothie at the breakfast counter."

"Why do you always say such amazing things to me?"

"Because I know the way to your heart and it's definitely through strawberries."

"That's how simple you think I am? Give me great sex, advice from a hot blond woman who knows racing, and a few strawberries, and I'm sold?"

"Yes," Sloane said without considering the question.

"Fine. You're not wrong." Reese grinned because she very much liked that Sloane had gotten to know those little details.

Sloane walked to her and slid her arms around Reese's neck, going up on her tippy-toes so they were eye to eye. "I might be generalizing. Because you're a lot more complex than that. I happen to love … your intricacies."

Record scratch. Reese raised an eyebrow. She knew what she almost heard. She also watched Sloane change course midsentence, and it made her heart dance. They were on the same page.

"What?" Sloane asked, the sides of her mouth tugging.

"Nothing. Just taking a sec to enjoy this moment."

"Good. Come here for it."

"Me?" Reese employed her sexy grin.

"No one else." Sloane angled her head and kissed Reese slowly, longingly, and with intention. When they parted, she held her eyes closed for an extra few seconds. "You also kiss like no human should be allowed to kiss. You'll ruin me for all others."

"That's exactly the point," Reese said, going in for more. "Others? What others?" Reese said, doing Sloane's voice. "That's what I want you saying."

"Is that how I sound?" Sloane asked with a laugh. "Others? What others?"

"That was the best impersonation of me impersonating you that I've ever heard. Do it again. Maybe with your clothes off."

"No," Sloane said, jabbing her ribs with a finger. "I will not. There is a smoothie with my name on it. Get me there."

They took their time on the way to the circuit, holding hands until they approached the driver's entrance. No need to attract extra attention, but secretly, Reese wouldn't have minded at all. She wanted to announce to every human they passed who they were becoming to each other. She'd write it in the sky or make Samara put it smack in the middle of her documentary, complete with subtitles. But she could be patient, because she sensed it was what Sloane needed. Their day would come, though, and Reese was feeling ready for the leap. She watched as Sloane stopped for a selfie with a group of diehards along the fan zone, and the way she rocked each interaction with such grace and poise. Reese seemed like a loping golden retriever in comparison, energetic and bouncing from person to person. How could two people with such different approaches be so ridiculously compatible?

Reese spent the day checking the boxes required of a reserve driver, none of which put her behind the wheel of a car. She passed Marco Faz in the Laurens garage shortly before the race. Continuing her efforts, she offered a nod, and he provided her a full-body once-over that made her cringe. Teammate or not, she found it hard to root for the guy.

The race was a highlight. Simply being that close to the action made her pulse kick up, the sound and vibration of the cars bleeding straight into her bones. She stood near the pit wall, headset hanging uselessly around her neck, eyes tracking apexes and exits on instinct, mentally correcting lines she couldn't drive. Every start, every late brake, every clean overtake landed like both a gift and a taunt. This was where she belonged, inside the action, not hovering on the edges, smiling for cameras and waiting for permission.

When the race ended, the adrenaline had nowhere to land. She'd watched both Marco and Ezra finish in the middle of the pack, with Ezra just inside the points. Marco had delivered none. She couldn't help but wonder if maybe, just maybe, she'd have done a better job for Laurens.

"You have good instincts. I heard you talking with Shanelle during the race."

Reese turned at the sound of the voice to see Damon Mendoza looking her way. As Ezra's engineer, she'd listened to his counsel on the radio for much of the race. He was no Julie, but still very good at his job.

"Yeah? I hope I'm not in the way up here. I'm trying to soak up as much as I can. I feel like I learn something new every race," Reese said, flashing a guilty smile. "Also, sorry if I was talking too much."

"No, no, no. Never apologize for ambition. Hopefully, we'll see what you can do soon. Keep up the good work."

"You don't have to worry about that." The truth was, she had been working her ass off, with discipline now her most important asset, a valuable lesson she'd learned that year. The words from Damon had been the pat on the back she needed to keep going because this wasn't a short journey, it was a long one.

When she headed to the driver's room to reclaim her phone, she discovered something remarkable that stopped her in her tracks.

CASSIDY

Is this thing on?

Reese crushed the phone to her chest, relief infusing every inch. Cassidy had just messaged The Starting Grid, and they were the most glorious four words Reese had ever read in her life. Her eyes filled as she typed, apparently at the same time as the other two. All of their messages appeared right away.

Relief arc activated. Never do that again!

MARISSA

OMG. Best message ever. The people want more.

DELANEY

Dammit, Simms. I'm crying in the paddock bathroom now.

CASSIDY

Love you guys. Thanks for caring about me.

It got better from there. The news from the doctors was amazing. After another day or two in the hospital, Cassidy would be able to fly home to Florida to rest and heal. She was likely out for the season, but seemed to have no intention of letting this little setback stop her.

CASSIDY

Miss you guys already. But I'll be back. Guaranteed.

How are you feeling?

CASSIDY

> Hands are healing. Midsection is really tender.
> Docs say I'm grounded for a bit. Which means
> I'm appointing myself The Starting Grid race
> control.

Reese smiled. Of course she was.

The paddock was already thinning as Reese stepped back out, transporters closing up, crews shedding lanyards and fireproofs. Sunday always felt like this once the race was over—everyone exhausted, hollowed out, quietly forward-looking. Drivers scattered, crews packed up, and teams already shifted their focus to the next stop on the calendar. In this case, Zandvoort, Netherlands.

But for Reese, the day wasn't done. In fact, the best part was still ahead.

As the reserve, she got a small window to practice in the Laurens car once the chaos cleared. A short session when the track belonged to whoever still had a reason to be there. It wasn't glamorous, and it certainly wasn't public, but it mattered. Laps were laps. Data was data. Seat time was absolutely priceless.

Her phone buzzed again.

DELANEY

> You got your Sunday laps today?

> Yeah. Thirty minutes.

DELANEY

> 🔥 Use every second.

MARISSA

> What I wouldn't give to drive that car.

And it was a glorious car, too. She'd never driven anything like it. A short time later, Reese paused at the edge of the pit lane, watching a marshal wave a car through. The teams that stayed were the ones with something extra scheduled—test data to gather or rookies to keep sharp.

The Formula 1 car had felt different from the first moment Reese pulled onto the track. In karts, speed came from being aggressive. In rally, it was about reacting fast and trusting instinct. Even the other open-wheel cars she'd driven let her fight them a little. This one didn't. It wanted calm. Smooth hands. Patience. There was enormous power beneath her, but it only showed itself when she stayed controlled. Reese realized quickly that driving this car wasn't about going as hard as possible—it was about not making critical mistakes.

"Just keep it on the track," Shanelle had told her. "The rest is all tweaking. We can't tweak a drive once you're in the wall."

"Got it. Don't bust up the multimillion-dollar car my first month on the job."

Shanelle smiled and crossed her arms. "Now you've got it."

The session left her on a high and craving more. The thirty minutes had flown by in a flash, making her reluctant to get out of the car. She climbed out and peeled off her gloves, the adrenaline slowly ebbing. When Reese looked up, Sloane was standing along the railing, blond hair lifting in the wind.

"You're looking good out there, Hotshot," Sloane said, quiet but certain.

"Thank you." Reese tucked her helmet under her arm and stepped closer. "Any tips?"

"Pay attention to your braking points," Sloane said easily. "The more consistent you are, the more the car gives back."

"You got it." Reese paused, a grin slipping free before she could stop it. "I love it when you watch me drive."

Sloane's mouth curved, small and unmistakable. "I know," she said. "I love getting to."

"When do I get to see you behind the wheel?"

Sloane's eyes widened just a fraction before she caught herself. She opened her mouth, then closed it. "I don't know," she said finally. "It's been a while."

"Yeah?" Reese asked. "How long?"

Sloane paused, as if counting backward. "Six years. Maybe."

"I'm sure Veronica could make it happen," Reese said easily. "We could take a car out and—"

Sloane drew in a slow breath. "Let's hold off on that for now."

Reese nodded immediately, the answer landing before the reason. She hadn't meant to push. She hadn't meant to touch anything still bruised. "Of course," she said. "Whenever you're ready."

She didn't say that she'd watched Sloane's old races more times than she could count. Didn't mention Abu Dhabi, where Sloane had carved through the field from thirteenth to first and won the whole damn thing. That history belonged to Sloane. Reese could wait to be invited into it.

"I did have a question for you, though," Sloane said.

Intriguing. "And what is that?"

"Have you ever been to Venice Beach?"

Reese smiled, seeing where this was going. "Not since I was in karting."

"Wanna go?"

CHAPTER 24
BEACH ADJACENT

Sloane leaned against the doorframe, letting the sun warm her shoulders, and watched the street for Reese's car. Why wouldn't she get here already? Every part of her missed Reese, craved her in so many different ways. Her humor, her body, the soft way her hair tickled Sloane's shoulders when she leaned in close. Sloane had been anticipating having her here, in her actual space, for a long time now. She'd spent the morning tweaking the details, turning the tricky shelf plant to the right, adjusting the Race Hair, Don't Care magnet on her fridge, fluffing the turquoise pillows on her cream-colored couch, and wholly looking at her home through Reese's eyes to be sure it checked out. It was more than silly, she knew, because Reese was a very easy-to-please human who smiled at least once every thirty seconds and sank into new experiences like her favorite pair of shoes. She would love Sloane's place and make herself comfortable in record time. It was one of Sloane's favorite things about Reese. She relished life and found the dollop of awesome in most everything.

Sloane checked her watch and exhaled, realizing she felt looser than she had since Cassidy's accident. California had shown up for the occasion. The day was impossibly good—sun bright but not harsh, the air warm without too much weight. On her walk that morning, the boardwalk had shimmered in the new light, the canal just beyond it twirling into small, dancing ripples. The palm trees swayed lazily in the ocean breeze, as if even they had nowhere urgent to be.

Now, sitting on the top step in front of her place, a few pedestrians drifted by, skateboards clattering over concrete, a dog barking at nothing in particular, but Sloane barely registered any of it. Her attention stayed fixed on the driveway, on the exact moment Reese would arrive. She rolled her lips inward, a quiet hum of happiness moving through her as she imagined Reese's arms around her, the familiar weight of her body, the kiss that would follow after several very long days apart.

The distance was becoming a problem. Even a few days hurt. And yet, even as she ached for that closeness, Sloane hesitated. Wanting Reese this much felt like leaning into something that could vanish without warning, and Sloane had learned how quickly solid ground could give way.

When a black SUV paused in front of her house, Sloane stood and looped a strand of hair behind her ear. Reese emerged with a bag slung over her shoulder, hair down, eyes bright, and looking more beautiful than ever. "Does this place have any vacancies?" She called from the bottom of the sidewalk.

"Yes, but there's a problem," Sloane called back.

Reese walked toward her, head quirked. "What's that?"

Sloane shrugged. "Only one bed."

"You're kidding."

"I'm not."

"I don't know what we're going to do about that," Reese said, pressing her forehead to Sloane's. "Except I definitely do. I've missed you. Hi."

"Hi, you," Sloane said quietly, drinking in the moment. Everything in her went warm and soft. This, this right here, was her happy place. She cradled Reese's face, and they stayed just like that, foreheads pressed, for an extended moment. The best one, really.

"I talk to you nonstop, yet I feel like it's been a year since I've seen you."

"Half a week: cruel. Do you want to come inside? It's almost four. In California time, it's happy hour."

"It is?"

"Oh yes. If you just say California time, you can make anything true."

Reese laughed. "So noted." She followed Sloane inside, seemingly taking in every detail as they walked. "You collect art," Reese said, pausing in front of a painting of a woman turned half away, sunlight breaking across her face, unfinished in a way that felt deliberate on the artist's part.

Sloane placed her hands on her hips and studied the piece she'd found in Florence in a tucked-away shop five years ago. "I don't know about *collect*. That's probably too generous. But I pick up pieces here and there. When something compels me to pause and stare for a while, I know it's good." She dropped her hands, and Reese threaded their fingers. "And that's the extent of my art knowledge."

"Well, you have good taste. But we already knew that."

"Thank you. Oh! And technically, I am collector adjacent. My father has a Rembrandt. Probably several."

"He probably has more than one bed, too."

Sloane laughed and gave Reese's arm a tug. "I'll give you the grand tour." The house wasn't big because Sloane was raised in excess and never really understood the point of too much space. Cozy chic was more her vibe. She'd decorated the living room with a softness in mind, leaning into creams and blues and turquoises that reminded her of the ocean just yards away.

"I love this place. And right on the water. Wow."

"I haven't touched my Foster trust fund, but the F1 money was good. You'll likely find that out soon enough. Plus, my automotive consulting work is fairly specialized."

"So you can be neighbors with the ocean because you're Moneybags McGee."

"Well, my friends just call me McGee."

Reese turned. "I like it. And I like you. End of story." She gave Sloane's arm a tug, and it brought her closer. They could hear the waves rolling in from the back deck, which felt more romantic than she'd ever fully realized on her own. She wanted to be kissed so badly. She wanted to be taken. She wanted to escape the world with Reese Maddox because, with her, the world seemed so much more interesting. Details snapped sharply into focus like the sound of the waves. Jokes were funnier. Even food tasted better.

"Have you ever had sex on the beach?" Reese asked, running her thumb over Sloane's bottom lip.

"Once, years ago. Sexy in theory. But a lot sandier than I would have guessed."

Reese winced. "Maybe we stay beach adjacent then."

"Are you making plans for the next few days?"

"And every day after that," Reese said quite seriously. The declaration sent a flutter through Sloane's midsection. "Does that scare you?"

"Nothing about you scares me." She hesitated. "But what you do for a living hits pretty close to home."

Reese nodded, absorbing. "You've been quieter since Cassidy."

"What if it had been you?" The rush of emotion that nearly toppled her wasn't new. She'd been battling it for a while now, but it was gaining ground. She felt tears prickle, hating that the mood had shifted, but knowing it was important to communicate. "It scares me that I grow closer to you every single day, knowing the kind of heartbreak that might be waiting for me that very next weekend."

Sloane swallowed hard. The words had tumbled out before she could sand down their edges. "Every time you strap into a car, I'm bracing for the call. And I hate that part of myself, the part that counts risk like it's some kind of debt I'll eventually have to pay."

Reese's hand slid beneath her jaw, grounding and warm. "Hey," she said softly. "Look at me." When Sloane did, Reese's expression was open, unguarded in that way that always undid her. "I don't pretend it isn't dangerous. I know exactly what it is. But I'm careful. I prepare. I listen. And I love what I do." She took a breath. "I also love us."

The words landed with a quiet weight between them. Sloane laughed weakly, the sound breaking around the ache in her chest. "You say things like that like it's easy."

"It isn't easy," Reese said. "It's just worth it." She leaned in, pressing a kiss to Sloane's forehead, then her temple, a trail of gentleness that felt deliberate. "And for the record, I worry too. About you. About losing time. About all the ways life can blind-side you." She smiled, small and earnest. "We're both brave in different directions."

Sloane rested her hands at Reese's waist, grounding herself there. The waves rolled in behind them, patient and constant, as if reminding her that fear didn't get to be the only thing that stayed. "I don't want to hold you back," she said. "I just ... want you to come back."

Reese's smile softened. "Then that's the deal," she said. "I go fast. Then I come back." She nudged Sloane's nose with her own. "And right now, I'm very much here."

That was enough. It had to be.

Sloane pulled her closer and kissed her—slow, unhurried, the kind of kiss that communicated everything Sloane was feeling. Reese responded in kind, hands firm at Sloane's back, like she was anchoring them both to the moment. When they finally broke apart, Reese rested her forehead against Sloane's again, grinning. "So. Happy hour?"

Sloane smiled through the last of the sting in her eyes. "On the deck," she said. "Beach adjacent."

"Perfect," Reese replied. "I knew this place had potential."

It was dinnertime in Venice Beach, and Reese's mouth watered. For more reasons than one, if she was being honest.

Sloane stood at the stove, barefoot, weight shifting easily from one foot to the other as she worked, knowing the rhythm of her own space. The stir-fry chicken and vegetables she'd tossed together made the kitchen smell heavenly of garlic and ginger, and a bite of citrus cutting through it all. Sloane's hair was pulled up in a careless twist, the kind that suggested it hadn't been meant to last, wisps escaping at her temples and along the elegant line of her neck. That neck—bare, vulnerable, impossibly distracting—caught the late light pouring through the windows and turned it into something Reese felt low in her body.

She didn't even realize she'd gone still until a second passed. Then another.

There was something almost obscene about how good Sloane looked doing something so ordinary. Cooking and simply existing casually in her own home. Reese had seen her in race gear, in pressed jackets, in rooms where power clung to her, but this? This was different. This felt private. And Reese knew how incredibly lucky she was to experience it.

Sloane shifted, reaching for a lemon, and Reese had to bite the inside of her cheek. Desire rolled through her, sharp and immediate, but threaded with something warmer. A sense of landing right where she was supposed to be.

Sloane glanced over her shoulder, smiling like she'd heard her anyway. "You're staring."

"That's because you're so fucking sexy right now that I don't know what to do with myself."

"Me? Really? Like this? Well, I have an idea."

"Yeah?" Reese leaned against the counter, facing Sloane. "And what is it?"

"You can start by grabbing the sesame oil from inside the fridge door. I'd be very appreciative."

"I can do that." After a successful sesame mission, Reese stepped in behind her, hands settling at Sloane's waist, her chin brushing Sloane's shoulder as she leaned in. Up close, the temptation was almost unbearable. The heat of her skin, the curve of her body, the quiet intimacy of the moment. "Just how important is it that this food finishes cooking?"

Sloane grinned as she stirred. "I mean, this is a very important stir-fry, Reese. Our nightly nourishment depends on it."

She kissed Sloane's neck slowly, feeling her muscles relax beneath the touch. "What if I promised another kind of nourishment?" She encircled Sloane's waist and placed her palms flat against her stomach, then slid them downward toward her thighs.

"Reese Maddox, you're instigating."

"Because you look so good. What about after dinner?"

"Hmm. I think I'm free," Sloane said, reaching behind her and touching the back of Reese's neck.

The stir-fry finished cooking, plates were filled, and they carried everything to the small table near the windows where the light had softened into evening. Conversation drifted easily, bits of the day, a story Sloane told that made Reese laugh, the quiet comfort of sharing food in a space that already felt familiar. At some point, between bites and shared glances, Reese felt it bloom fully in her chest—this sense that this wasn't just a good night, or even a good relationship. It was something rarer. Something reliable. She set her fork down, suddenly needing to say it out loud.

"I've never had this before."

Sloane watched her like she knew exactly what Reese meant. "Me neither."

She picked up Sloane's hand and studied it. "You understand me. You challenge me. You thrill me. And you make everything matter."

Sloane swallowed.

"Since I met you, I'm the best version of myself, and I only see that continuing."

"So, what do we do?" Sloane asked.

"We're honest with each other, which means I need to be honest right now."

"Okay," Sloane said, sweeping a strand of hair from Reese's forehead. "I'm right here. Tell me."

"I'm in love with you."

"You are?" A small smile debuted.

"Oh, there is zero doubt in my mind about that. In fact, I'm so confident in my feelings that I want to tell everyone. I'd be so annoying about it, too. I'd boast about it." Sloane laughed as she listened. "I want to walk down the pit lane holding your hand and kiss you in front of the whole world the next time I have a podium finish." She threaded their fingers. "And then I want to come home and have chicken stir-fry and watch a movie or explore whatever city we might be in that week." She took a deep breath, seeing the whole thing playing out like a movie in her mind. She wanted it all for them so badly. "And when it's time to retire from racing, I want to find our own little corner of the world and be boring and happy and laugh and make love and maybe get a dog or two. Maybe three. I might want three dogs. We'll see." She exhaled. "There. That's the life that I want. And it's with you."

Sloane laughed. "Wow."

"I know. Three dogs *is* a lot." She blew out a breath. "Seriously though. I hope I didn't freak you out. But you should know where my brain is. What my heart is telling me without question."

Sloane placed a hand on Reese's cheek as the sun set over the water through the picture window, showcasing purples and oranges. "Well, here's the thing." She looked into Reese's eyes. "I have fallen very much in love with you, Reese Maddox. I'm gone on you. I mean that with every ounce of conviction in my body. And I want it all, too." She closed her eyes as if steadying herself.

"And it's a big step for me to admit it out loud, because it's scary for me at the same time. But I love you too much to let anything get in the way of telling you."

The smile that took shape on Reese's face was a manifestation of sheer joy like nothing she'd ever experienced. Racing highs were a real thing, but they didn't compare in the slightest to what she felt in this moment. "Come here," Reese said, giving Sloane's arm a tug. Sloane allowed herself to be pulled onto Reese's lap, where she cradled the back of her head, leaned down, and captured Reese's mouth in a kiss that began soft and heartfelt and shifted steadily to hot and urgent. As their mouths danced, Sloane went up on her knees, straddling Reese, for better access, the movement knocking the breath from Reese's lungs in the best way. The kiss deepened, mouths fitting together like they'd been practicing for all time. Sloane tasted like citrus and ginger, and the wine from dinner, and Reese knew she'd never get enough.

"God, you feel good," Sloane breathed.

Sloane's hands fisted in Reese's shirt, grounding herself there, and Reese answered by holding her closer, as if distance had become an intolerable concept. When Sloane sighed into her mouth, low and unguarded, Reese felt it everywhere.

"Should we?" Reese asked around kisses.

"Definitely should." Another mind-blowing kiss. "Let me give you a tour of the bedroom."

Reese arched a brow. "And by tour, you actually mean ..."

"Hundred percent."

When you love someone, the touches linger longer, the kisses grow more insistent, and the release carries a depth that feels almost overwhelming. Sloane felt it immediately—that everything between them had slowed and sharpened all at once, as if saying the important words had tuned her senses to a finer frequency.

Reese's hands explored her with intention now, not searching, not guessing, but learning her again through the lens of certainty.

They stayed up into the early morning hours, bodies moving together in a quiet, reverent rhythm, the night unfolding without urgency. Sloane let herself sink fully into it, into the way Reese held her like something precious, into the way every kiss anchored her to this woman who was nothing short of amazing. Pleasure built patiently, wave after wave, until it left her undone in Reese's arms, breathless and trembling, held through it all.

Later, when the world outside had softened toward dawn, Sloane lay tangled with Reese, limbs warm, heart impossibly full. Love changed everything, she realized, and she would always remember the night they'd finally claimed it.

The lazy morning belonged to them, and the idea that they had absolutely nowhere to be was not only novel, but it was also cause for celebration. Sloane was up first. She threw on jeans and a faded yellow T-shirt, then walked the couple of blocks to the Cat's Pajamas, where she grabbed them lattes to go and a variety of amazing pastries Autumn had assembled in a cute little blue box.

"What is that?" Reese asked when she arrived back at the house. She was awake and stood in the kitchen, wearing only her underwear and a blue T-shirt featuring a duck wearing glasses. Her hair was wild from a good night's sleep, and her lips slightly swollen from, well, everything they'd done right before. She looked absolutely perfect.

Sloane smiled, shifting the box to one hip as she nudged the door closed with her foot. "Breakfast. Or possibly brunch. Time is a suggestion today."

Reese crossed the kitchen barefoot, peered into the blue box, and made a low, appreciative sound. "You went to a place called the Cat's Pajamas?" She looked up, eyes warm and amused. "You're trying to make me fall in love with you all over again."

"Too late for that," Sloane said easily, setting the lattes on the counter. She handed one over, fingers brushing Reese's, the contact still sending a quiet thrill through her. It felt different this morning, lighter somehow, but deeper too. Like everything fit just a little better.

Reese took a sip, sighed, and leaned in to kiss her, slow and unhurried, as if they had all the time in the world to get it right. "This," she said, gesturing vaguely between the coffee, the pastries, and the two of them, "might be my favorite version of us."

Sloane bumped her shoulder. "Mmm. Mine, too."

They ate at the counter, sharing bites, laughing when powdered sugar ended up on Reese's nose without her realizing it, talking about work, their favorite vacation spots, and why Sloane believed she could absolutely outrun a goose if it came down to it. Outside, the day stretched open and unclaimed. And for once, Sloane didn't feel the need to plan ahead or brace for what came next. She just sat there with the woman she loved, sunlight creeping into the room, thinking that if this was what the morning after looked like, she was more than ready for whatever followed.

"What if we took a walk around the neighborhood after this?" Sloane asked. "We can end up on the beach. Watch the waves. Grab a lemonade. I guarantee you the people-watching alone will be well worth it."

Reese pulled off a section of croissant. "I want to do all of that. The answer is a resounding *you're on*." She popped it in her mouth.

"Stop making croissants sexy," Sloane said.

"I will not. And now that I know I can, I'm going to do it more." And oh, she did, too. Deliberating, tugging a flaky bite of the freshly baked middle and placing it slowly in her perfect mouth, the same one that had Sloane clawing the sheets and screaming her name last night.

"You're out of control."

"What are you going to do about it?" Reese asked, blinking innocently, and showing off her long lashes.

"Come here. Let's find out." Sloane turned her around and backed her against the counter as the smile faded from Reese's lips and her eyes darkened with a look Sloane recognized: desire. She placed a soft hand between Reese's legs and watched her face as she stroked softly once. Twice. "Oh, you're quieter now," Sloane said. "And this is in the way." She slid the rectangular piece of fabric to the side and began to play. Reese dropped the croissant onto the counter and grabbed the edge with both hands.

"Fuck," she breathed, eyes closing.

"Yes, I am about to fuck you," Sloane said. Reese's body was always so responsive in the morning, and today was no different. "But I want to make sure you want it first. Do you want it?" Sloane asked, trailing a finger down Reese's cheek. She kissed the smooth skin on her neck, inhaling her scent.

Reese was already rocking against her other hand, the T-shirt riding up with each small movement, offering a glimpse of her abdomen. "I do want it."

Sloane began to move her fingers in a circular pattern between Reese's legs, purposefully avoiding her clit, getting ever so close and moving off again, reveling in what it seemed to be doing to Reese. "You're even wetter now. You must like this."

"I love it when you touch me." Reese's voice was breathy, her breathing shallow. Her hips began to move faster, seeking Sloane's hand, pressing into it, desperate for more attention, more pressure.

"What is it you want?" Sloane said in her ear.

"I want you to fuck me," Reese said. "I need you to."

"How bad?"

"So bad. Baby. Please." Reese bit her bottom lip and closed her eyes. Sloane liked the image very much. So much that she slid inside, filling Reese, pumping her with two fingers and then three. She allowed her thumb to brush Reese's clit ever so briefly, nodding when Reese twitched and whimpered.

"Was that good?"

"Mm-hmm," Reese said, eyes still closed as Sloane moved in and then out again in a rhythm that left her very much in control. Reese's quiet little cry that accompanied Sloane's every thrust was extra motivation. She brushed her clit again. "Please. More."

Sloane began to pass over it and back, softly with her thumb at first until accelerating as Reese's hips moved faster in a frenzy. "Yes. Just like that. God. Oh, fuck. Yes, Sloane. More, more." She rode Sloane's hand, leaning back against the counter. Finally, Sloane increased both her pressure and her speed until Reese bowed and cried out as she tumbled. "Oh fuck, oh fuck. That was too good." She slid her hand under Sloane's jaw, her breathing still ragged. "God, your voice does things to me."

"Yeah, well, your body does things to me. She palmed Reese's breast through the T-shirt. "I don't ever think I've known a sexier person. Especially one with a duck on her shirt."

Reese laughed quietly. "I hope that means we can do lots more of this."

"Breakfast sex?"

"All of it."

Sloane smiled sincerely. "You have no idea how much more I want of this." She stepped in, and they shared a lingering kiss that made Sloane go up on her tiptoes for maximum access to those lips that drove her wild. Her midsection fluttered, her thighs quivered, and she wanted to live in this moment forever. Alas, they had the day ahead of them, and with as little time as they had together over Reese's visit, she didn't want to miss showing Reese her little piece of the world. "Should we take a walk to see the neighborhood?"

"We have to, or I'd be hugely sad. Let me shower and change, then we can see what this ridiculously pretty neighborhood has going on."

"Perfect. I'm going to sit here and drink coffee and watch you walk away."

Reese understood the assignment because the walk was something to behold. The way the T-shirt shifted to the side with each sway of her hips, revealing the tight cling of the baby blue underwear to the bottom of her ass.

Sloane took a sip of her still-warm coffee and smiled. Yeah, this was going to be a great day.

CHAPTER 25
EXCITEMENT FIRST

Reese slid into a pair of her favorite jeans just as her phone began to dance on the creamy gray marble of the bathroom counter. She hopped toward it, one leg still fighting to make it inside, hair damp and loose around her shoulders.

"Oh shit," she said, catching sight of her agent's name on the readout.

She grabbed the phone and fumbled with the last button of her jeans. "Jeremy, hi," she said, trying—and failing—to hide the breathlessness from the hop over.

"Hey, superstar," Jeremy said, voice already pitched somewhere between excitement and restraint. "You got a minute?"

Reese's pulse kicked. *This is it. Or it's nothing. Don't get ahead of yourself.*

"Yeah," she said, leaning her hip against the counter. "What's up?"

A pause—too deliberate to be casual.

"Okay," Jeremy said. "So. Ezra Fernandez is having his gallbladder out. Emergency surgery. He's fine, but he's out for next weekend. Possibly the weekend after that. We'll have to wait and see."

Reese went very still.

Out in the other room, Sloane laughed at something probably on her phone. The sound threaded straight through Reese's chest.

"So," Jeremy continued, "they're putting you in. This is it!"

The words landed with a weight Reese felt all the way down to her bones. Not a spark or a jolt. A *settling*. Like something sliding into place that had been waiting there the whole time.

"They want you back tonight," Jeremy said. "Prep starts immediately."

Tonight.

Her first instinct was a grin so wide it almost hurt. Her second was the image of her hands on the wheel, the smell of rubber and heat, the sound of the engine.

Her third was Sloane.

"Tonight," Reese repeated, just to hear it out loud. She blinked, shoving a hand into her wet hair.

"You good?" Jeremy asked. "Because if you're not—"

"I'm good," Reese said quickly. Too quickly. Then she steadied herself. "I'm really good."

She walked to the doorway, watching Sloane pull on her shoes, sunlight catching in her hair. Venice Beach. Downtime. A walk she'd been looking forward to more than she'd admitted.

"Ezra's okay?" Reese asked. She needed that part nailed down.

"He'll be back," Jeremy said. "Just needs recovery time."

Reese nodded, even though Jeremy couldn't see her. "Tell them I'll be there tonight."

"I already did," he said, pleased. "You don't let people wait, Reese."

She smiled. "Thank you," she said, and meant it for more than just the call.

When she hung up, the house felt suddenly smaller, tighter, like it knew she was about to leave.

Sloane looked up and frowned. "That look," she said. "What's going on?"

Reese inhaled. "They're putting me in."

Sloane's face lit up instantly, pride and happiness crashing together so cleanly it made Reese's chest ache. She crossed the room and took Reese into her arms, warm and solid and real.

"Baby. That's incredible," Sloane said. "I knew this was coming."

Reese hugged her back, breathing her in, already feeling the pull of what came next. Studying the track. Strategy sessions. A practice session behind the wheel.

"They want me there tonight," Reese said softly. "That's the hard part."

Sloane didn't hesitate. Not outwardly. "Oh." A pause. "Okay. Well, what do we need to do?"

But Reese felt it—the tiniest shift. The weight behind the words.

And there it was. The part Reese didn't let herself dwell on. The truth she carried quietly, like a fragile thing she didn't want to drop.

I get to do the thing I love. And the person I love has to live with it.

She kissed Sloane's temple, held on for one more beat than necessary. "Hey. Look at me."

Sloane did. Her lips were pressed together, and she blinked several times.

"Are you okay? I'm sorry we're getting cut short."

Sloane brightened again. "No, no, no. I'm good. I'm incredibly happy for you. And we will have plenty of time to be ... us. Right?" There was a quality behind her eyes that Reese couldn't quite name. She'd not seen it before. Hesitancy maybe? Unease, perhaps? It made Reese linger an extra moment.

"Do you need to pack?" Sloane asked, placing a hand on the back of her hip, almost like she didn't know what to do with it.

"Probably," Reese said, still not ready to move away from Sloane if there was anything they needed to talk through. "But ..."

"Go, Reese. I mean it. You've got a race to train for."

The smile that took over Reese's face was immediate, unstoppable. Because there was no sentence as thrilling as that one. After being out of the driver's seat for far too long, she was back.

She was racing. And in her first Formula 1 race.

Reese pressed her forehead briefly to Sloane's, grounding herself in the warmth of her, the reality of this moment, before the world shifted again.

For the first time, she wasn't chasing the dream.

She'd caught it. It was here.

And in just a few days, she was going to climb into an F1 car and finally show the world exactly what she could do.

Sloane stacked one hand over the other and pressed them together until the tremor eased. The apartment felt suddenly too quiet, the air thick with the aftermath of the call, with everything it had set in motion. Reese was in the bedroom packing, the soft rasp of zippers opening and closing carrying down the hall like a countdown.

She forced her breathing to slow. In through her nose. Out through her mouth. *Get your head right.*

She knew what this moment meant and had known it long before Reese ever let herself hope for it. A first Formula 1 race wasn't just an opportunity; it was a threshold. A once-in-a-lifetime crossing. Sloane refused to be the person who dimmed that. She would not let her fear reach Reese's joy, even if it meant locking it away where it could bruise her in private.

She'd always known the call would come. There were too many eyes on Reese now, too many people who understood what they were seeing. If it hadn't been Laurens, it would have been someone else, some other team, next season at the latest. Sloane had just believed—wrongly—that she would have more time to prepare herself for it, get some safeguards in place.

She'd already left a message for her old therapist, the one

she'd walked away from back when she thought she had everything under control. She'd been so sure she could build a safety net before the ground gave way again.

Now the moment was here, and she was standing without one.

"Okay, so apparently Jeremy's assistant managed to snag me the last seat on a flight to New York," Reese said, bursting into the room with a duffel slung over her shoulder, words tumbling out in a rush of adrenaline. "There's a tight connection to London, but it's the best they could do."

Sloane turned toward her, letting her face soften into something calm and open, even as her pulse skittered.

"I'll probably need to sleep on the plane," Reese went on, already pacing. "I just talked to Shanelle—she's excited but wants to get straight to work. Use every second we have and maximize every practice session they'll give me." She paused, eyes bright, grin breaking through. "I know the circuit, though. I mean, it's Silverstone for God's sake. Couldn't be more full circle."

Sloane nodded. "That's where Veronica recruited you, right?"

"Exactly." Reese shook her head slowly, wonder creeping into her voice. "I had no idea how much that moment would change everything. Not just my career. My life."

Her gaze found Sloane's, purposeful and earnest, and something in her expression softened.

"Can you imagine if I'd said no?" Reese said quietly. "I never would have met you."

"Who would have taught me about racing in a bar?"

"I thought we were never going to talk about that again?"

"Oh, I don't know if I can agree to that," Sloane said. "Lore is lore."

Then Reese crossed the space between them and wrapped her arms around Sloane, holding on longer than necessary. Sloane closed her eyes and held Reese back, anchoring herself in the weight of her, the truth of this. It was love and fear braided so tightly she wasn't sure where one ended and the other began.

But joy still mattered, right?

And for Reese, today, that came first.

Reese pulled back just enough to find her eyes. For a moment, neither of them spoke. The house held its breath with them, the sound of the ocean drifting in through the open window, wholly indifferent.

"They're sending a car," Reese said softly, like saying it too loud might make it real too fast. "It should be here soon."

Sloane nodded. "Yeah. I figured you'd have to head out fast."

"Fuck. I hate this part."

"It's definitely getting zero stars from me." Sloane sucked in air. "C'mon. Let's get you ready."

She helped Reese with the last few things. She folded a sweatshirt, handed over a charger, and tucked a forgotten toothbrush into a side pocket. Ordinary motions, muscle memory filling the space where words felt too big.

At the door, Reese hesitated, one hand on the handle. "You'll be there in a few days," she said, more statement than question.

"I arrive on Thursday," Sloane replied. "Not too bad, right?"

"Any time away from you is rough," Reese said, misting up. "Ah, shit." She looked at the ceiling and shook her head, smiling at her own obvious emotion. "Turns out I'm a softy."

"I won't tell the other drivers."

"I'm forever indebted." Reese took a breath. "Will I see you at my first race?"

"Are you kidding? Front row if they'll let me. I plan to be obnoxious."

Reese smiled, relief flickering across her face. "Good. I want to hear you yell my name."

"You will," Sloane said. She meant it in every possible way.

Reese leaned in and kissed her. Slow this time, unhurried, like she was memorizing the feel of Sloane's mouth, the shape of her sigh. Sloane slid her hands up Reese's arms, grounding herself in the warmth of her, the simple fact of her being here now.

"Hey," Reese murmured against her lips. "It's going to be fine. I'll be careful. Promise."

Sloane swallowed. She'd learned long ago not to ask for promises no one could keep. "I know you will," she said instead. "And you're ready. You always have been."

Reese searched her face, like she was looking for something, trying to decode how Sloane really felt. Sloane let herself smile, real and honest, even as something tight coiled in her midsection.

They stood there another beat, arms wrapped around each other, neither quite willing to be the first to let go.

Then Reese kissed Sloane's temple. "I love you."

"I love you," Sloane said back, the words anchoring her.

Reese finally stepped onto the porch, bag slung over her shoulder, suitcase waiting at her side. She turned back once more, eyes bright and full. "I can't believe this is actually happening."

"It damn well is, and you should memorize every moment. Text me when you land," Sloane said.

"Of course. And a whole lot before that. Bye."

The door closed quietly behind her.

Sloane stood there for a moment longer, listening to Reese's footsteps fade, the apartment settling into stillness around her. In a few days, she'd be trackside again, headset on, heart in her throat, cheering for Reese with everything she had.

She pressed her hands together once more, anchoring herself.

Excitement first, she reminded herself.

Fear could wait.

CHAPTER 26
HERE WENT EVERYTHING

Race day arrived like something holy.

Morning light filtered through the thin hotel curtains, soft and gray, and Reese woke with the strange calm of someone standing at the edge of something enormous. For years, she had imagined this day in fragments of helmets, anthems, and the heat of the grid. Now it was here, ordinary and extraordinary all at once. Surreal in the way she couldn't believe it was hers.

She pressed her palm flat against her chest and felt her heart beating evenly beneath it, then reached for her phone before she even checked the time.

There was already a message from Sloane:

SLOANE

Morning, Hotshot. You were born for this.

Reese grinned, internalizing the words. They meant everything to her.

Sloane had snuck out early that morning to start work at the academy, whose feature race was scheduled first of the day. They'd agreed that Reese would sleep in and get as much rest as possible. She remembered distinctly the moment the warmth that had been curled into her back had disappeared, and a kiss had been placed softly on her cheek.

Now, alone and awake, Reese smiled into the quiet room, nerves humming beneath her skin. "Just keep the car on the track," Shanelle had said.

The few days since she'd landed in the UK blurred into a montage. There'd been factory briefings over video on the flight, simulator sessions that stretched late into the night, engineers firing data at her in rapid succession as if testing whether she could swim in it or sink. It had left her feeling overloaded, overwhelmed, and in need of a break. To calm her nervous system, she'd walked Silverstone twice—once alone at dusk, tracing the racing line with her steps, and once with Shanelle, dissecting braking zones and wind direction like surgeons. Every practice session had been measured, every radio exchange intentional. No wasted laps. No ego. She'd pushed without overdriving, listened more than she spoke, and memorized the car's personality, which was so much more heightened than any car she'd ever driven. The way it rotated under throttle, the way it twitched in high-speed corners, and the way it reacted so sensitively to each driver's request.

Sloane had arrived three days prior, but their busy schedules always seemed to be in opposition, and Reese had to focus on qualifying, which, in the end, had placed her in P13 to start the race. At least she wasn't last in P22. Falling into bed with Sloane at the end of a long day had become the moment Reese looked forward to the most. They'd decompress with the lights off, wrapped around each other, talking until one of them couldn't keep their eyes open anymore.

The night before the race, most of The Starting Grid ended up squeezed into Marissa's hotel room, which looked like it had been decorated by someone deeply committed to retro glamour —mustard and teal accents, a low-slung leather headboard, abstract art that tried very hard to mean something, and a floor lamp that leaned at an angle like it had opinions. Reese sat cross-legged on the carpet with her back against the bed while Marissa paced like an overcaffeinated team principal.

"Okay," Marissa said, pointing a hairbrush at her like a microphone and tossing her sassy curls back like a supermodel. "Opening lap. What's the plan?"

"Survive," Reese deadpanned.

"Incorrect," Cassidy's voice chimed in through the laptop propped on the desk. Her screen froze for half a second before catching up. "You're not surviving. You're belonging. You should maybe write that down."

Reese glanced at the screen. "Easy for you to say from your couch."

Cassidy smirked. "I've studied Silverstone. It rewards patience. Don't try to win it in Sector 1. Let the race come to you. Write that down, too."

"Listen to her," Delaney added, dropping down onto the edge of the bed. "You don't have to prove anything in the first corner. Your name's already on the grid."

Marissa squeezed Reese's shoulder. "And isn't that the coolest?"

"You've done the work," Cassidy said more softly now. "Trust that."

Reese exhaled. For a moment, it wasn't about headlines or history or firsts. It was just this—friends who understood exactly how much tomorrow meant.

"Okay," she said, nodding once. "I'll let it come to me."

"And if you don't," Marissa grinned, "we'll still claim we knew you when."

"Speak for yourself," Delaney said, as she pulled Reese into a headlock, which of course shifted into a wrestling match that Delaney, in typical fashion, won.

Laughter rolled through the room, warm and grounding. Reese had needed that time with her friends to relax away from the stresses of training. She knew her friends would be watching the race as if it were their own. Her family would tune in, too.

But that morning, the race day was no longer abstract.

Here went everything.

Silverstone on race morning felt different from how it had all week. Heavier. Charged. Almost like it was ready to go. The low gray sky stretched wide and endless above the circuit, the kind of English morning one could expect. The grandstands were already a living thing—color and flags and sound folding in on itself from the die-hard fans, ready to spend the whole day there.

She blinked at her name on the timing screens. That hit harder than she expected.

As the day moved forward, she adjusted the collar of her race suit as she walked, helmet tucked beneath her arm, the weight of it familiar and sacred. Engineers moved around her in practiced choreography. Cameras tracked her steps. Somewhere, an announcer said her name again, stretching it slightly, making it larger than it felt inside her own head.

This is real.

The car sat waiting at the end of the grid, nose pointed toward Turn 1, impossibly sleek under the muted light. Mechanics hovered around it like guardians, tire blankets humming softly, heat rising in faint waves. The smell met her first: fuel and rubber baked into asphalt.

She slowed as she approached.

For years, she had watched this walk from the outside. From hospitality balconies in F2. From the academy paddock. From behind pit walls where her access badge hadn't quite matched her ambition.

Now the path cleared for her.

Damon met her halfway. "All good," he said, voice steady in her earpiece. "Just another race."

Reese almost smiled. It wasn't just another race.

She ran a hand briefly along the halo as she reached the car, grounding herself.

Her first Formula 1 start.

The noise of the crowd swelled as more drivers emerged onto

the grid. The national anthem would come next. The formation lap. The lights. This was happening.

Reese eased her helmet on, the world narrowing instantly to the sound of her breath and radio chatter.

She lowered herself into the seat, hands finding the wheel like they'd always belonged there. It was go time.

As they grew closer to race time, Sloane stared at the clouds inching in on the circuit, willing them to stay in the distance. The weather scanner predicted a small shower a few minutes into the race, but the precipitation was scheduled to move off after that. She was holding those problematic clouds to the bargain. Reese had enough to contend with on her first race and didn't need wet conditions and unplanned tire changes to worry about as well.

She'd attempted a light breakfast that morning, and had even walked around with a toasted bagel on a plate for a good half hour before she had to surrender it to the trash can. Her appetite had stepped out and probably wouldn't return until Reese had successfully finished the race and could move safely back to her status as the reserve driver. Sloane just had to make it through today, and then she could regroup and figure out how to be better prepared for these feelings in the future.

She had checked the radar twice before the start and then once more on her phone during the formation lap, as if vigilance alone could influence weather patterns. The system had looked small. Fast-moving. Five minutes of inconvenience, the commentators had said.

But from her place near the Laurens garage, she could see the sky deepening instead of clearing. *Dammit.* The gray thickened, low and stubborn. The air felt heavy against her skin, charged in a way she remembered too well. When the first drops hit the track, they didn't seem tentative. They came down with intent. Leave it to Silverstone to make this harder.

She folded her arms to contain the unease pressing outward from her chest. She would not devolve into anxiety. She would not give in.

When the lights went out, Sloane's breath caught anyway. Reese launched cleanly without spin or hesitation, slotting neatly into the rhythm of the pack as the field surged toward Turn 1. She held her line, gave just enough room, and came out the other side exactly where she'd started, intact and unbothered. Sloane grinned. Reese Maddox doing exactly what she'd been trained to do, surviving the chaos and keeping her place among drivers who'd been here for years.

On the screens, Reese was composed. That was what struck Sloane first. The steering inputs were clean. The throttle application was controlled, and there was no panic in the corrections. No trace of ego. Reese was adapting really nicely to the conditions.

"Good girl," Sloane murmured, hand on her chest. It seemed to be living there. "You got this, baby." She exhaled slowly, an attempt to release some of the muscle tension. It didn't work.

Sloane had told Reese a hundred times that races were won in small decisions, not bold declarations. Watching Reese make those little, disciplined choices should have felt like triumph. But it didn't. Why? Because if Reese could do this, if she could thrive here, then she truly belonged in this world, the very one that had Sloane so far back on her heels that she felt like she might fall over at any moment.

Behind Reese, Marco Faz began to close in. The gap shrank to tenths of a second. Marco had never been good at patience, plus he was hotheaded and sexist as hell. Sitting behind anyone irritated him, but sitting behind his teammate, who was female, would be intolerable. Sloane could scarcely blink, watching his proximity to Reese. "Fuck that guy." She walked a few steps to her right and then back again.

To make things worse, the rain intensified, thick enough now that spray rose in sheets behind the cars. She knew firsthand how difficult it would be to see the track, adding tons of guesswork into the mix. Even Sloane couldn't follow the action of the race clearly, and she had perspective. She squinted as the straightaway disappeared into a white corridor, visibility collapsing with every passing second.

Marco tucked into Reese's slipstream. *Dammit.*

Sloane's jaw tightened. He didn't need to do this. They were both running in the points, the season was long, and they were teammates. There was no prize for bravado in fucking standing water. Why would he risk both cars?

The two red Laurens surged forward, nearly fused in the haze. For a moment, they were indistinguishable, twin flashes of color swallowed by spray as they barreled toward Turn 11.

Sloane stepped closer to the monitors without realizing she had moved.

She told herself it was fine. Drivers went wheel-to-wheel in worsening conditions every year. She had done it herself. It required precision and trust. The cars vanished into the corner, and Sloane lost them. She swallowed and waited.

Then the garage gasped.

Sloane swiveled her focus. On the broadcast screen, a red car snapped sideways in a violent arc. The rear stepped out, overcorrected, and the car rotated through the spray like something knocked loose from gravity.

For half a heartbeat, both Laurens cars occupied the same blurred space. There was no visible number. No clear identifier of who was who. Just color and chaos. Sloane couldn't process just what she was seeing.

The timing tower flickered as the system recalculated. One Laurens entry shifted. Then both did. For two disorienting seconds, the data seemed to hesitate, and Sloane couldn't tell which name belonged to the spinning car. *God, help her. Please. Oh, please.*

Her breath stalled in her chest. She knew this sensation, when your body understood something your brain hadn't accepted yet.

The spinning car hit the wall.

The sound came through the broadcast a fraction later, hollow and violent.

Sloane gripped the back of an engineer's chair, securing herself as her vision tunneled. She didn't ask which driver it was because she couldn't form the words. The question lodged somewhere beneath her lungs, heavy and unmovable.

On the GPS tracker, the two dots that had overlapped began to separate. One continued forward. The other stopped.

Someone said, "Car 24 is out."

Marco. That was Marco. Marco was car twenty-four.

Relief struck so intensely it felt almost painful. She bent at the waist and held the position as she floated back into herself.

"Hey, she's okay. She's still going," Shanelle said, spotting Sloane in distress and moving to her from the pit wall. She placed a hand on Sloane's back until she straightened and nodded, grateful for the reassurance.

But the relief was incomplete. Reese was still out there, driving in worsening rain, threading a car through the same standing water that had just swallowed her reckless teammate, and it was Sloane's job as her girlfriend to stand here and watch. She tried to draw in a full breath and realized she couldn't. The air felt thin, insufficient. Her body had already decided this was happening again.

On screen, Reese's onboard camera flickered up. Rain streaked across the visor. Her breathing came steady over the engine noise.

"Reese. You okay?" Damon asked.

"I'm good," Reese said over the team radio. "Continuing, but what the fuck was that?"

"Just focus on this lap."

"You got it."

It helped to hear her voice.

Sloane's pulse still hammered against her throat, and a faint tremor moved through her hands. She pressed her tongue to the roof of her mouth, grounding herself the way she'd practiced in therapy. She reminded herself that she was not in a cockpit. She was not trapped in smoke and fire. She was standing on solid ground in a brightly lit garage in England.

But her body refused to fully believe it.

The safety car bunched the field, and the garage erupted into a flurry of strategy discussions. Sloane heard none of it clearly. She was watching only Reese and the tilt of her helmet, the steadiness in her hands, and the absence of desperation.

As the race resumed, Reese did not force the issue. She let others overcommit. She positioned the car carefully. She climbed into ninth without spectacular or unnecessary big moves.

By the time the checkered flag fell, the Laurens garage exploded into celebration. A ninth-place finish in those conditions with a new driver was enormous. Reese had finished *in the points* her first time out. It was a huge victory.

Sloane remained still for a beat too long, feeling as though she'd driven the race herself. Her muscles were tight, her chest aching with the aftershock of adrenaline.

Then she forced herself forward.

When Reese climbed from the car, rain-matted hair clinging to her forehead, her grin was incandescent and disbelieving. It was everything. She looked straight toward the garage and found Sloane immediately.

Sloane moved to her and opened her arms before she could overthink it, and Reese moved straight into them, in one piece. She held Reese tightly—more tightly than she meant to—and felt the solid warmth of her through the damp race suit. Tears sprang into her eyes, and she sent up a silent thank you to the universe for returning Reese to her. She savored the dependable rise and fall of her breathing. The undeniable proof of her aliveness.

Reese pulled back slightly, studying her face.

"You okay?"

The question was gentle, layered with concern beneath the triumph.

"I'm so proud of you," Sloane said, and she meant it with everything in her. "Do you know what an accomplishment this was?"

Reese's eyes lingered. "You're shaking."

Sloane hadn't realized she was.

"I'm fine," she answered, but the word felt like it was built out of cardboard.

The rain had passed. The track was already beginning to dry.

But inside her, nothing had settled at all.

Reese had just finished her first Formula 1 race and the world felt slightly unreal, as if someone had turned the saturation up too high and forgotten to dial it back. Beer tasted better. Laughter came easier. Even gravity seemed optional. If this was what success felt like, she understood why people chased it so recklessly.

The Starting Grid had joined her and Sloane at the Laurens gathering at a local pub, The Fox and Hound, which was more than enthusiastic about hosting.

"Anything you need, you just yell for Sal," a woman with luxurious red hair piled upon her head told them. She had an English accent that Reese thought came right out of a movie. "Because I'll probably be having a pint with all of ya. Not every day we get a team into the pub."

"Are you racing fans?" Reese asked.

"Is wombat poop cube-shaped?"

Reese paused. "I don't know. Is it?"

The woman clapped her on the back. "It bloody well is! Cheers to ya. I'm sending over another beer."

The pub filled fast, noise layering on itself. Marco was noticeably absent, but that was okay with Reese. Laughter, boots on wood, glasses clinking, the low hum of people who were pleased to have something worth celebrating. No one had expected her to finish as high as she had. Reese was floating. But every few seconds, her attention drifted back to Sloane like a reflex she didn't yet understand.

Sloane stood near the bar, pint in hand, posture relaxed enough to pass inspection. She smiled easily when someone congratulated her, nodded along when Marissa launched into an animated retelling of Turn 4 like she'd personally wrestled the corner into submission. But there was something off. A tightness Reese couldn't name. Like Sloane was braced against something only she could feel.

Reese's phone buzzed. Cassidy again. She'd blown up her phone during the race, leaving Reese to return to a literal running commentary from her own personal phone cheerleader. It was awesome.

CASSIDY

I screamed so loud my neighbor knocked.

CASSIDY

IN THE POINTS.

CASSIDY

YOUR FIRST F1 RACE.

CASSIDY

I AM YOUR PROUD PROBLEM CHILD.

Reese smiled to herself, thumb flying.

You okay? You sound feral.

Cassidy didn't hesitate.

CASSIDY

FERAL WITH PRIDE.

CASSIDY

I'm framing this weekend.

CASSIDY

I don't even care if I'm on the couch for another couple of weeks anymore.

Reese locked her phone and slid it into her pocket just as Delaney bumped her shoulder.

"You realize," Delaney said, lifting her glass, "that you've officially made the rest of us look bad."

Reese snorted. "Well, that didn't take much."

"Oh, please," Marissa cut in, grinning. "In this morning's race, I was graceful. Elegant. Untouchable."

"Untouchable because no one could catch you," Delaney said. "Which is rude, by the way. Work on that."

Marissa raised her brows. "That's racing, Baby D."

Reese laughed, but her eyes flicked again to Sloane. She was talking to Damon now, smiling, head tilted, listening intently. She looked present and engaged. And yet, when Reese caught her eye, the smile sharpened, brightened, like a light turned up deliberately.

There it was again.

Reese excused herself from Delaney and Marissa and crossed the small space between them.

"You good?" she asked casually, leaning in just enough to be heard.

Sloane's smile came instantly. Too instantly. "I'm great. You were fantastic out there."

Reese narrowed her eyes playfully. "You already said that. Two or three times."

"And I'll say it again," Sloane replied. She took a sip of her beer, gaze drifting somewhere over Reese's shoulder, like she was tracking something invisible.

Reese followed her line of sight without thinking. Nothing. Just noise and warmth and the aftermath of a good day.

"You're not actually here," Reese said, quieter now.

Sloane looked back at her, surprised. "What are you talking about? I am."

"No," Reese said. "You're *performing*. It's not like you."

Sloane's mouth twitched. "Is that a driver's assessment?"

"Call it instincts," Reese said. "They're pretty reliable."

Sloane raised a shoulder and let it fall as the propped-up smile faded. Her eyes said that she didn't have the words or understanding to explain. Or maybe it was that she was holding it in for the sake of Reese's celebration.

She could fix that part. "I have a wild idea. Let's get out of here," Reese said. "Spend some time together and unwind. We can go back to the room and talk." Because all she wanted in the world was to be there for Sloane in whatever she was feeling, to hold her and make it clear that she wasn't alone. More than anything, she just wanted things to be okay again.

"No. Today isn't about me. You drove an amazing race and should get to celebrate with—"

Then Shanelle's voice cut in from behind them.

"If I could grab your attention, everybody. I think we should all raise a glass to Reese Maddox," she called, raising her glass. "First F1 race. First points. Zero damage to the car."

"That last part's a goddamn miracle," Delaney said loud enough for most to hear.

Laughter rippled through the group.

Reese nodded and tipped her beer in acknowledgment of Delaney's point. "Couldn't have done it without my charming critics," she said.

"Cheers to Reese," Shanelle said, glass held high.

The rest of the pub raised their glasses before turning back to their private conversations. Marissa leaned in. "And let's hear it for how you defended Turn 7."

"I can second that," Sloane said. Then, after a pause, "That was the moment I stopped breathing."

Reese blinked. "You what?"

Sloane waved it off quickly. "Momentary lapse. Occupational hazard."

With Marissa and Delaney having a conversation of their own, Reese stepped closer to Sloane and tilted her head. "You should have told me."

Sloane met her gaze then, something unguarded flashing through before it disappeared. "This doesn't get easier," she said, carefully. "Watching. Wanting to step in. Knowing you can't." The fear behind Sloane's eyes was now clearly visible.

Reese felt that land somewhere deeper than expected, because now what? "I thought you were managing."

"I was," Sloane said. She took another sip, then set the glass down. "I think."

The noise around them surged again. Marissa laughing too loudly. Delaney arguing about tire preferences. Sal yelling from behind the bar about last call for food. Life was pressing in.

Reese leaned closer, voice low. "You don't have to be used to it tonight. I'm sure this is going to be a process."

Sloane's smile returned, softer this time. Realer. "You did beautifully, Reese."

Not *you're right*. Not *it's going to be okay*. Just that.

Reese nodded, accepting the praise, but she didn't miss the way Sloane's eyes drifted again, distant, already bracing for the next weekend, the next moment when control would be tested all over again. Reese took a pull from her beer, joining the celebration, but the thought stayed with her. This wasn't just about racing anymore.

And whatever this thing was between them, it was going to ask more than either of them was likely ready to give.

CHAPTER 27
THE CROISSANT QUOTIENT

Sloane felt like she was held together by paper clips and Scotch tape, capable of crumbling in on herself at any point. When they returned to the hotel that night, she tried her best to steer them clear of the conversation she was too afraid to have. But Reese was astute and too attuned to her shifts to just let it go.

"Do you want to talk about it now or later?" Reese asked as she stepped out of the jeans Sloane had decided were her favorite. The lamp on the bedside table glowed, but they'd left the overhead lights off, giving the room a calming, end-of-evening feel. Sloane loved the domesticity that was uniquely theirs, even as it moved from one city to the next.

"I had a moment today," Sloane said simply with a shrug. She wasn't sure how else to describe it.

Reese stilled, jeans pooled around her ankles. "On the pit wall?"

"Yes." Sloane folded her arms, suddenly unsure what to do with her hands. "In front of the screens."

Reese nodded slowly, like she already knew where this was headed but was letting Sloane set the pace. She finished changing and sat on the corner of the bed, elbows resting on her knees. "Talk to me about it."

Sloane stayed standing. If she sat, she wasn't sure she'd be able to get back up. "I've watched hundreds of races," she said. "Thousands, probably. I've analyzed incidents frame by frame. I know what a near miss looks like." Her voice tightened. "This one didn't feel like data because it was you, and it's always going to be you. That won't change."

Reese's brow furrowed. "It was under control."

"I know it was," Sloane said quickly. "You handled it beautifully. You always do." She exhaled, slow and shaky. "That's the problem."

Reese looked up at her fully now. "Okay. You're going to have to explain that part."

Sloane crossed the room but didn't sit. She stopped a few feet away, close enough to feel the warmth of Reese's body, far enough to protect herself. "I realized today that this is what it will forever be. Me watching and waiting and hoping the car keeps moving. Hoping the radio crackles and tells me you're still fine."

Reese straightened. "Sloane. It doesn't have to—"

"I stood there," Sloane continued, words picking up speed like she might lose them if she slowed down, "and it hit me that every weekend, every series, every step up the ladder just raises the stakes. And I don't get to do anything about it. I don't get to help. I don't get to intervene." Her throat burned. "I just have to hope."

Silence settled between them like the scratchiest blanket.

Reese stood. "That was one moment," she said gently. "It happens. It didn't even make the stewards' notes."

"I know." Sloane nodded, eyes bright. "I know all of that. The logic is right in front of me, but I can't grab hold. I know the statistics, the margins, and the safety improvements. How many things have improved since I was driving." Her voice softened and broke just a little. "I didn't know what it would feel like to watch it happen to someone I love."

That landed.

Reese took a step back this time, hand dragging through her hair. "So, what are you saying?"

"I'm saying I don't know if I can live like this," Sloane said. She forced herself to meet Reese's gaze. "Loving you and waiting for the worst thing not to happen. I'm just being honest."

Reese's jaw tightened. "Are you asking me to stop?"

"No," Sloane said immediately. "God, no. I would never ask that. This is who you are." Her hands dropped uselessly to her sides. "That's what scares me."

Reese paced once, then turned back. "You knew racing was my life."

"I knew it intellectually," Sloane said quietly. "I didn't know it viscerally. I didn't know how much I'd have to lose."

"I don't know what to say." Reese's voice dropped. "I can't promise you safety."

"I know."

"I can't promise this gets easier."

"I know."

They stood there, neither reaching for the other. The want was there, familiar, aching, but so was the fault line running straight through the middle of it.

Outside, laughter drifted up from the street below. A car passed. Life went on, unaware.

"I don't want to lose you," Reese said finally. "I can't."

Sloane swallowed hard. "Neither do I."

But nothing was decided. Nothing was solved.

Neither of them moved at first. The space between them felt fragile, like one wrong motion might shatter what they were still trying to protect.

Finally, Reese reached out to hook her fingers into the hem of Sloane's shirt. A quiet question. A plea without words.

Sloane went willingly.

They didn't talk anymore after that. There was nothing left that wouldn't hurt to say. Reese climbed under the covers first, and Sloane followed, fitting herself against Reese's back like muscle memory knew exactly where to land. Reese reached behind her, lacing their fingers together, pulling Sloane close until there was no daylight between them.

Sloane pressed her face into Reese's shoulder, breathing her in. Warmth. Familiarity. The even rise and fall that told her that right now, at least, everything was okay.

They lay there wrapped around each other, holding on to what they knew to be true. That they loved each other. That this was real. And whatever waited for them down the road hadn't arrived yet.

Tomorrow would come with its questions and its choices and its impossible asks. But for tonight, they stayed exactly where they were, anchored in the quiet certainty of each other, neither ready to let go.

Not yet.

Morning came too soon. Sloane woke with the sense that something had already gone wrong, even before she remembered what it was. Reese lay warm and solid beside her, breathing evenly, an arm slung across Sloane's waist like always. For a few fragile seconds, Sloane let herself believe they were still suspended in last night, untouched by consequence.

They were both flying out that day, but had purposefully booked flights for the early evening so they could enjoy as much time together as possible. Sloane was off to meet with a client in Munich, and Reese was heading to Florida with The Starting Grid to visit Cassidy and unwind with her friends.

"Hey, Hotshot," Sloane said as Reese's eyes fluttered open. When she saw Sloane, she relaxed into a smile.

"That's me. Hi."

Sloane touched her cheek. "Hi. Want to sleep a little more or grab some food? Your choice."

Reese's eyes lit up. "Can we have bread?"

Sloane laughed quietly. "Baby. We can have anything you want. There's a bakery on the corner. I can grab some croissants and bring them up. How would that be? That way, you can take your time. Wake up slowly."

"I love it when you wake up and get us baked goods." Reese grinned fully and sleepily, which meant Sloane had to kiss the full and adorable lips.

"Stop being cute."

"Can't."

"Good." Sloane found her smile. She slipped out of bed carefully, easing Reese's arm back into the warmth of the sheets, and dressed quietly. "Be back in a few minutes."

"Can we have really good morning sex when you do?"

She turned back around. "Wow. Bread *and* sex? Hmmm. Tall order, but I bet we could work something out."

Reese closed her eyes, already drifting off again. "I love you," she murmured.

"I love you, too, Reese."

Even in the midst of that warmth, that ever-present connection between them, there was a heaviness hanging on from the day before, a tax still owed. Sloane felt it weighing heavily on her shoulders.

The hallway outside their room was hushed, that peculiar hotel-morning stillness where even footsteps seemed to apologize for existing. She took the stairs down instead of the elevator, needing the movement, the brief anonymity of being just another person heading out for breakfast.

The bakery was exactly what she'd hoped for—small, unassuming, tucked into the corner like it hoped to be discovered rather than advertised. The door chimed softly when she stepped inside, and the scent hit her all at once. *Amazing*. Butter. Yeast. Sugar caramelizing just enough at the edges. It wrapped around her chest and loosened something tight.

Sloane breathed it in, slow and deep, like it might actually fix things.

A glass case displayed neat rows of croissants, their layers visible even before they were cut, golden and impossibly flaky. There were loaves cooling on racks along the wall, crackling faintly as they settled, and a woman behind the counter humming to herself while she worked. No screens. No urgency. Just bread and time and the gentle certainty that this place would exist whether the world was racing or not.

She ordered more than necessary because it somehow felt like medicine—four plain croissants, one almond, because Reese would pretend she didn't want it and then absolutely steal half, and a small loaf she didn't recognize but trusted anyway. The paper bag was warm when she took it, comforting in a way that felt almost indecent given how knotted her thoughts had been since yesterday.

For a few minutes, standing there with the bag cradled against her chest, Sloane started to believe this could be enough. That maybe life was allowed to be this simple sometimes. Bread. A quiet morning. The woman she loved resting upstairs, hair tangled, smiling as she waited for Sloane to return. Maybe that's how they did this thing. One step at a time.

By the time she pushed back into the hotel, she felt steadier. Not wholly fixed. But steadier.

The room was no longer soft with sleep when she let herself in. Reese stood near the bathroom mirror, hair dryer humming in her hand with more intention than a lazy morning warranted. She was dressed in jeans, her team hoodie, and her sneakers laced. Focused. Dialed in.

Sloane paused just inside the doorway, the bakery bag rustling softly in her grip.

"Well," she said lightly, forcing a smile. "Someone looks like she's about to be late for her own life."

Reese turned off the hair dryer and met her gaze in the

mirror before turning fully around. There was an apology in her eyes before she even spoke.

"Hey," Reese said. "God, that smells incredible."

"Bread oasis," Sloane said. "You should see this little place. I was hoping we could—"

"I know." Reese crossed the room and kissed her quickly, warmly, but with momentum still pulling her forward. "I wanted that too. I really did."

Sloane's stomach sank, just a little.

"What's up?"

Reese exhaled, running a hand through her hair. "Shanelle texted while you were gone. She wants to see me. Now-ish. Go over a few things from yesterday." She hesitated, then added, "I told her we were having a morning, and she told me to bring you along."

"Oh. Well, that was nice of her." Sloane tightened her fingers around the paper bag, the warmth seeping into her palms.

"Right?" Reese ran her fingers through her hair and gave it a final look.

"Okay," Sloane said, after a beat. "Then we'll go."

Reese searched her face. "You sure?"

Sloane lifted the bag slightly, managing a small smile. "We'll bring croissants. If we're about to have a serious debrief with a higher-up, at least we'll be armed."

Reese laughed, relief flashing across her features, and leaned in to rest her forehead against Sloane's. Just for a second.

"I'm really glad you're coming with me," she said softly. "And you look really hot in this white zip."

"Thank you." Sloane closed her eyes, breathing in the scent of Reese and butter and morning all at once, and held onto the delicate, stubborn belief she'd found in that little bakery, that maybe, somehow, everything just might be okay.

"I don't think I've ever had a driver bring breakfast before," Shanelle Laurens said, as she peered into the bag and helped herself to a plain croissant.

"Well, then you've been working with the wrong drivers," Sloane said with a wink. She looked behind her to the office door. "And if you'd rather speak with Reese privately, I can bother Jesse out front. He used to tease me about my hair peeking out of my helmet when I finished a race, and I'd be happy to pick on him a little while you two debrief."

Shanelle scoffed. "Sloane, you and I go way back, and you're a bigger help in this room than out of it. We both know that."

Reese raised a brow from her seat across from Shanelle's desk.

"Then I guess I'll stay," Sloane said, taking a seat in the chair next to Reese's.

"I think you had a fantastic first race yesterday," Shanelle said. "Everyone was impressed, from the press to the team of owners to the pit crew cheering you on."

"I'm glad to hear that," Reese said, lighting up. "It was a day I'll never forget, and I'm honored that I was given the chance to drive for Laurens."

Shanelle paused and adjusted her posture before addressing them both. "I don't know if you saw the comment Marco made online overnight, but I want to make it clear that it doesn't reflect our team culture and it's been addressed."

Reese looked at Sloane and back to Shanelle, uneasy. "I haven't been online much since the race."

Sloane frowned. "No, me neither. What did he post?" She already felt her defenses flaring on Reese's behalf because *that fucking guy.*

Shanelle slid a print capture of a post across the desk. Reese picked up the sheet of paper, stared for a minute, and then passed it to Sloane without saying a word.

@F1poletoflag:

History made. Reese Maddox becomes the first woman in years to score points in Formula 1.

@MarcoFaz:

Amazing what happens when the rules bend for a good storyline. Guess crashing out so the female marketing experiment can cruise to a P9 is just part of the show now.

Sloane shook her head, her anger rising the longer she processed. "Classy guy."

"I'm going to guess he was having a hard time with the results," Reese said diplomatically. Big of her.

"He deleted the post ten minutes later," Shanelle said, "but it was too late. Screenshots are everywhere. Racing fans are weighing in this morning."

"I'm sure in both directions." Reese shook her head. "I think that's my cue to stay off the internet this morning."

"What happens to Marco?" Sloane asked, hoping for nothing less than being fed to a hungry hippopotamus in a remote jungle.

"Well, it's been a string of incidents with Marco, and we feel it's probably time to move on. Which brings me to the real reason we're here. How would you feel about stepping in, Reese?" Shanelle placed one hand over the other and waited. Sloane blinked. Was she asking what it seemed like she was asking?

"Filling in for Marco? I don't understand," Reese said. "How would I fill in for both Ezra and Marco?"

"There were a lot of phone calls this morning. A true flurry, if I'm being honest. But everyone was of the same opinion. We'd like to offer you Marco's seat for the rest of the season."

The room went quiet.

"For the rest of the season," Reese said carefully. "In Formula 1."

Shanelle nodded. "Yes."

Reese leaned back in her chair and exhaled slowly. Processing. "You're serious?"

"I wouldn't insult you by floating it otherwise," Shanelle said. "You proved yesterday that you belong on that grid. You raced smart. You adapted. And you finished in the points without putting the car, or anyone else, at risk."

Reese's gaze slid sideways to Sloane.

She attempted to contain her emotion for Reese's benefit. But excitement flashed within her, bright and undeniable, followed by something quieter. Fear.

"That's a massive leap," Reese said. "Midseason. New engineers. New expectations."

"And more eyes," Sloane added softly.

Reese nodded. "Yeah. That too."

"I won't pretend otherwise," Shanelle said. "You'll be scrutinized in ways Ezra never was and Marco never had to be. But I also won't pretend you aren't ready. And you wouldn't be doing this alone."

Her gaze moved to Sloane.

"We'd want Sloane involved," Shanelle continued. "Publicly. Strategically. As support and mentorship. The paddock knows her. They trust her. That matters."

Sloane's heart gave a hard thump. She'd known this was coming, had prepared herself for it, but hearing it said out loud was something else entirely.

"When would this start?" Reese asked.

"Next race," Shanelle said. "You'd test immediately. We'd announce within forty-eight hours."

This was everything Reese had worked for. It was also the thing Sloane had been dreading since the first time she'd watched her drive.

Sloane nodded along, professional and seemingly present, but didn't trust herself to speak.

Forty-eight hours. Flights. Briefings. Headlines. The way Reese's life would compress and accelerate all at once.

"I'd need a few days to get ready," Reese said finally. "To see my friends as we'd planned. To get my head on straight. To call my family."

Shanelle smiled respectfully. "Of course. You've earned that."

Reese blew out a breath. "Okay. Let's do this."

"I'll talk to your agent and get the paperwork together. I have a feeling this is going to be a fruitful partnership, Reese," Shanelle said.

"I really think so, too. I won't let you down."

Sloane reached over and squeezed Reese's knee. Just once. A silent show of support.

Sloane kept her hand where it was, light and supportive. She let Reese have the moment without adding her own weight to it.

There would be time later to reckon with what this meant.

Forty-eight hours.

Sloane held on to Reese and tried not to think about how fast everything was about to move, and how Reese was already slipping through her fingers into a world that Sloane simply could not follow.

CHAPTER 28
THE DEEP END

There was something profoundly grounding about stepping off a plane and into the orbit of people who knew you before the headlines did. Florida greeted Reese with thick heat and salt air, but it was the familiarity waiting beyond baggage claim that steadied her pulse.

She saw Cassidy's blond hair first. Marissa was standing beside her holding a sign that said, "F1 Babes Only." Delaney was pointing to it like a bouncer at a nightclub.

"You did not," Reese said, swallowing back a laugh.

"Oh, we did," Cassidy said, opening her arms for Reese, who gave her the biggest, but also the gentlest, hug she could manifest. "The Grid's all here!"

"How are the hands?"

"So much better. No more bandages. Full recovery on the way. I'm told as long as I stick with my OT, I should be back next season."

"Seriously? I will be screaming my face off for you, Cass."

Marissa was next in line for a hug. Reese wrapped her arms around her friend, and they rocked back and forth to exaggerated extremes. "Do F1 drivers fly first class?"

"Not when it's on their own dime," Reese said, releasing her. "I saw that overtake on Turn 7 last week. That was sick."

"Thank you. My academy mentor helped me with a few new tricks."

"The really hot one?" Reese asked with a wink.

Marissa frowned. "Yeah, but I hear she's all girlfriended up."

"Damn right she is."

Delaney waited for her turn patiently, but didn't hold back on her hug when it came. "There's my teammate."

"Hey, buddy. Have you scouted all the best spots in Fort Lauderdale?"

"No, because I'm not sure I want to be far from the couch or the pool."

"That's actually logic I can get behind." The few days they were stealing between races were much-needed rest and decompression time, and if all they did was sit in Cassidy's parents' guesthouse and watch movies, mainline all varieties of Pop-Tarts, and catch up on each other's little details, it would be a welcome getaway.

They'd chosen Cassidy's neck of the woods since she was still in recovery, but happily accepted the bonus of sun-bleached docks, slow afternoons, and nice, easy weather. They hadn't all been in the same place since the hospital in Europe, when everything had been heavy and uncertain. Seeing Cassidy in person, upright and healing, felt like closing a loop on something Reese would rather not remember. With Formula 1 looming, contracts signed, expectations towering, this pocket of time felt less like a vacation and more like a salve. True friends had a way of stripping the noise away, of reminding her who she was beneath the fire suit and the scrutiny. And for the first time in weeks, Reese let herself exhale.

"Let's get out of here," Cassidy said. "We've spent enough time in airports this year."

Later that afternoon, when the sun shone down, the pool became the center of gravity. Mai tais sweated on the edge, their citrus bite much needed and perfect, while Cassidy drifted lazily on a ridiculous dinosaur floaty, sunglasses tipped just so, issuing commentary like a benevolent queen in recovery. Marissa owned her va-va-voom bikini with zero apology, all confidence and laughter, while Reese's bikini cut a clean, sleek line in black. She leaned her head back, hair touching the water, feeling lighter than she had in months. Delaney lounged nearby in ultracool shades, feet in the water, offering dry observations that landed expertly every time. They caught each other up on life, talked about everything important and not, letting the day stretch long and loose, just friends, warmth, and the quiet luxury of nowhere else to be.

"Did I hear you correctly that Sloane was with you when you got the offer?" Marissa asked.

Reese nodded. "Yeah, that part was really cool." A pause. "At least, for me."

"Her, too, I'm sure," Cassidy said.

Instinctually, Reese checked her phone to see if Sloane had responded to her last check-in text. She had not. She'd tried not to let that bother her. Sloane was probably juggling client calls and a busy afternoon. That's what she told herself anyway. She'd been quieter since their meeting with Shanelle. There was no denying that, and Reese knew why. She just wasn't sure how to reconcile her new job with what Sloane needed to feel secure.

"I think she wants F1 for me, but not her."

Delaney frowned. "What do you mean?"

Reese went on to explain how Sloane's accident had shaped the way she handled risk in her life. She talked about the fear that never fully loosened its grip once it got its hands on you. How Sloane never said *don't go*, but it was there all the same.

The pool had gone quieter, the soft lap of water against tile suddenly louder.

Cassidy let her dinosaur drift closer, resting her forearms on the edge. "That kind of fear sticks," she said. "Once you've been on the wrong side of luck, it's hard not to see it everywhere." Reese understood that Cassidy was speaking from experience.

"And she loves you," Marissa added. "Which honestly makes it worse. Love gives fear more material to work with."

Reese nodded. "She wants this for me. I know she does. I just don't think she wants it around *her*."

Delaney pushed her shades up onto her head, finally meeting Reese's eyes. "Okay, but here's the thing," she said. "You're not asking her to be reckless. You're asking her to trust *you*. And that's different."

Cassidy hummed in agreement. "This might take time, Reese. Big transitions don't come with easy or tidy timelines."

"And," Marissa said lightly, though her gaze was sincere, "you're allowed to want the thing you've worked your entire life for *and* the woman you love. That's not greed. That's being human."

The tightness in Reese's chest eased just a fraction. Talking to her friends helped. "I hate that it feels like I'm choosing," she admitted.

"You're not," Delaney said immediately. "You're moving forward. The people who love you will figure out how to move with you."

And what if Sloane didn't, couldn't? Reese would attack that bridge when she came to it, because the idea of it was almost too much for her brain to handle. *Don't get ahead of yourself.*

The sun dipped lower, turning the water gold. Cassidy kicked her floaty lazily, Marissa reached for her drink, and the moment softened again, the weight redistributed among them.

Reese leaned her head back, eyes closed, letting the warmth of the sun wash over her body. She didn't have answers yet. But for now, she had this. Friends who knew her, who held space without trying to steer the wheel.

She checked her phone and smiled because she had a message from Sloane.

SLOANE

I love you. I miss you. I hope you're having the best time.

She exhaled and held the phone to her chest because Cassidy was right. Things were going to work themselves out.

Sloane discovered, by accident, really, that if she stacked enough work on top of her thoughts, they stayed mercifully quiet.

Her calendar became a study in saturation that week. Morning calls with automotive clients on three continents, afternoons with the academy reviewing data, sitting through Zoom meetings where the dividing lines between *acceptable risk* and *career-ending disaster* were discussed in clean, unemotional language. She thrived there because numbers behaved. They were easy to understand. Problems always had solutions if you stared at them long enough.

Unlike everything else.

She told herself she was being professional by working so much. Efficient, even. She did not tell herself that she was afraid of silence, of giving herself too much time to think, because that's when things got dangerous. It was in those spare moments that the same image crept back in: her car splintering, fire blooming where it shouldn't, the long wait between impact and movement. She didn't let herself dwell on the fact that loving a woman who now belonged to Formula 1 felt like standing too close to the edge of something she'd already fallen from once.

So, she worked.

She worked until her eyes burned and her coffee went cold. She worked until Reese's texts sat unanswered for longer than she meant them to. *Busy*, she told herself. *Just busy. That's all.*

It almost held.

Until the night before travel, when she was scheduled for another race weekend. The academy's. And, of course, Reese's.

Her suitcase sat open on the bed, half-packed, the academy credentials tucked neatly into the side pocket. Everything about the trip was routine. Same airports, same security lines, same practiced efficiency. She'd done this dozens of times. Hundreds, maybe.

But this time was different. The stakes were.

Sloane sat on the edge of the mattress and tried to picture it all unfolding: the F1 garage, the speed, the monitors. The way the whole world watched now. The way *she* would have to watch. Her chest tightened, breath turning shallow before she even realized she was bracing.

I can do this, she told herself.

The words didn't land. So she tried again. And again.

Morning came anyway, and she somehow found her way to the airport, driven by love and determination, hand in hand. She was met with airport noise, rolling bags, stressed-out travelers, and the low hum of what felt like the inevitable. Sloane made it through security on muscle memory alone, heart beating too fast, palms damp. She stood at the gate and watched the waiting plane through the glass.

All she had to do was board. Just get on the plane and fly to Reese.

Her body refused.

It wasn't panic, exactly. No dizziness, no drama. Just a firm, immovable certainty settling in her bones: *If I get on that plane, something in me is going to break.*

She stepped away from the gate, phone already in her hand.

Veronica answered on the second ring. "You're early."

"I'm not coming," Sloane said. "At least not now."

There was a pause. "Okay," she said calmly. "Tell me why."

Sloane closed her eyes. The truth pressed hard against her midsection. "I can do the academy job," she said. "I can do the clients. I can do risk on paper and data and simulations." Her voice caught, just slightly. "I can't do *this*. Not yet."

Another beat. "This being Reese driving in Formula 1?

"Yes."

Veronica exhaled slowly. "You don't usually bail."

"I know." Sloane swallowed. "I don't want to punish her for something she's earned. And I don't want to punish myself by pretending I'm ready when I'm not. I'm not ready, Veronica."

Silence stretched.

"Can you throw a tennis ball around and get yourself to a better spot? This is your happiness we're talking about. I'll hold your hand, Sloane. We can get through this weekend, and the rest will get easier with time and practice. You've been so happy."

"I can't do it this time, Ronnie."

"All right," Veronica said at last. "I'll cover. Take the time you need. But Sloane—" She softened, just a fraction. "Don't disappear. From her, or from yourself."

Sloane opened her eyes, watching the final boarding call light up the screen. "I won't," she said. She hoped it was true. She had work to do on herself before she could properly show up for anyone else, and that included Reese.

She hung up as the line moved forward without her, the plane filling, the world continuing on schedule. She hoped there was a scenario in which Reese would understand, would forgive her. Their future had a question mark attached to it, and it was up to Sloane to fight like hell to erase it. She wanted Reese, but had to acknowledge that she just might lose her in the process of working on herself.

Sloane turned away from the gate, heart heavy but choosing, for once, not the fastest path forward, but the one she could actually walk.

CHAPTER 29
EATING AN ELEPHANT

Reese was already making a list of all the things she wanted to see, do, visit, and experience with Sloane while they were in Budapest. A walk along the Danube, hopefully in the evening when the city would be lit up. Maybe visit a little ruin bar tucked into a courtyard. Coffee on a terrace where no one cared who she was, just that the espresso was strong and the pastries were perfect. Oh, and she wanted to show Sloane the circuit from the outside, the way the hills cradled it. There wouldn't be enough time for all of it. There never was. But they'd get to what they could.

Reese had arrived a couple of days earlier to shoot promos and photos in preparation for her official debut with Laurens. The PR people wanted to make sure they had everything they needed to give her a proper launch. Seeing her image stretched into a massive banner above the garage was a moment she'd never forget. The scale of it. The finality. The way it felt like the world was suddenly speaking her name at full volume. Did she Instagram the hell out of a photo of her standing in front of the banner in her race suit? Absolutely. She'd sent it straight to Sloane, captioned with something breezy and untrue about how totally chill she felt.

But today was different. Today, Sloane was arriving, and it had Reese on a complete high.

She had dashed back to the hotel to change, nerves buzzing under her skin in a way that had nothing to do with racing. She checked her phone for the hundredth time. Still nothing. Sloane hadn't responded since boarding her first flight, but the connection was tight, and Reese figured she'd stayed in airplane mode, chasing sleep where she could. It made sense. It was fine. If everything was on time, she'd have landed an hour ago, probably already in a cab, probably rolling her eyes at Reese's *come straight up* text and smiling anyway.

She paced the room, tugged on a clean shirt, then abandoned it for another. Sent one more message.

> I'm here in the room. Can't wait. I want to kiss you already.

No reply.

When the knock finally came fifteen minutes later, it hit her like a jolt of happy electricity.

Reese didn't bother checking the peephole. She crossed the room in three long strides, heart already racing, joy rushing up so fast it almost hurt. She was halfway through imagining the weight of Sloane's arms around her, the familiar kiss that always made the world click back into place when she opened the door.

It was Veronica.

The smile froze on Reese's face, confusion flashing so fast it barely registered before something colder slid in beneath it. "Hey," she said, already knowing something was wrong. "I thought you were …"

Veronica's expression was gentle in a way that scared her more than anything else. "Hey, Reese. Can I come in?"

Reese stepped back automatically, the room suddenly too quiet. Veronica didn't rush. She closed the door carefully, like she was containing something fragile.

"She's not coming," Veronica said, her eyes apologetic.

The words landed wrong. Like they'd missed their mark entirely. Reese shook her head once. "What do you mean she's not coming? She's—she was flying today."

"I know." Veronica met her gaze. "She tried. She really did."

Something inside Reese dropped hard, like she'd missed a gear. Her chest tightened, breath turning shallow as the implications stacked up too quickly to process. "Hold on. Did something happen? Is she okay?"

"She's safe," Veronica said immediately. "Physically. This isn't an emergency."

That somehow made it worse.

"She said she couldn't wait to see me," Reese said. "There have been hiccups about my driving, but she said she was working on things."

"I know," Veronica said. "And she is."

Reese nodded, already reaching for her phone without thinking and having to stop herself because maybe that wasn't helpful. "Okay. Then I'll give her time. Or space. Or—whatever she needs. I don't need her at every race. I don't need—" She stopped, breath hitching as the words outran her certainty. "I just need her to know I'm here. That I'll be here."

Veronica watched her gently. "Reese ..."

"I mean it," Reese pressed, the urgency sharpening. "I don't need grand gestures. I don't need her standing on the pit wall every weekend. We can figure this out." She looked up, hopeful despite herself. "Right?"

The silence that followed was careful. Considered.

"Sometimes," Veronica said slowly, "what someone needs isn't something you can provide by offering more. Sometimes, it's something they have to sort through on their own, and she's taking time to do that. All of this happened really fast."

She nodded. The words slid into Reese's chest and stayed there.

She stared at the screen of her phone, thumb hovering uselessly above Sloane's name. All the ways she'd been prepared to bend—reschedule, rearrange, compartmentalize—lined up neatly in her head, solutions waiting to be deployed. She was good at that. At adapting, executing. At finding a way to make things work.

But this wasn't a line she could adjust with more practice.

"What if," Reese said quietly, "what she needs is a life that doesn't include … this?" Her voice wavered on the last word because what she really meant was *me*.

Veronica didn't rush to answer. "That's the question she's still trying to sit with."

The thought hollowed Reese out. She had always believed love was an action: showing up, adjusting, choosing each other again and again. The idea that love might also mean standing still, hands empty, felt unbearable.

"I can't lose her," Reese said. Because to Reese, that was her thesis statement. All the rest were just details.

"I know," Veronica said softly.

The room felt suddenly enormous. The future she'd been moving toward might happen without the one person she'd been picturing beside her. Reese pressed her palm flat against her sternum, grounding herself as best she could.

"She might never come back," Reese said.

Veronica didn't contradict her. She couldn't.

After a moment, Reese lowered her hand, shoulders settling with the weight of it. "I still have to drive this weekend," she said with disbelief. Because how was that going to happen? How was she just supposed to go about her weekend like everything wasn't upside down?

"You do," Veronica agreed. "And you don't have to know how you'll do it yet. Just that you will. You're a pro, Reese."

She nodded, though it felt like agreeing to something she didn't fully understand. The ache didn't lessen, but it settled in. Somehow, she was just going to have to move forward without knowing whether the person she loved would ever be standing beside her again.

Veronica lingered for a moment, like she might say something else, then thought better of it. She squeezed Reese's shoulder once before letting herself out, the door clicking shut with a finality that felt too loud in the quiet room.

Reese stood there long after, phone still in her hand, the last message she'd sent glowing faintly on the screen.

Eventually, she sat on the edge of the bed and stared at the floor, at the scuff marks in the carpet, at the place where Sloane's bag should have been. She tried to imagine the weekend unfolding without her, and for the first time since Budapest had come onto the calendar, the city felt impossibly far away.

Reese lay back fully dressed, arms crossed over her chest, and let the ceiling blur.

She didn't cry. She didn't break.

She just stayed there, breathing, waiting for the ache to become something she could live with.

Back in Venice Beach, Sloane let her days take on a different shape.

She'd been home a little over three weeks, which was long enough for the salt air to feel normal again. Also long enough that she'd missed two race weekends she should have traveled for. Academy obligations she'd handed off. Formula 1 paddocks she'd stayed away from. That was hard.

But she'd been busy.

Therapy came first. Twice a week at the start, then a standing slot she agreed to treat like any other nonnegotiable commitment. Lindsay, her therapist, sat across from her with a legal pad she barely used and a way of listening that made silence feel productive.

"What does your body do," Lindsay asked one morning,

"when you imagine standing in the garage while she's out there racing?"

Sloane didn't answer right away. She closed her eyes, checked in. "My chest tightens," she said finally. "Not panic. More like ... bracing."

"Okay," Lindsay said. "So, your body's talking before you are. That's helpful to know. That's a starting point."

They talked about timing and proximity, about how Sloane's instincts shifted when risk stopped being theoretical. Loving racing had never been a problem because she did love it. It was loving Reese that had changed the math. Together, they made plans for how she could handle any difficult moments ahead: regular check-ins even when Sloane was on the road, a clear agreement that she wouldn't disappear and then pretend she was fine. Falling off the therapy wagon wasn't an option anymore.

"Not attending a race," Lindsay said later, "doesn't mean you're retreating. It means you're listening. We can take this case by case."

Sloane leaned in. "Don't you mean race by race?"

Lindsay smiled. "Actually, I do."

Some days, Sloane walked out feeling steadier. Other days, wrung out. Lindsay had told her both counted.

Late mornings often found Sloane at The Cat's Pajamas, the coffee shop tucked a block off the boardwalk, where the windows were always open and the air smelled faintly of salt and espresso. Autumn was behind the counter every time—curly red hair wild, smile immediate, pulling shots with the precision of a scientist and the joy of someone who loved what she did.

"You look better," Autumn said one morning, sliding a mug across the counter without asking.

Sloane wrapped her hands around the cup. "I feel better," she admitted. "Which is ... new."

Autumn lifted a brow. "But?"

"But I don't want to rush it, ya know?" Sloane said.

Autumn nodded slowly. "Nor should you. You just sip your coffee and enjoy all you're doing to get back to that girl of yours." She placed a hand on her hip. "I saw the end of her race on Sunday. Ouch."

Sloane deflated. "I caught the highlight show after the race. Yeah, not her best. I'm not exactly sure what's going on." Reese had finished out of the points and had slow starts in both of her last two races. Sloane had thoughts, but she was worried the problem went beyond racing, and that sat uncomfortably on her chest. "Hoping she rallies next weekend."

"Of course she will," Autumn said without a beat of hesitation. "She's a badass hottie, and those always triumph in the end. I should know. I'm married to one." A pause. "What else?"

Sloane exhaled. "I talked to Veronica. We made a plan. Next time I watch Reese race, she'll sit with me. Just … be there. And she'll keep sitting with me until I get the hang of the whole thing again. And I will. I know it."

Autumn smiled, soft and proud. "You're making things happen a little at a time."

Sloane huffed a quiet laugh. "I am. What is it they say about eating an elephant?"

"Oh, sweetie, I have some freshly baked chocolate chip muffins that will taste much better."

Sloane laughed. "Probably wise."

"Well," Autumn said, tapping the counter lightly, "from where I'm standing, it looks like tons of progress. You love her," she said, her eyes soft and big. "That part is more than clear."

"I really do," Sloane said.

When she imagined returning to a race weekend, she imagined doing it differently. Not proving anything. Not forcing herself through moments her body wasn't ready for yet. Choosing presence when she could … and honesty when she couldn't.

Every few days, she texted Reese. Nothing heavy. Nothing evasive.

> Thinking of you.

> Hope the weekend went okay.

> I love you.

> I'm here. Hopefully, we can talk more soon.

Reese always replied. It wasn't always right away, but she got there.

That mattered.

REESE

> I love you. Thank you for checking on me.

At night, Sloane stood barefoot on her balcony, ocean air cool against her skin, and practiced staying present, which meant neither retreating into the past nor racing ahead to a future she wasn't ready to inhabit yet. She wasn't fixed. She wasn't finished. But she was closer than she'd been.

And for now, that was enough to keep going.

CHAPTER 30
SIXTEENTH

The next race weekend felt wrong from the start. And it reminded her of the last.

Reese noticed it in the small things first—the missed braking point she never missed, the hesitation in a corner she usually trusted without thinking. The car was fine. The track was familiar. She wasn't. Her lap times hovered close enough to respectable to keep anyone from panicking outright, but the stage was set, and the data was adding up.

"I don't know what's wrong," she told Shanelle, as they sat in her office later that day. "Other than I'm in my head a little more than usual." She couldn't argue that part. She missed her girlfriend immensely and walked around on autopilot, hollow and worried and second-guessing everything she'd done and said up to that point. But when she got behind the wheel, she focused, she executed, and none of it was paying off the way she was used to.

"Here's the thing. The change in your driving is small, but those quarters of a second add up," Shanelle told her. "A tiny shift in your mindset makes incremental differences lap after lap after lap until you're finishing three seconds behind your competitor."

Reese nodded. "Fewer hesitations. I have to process quicker."

"Do I look worried?" Shanelle said, sitting back in her chair like a woman waiting patiently on a martini. "I know who I hired, and she'll be back. Let's see how you do in your practice session today and come up with a workable race strategy with Geoff." The new engineer she was working with, now that Damon was back with Ezra, was patient and smart, but they had yet to develop a rhythm.

"Okay, let's hope for a good session."

Shanelle's confidence was helpful, the way it always was. Reese left the office, telling herself to simplify. Brake later. Commit sooner. Trust the muscle memory that had carried her this far.

The practice session was cleaner. She hit her marks more consistently, stayed out of trouble, and finished without incident. On paper, it looked like progress.

Inside the car, it felt like holding something together with both hands.

When she climbed out, Delaney, Marissa, and Cassidy were waiting near the back of the garage. There was no academy race that weekend, no overlapping obligations—just three familiar faces she'd invited as guests, guest passes clipped visibly at their waists. They stayed deliberately out of the way, like people who knew the rhythm of a paddock and respected it.

Delaney didn't bother easing into it. "You're late on turn-in."

Reese gave a tired half-smile. "Cool. Hello to you, too."

"Sorry. Hi. But, I mean it," Delaney said. "You're not committing when you should. You hesitate, then overcorrect."

"And that's new," Marissa added. "You usually trust your first instinct."

Cassidy watched her quietly for a beat. Her friends knew everything that was going on with her and Sloane, but Cassidy was the most attuned to her feelings, checking in on her multiple times a day. "You're not distracted," she said. "You're guarded, which makes sense when you think about it. Given everything you have going on."

Reese leaned back against the wall, helmet tucked under her arm. "I don't know how to stop thinking long enough to drive."

"You don't," Delaney said. "You stop trying to think your way through it."

"That's not helpful," Reese muttered.

"It is," Marissa said gently. "You're trying to solve something that isn't a driving problem while driving. Your brain keeps wandering because it doesn't feel settled."

Reese stared at the concrete. "Well, I don't know how to settle it."

Later, as the garage thinned and the day wound down, Reese found herself alone again—too quiet, too much room for the thoughts she'd been keeping at bay. Sloane's absence pressed in on her from every direction. The empty space where she should have been. The unanswered questions Reese was trying not to ask yet.

That night, Reese sat on the side of her hotel bed, phone in her hand, thumb hovering over Sloane's name. She didn't text. Not because she didn't want to, but because she didn't know what she could say that wouldn't sound like pressure.

I miss you felt obvious.

I'm not okay felt unfair.

Please come back felt like too much.

She set the phone down and stared at the wall instead.

The thought came to her slowly, without drama. If this—*this life*—meant losing Sloane, then no amount of speed or success would make it worth it. Ever.

She would race this weekend. She would show up. She would do her job. But if the choice ever became real, if the cost became final? She already knew the answer.

And that knowledge, heavy as it was, finally let her breathe.

Sloane was already packing when Veronica answered the phone.

The suitcase lay open on the bed, and she moved around it with purpose, tossing clothes inside without folding. She took stock. Jeans, a soft T-shirt, her academy polos, the jacket she always grabbed when she didn't know what the weather would be like, but needed something familiar.

Her phone sat on the nightstand, Veronica's voice coming through on speaker, even and unhurried. "You don't have to rush," Veronica was saying. "Take another week if you want. We're not racing this weekend anyway. I feel like this time has been good for you, and I want to see that continue."

"It has," Sloane said, tugging open a drawer and scooping up socks. Veronica was worried because she was a good friend, but Sloane felt emotionally stronger than she had in years, and now was the time. "It's not that I'm undoing the work. If anything, I'm acting on it."

There was a brief pause on the other end of the line. "Okay," Veronica said. "Tell me what changed."

Sloane stopped moving for a moment, one hand braced on the bed. Her chest tightened with certainty, the panic gone.

"I saw qualifying."

Earlier that day, she'd been sitting on her couch, coffee cooling on the table. She'd had the broadcast muted and her laptop open so she could check in on the progress, monitor the timing graphics. It had turned into more than that.

Reese's turn came early in qualifying. The first lap was messy. Nothing catastrophic, but off, almost like she wasn't warm yet. The second attempt was worse. A snap of overcorrection, a missed apex, momentum bleeding away in places where Reese usually gained it.

Sixteenth.

It was an abysmal result, and Sloane knew how devastated Reese had to have been.

The number had sat there on the screen, stark and undeniable. She'd have an uphill battle going into the race, and a third poor showing was going to start voices behind the scenes talking. The media would join the speculation. Had Laurens acted impulsively when they'd brought Reese on? Would they correct the mistake before the season was too far gone to save?

Sloane hadn't felt fear then. She'd felt something colder and sharper. Recognition. Reese was so much better than what she was showing, and it was time to step up and support the woman that she loved.

"She's in her head," she said quietly. "She's drowning, and I know I can help."

Veronica didn't argue.

Standing in front of her suitcase, she stared at the ceiling, hands on her hips. "She needs me, Ronnie, and I need her, and for the first time in a long time, I feel like I can truly be there to cheer her on, hold her hand, and help. And I can do it in the right way."

"She has been struggling. That part's true. She misses you."

"I miss her, too." She took a deep breath. "And I'm ready."

Sloane exhaled and reached for her passport, sliding it into the outer pocket of the suitcase. There was a flight late that afternoon that would have her in Barcelona by midmorning their time, in plenty of time for the race.

She zipped the suitcase closed and rested her palm on it for a moment, grounding herself. No rush in her body. No spike of adrenaline. Just intention.

"I'll text you when I land," she said into the phone.

"I'll be there," Veronica replied. "In more ways than one."

"I know." Sloane smiled, small but real. "Thank you for trusting me to know when it was time."

"That's the thing," Veronica said gently. "You didn't rush back to the fire. You learned how to stand near it again. Proud of you for that. Travel safe."

"Thank you, Ronnie. See you soon."

She moved through the apartment slowly, deliberately—checking the back door, setting the coffee mug in the sink, straightening the throw blanket on the couch without thinking about it. Ordinary motions. Anchors.

She paused at the doorway, one hand on the frame, and took stock of herself the way Lindsay had taught her to. Chest open. Breath even. No bracing. No rehearsal of disaster.

This wasn't about proving anything. It wasn't about erasing what had happened or pretending she was fixed. It was about showing up honestly.

She rolled her suitcase down the hall, the sound soft and ordinary, and stepped out into the day.

By the time the plane lifted off, Sloane felt settled in her seat, hands resting easily in her lap. She looked out the window as the city fell away, not replaying the past, not racing ahead.

Just moving forward.

Toward Reese.

Toward the life they were still building, one step at a time.

CHAPTER 31
ONE STRAWBERRY SMOOTHIE

Reese wanted to start race morning by looking through the photo album on her phone, the one that contained photos of her and Sloane from various cities. Her favorite was the one in Monza at the little wine and cheese place where Sloane was smiling into the camera with her arms around Reese's neck, and Reese was smiling at Sloane. A little crooked, like she'd forgotten the camera was even there. It was a memory she held onto and pulled out when she needed to drift away to a happier moment.

But she wouldn't be doing that today because the stress of her current reality was adding fractions of a second to her lap time, so anything that would tug on her brain had to be shelved until after the race.

She had prep to get through and that started now.

Barcelona's morning air carried a hint of salt from the Mediterranean, warm already despite the early hour. The paddock hummed with its usual race-day rhythm—generators buzzing, radios crackling, the low thrum of engines being woken up. Somewhere, an air wrench barked to life, sharp and sudden. Reese moved through it all like she was stepping across thin ice. Careful. Deliberate. Not allowing herself to fall through.

Sixteenth.

The number had sat beside her name on the timing sheet yesterday like an accusation. She'd told the media it was "a learning weekend." She'd told Julie they were "still dialing it in." She'd told herself to stop spiraling.

Two races out of the points. Sixteenth on a circuit where overtaking wasn't exactly a gift. And a brain that insisted on replaying every almost-text, every unfinished conversation with Sloane.

She adjusted the strap of her backpack higher on her shoulder and ducked into the hospitality unit, grateful for the blast of air-conditioning. Fuel first. Smoothie. Hydrate. Review data. Visualize starts. Brake markers into Turn 1. Stay out of chaos.

Simple.

The smoothie counter was tucked into the corner, half-hidden behind a column wrapped in sponsor decals. Reese stepped into line, eyes already scanning her mental checklist.

Strawberry. Always strawberry on race mornings. Predictable. Familiar. One thing she didn't have to think about.

"Hey," a voice said softly.

Everything in her body stilled.

It was ridiculous how quickly she knew. Not just the sound of it, but the way it landed—like it belonged to her.

Reese turned.

Sloane stood there, hair pulled back, academy jacket unzipped, a smoothie cup already in her hand. Strawberry pink, unmistakable even through the clear lid. She was smiling, not carefully or cautiously, but the way she did when she'd been counting the minutes to see Reese again.

For a second, Reese forgot where she was. Forgot sixteenth. Forgot Barcelona. Forgot the careful walls she'd built around her heart for three weeks.

She didn't think. She just moved.

Reese stepped forward and reached for Sloane, one hand sliding around her waist, the other coming up to her shoulder, pulling her in. It was instinct. Muscle memory laced with relief.

Sloane came easily, like she'd been waiting for permission and now had it. The smoothie was set down on the counter without a second thought as Sloane wrapped her arms around Reese's back, holding her close. Reese caught the faint scent of Sloane's citrus shampoo and the last of the tension in her chest finally loosened. If there was ever a metaphor for home, Reese had found it in this moment.

"There you are," Sloane murmured, lips brushing Reese's temple.

"Hi," Reese said, her voice smiling into the word.

They stayed like that longer than was strictly professional, but neither of them rushed it. The paddock would get over it. Sloane's hand slid up and down Reese's back once, grounding her and reminding her she wasn't alone.

When they finally pulled back, Reese kept her hands where they were, thumbs brushing lightly against Sloane's sides like she needed the contact to stay upright.

Sloane picked up the smoothie and pressed the cup into Reese's hands. "Strawberry. Race morning. I know the rules."

Reese laughed, bright and surprised by how freely it came. Her chest felt lighter, like something tight had finally unclenched.

"Thank you," she said. "I've missed you so much."

Sloane's expression softened. "Same. A lot."

Reese took a sip, the cold sweetness hitting her tongue, familiar and comforting. She closed her eyes for half a second, then opened them again, feeling for the first time in a while that she was on solid ground.

"I qualified sixteenth," she said, matter-of-fact.

"I know," Sloane said. "That doesn't change anything." They stepped out of the way of people entering the smoothie line and found their own spot along the wall.

Reese searched her face. "Doesn't it?"

"No," Sloane said firmly. "It means you have an uphill battle and you'll have to work if you want to get into the points and P10. Which you're very good at." She brushed her thumb along Reese's jaw, quick and subtle but intimate all the same. "And it means I get to watch you fight forward."

Reese's heart lifted, buoyant, soaring in her chest. This—*this*—was what she'd been missing.

"Don't go anywhere," Reese said.

"I'm not," Sloane promised. "I'll be right here. When you get back."

Reese nodded, gripping the smoothie like a talisman, then leaned in and pressed a quick kiss to Sloane's lips. It was soft, sure, and full of all the things they didn't need to say out loud.

When she stepped away, she felt different, like she was ready to take on twenty-one other drivers, knowing that at the end of the day, something even more important was waiting for her. They hadn't had a conversation yet, but Sloane's presence alone, her entirely open demeanor, communicated a lot.

Sixteenth no longer felt like a sentence, but a problem to solve.

When Reese walked back to the garage, prized smoothie in hand, she nodded to the crew members she passed, some offering words of encouragement. Others knocked lightly against her shoulder or lifted a wrench in greeting. One walked out from behind the car with a big smile on his face. She nodded to him as she passed before pulling up short.

She turned back immediately and found herself face-to-face with her brother, dressed in Laurens team gear, no less.

"What is happening right now?" Reese asked.

"I couldn't let you have all the fun," Luke said, shuffling over in that ridiculous walk he put on that took six inches off his height.

He wrapped her in a soft hug that brought tears to her eyes. For half a second, she smelled grease and laundry detergent, and suddenly she was five years old again, being lifted into the kart.

"But you're working?" She looked behind him to the car and the tools off to the side.

"Got the call a couple days ago, and wanted to surprise you."

"I have so many questions," Reese said.

"And I have answers for you. Later," Luke said, heading back behind the car. "You have a race ahead of you and I'm gonna get you ready for it."

He wasn't wrong. She had to get started on her checklist and make the strategy meeting in time.

"Reese, can I grab you a minute in my office?" Shanelle said, from around the corner.

"Um, yeah. Of course." Reese turned to Luke, and they exchanged a smile. "I can't believe you're standing here and we will catch up after this."

He nodded and went back to work.

Having Luke in the garage again was not only surreal, it was so far beyond the realm of what she'd thought possible that her brain still hadn't fully caught up.

She arrived in Shanelle's office to find Julie sitting in one of the leather-backed chairs across from Shanelle's desk. She met Julie's gaze and turned back to Shanelle. "Okay, what is going on around here?"

"Julie will be shadowing Geoff today to learn the intricacies of our operation."

"Okay," Reese said, the smile on her face growing.

"The expectation is that she'll take over as your engineer shortly after she's completed that training."

"You're kidding."

Shanelle folded her arms. "I don't do that very well," she said with a wink.

"My brother is out front. My favorite engineer on the planet is sitting in your office."

"Thank you, Reese," Julie said, touching her glasses.

"No problem. It's true." Reese gave her head a shake of

disbelief. Her and Julie. Back together again. It didn't get much better. "How did this happen?"

Shanelle folded her arms. "Veronica thought bringing some of your people on board might be a good idea."

Leave it to Veronica Vance, maker of miracles, to swoop in and change her life once again. It was starting to make sense.

"Please tell me Danielle Todd is still racing for the academy and is not going to pop out from behind your desk."

"No. I think Veronica had standards," Shanelle said.

Reese nodded. "She arranged a support system."

"That's what she does. She's an arranger." Shanelle smiled. "How does this sit with you?"

"Are you kidding? That's not even a question. I'm thrilled with the idea."

Shanelle clapped her on the shoulder. "Great. Now, get out there and figure out what you can do with sixteenth."

Reese deflated again when she remembered what she was working with today. "I'll do my best for you, boss."

"Oh, and I passed Sloane in the hallway."

"I still can't believe you rebounded from that first night in the bar," Julie said, as if alone in her own room.

"Well, I'm going to need that story one day," Shanelle said, turning to Julie.

"I'm your woman," Julie said. "It was epic."

Reese laughed and made a gesture as if erasing a whiteboard. "No need. Nope. Nothing to see here."

"Now I really need to hear."

"Then I'm gonna go start reaction drills."

By the time Reese stepped back into the garage, the world felt different. The noise of the paddock sharpened into something electric instead of overwhelming. The clatter of tools, the murmur of strategy calls, the low growl of engines coming to life invigorated her in a way it hadn't all weekend.

Sloane was here. Luke was here. Julie was coming back to the pit wall.

Somehow, the universe had lined up every person who'd ever believed in her and placed them exactly where they belonged.

Sixteenth wasn't a setback anymore.

It was an invitation.

Her mind flicked automatically to the run into Turn 1—her braking point, inside line, who might overcook it ahead of her. Opportunity lived there.

Six drivers stood between Reese and the points. Six cars to hunt down. And for the first time all weekend, she couldn't wait to go find them.

CHAPTER 32
RIDICULOUSLY HERS

From the Laurens hospitality suite overlooking the main straight, the Circuit de Barcelona-Catalunya looked almost peaceful for a moment. The late morning sun washed the grandstands in pale gold, thousands of fans shifting in their seats, flags snapping in the warm breeze coming off the Mediterranean. It was the last quiet breath before everything exploded.

Sloane stood beside the glass railing, one hand curled lightly around the metal edge, her eyes fixed on the grid below.

Twenty-two cars sat in perfect formation, engines already rumbling through the pavement and up into her chest. Mechanics stepped away one by one, tire blankets peeled off and rolled away, leaving the cars gleaming under the Spanish sun.

Reese's red-and-black Laurens Racing car sat three rows from the back, angled perfectly in its grid box. Even from this distance, Sloane could spot it immediately, the bright red bodywork flashing whenever sunlight hit the nose.

A few weeks ago, watching from this close would have tightened every nerve in her body. She would have been bracing herself for something to go wrong, for the sharp, familiar dread that came with seeing someone you loved hurtling toward danger at 200 miles an hour.

But today was different. The tension in her chest didn't feel like the kind of terror she'd expected. It felt like anticipation. The nerves were still there, of course they were, but they felt lighter somehow. Manageable. Like a hum beneath the surface rather than a storm, which she'd take any day.

Veronica leaned against the railing beside her, calm as ever, sunglasses perched low on her nose as she studied the grid.

"You're doing all right," Veronica said casually. "Just look at you."

Sloane exhaled a small laugh. "Right? It feels a little like the old days if I'm being honest. Only I don't have to drive. A bonus."

Veronica smirked. "I'm sure we could arrange something, if you're up for it."

"No, thank you. I'm good. I'm gonna sit here with my popcorn and emotional support Ronnie and watch the others race it out."

"That's fair," Veronica said and sipped her Pellegrino.

Sloane shifted her weight, rolling her shoulders once to loosen the lingering tension there. And she had made a quiet deal with herself. If at any point the old fear crept back in—if the anxiety tightened its grip and made it hard to breathe—she would simply step away. No guilt. No shame. Reese would understand. Reese always understood.

The formation lap began with a rising metallic scream as engines surged to life. One by one, the cars rolled away from the grid, weaving back and forth to warm their tires as they disappeared into the first sector.

Sloane followed the red Laurens car as it swept through the final corner and returned to its grid slot moments later.

Veronica nudged her lightly. "All right," she said. "Here we go."

"C'mon, Reese," Sloane murmured. "We need a clean start."

The five red lights illuminated above the track.

One.

Two.

Three.

Four.

Five.

And then finally … the lights went out.

The grid detonated.

The roar that followed was enormous, a wall of sound that swallowed the crowd's cheers and shook the glass beneath Sloane's hands. Twenty-two cars surged forward in a blur of color and speed.

Sloane's eyes locked instantly onto Reese's car and held.

The red Laurens launched cleanly, threading between two rivals as the field barreled toward Turn 1 in a tight, chaotic pack.

"Oh, that's brave," Veronica murmured beside her.

Cars fanned out across the width of the straight, everyone searching for the smallest gap. Three cars ahead of Reese braked too late, overshooting the corner and sliding wide as tires protested in a burst of smoke.

Reese slipped inside them. "Good girl," Sloane said, tightening her hand into a fist.

By the time the field exited Turn 1, she had already gained two positions.

Sloane blinked.

"Well," Veronica said with a hint of amusement, "she didn't waste time. I think maybe Reese just needed a little reassurance from the people who matter." She bumped Sloane's shoulder with hers, pulling a smile.

Lap by lap, the race unfolded, the rhythm settling into something almost hypnotic.

Reese was patient at first, seeming to study the cars ahead and choosing her moments carefully. The red-and-black Laurens car appeared again and again in places it hadn't been the lap before, inching forward through the field with quiet determination.

A clean overtake into Turn 5 had them screaming their faces

off. Sloane was confident she'd have half a voice when this thing finished. One thing was for certain. She was definitely enjoying herself, even more than she'd expected.

Another takeover along the back straight, where Reese tucked into the slipstream before darting past at the braking zone. Each time she gained a position, cheers erupted from the Laurens garage below them, the mechanics crowding around the pit wall monitors.

Sloane found herself leaning farther over the railing with every passing lap, following the car as if her focus alone could keep it moving forward.

But the fear never came. No panic attack took over. And gradually, she realized something that surprised her. Watching Reese race didn't feel terrifying anymore. It felt exhilarating. Because Reese wasn't reckless. She was extraordinary.

By Lap 32, the timing board showed Reese in eleventh place.

Veronica leaned forward beside her, her attention narrowing. "One more," she said quietly. If Reese could move into P10, she'd finish in the points. The higher up she went, the more points she pulled.

The car ahead defended aggressively, forcing Reese wide through the final corner and squeezing her toward the curb on the straight.

Sloane felt her breath hitch despite herself.

For two laps, the battle continued, the cars dancing around each other in a delicate balance between aggression and restraint. It was a nail-biter to say the least.

Then Reese made her move.

She braked later than anyone expected into Turn 1, slipping neatly along the inside line and emerging from the corner with better traction on the exit. The red Laurens car surged forward.

Half a car length.

Then a full one.

The timing tower flickered.

P10.

The Laurens garage exploded in cheers.

Someone shouted Reese's name. Even Veronica allowed herself a satisfied grin.

"Points," she said.

Sloane laughed softly, relief flooding through her.

"Points," she echoed.

When the checkered flag waved twenty laps later, Reese crossed the line still holding tenth place.

And judging by the eruption from the Laurens garage, you would have thought she'd just won the race.

Sloane and Veronica made their way down through the paddock as the cars rolled into parc fermé, the air buzzing with adrenaline and celebration.

Reese climbed out of the car moments later.

Sloane stopped walking. The sight still hit her like lightning.

Reese pulled off her helmet and shook out sweat-damp hair that flattened briefly before springing free. Her cheeks were flushed from the heat of the cockpit, her grin wide and triumphant as she pushed her gloves off and wiped her forehead with the back of her hand.

Ridiculously sexy.

Ridiculously proud.

Ridiculously hers.

The Laurens crew surrounded her almost immediately, hands clapping her shoulders as congratulations flew from every direction.

"Sixteenth to points!"

"What a drive!"

Reese laughed, still catching her breath as she looked up. And spotted Sloane. For a moment, everything else seemed to fade away.

Sloane walked toward her before she could second-guess the decision.

Reese met her halfway.

"You saw that?" Reese asked.

"I might have noticed."

Reese's grin widened, and this time, Sloane didn't hesitate. She reached up, grabbed the collar of Reese's race suit and kissed her. Right there in the middle of everything and absolutely everyone. The cameras erupted instantly, flashes firing like a lightning storm around them as photographers scrambled to capture the moment.

Someone whooped.

Someone else yelled something that sounded suspiciously like, "About time!"

But Sloane barely registered any of it. Because Reese was kissing her back, laughing into the moment as one hand slid to the back of Sloane's neck, warm and solid and very much real.

When they finally pulled apart, Reese rested her forehead against hers.

"You liked the race then?" Reese asked.

Sloane didn't hesitate. "Baby. I loved it. That drive was incredible."

Reese's eyebrows lifted slightly, and her cheeks dusted with a proud blush.

"You started sixteenth and carved your way into the points like it was nothing," Sloane continued, her voice warm with pride. "You were patient when it mattered, aggressive when it counted, and that move into Turn 1 was beautiful."

Behind them, the Laurens crew erupted again, several mechanics clapping Reese on the back as someone waved a timing sheet over their heads like a victory flag.

"Sixteenth to points!" one of them shouted.

Reese finally turned toward them, still smiling, raising both hands in mock surrender as they crowded around her again.

Sloane stepped back a pace, watching the scene unfold.

The car still ticked quietly with heat behind them. Engineers leaned over laptops. Someone popped open a bottle of something that absolutely wasn't on the official hospitality menu. And Reese stood in the middle of it all, glowing and laughing with her team.

For the first time since she'd fallen in love with a driver, Sloane didn't feel the old knot of fear tightening in her chest. She just felt proud.

Veronica appeared beside her again, folding her arms as she surveyed the celebration.

"Well," she said with an appreciative grin. "That was subtle."

Sloane didn't even try to hide her smile.

"She deserved it. She drove a hell of a race."

Veronica nodded once toward the garage floor, where Reese was still being congratulated by half the team.

"I can't argue with that," she said.

Sloane watched Reese for another moment before Reese glanced up again, catching her eye through the crowd. And even from across the garage, Sloane could see the promise in her smile.

The race was over.

But somehow it felt like everything else was just getting started.

***

By the time they reached the hotel, the adrenaline of the night still hummed through Reese's veins. The elevator ride up had been quiet but charged, Sloane's hand resting lightly at the small of her back as if neither of them quite trusted the moment to be real yet. The hallway smelled faintly of carpet cleaner, and the space was completely still, a sharp contrast to the noise and warmth of the celebration they'd just left behind.

Reese unlocked the door and pushed it open, flicking on the lamp near the bed.

"Your brother was adorable," Sloane said as they stepped inside.

Reese glanced back at her, smiling as she noticed the hotel had already honored their request. Sloane's suitcase sat neatly beside the dresser where the bell staff had delivered it earlier.

"He was starstruck," Reese said, toeing off her shoes. "I don't think I've ever seen him at a loss for words. Enjoy it. It was probably the last time."

The celebration had stretched late into the evening, the team still buzzing from the race and the unexpected result that had everyone talking at once. Not to mention, Ezra had finished in P6, pulling in additional points for Laurens. Glasses clinked, stories grew more exciting with every retelling, and Reese found herself pulled into a steady stream of congratulatory hugs she still wasn't sure how to gracefully accept.

"I think we're going to do a lot of damage together," Ezra said, touching his pint glass to hers.

Reese grinned. "I can't tell you how much I'm looking forward to racing with you."

Across the room, Sloane stood in easy conversation with Marissa and Delaney, one shoulder resting against the bar while Marissa animatedly told a story, her hands moving as much as her words. Sloane laughed, bright and relaxed, and Reese felt the familiar pull in her chest that always seemed to lead her back to that exact spot.

She drifted over, still riding the energy from the race.

"There she is," Marissa said, smiling as Reese approached. "We were just saying that drive deserved its own highlight reel. I should be heavily featured, screaming like a maniac muppet."

Reese laughed. "I can make that happen. Did you guys see that start though? I got boxed in for a second and thought, well, that's it, race over."

"Oh, we saw it," Delaney said. "Then you just kept going like some kind of contracted killer."

"Dark," Reese said, "but I like it."

Sloane laughed along, their eyes meeting and holding for a moment longer than called for. Eventually, Reese finished her drink and offered a few last grateful smiles to the people nearby. When Sloane's hand found hers in the easy chaos around the bar, the decision felt natural rather than deliberate. "Let me grab Luke real quick."

She found her brother in the corner, engaged in a round of darts with some of the crew members. "I think we're going to sneak out, but I wanted to tell you how awesome today was. Seeing your face." She gave his chest a thump, just so he wouldn't think she was too soft.

"I think we have a lot of great races ahead of us, Roo."

"Oh, I think I need to hear about Roo," Sloane said, her eyes dancing.

"So many stories for you," Luke said, and took her hand in both of his. "And it was an honor meeting you earlier. I hope I wasn't too enthusiastic."

"Not at all."

Luke looked to Reese and back. "It sounds like we have more good times ahead."

"Yeah, we definitely do," Sloane said.

They slipped away with quiet goodnights and soft laughter, stepping out into the cool night together, both of them perfectly content to trade the noise of the celebration for the quiet promise of time alone.

Now nestled in the quiet of the hotel room, Reese took a seat on the edge of the bed. Her body was still wired, muscles thrumming from the g-forces that left her arms heavy, but the ache felt distant now. Sloane was here. That was the only thing registering.

Sloane didn't rush. She kicked off the heels she'd changed into for the gathering, crossed to the minibar, and pulled out two bottles of water. When she turned back, her eyes were soft, steady, tracing Reese like she was memorizing her all over again.

Reese managed a tired grin. "You're really here."

"I'm really here," Sloane said, handing her one of the waters before sitting on the bed beside her. Their knees brushed. "You were unreal today. I've watched a lot of races, but watching you claw through that field … I forgot how good it feels to see you do that."

"It felt different with you here again. Everything was a blur these last few races, like a part of me was missing. And it was."

Sloane reached out, threading her fingers through Reese's, her thumb brushing over her knuckles. "I was thinking of you the whole time. Missing you. Every single day. I just … needed to get my head right first." She paused, exhaling slowly. "I did the work. Or at least the start of it. Therapy, breathing exercises, planning for when it hits, all of it. But today? Sitting in those stands, watching you fight for every tenth … it wasn't terrifying. I was in it. I was proud. Not just of you, but of me, because I could finally be there for you without my past choking me. It felt like a step. A real one."

Reese's throat tightened. She lifted their joined hands and pressed a kiss to Sloane's knuckles. "I'm so fucking glad you're here."

Sloane's free hand cupped Reese's jaw, her thumb tracing the line of her cheekbone. "Me too." She leaned in and kissed her—slow at first, almost careful—then deeper, hungrier, like the month apart had finally snapped its restraint. Reese groaned into the kiss, the sound vibrating low in her throat as her fingers tightened on Sloane's hips, yanking her flush until their bodies locked together with a soft, urgent thud. The weeks of absence crashed through them: every phantom brush of fingertips she'd imagined in empty hotel rooms, every clipped goodnight that had left her staring at the ceiling, every cold sheet that had mocked her loneliness. Now it all ignited—hot, immediate, electric.

They stumbled toward the bed without breaking the kiss, mouths sliding wet and greedy. Reese's team jacket slithered to the carpet with a hushed rustle. Sloane's shirt came next—each button popping free with a tiny, satisfying click until the fabric parted and warm skin met warm skin. The air carried the faint, intoxicating mix of Sloane's perfume—something sharply citrus and clean—layered with the lingering warmth of sunbaked grandstands.

Reese's mouth chased the pulse in Sloane's throat, lips parting to taste the faint salt of the day still clinging to her skin, the rapid flutter beneath like a trapped bird. When her teeth grazed the tender spot just below Sloane's ear, Sloane's breath hitched sharply—a quick, ragged inhale that sent a fresh jolt straight to Reese's core. Sloane's fingers dug into Reese's shoulders, nails pressing crescent moons through the thin tank top, urging her closer, harder.

"God, I missed your mouth," Sloane murmured, voice rough like gravel, lips brushing Reese's as she spoke.

Reese pulled back just enough to meet her eyes, darkened with desire. "I missed everything about you."

Sloane pushed her gently backward, the cool sheets pressed against her now overheated skin, then crawled over her, straddling her hips. The weight of her, solid, familiar, and perfect, pressed Reese deeper into the mattress.

Reese looked up, chest heaving, the rapid rise and fall brushing her breasts against Sloane's bare stomach. "You have no idea how many times I replayed this in my head. Just … this. You on top does me in every time."

Sloane's gaze darkened to near-black. She leaned down and kissed her slowly, tongue sliding in a lazy, deliberate rhythm that made Reese arch up, her hips seeking friction against the seam of Sloane's underwear. Sloane's palms skated over Reese's ribs, thumbs brushing the sensitive undersides of her breasts through the thin sports bra before tugging it up and off in one smooth motion. Sloane's mouth followed instantly—hot, wet, closing over one nipple with a firm suck that pulled a sharp gasp from Reese's lungs. Fuck, that lit her whole body up. Sloane's fingers teased the other peak, rolling and pinching just enough to make Reese arch her back.

"Fuck—Sloane—God."

Sloane hummed against her, the low vibration rippling straight down Reese's belly and pooling between her thighs like liquid heat. She switched sides, sucking harder this time, tongue flicking in tight circles before soothing with slow, broad licks that left Reese trembling, skin prickling with goosebumps.

Reese's hands fisted in Sloane's hair, the silky strands slipping through her fingers, as the pleasure built in thick, deliberate waves, every nerve singing and reaching for more.

When Sloane finally kissed lower, open-mouthed and unhurried, tracing the quivering line of Reese's abs with her tongue, the muscles jumped under the wet heat. Reese's hips lifted instinctively, chasing contact. She was throbbing and nearing desperation. Sloane paused at the waistband of her underwear, breath skating over damp cotton, and looked up with that confident, knowing smile that always unraveled Reese completely.

"Tell me what you want, baby."

Reese swallowed hard, voice wrecked and hoarse. "Everything. All of you. Don't stop."

Sloane peeled the last scrap of fabric away with deliberate slowness, cool air hitting slick skin for only a heartbeat before her mouth returned. Sloane settled between Reese's thighs, her shoulders nudging them wider. The first slow, flat drag of her tongue made Reese's whole body jolt, a current snapping through her. The second drew a broken curse from her lips. Sloane took her time with long, languid licks that explored every inch, circling her clit with featherlight pressure before sucking gently, rhythmically, building Reese higher until her thighs shook violently and her hands clawed at the sheets, knuckles white.

The orgasm hit like the lights out on a grid. Her back arched sharply off the bed, a raw, shattered cry tearing from her throat as pleasure crashed over her in blinding waves. Sloane didn't pull away until the aftershocks ebbed to soft tremors. She pressed tender, open-mouthed kisses to each inner thigh before crawling back up to claim Reese's mouth again.

"Oh, don't think we're done yet," Reese whispered against her lips, already rolling them so Sloane lay beneath her. "Not even close."

Sloane laughed—soft, breathless, the sound vibrating against Reese's chest. "Thought you were tired."

"As if that would ever matter." Reese's hands roamed everywhere—cupping the warm weight of Sloane's breasts, thumbs circling pebbled nipples until Sloane hissed through her teeth, then sliding down to shove Sloane's jeans and underwear off in one impatient tug. The fabric caught briefly on Sloane's ankles before she kicked it free. When Reese's fingers finally slipped between Sloane's legs, she found her drenched—hot, swollen, slick enough that Reese's breath caught.

"Jesus," Reese breathed, fingers circling slow, teasing, gliding through wetness that coated her hand. "You feel amazing. So ready for me."

"Been thinking about this all day," Sloane admitted, hips rocking up into the touch with a needy little roll. "Watching you fight for every position ... knowing I'd get to feel you like this after."

Reese slid two fingers inside her, taking her slow and deep, curling just right against that sensitive spot that made Sloane whimper. Her thumb pressed steady, firm circles over Sloane's clit. Sloane's head fell back against the pillow, her neck exposed, another cry spilling out as her hips rolled to meet every thrust. Reese matched the rhythm of Sloane's body, deliberate and unhurried, as she kissed the column of her neck.

"Come for me," Reese murmured against that racing pulse. "Let me feel you."

Sloane did—hard and sudden, thighs clamping tight around Reese's hand, her whole body bowing off the bed as pleasure ripped through her in shuddering waves. Reese worked her through it, bringing her down gently, her fingers slowing but never stopping until Sloane's gasps melted away and her muscles relaxed.

"Come here," Sloane said.

They collapsed together, limbs tangled, breaths ragged and mingling in the quiet room. Reese pressed lazy kisses along Sloane's shoulder, up the side of her neck, to the corner of her mouth. Sloane's fingers traced idle, soothing patterns up and down Reese's spine, nails grazing just enough to raise pleasant shivers.

"I love you," Reese whispered, voice already thickening with sleep but arms tightening like she'd never let go.

Sloane kissed her temple, lips lingering. "Nowhere else I'd rather be. I love you, too."

Reese shifted closer somehow, tucking herself more fully against Sloane's side. Outside, the city hummed faintly beyond the windows, distant and unimportant. In the quiet cocoon of the room, the night felt suspended—no races to worry about, no expectations waiting for them in the morning, just the steady rhythm of two heartbeats.

Sloane brushed her thumb along Reese's arm one last time before sleep claimed her. Reese was left marveling at the simple truth of it all. After everything—the distance, the doubt, the chaos of the season—they had found their way right back here.

She drifted off like that. They were spent and happy and wrapped tightly around each other, the world outside dimming while the certainty between them burned warm and bright.

The next morning in Barcelona arrived slowly, the city still quiet beneath a pale wash of early sunlight. From the balcony of the small hotel suite, Reese could see the tops of palm trees swaying along the boulevard and the faint shimmer of the Mediterranean beyond the rooftops.

She stepped outside with two cups of coffee balanced carefully in her hands.

Sloane was already there, leaning against the railing in one of

Reese's oversized team sweatshirts, her hair still a little sleep-tousled. She turned when she heard the door slide open.

"Morning," Reese said, handing her a cup. "Please always wear my clothes."

"Morning." Sloane took it, fingers brushing Reese's in a small, familiar touch that made Reese smile. "I can make this deal." She snuggled further into the shirt as if it was her favorite.

For a while, they stood there without saying much, watching the city slowly wake up. The street below was still quiet, except for a singular delivery truck rumbling on its way somewhere. Nearby, the smell of bacon and eggs from the café on the corner wafted over.

Reese exhaled, stretching her shoulders. "Hard to believe yesterday was real."

"You mean the part where you carved through the field like it was a Sunday drive?" Sloane asked lightly.

Reese laughed. "That's not how it felt in the car."

Sloane glanced at her. "It looked exactly how it was supposed to."

Reese leaned her hip against the railing beside her. The quiet between them had always felt so easy, like they'd been together their whole lives. Reese adored that part of them. They just fit.

"You heading back to California after this?" Reese asked.

Sloane nodded slowly. "Yeah. A few remote meetings. Some work to catch up on." She took a sip of coffee, then looked out toward the water again. "Venice Beach is going to feel very quiet after this weekend."

"Because I'm so chatty?" Reese tilted her head in a playfully exaggerated display.

"Well, you are that. But I happen to love it."

Reese huffed a small laugh, reflecting. "Quiet sounds pretty good right now, if we're being honest."

"Baby. You need to unwind on your days off. Really take advantage so you can come back renewed and refocused."

"I need to do a better job of that."

Sloane was quiet for a moment.

"You know," she said eventually, "drivers always need a solid home base."

"Yeah," Reese said. "Somewhere to leave your stuff for three days before the next airport."

"Somewhere warm and comfortable that feels like a true home." Sloane glanced at her. "You've basically been living out of a suitcase for years."

"Yeah. Part of the job."

"Maybe," Sloane said. "But it doesn't have to be the only way."

"Okay." Reese tilted her head. "What are you getting at?"

Sloane shifted so she was facing her fully now, one elbow resting on the railing.

"You could use Venice Beach as your base," she said. "Between races."

Reese blinked.

"Come back with me when you're not on the road," Sloane continued, voice steady but warm. "Leave your gear there. Your clothes. Whatever you want."

Reese studied her for a second, the meaning settling slowly. Wonderfully.

"You realize," Reese said, carefully, "that sounds a lot like you're asking me to move in."

Sloane's mouth curved. "Yeah," she admitted. "I guess it does."

Reese let out a soft breath, glancing out toward the distant line of the sea. For so long, her life had been airports, hotel rooms, and temporary addresses that never really belonged to her.

But the thought of Venice, of sunlight on the Pacific, of Sloane waiting there, felt different. It felt like something solid.

She looked back at Sloane and slipped her hand into hers.

"Good," Reese said quietly. "Because having somewhere to

come home to sounds pretty great." Sloane squeezed her fingers, her smile easy and certain. "Especially if it's with you."

Sloane was quiet for a moment after Reese finished speaking. The city hummed below them, but the space between them felt strangely still.

"Reese," she said softly.

Something in her tone made Reese turn fully toward her.

"I need you to know something." Sloane rested her forearms on the balcony railing, then reached for Reese's hand like she needed the contact to say the next part. "I've been thinking a lot about the future lately. About what this life looks like for you, and what it means for me to be part of it."

Reese's chest tightened slightly, but she held Sloane's gaze.

"I know racing is chaos," Sloane continued. "Flights, time zones, pressure, the whole world watching. And I know there will be hard moments. For both of us." She paused, her thumb brushing slowly across Reese's knuckles. "But I'm not here temporarily. I'm not dipping a toe in to see how it feels."

Reese's heart kicked hard, and her palms tingled.

"I'm in this," Sloane said quietly. "For the long haul. For the messy parts, the scary parts, the incredible parts. All of it." She took a breath, her voice softening even further. "I've never been this certain about anyone before. But I am about you. I love you that much."

For a second, Reese couldn't speak. The words settled over her slowly, but when they did, they landed deep. She'd spent years moving forward at full speed—career first. Relationships tried to keep up, but never quite could. She'd told herself that was just the price of the life she'd chosen.

But Sloane wasn't trying to keep up. She was choosing to stand beside her.

Reese squeezed her hand. "Good," she said softly.

Sloane's brow lifted slightly. "Good?"

"Yeah." Reese smiled, a little crooked but full of something steady and real. "Because you should probably know something too."

"And what is that?"

Reese looked out toward the Mediterranean for a moment, gathering the right words, before turning back to her.

"I've experienced love," she said. "But never like this. Never with someone who makes everything feel … clearer. Like the rest of my life actually makes sense with them in it."

Sloane's eyes softened.

"You're it for me," Reese said simply. "However long this crazy career takes me around the world, however many races are ahead … I know, with absolute certainty, that I want you at the end of every one of them."

For a moment, neither of them moved.

Then Sloane leaned forward and kissed her, slow and certain, the kind of kiss that you remembered.

When they pulled apart, Sloane's smile was softer now, but brighter. "Well," she said, "in that case …"

Reese squeezed Sloane's hand, the decision settling into her chest faster than she expected. It didn't feel reckless or rushed.

It felt right.

Sloane bumped her shoulder lightly. "Looks like I'm going to have to clear out some closet space."

Reese smirked. "You're the one who fell for a woman with a designer jacket problem."

"That wasn't a problem."

"Oh?"

"That was one of the selling points. Because you know I'm going to wear them."

Reese shook her head, smiling, and leaned her forearms on the balcony railing beside her. Barcelona stretched wide and bright below them now, the city fully awake in the morning sun. Somewhere down the street a scooter buzzed past, and the smell of fresh bread drifted up from a bakery in the distance.

In a few days, Reese would be back in the car again, chasing hundredths of a second around another track somewhere else in the world. That part of her life wasn't slowing down. But for the first time in a long time, it didn't feel like everything.

Reese glanced sideways at Sloane, who was watching the city with that calm, thoughtful expression she always wore when she was taking the world in.

Loving her had changed something fundamental inside Reese.

For years, racing had been the center of everything. It had been the goal, the obsession, the thing that made every sacrifice make sense. Airports, hotel rooms, missed birthdays, lonely nights staring at unfamiliar ceilings. She'd accepted all of it as part of the deal.

But somewhere along the way, without Reese even realizing it, Sloane had become the reason the rest of it mattered. All of it led back to her. To someone waiting at the end of the race.

Reese reached for Sloane's hand again, lacing their fingers together. She looked down at their hands. "We just fit," she said simply. The sentence she'd never get tired of saying.

Sloane turned toward her immediately, smiling that soft, certain smile Reese knew she'd spend the rest of her life happily chasing.

"And you're really feeling okay with all of this?" Sloane asked.

Reese pulled her closer and kissed her, slow and easy, the kind of kiss that didn't need urgency anymore. Instead, she used it to communicate every damn thing she was feeling.

"Yeah," Reese murmured when they parted. "I'm more than okay. I just can't believe this entire year. I'm happier than I've ever been in my life."

"Me too." Sloane rested her forehead against Reese's and sighed a happy sigh. "Venice is going to look so good on you."

Reese smiled. "Yeah," she said quietly. "If it means I get to wake up next to you every morning, in *our home*, then it definitely will."

"Our home," Sloane breathed. "Best words ever."

Below them, Barcelona hummed with life, the rest of the season stretching ahead with more races, more flights, more hangouts with The Starting Grid in someone's hotel room. But for the first time since she'd climbed into a kart as a kid, Reese knew exactly where the road would lead her back to.

And she couldn't wait to get there.

EPILOGUE

Six Months Later

The Mojave Desert stretched wide, and around Willow Springs International Raceway, the asphalt ribbon of track cut through the surrounding pale sand, as if someone had drawn it there with a marker. It was quiet there that day. Just their group, there for a little fun during the offseason.

Reese leaned against the pit wall, sunglasses pushed up into her hair as the wind, warm for February, rolled across the valley.

Six months ago, she'd been standing on a balcony in Barcelona, trying to imagine what her life might look like with Sloane fully in it.

Turns out the answer was: better than she'd even dared to picture.

Venice Beach had quietly become home. Not just her address between races, and the three months of the offseason, but something real. Their mornings started slow—sunlight spilling through the windows while they stayed tangled in bed far longer than either of them intended. Some days, they ran along the boardwalk before the crowds woke up. Other days, they didn't bother leaving the beach house until noon.

Afternoons meant sand and salt air, lying side by side on the beach with the Pacific stretching endlessly in front of them.

But evenings were the best part.

The smallest outdoor cafés with string lights and tables squeezed onto sidewalks. Shared plates. Cold wine. Sloane's hand resting casually on Reese's thigh like it belonged there.

And the nights …

Well.

Reese smiled to herself.

Safe to say neither of them had suffered from a lack of enthusiasm in that department. They were adventurous in bed, loving, and deeply satisfied.

Life had settled into something warm and bright and very much what they made it.

And in a few weeks, the new Formula 1 season would start again. Reese would be back in the Laurens car, chasing the other drivers around the world, and seeing if she could advance Laurens's spot in the Constructors' Championship. Sloane was headed back to the academy for another season, which meant they'd be together in almost every city on the schedule. She couldn't wait to explore each one with her hand in Sloane's.

Behind Reese, the rest of the crew had taken over the garage like it belonged to them.

Marissa and Cassidy were arguing about who'd had the cleanest lap of the afternoon. Delaney was sprawled across a stack of tires, insisting she could definitely beat Marissa if she got "just one more go."

And a few yards away, Samara had a camera perched on her shoulder, documenting the chaos with obvious satisfaction. Her film was almost complete and off to editing, but she wanted to grab a few extra shots of Reese gearing up for the season ahead. Some unofficial car time with her friends should fill out the story nicely.

"Don't look at me like that," Samara said when Reese noticed the cameras on her … again. "You're the one who made the story so compelling. I'm just seeing it through."

Reese laughed.

Veronica clapped her hands once, drawing everyone's attention.

"All right," she said brightly. "Everyone's had some time to play behind the wheel. Should we head to dinner, maybe?" Even Veronica had slid behind the wheel of the retired F1 car. She'd borrowed it from a friend who'd picked it up at auction. The car could move. Reese was impressed.

Delaney pointed toward the far end of the garage. "Not everyone."

All eyes shifted to Sloane, who stood near the car, looking relaxed and happy.

"Oh no," Sloane said immediately. "Today is for you all. I'm literally the cheerleader."

Marissa folded her arms. "Sloane. Can you honestly walk away from this without driving a lap or two? No crowd. No media. Just friends hanging out."

Cassidy nodded calmly. "No pressure. You can set your own pace."

"It would be disrespectful to motorsport not to have a little fun," Delaney said.

"Oh, I had no idea," Sloane said with a laugh. "I would hate to offend motorsport, but … I'm not sure I want to go there."

Veronica grinned like a proud mastermind. "Well, the car's privately owned and fully insured." Sloane raised an eyebrow. Then she looked over at Reese.

Reese shrugged, a slow smile spreading across her face.

"Totally your decision."

Sloane studied their faces, clearly teetering, almost like the temptation was too much. "Well, why not?"

"We're doing this," Delaney said, clapping her hands.

A few minutes later, Sloane was lowering herself into the

cockpit of the old single-seater, sliding into the seat like her body remembered every inch of the motion. The engine fired with a sharp mechanical growl that echoed across the open desert.

Everyone drifted toward the pit wall.

Even Samara lowered her camera slightly, suddenly very interested, before raising it again, realizing what she might be about to capture.

The car rolled out onto the track.

The first lap seemed cautious. Sloane was feeling the brakes, testing them out. Then, the steering. The grip.

"She's rusty," Delaney predicted.

"Well, yeah. Give her a minute," Veronica said, hands on her hips, dark hair blowing in the breeze, as she stared out at the track.

Second lap. Faster. Cleaner.

Reese felt something tighten pleasantly in her chest. Things were looking good out there. The way Sloane placed the car through the corners had her breath catching—smooth, controlled, and effortless.

Cassidy leaned forward slightly. "Okay."

Marissa's eyebrows lifted. "Oh."

Third lap. Sloane decided to stop being polite. The car exploded down the straight, engine screaming as she braked impossibly late into the corner and snapped the car toward the apex with surgical precision.

Delaney blinked. "Holy shit."

"And there's Sloane," Veronica said with a nod of her head.

Marissa laughed in disbelief. "Are you fucking kidding me?"

Cassidy shook her head slowly. "That's … absurd."

Reese just stood there, grinning like an idiot.

Because watching Sloane drive like this—confident, fearless, completely in command—was the sexiest damn thing Reese had ever seen in her life.

Veronica beamed like a proud parent. "That's my girl," she said. "That's my best friend."

Sloane finished the lap like she had something to prove, carving through the final corner before coasting back to the pit lane.

The car rolled to a stop in front of the garage. The engine shut off. And suddenly everyone was talking at once.

"Did you get that?" Delaney asked, turning to Samara.

"Every second," Samara said. "Wow."

Sloane climbed out of the cockpit, pulling off her helmet and shaking out her hair like she hadn't just stunned the entire group.

Reese didn't think. She just walked straight over, grabbed the front of Sloane's race suit, and kissed her. Hard. The pit lane erupted.

Delaney whooped loudly. "That's the kind of energy we need today."

Marissa laughed, clapping once. "Iconic."

Cassidy shook her head with a small grin. "Honestly? Relationship goals."

A few feet away, Samara kept filming, clearly delighted with what she was capturing.

When Reese finally pulled back, Sloane was smiling that easy, confident smile that had undone her from the very beginning.

"You liked that?" Sloane asked softly, squeezing Reese's hand and then heading over to the group.

"Liked it?" she called, hurrying to catch up. "Are you kidding me? That was the hottest thing I've ever seen. You're a badass. I mean, I *knew* you were a badass. But you *still are* a badass. As in presently."

"Thank you, baby." Sloane leaned over and kissed her again, quick this time, but just as certain, her hand settling warm and steady at the back of Reese's neck.

Standing there in the middle of the desert, surrounded by engines, sunshine, and the people who had become their family, Reese had the quiet, unmistakable feeling that everything had landed exactly where it was supposed to.

Around them, their friends were still buzzing, arguing about lap times and replaying the moment Sloane had rocketed through the final corner like she'd never left the sport at all.

The desert wind moved across the track, restless beneath the afternoon sun, carrying the sound of laughter and the engine ticking as it cooled. This was the kind of night Reese lived for right along with the people she loved most. She wanted to bottle the moment and save it forever.

Reese slipped her hand into Sloane's, their fingers slotting together easily.

Six months ago, she'd been hoping this life might work. Now she knew it did. And on the horizon, the new season was waiting like a fresh page about to turn.

More races. More cities. More miles.

But this time, Reese stepped into it with not just ambition, but something she'd never had before: the woman she loved beside her.

And honestly?

Reese couldn't wait to see where they went next.

ACKNOWLEDGMENTS

This book, in particular, stretched me in new ways. I stepped into a world I'd long admired from afar—the high-speed, high-stakes world of racing—and came out the other side with a whole new appreciation for the sport and the people who live and breathe it. I learned more than I ever expected, and I loved every minute of it. (I might drive a little faster now, too.)

To my readers—thank you for continuing to show up for these stories, for caring so deeply about the characters who live in my head, and for reminding me every day what a privilege it is to do this. I never take it for granted, and I treasure our interactions.

To Lynda, thank you for your steady hand, your insight, and your ability to make a good book better every single time. I'm so grateful for you and never stop laughing as I move through your notes, especially when you say you're going to punch me in the face.

To Avery, thank you for your thoughtful and meticulous copy editing—your attention to detail makes all the difference, and your catches amaze me. Who knew commas could be used in so many ways?

To Nikki and my team of proofreaders, thank you for your careful eyes and the time you dedicated to helping polish this story. You save me every time.

To Sam, thank you for the gorgeous cover that captured the heart of this story so perfectly. I can't wait to create the rest of the series with you.

To Quinn, thank you for your amazing ability to breathe life into these characters and for lending your voice to their story. Your talent continues to astound me. I bow down!

To my family, thank you for the love, the patience, and the constant support. Alan, you are my calm in the chaos and my soft place to land. Everett and Camryn, you are my greatest joy, always.

And finally, to anyone still waiting for their moment, still chasing the thing that sets their heart on fire—this one was for you. You got this.

ABOUT THE AUTHOR

Melissa Brayden is the multi-award-winning author of too many sapphic romance novels to count and loves her job. She's a dedicated fan of all kissing scenes, enjoys gallivanting on TikTok, and spends most of her time chasing two short humans around her home. Though writing romance is her full-time job, much of it is spent on donuts, wine, coffee, and staring off into space.

ALSO BY MELISSA BRAYDEN

Waiting in the Wings

Heart Block

How Sweet It Is

First Position

Strawberry Summer

Beautiful Dreamer

Back to September

To the Moon and Back

Marry Me

Exclusive

The Last Lavender Sister

The Forever Factor

Lucky in Lace

Marigold

You Had Me at Merlot

When You Smile

Dream a Little Dream

Soho Loft Series:

Kiss the Girl

Just Three Words

Ready or Not

Seven Shores Series:

Eyes Like Those

Hearts Like Hers

Sparks Like Ours

Love Like This

Tangle Valley Series:

Entangled

Two to Tangle

What a Tangled Web

Read It and Weep Series:

Can We Skip to the Good Part?